Love. Set. Match.

by

Taylor Lunsford

Match Set Series, Book 1

Love. Set. Match.

Cover Art by *Diana Carlile*

The Wild Rose Press, Inc.
PO Box 708
Adams Basin, NY 14410-0708
Visit us at www.thewildrosepress.com

Publishing History
First Champagne Rose Edition, 2019
Print ISBN 978-1-5092-2753-2
Digital ISBN 978-1-5092-2754-9

Match Set Series, Book 1
Published in the United States of America

"I'm sure Rob won't hold your past…sparring matches against you. I can certainly see why they hired him. Between his pedigree and good looks, he could be a big numbers boost for them. So much more attractive than Bruno with all that golden Ashton hair and those lean muscles. He wouldn't look out of place in one of Papa's movies."

Emerson struggled to nod, the knot in her stomach dancing a polka—a really painful polka. Dera didn't know the truth about her history with Rob. No one did, not even her long-time coach, Zoe, or her grandma. Only her grandpa had known.

Dera was right about one thing—Rob's movie star looks made him an ideal candidate for the job. If she pushed through the crashing waves of anger and worry and hurt, she couldn't deny that the eye-candy factor was off the charts and ideal for a network more focused on gossip than the game. But that didn't make the situation any better for her.

Stepping onto the court tomorrow terrified her, more so now than it had when she woke this morning. Playing in her first tournament without Papa Vic broke her heart, but in the last few weeks she'd found a way to push past her grief and focus on the game.

Dedication

To Angela
for always geeking out with me
even if we have different favorite players
~
And to Andy Murray
for inspiring my love of tennis

Chapter 1

Thunk. Thunk. Thunk.

The hollow rhythm of the bright ball hitting the taut racket strings had haunted Rob Ashton's dreams for almost a year and a half. This time last year had been tough, but not this tough. At least then he'd been alone in his apartment with copious amounts of alcohol and no cameras around to watch him wallow in self-pity.

Every year for twelve years, he'd stood on the tennis courts surrounding him, ready for the first Grand Slam—the four most prestigious tennis tournaments—of a new season. Now, in the cool early morning as the sun started to stretch across the sky, he watched on the sidelines as the tournament came to life. Ball boys and girls scurried down the paths to their assigned courts. Line judges and referees moved at a more sedate pace, wearing their years of experience like a second skin. The stage production of the Australian Open was about to raise the curtains, and he was stuck in the audience for good.

But if the last eighteen months had taught him anything, it was that he couldn't stay away from tennis for too long, or he'd go stark raving mad. He missed the adrenaline high of sitting in the locker room, preparing to step out there before the world in the first big tournament of the year. Someone who hadn't played the game didn't know how the anticipation and energy tugged at him until he thought he'd jump out of his skin if he didn't grab his racket and wail on the ball for his first serve.

But all that was gone for him. Finished. The career he'd worked for since age four, gone in a blink, and he was still trying to pick up the pieces.

"Ah, the great Rob Ashton returns. I heard you were back, but I couldn't believe my best friend would take a job on a third-rate network like Tennis World Wide without telling me."

Rob turned. A tall Spaniard decked out in Adidas workout gear stood off to one side, his hazel eyes harder than the surface of the practice courts in front of them. Cruz Guerra, the number one Spanish player on the tour, nodded to the older man behind him, his uncle and long-time coach, waving him off. "*Estaré allí en un momento, tío.*"

"So on a scale of one to ten, how pissed are you?" Rob didn't pull any punches because his friend wouldn't either. They'd built their friendship on the bluntness of teenage boys away from parents, and that bluntness remained even as adults.

Cruz's jaw tightened. "*Seis o siete.* It'd be higher, but you did have surgery and a long recovery, so I give you some grace."

"That's fair." Rob's shoulders sagged, and he loosened his tie. "I should have called. I'm an asshole and a shitty friend."

"Maybe. I'll reserve judgement on that until I hear what the hell you were thinking going to work for TWW. You could have been a coach or a lawyer or anything. Why a reporter?" Cruz set down his travel mug of tea to pull out his racket and a spare ball. He bounced the ball, then tapped it with the racket, carefully controlling the ball's motion. "You've got exactly fifteen minutes before I'm scheduled on the practice court."

"Coaching? With my shoulder? Besides, TWW's not that bad. Except for Bruno." He watched Cruz, a small twinge of envy ricocheting through him. Although he'd gotten most of his strength back, he still struggled with gripping a racket for more than a few minutes, and he woke up every morning with a dull ache in his shoulder.

"You could coach kids. You'd be amazing at it. And Bruno Watson spent all last season trying to convince the world that I was a—what's the word?—manwhore. Any woman who I'd even smiled at after a match, he would try to get an interview with them." Cruz continued to tap the ball, dark eyes flashing with temper. "He's gone after Dera, Chessa, Owen, every top player, really, except for Naumov. That *hijo de puta* can do no wrong in Bruno's eyes."

He opened his mouth to make a snarky comment when movement out of the corner of his eye caught his attention. He turned to watch a woman run past, her powerful legs telegraphing barely contained anger with every stride. Her ebony locks were shorter than he remembered and her skin more golden, but he'd recognize that compactly curvy body anywhere.

Emerson Grace.

It'd been almost two years since he'd seen Em in person, but he'd thought about her every day. He'd thought about her and the unanswered questions and the what-ifs that plagued his nightmares for seven long years.

"She must have seen Kole's interview with Bruno from last night," Cruz commented, shaking his head in disgust. "Still can't believe she dated him."

Nausea and rage mingled with the coffee Rob had hastily chugged down this morning before leaving his hotel room. He'd last seen the world number one when he faced the Serbian champ across the court at the US Open almost a year and a half ago. All it would have taken was one last point, and Rob would have won the title and the world number one ranking. Instead, all he won was blinding, gut-wrenching pain, a new shoulder, and a new career. And while he was recovering, Kole had apparently dated the one woman Rob thought he wanted to spend the rest of his life with.

"Kole and Emerson? Seriously? What's a nice girl like her doing with a jackass like Naumov?" Rob kept his words casual, not letting on what he really felt.

"Nice girl?" Cruz raised one dark eyebrow as he switched to bouncing the ball in the air with an easy flick of his wrist. "Since when do you think Emmy's a nice girl? You two fight to the death every time you get within five feet of each other."

"We do not," Rob said, grimacing. Cruz was only slightly exaggerating. "We express our differing opinions and debate heatedly on occasion."

They used to do other things heatedly—for three incredible weeks seven years ago—but then he'd screwed things up and let her go. His anger simmered, thinking of Em dating a guy like Kole Naumov. The world number one had a reputation on the tour, both for ego and his numerous liaisons.

"Right. I'm surprised she didn't stop to slap you or

something." Setting aside his racket and the ball, Cruz pulled one of his arms across his chest, stretching out his triceps. "Well, Bruno's been going after her pretty hard since the breakup. He's taken some swipes at your sister too. You really want to work with a guy like that?"

Shoving his hands through his hair, Rob sighed. "Bruno's definitely a downside to the job, but I feel like this is something I need to do. We've spent years bitching about how awful the tennis coverage is, especially on TWW. I want to try to change that. Make it about the game and the players' skills, rather than the behind-the-scenes gossip and intrigue."

"TWW's all about the gossip," Cruz argued, moving to stretch his quads. "Do you honestly think you can change the network's tennis coverage as the junior correspondent?"

Damn Cruz for giving voice to the worries Rob had wrestled with since he agreed to take this job three weeks ago. Every time he almost talked himself out of taking the job, he'd reminded himself this was his chance to try to protect his sister and his friends from the type of negative coverage TWW usually thrived on. "I don't know. But I want to try. I missed being part of the tennis scene, and I'll never play again, so this is the next best option."

Cruz shrugged. "It's your life, amigo. I just hope you don't expect this to be easy."

"I stopped expecting easy the second I felt my shoulder go, man." He straightened his tie. "So are we good?"

The Spaniard studied him for several minutes, dark eyes assessing as he braced his hands on his hips.

Finally, he gave a small nod. "We'll get there now that you're out from under your rock. Just make sure you don't fall into the muck with Bruno, or I'll have to reconsider punching you."

****

Thunk. Thunk. Thunk.

The echo of the ball hitting the sweet spot of her racket as she aimed it toward the backboard lulled Emerson, soothing some of her anger and grief, but not completely dampening it. Few people ventured this far out so early in the morning, but she enjoyed the solitude as the sun sent small tendrils of light into the Melbourne sky. This was what she was here for. Tennis. Her career. She couldn't afford to forget that. Now more than ever, she needed to be on top of her game.

Staying off tennis courts—even when she'd torn her MCL last September—wasn't an option. The tennis court was the only place that gave her a modicum of peace, that made the rest of the world fade away. She could find her center, and for a few hours, nothing would exist but her, her racket, the ball, and her opponent. She'd clung to that feeling as she fought to get back in shape for this season, but she'd rejoined the tour at the Australian Open less than twenty-four hours ago, and already the outside world hit her like a battering ram.

After a few minutes, the squeak of someone else's athletic shoes echoed across the blue-paved court. Emerson didn't turn toward the sound, keeping her eye on the fuzzy green ball that could be her greatest ally or her greatest enemy. With a furious backhand swing, she sent it hurtling at the backboard again. Unfortunately, the ball went wide, and she missed it.

She turned to follow it and found her best friend, Dera Calvet, retrieving the ball with long-legged grace, her soft brown skin gleaming in the fresh light, her hair a wild mass of curled braids spinning from her high ponytail.

Instead of trying to talk, Dera picked up Emerson's spare racket and nodded toward the court.

Before long, the two were hitting the ball back and forth as fiercely as they had in every one of their matchups for the last ten years. They played all out, making trick shots when possible and trying to ace every serve.

When the ball finally sailed past her on a carefully crafted angle, the French woman waved her racket. "Enough."

"Oh, come on, Calvet. You can do better than that," Emerson teased.

"Not all of us have been here for two weeks getting ready, *Mademoiselle* Energetic. Some of us didn't see our beds until the early hours of the morning for the last two nights." Dera made her way to the chairs that held their bags and dug out a bottle of water.

Emerson shrugged, a smile tugging at her lips. Dera was usually a morning person, but the start of the tour always left her cranky. Getting used to the grueling schedule of press appearances, practice, and matches took some time.

"Some of us know how to get ready to kick ass and take names," Emerson said, the bravado in her voice false even to her own ears. She didn't know if she could really do this. The weight of anxiety over the upcoming season, the anger of her recent breakup, and the grief of losing her grandfather in November threatened to bog her down. She'd thought coming down here right after Christmas and avoiding the lead-up tournaments would be enough to get her into shape, but now the Australian Open, the first of the tournaments that earned a tennis player the most points toward world-wide ranking, the most money, and the most prestige of the year, was starting, and she couldn't get her head on straight.

"Even with little sleep, I still predict I will have a shorter first round match than you," Dera teased. "My bracket is easy until fourth round. The benefits of being number two in the world."

"Why is it your father's arrogant side only comes out when we trash talk?"

"Come, you know my arrogance comes from them both. *Maman's* supermodel blood helps me look so stylish when I kick your ass on the court." Dera set the racket back in Emerson's bag and turned to study her. "You saw it, didn't you, *cherie*?"

In the way of best friends, Dera could always read Emerson's moods. She was also one of the only ones who knew the whole story behind the end of Emerson's relationship with Kole Naumov, current men's number one tennis player and world class asshole.

Emerson had spent the last six weeks avoiding any form of media, focusing only on her game. Letting the world in meant acknowledging that her Papa Vic was really gone, that she was starting her first tennis season without her grandfather by her side. He'd been so proud when she and her brother turned pro, but he hadn't lived to see either of them reach the ultimate goal—winning a Grand Slam.

"When did he start saying I cheated on him?"

Emerson asked, grabbing the spare ball from the pocket of her bright-yellow skirt, tossing it from hand to hand, unable to stay still.

Dera sighed. "Kole's been a complete *conasse* since the breakup, but he started to amp up the nastiness over the last few weeks. For the first month, he claimed you were merely on a break, but when you stayed under the radar too long, he started to pull out the daggers."

"Damn it. Why couldn't he be an adult about this?" Emerson tossed up a serve and took a vicious swing at the ball, ignoring the slight twinge in her knee. She should have wrapped it before she started hitting the ball, but she'd been too worked up to think of practicalities.

"You hurt his pride, choosing your family over him." Dera took a seat on a nearby bench, stretching her legs out in front of her, her neon-blue shorts gleaming in the sun. "Watch yourself with him. I've never seen him so…wounded. He'll continue lashing out until he feels better."

Emerson set her racket aside. "Great. Just great. So I'm mature and don't tell the world he threw a diva-level tantrum when I wanted to go be with my dying grandfather instead of him, but I'm the one who gets painted as the bad guy in this?"

Dera held out a water bottle for Emerson. "Men are idiots. Surely you know that by now. They have their uses, but there's a reason I prefer to date women. They're usually so much more logical, especially when it comes to emotions."

"Speaking of idiot males, was that Rob Ashton I saw talking to Cruz on my way over here? Last I heard, he'd disappeared. Even Maren's barely seen him since his shoulder surgery, and she's his little sister." Emerson bent at the waist, going through a few stretches her physio had given her for when her knee started to ache. She'd had eighteen months of peace and quiet since his shoulder injury forced him to retire. No sniping matches in the players' lounge, no crossing paths on the practice courts. And absolutely no memories of her heart being ground up in a blender by him.

After seven years, she shouldn't care what he did or where he was. Except that every time she saw his strong jaw and silver-gray eyes, every time she took in that tall, lean frame of his, she couldn't help but feel that old flutter. The flutter was the ghost of a naive girl's first crush, she told herself. She'd kissed Prince Charming, and he'd turned out to be a frog. Twice, it seemed.

"He's TWW's new junior correspondent." Dera went into her own stretches, her hair falling around her head in a wild mass.

Anger flaring all over again, Emerson sat on the court, bending over her outstretched leg. "How could he go work for that rat hole of a network? Why did he have to come back in the first place?"

How long before he started spilling her secrets? She could only imagine him using those nights during her first Olympics as interview fodder. God, Kole shooting off his mouth was bad enough. Rob could make her life hell and do it all on camera.

"I'm sure Rob won't hold your past…sparring matches against you. I can certainly see why they hired him. Between his pedigree and good looks, he could be a big numbers boost for them. So much more attractive than Bruno with all that golden Ashton hair and those lean muscles. He wouldn't look out of place in one of Papa's movies."

Emerson struggled to nod, the knot in her stomach dancing a polka—a really painful polka. Dera didn't know the truth about her history with Rob. No one did, not even her long-time coach, Zoe, or her grandma. Only her grandpa had known.

Dera was right about one thing—Rob's movie star looks made him an ideal candidate for the job. If she pushed through the crashing waves of anger and worry and hurt, she couldn't deny that the eye-candy factor was off the charts and ideal for a network more focused on gossip than the game. But that didn't make the situation any better for her.

Stepping onto the court tomorrow terrified her, more so now than it had when she woke this morning. Playing in her first tournament without Papa Vic broke her heart, but in the last few weeks she'd found a way to push past her grief and focus on the game.

"I can't think about him. Or Kole. I came too close to finally winning a Slam last year to let them distract me." Em angrily threw a ball across the court. "I owe it to Papa Vic to win one this year. To show him everything he did for me wasn't in vain."

Men like Rob and Kole thought the world revolved around them, but she'd prove she wasn't going anywhere, no matter how many shots they fired at her.

Chapter 2

"Ah, Rob, there you are." The slightly accented tones of the tall, blond local head of production broke through the silence of Rob's temporary office.

He glanced up from his phone, smiling at the text his sister had sent him after her match, teasing him about their coverage. "Sorry, Joey. After all morning with Bruno, I needed some breathing room."

"Can't say I blame you. The man is great for ratings, but he does tend to suck up all the oxygen in the room and replace it with hot air." She flashed him a grin. "But I think we're ready to give you a chance to do an interview on your own. Bruno's got a meeting with some of the executives. Now, I know this will be weird for you at first, what with you knowing a lot of the players."

"I don't think it will be." He tried to sound convincing. He honestly had no idea what it would be like to be on the other side, interviewing the guys he'd once played against, the women his sister still played against.

"That's what I like to hear. Unlike Bruno, you're there to bridge the gap. You know, bring in the reporter and the former star angle; relax the players and have a little fun, but you'll still need to remain a neutral party. No old rivalries coming to the surface or anything like that, yeah?" Joey straightened the jacket of her smart suit, keen eyes taking inventory of him.

"No worries. I've been out of the game long enough that it shouldn't be a problem. I'm just a fan now, like everybody else." He flashed her a grin, one he'd perfected early on in his career. It was the smile of the golden boy of the great Ashton family, world renowned for their tennis prowess. The boy he could never be again. "So who's my first interview?"

She wiggled her eyebrows. "It's a juicy one."

"Tell me it's not Chessa Pavlich," he teased. "She chews interviewers up and spits them out."

"I'm not that cruel." The producer laughed. "No, you get the elusive Emerson Grace. Everyone's been trying to get Amir al-Tammar, her agent, to book her, but when I told him you would be her interviewer, he couldn't say no."

She might as well have punched him in the gut. Jesus, the universe had a funny sense of humor. Em as his first professional interview?

He still couldn't believe his luck—or was it misfortune?—as he settled into one of the two sleek, boxy chairs they'd set up angled toward the camera in the studio. One of the makeup artists fluttered around him, dabbing at his nose with more powder.

"I never thought I'd see the day when the great Rob Ashton sat around getting his makeup done."

He looked up to see Em standing there, looking as casually beautiful as ever. Seeing her in passing yesterday was nothing like having her standing here before him. A silky top of sunny yellow clung to her slim curves before giving way to dark-blue skinny jeans and those fashionable bootie things his sister loved. His heart sputtered at the sight of her, and it took every ounce of his self-control not to sweep her into his arms. Instead, he stared at her like an idiot until the makeup artist stepped back and he managed to get ahold of his scrambled wits.

"Hazards of the new job," he said easily. "It's good to see you, Emerson."

Her stubborn jaw tightened, and he caught the flash of temper he'd grown very accustomed to over the last few years. "Wish I could say the same. I can't believe you actually had the balls to take a job like this."

She sat down in the chair across from him, letting the makeup artist pat her face with powder too. He'd missed the crackle in the air around her, the passion she always kept a tight rein on. He'd sensed it that first time he saw her in the cafeteria of the Athletes' Village at the London Olympics. She hadn't realized the effect she had on men—on him—even then. He wondered if she even thought of their time together the way he did.

"Couldn't stay away," he returned. "Are you ready to do this?"

"No." She crossed her legs with a snort. "I can't wait to hear the questions they've given you to toss at me. Let me guess, something to do with my relationship with Kole, right?"

Jealousy flared up again at the mention of Kole, but he tamped down on it as his own anger bubbled to the surface at her insinuations. "They haven't given me any questions, Em. I—"

"Don't call me Em," she snapped.

Ah, so she did remember. To everyone else, she was Emerson or Emmy, but to him she'd always be Em. "Fine, Emerson. I'm not here to—"

"All right, everyone. Let's get in positions." Joey's

order interrupted him.

Biting back a growl of frustration, Rob turned his attention to the people buzzing around them rather than the woman who hadn't been far from his thoughts every day for the better part of eighteen months.

"We're here with Emerson Grace, world number four, fresh off her first match of the season." He fixed his practiced smile in place as he looked into the camera. "Emerson, I must say it's good to see you back on the court. It seems like you're back in fighting form since the injury that side-lined you after the US Open last year."

Her own public smile tilted up her lips, never reaching her eyes. "Thanks, Rob. It's good to be back. I've got a great team in my corner, and they all worked hard to help me rehab my knee."

"You could hardly tell you missed any time on the court from the looks of the match today. This was your first major injury in your career. Were there nerves about stepping out there again?" He watched her, studying to see if she realized his intent. He had no plans to take things where she—and probably Joey—expected him to. This was his chance to show Em and the other players on the tour that he didn't intend to fit the TWW mold.

Em hesitated. "Well, I'd be lying if I said there weren't a few butterflies. The end of last year was a little rough all around, and it was…strange to be back after everything that happened."

Sympathy tugged at his heart. He knew how much her grandfather meant to her. Victor Grace had been an unflagging presence on the tour for the last ten years. "I think I speak for everyone here at TWW when we offer you and your brother our condolences on the death of your grandfather. Do you think he'd be proud of your performance today?"

"I hope so," she said with a bittersweet laugh. "I'm sure he'd probably offer some armchair coaching on my second serve or on the fact that I let Kaye win three straight games in the second set, but even when he was in the hospital at the end, he was encouraging me to keep pushing through, to get back to the form I was in for most of last year."

Good girl. Reveal a little, then pivot. It was the best strategy to hold in her pocket in any interview.

"Is this your year? Are you going to win a Slam?" he asked, not missing a beat.

A soft look flitted across her face, a sadness that quickly disappeared behind her mask. "We all hope it'll be our year to win a Slam, you know that, Rob. But do I feel like I'm ready? Definitely. The time off gave me a chance to really get my head in the game. Zoe's had me training harder than ever and brought in a lot of different training styles we've never used before. As long as I don't lose focus, one—or maybe even all—of those titles are mine."

Looking at the ferocity in her eyes, he believed it. She was a warrior, ready to take on the world. Getting the answer he wanted from her, he led her through the rest of the interview, talking about her trips to the finals in all four Grand Slams the year before, then touching briefly on her second-round match against a wildcard player from Japan.

"Thank you again for joining us, Emerson. After break, we'll go to Christiane and Julia with coverage of the final matches of the day at Rod Laver Arena."

They stayed in place until the director gave the all-clear sign. Then Em shot to her feet, reaching behind her for her mic pack.

"Nicely done," Rob said.

She gave him a cool look. "Just doing my job, same as you."

"Would you like to have drinks with me tonight? Maybe catch up?" The words were out before he could stop them. God, he was an idiot.

"Drinks? Catch up?" Her body tensed, and temper sparked around her, but she kept her voice quiet so as not to be overheard. "Sorry, I don't meet socially with members of the press. Besides, the last time I had drinks with you, things didn't go so well for either of us."

With that, she turned on her heel and walked off, hips swaying and heels clicking against the polished studio floor, leaving behind a whiff of lemon and rosemary, her signature scent. Instantly, he ached for her to come back. Hell, he'd ached for her to come back the second they—okay, he—ended things seven years ago, and that ache had lingered despite both of them moving on. He'd missed that, even the sparring, because it meant she was near him. Over the years, their sparring matches had been the only times he felt truly alive when he wasn't on the court. Everything else had become a habit, a duty. When he was around Em, everything held more depth, more purpose, and he hated to let that go.

"I knew it," Joey said from behind him.

Shit. Had he been that obvious? He'd always been so careful about hiding his feelings for Em. First, because they hadn't wanted their fledgling relationship put on display, then because he'd made her hate him.

Fear spiking, he whirled around to face her. "What?"

"That you'd be totally brilliant at this." She grinned at him. "That interview was exactly what we're looking for."

"Really?" He frowned at her as he removed his mic. "I thought you'd be pissed that I didn't bring up Naumov."

She winced. "Yeah, we'll probably get some flak for that from the big bosses, but you read your subject so well. And you still got some personal moments out of her. We can build on that later. Emerson Grace has never been that open with one of our interviewers before."

"I just asked her the logical questions," he said, not meeting Joey's gaze as he moved past the cameraman. "Emerson's always been the consummate professional."

"Professional, sure, but everyone around here's always referred to her as an ice princess." Typing out something on her phone, she shrugged. "But not today. I knew hiring you was the right move. If you can get interviews like that from everyone, we can go really deep, dig into stuff we've never been able to get comments on."

Warning bells clanged in his head, but he pushed them aside. She wasn't saying what he thought she was. Was she? "I guess it's easier for players to talk about their game, about their sport, if they're talking to someone who's been in their shoes rather than a former football player."

"Exactly. It's like they're talking to a friend. A friend they want to spill their guts to."

Positively gleeful, Joey turned down the well-lit corridor and sauntered off with Rob glaring after her. Clearly, she was saying what he'd thought. He'd known going into this that TWW's motives for hiring him weren't pure, and he'd accepted that. It didn't mean he had to play along with them. Rob planned to do whatever it took to protect his friends from unnecessary invasions into their privacy, and that went double for Em.

Chapter 3

The insistent sound of her phone going off pulled Emerson out of a deep sleep. She'd stayed up late the previous night going to a party hosted by one of her sponsors, and her body craved more rest. Blinking, she squinted at the red numbers on the clock. 5:05 a.m.? Who the hell would call her so early? Outside the curtains, she couldn't even see a glimpse of dawn starting.

With a groan, she fumbled around on the nightstand until she grabbed her iPhone and blinked at her agent's face smiling back at her from the display. "Amir. I know you struggled with the whole different-time-zones thing, and I'm usually up early, but I have a match today, and I was stuck at a party you insisted I attend last night. I was counting on at least another hour of sleep. Why on God's green earth are you calling me at five in the morning?"

"Shit. I thought it was six there. Sorry."

She groaned, shifting to lay on her back, her eyes squeezed shut, and the phone pressed to her ear. "You're a middle-aged man. Do I really need to teach you how to use the little world clock app on your phone—again?"

"Not important right now." From the tension in his voice, she could almost see him pacing his office, his tie askew and his Armani suit coat slung over the back of a chair. Typically a snappy dresser, he only looked rumpled when someone got one over on him—a rare occurrence. "I'm assuming you haven't seen the blogs yet? Or the news?"

She yawned, not even trying to muffle it. "Amir, do I ever see the blogs or the news if you don't tell me to look?"

"Right. You need to fix that," he barked. "We've got a problem. A big one. Huge."

She struggled to sit up and reached for her iPad. "What site do I need to look at?"

"Pick one. TMZ. Tennis Beat. Perez Hilton. TWW. All of them have it."

She typed in a general search for her name and waited for the slow hotel Internet to load. What the image search delivered woke her up better than a gallon of coffee. "What the fuck? Who did this? How did they get these pictures, Amir?"

"That's what I'd like to know. Who took those? Tell me you didn't pose for them." He was in full crisis-management mode, so she tried not to get offended by his accusatory tone.

She struggled to see straight through the typhoon of emotions pelting her. The night she'd let Kole take those pictures appeared in her mind's eye, as clear as the hotel room around her. She and Kole had been together for three months, and they were still in that fun, sexy honeymoon phase. What had started as a publicity stunt had developed into something more real than she had anticipated. She'd splurged on some La Perla while they were in New York for the US Open, and Kole talked her into modeling the lingerie sets for him.

"I…Kole took them. In August. We were…I told him to delete them after. It was supposed to be for fun." Tears stung the backs of her eyes and clogged her throat. Shame and fear and the now familiar waves of hurt slammed into her. "How did this happen? Did Kole release them?"

Amir let out a long breath. "Too soon to know. I'm working on tracking it down now. I needed to confirm that they were authentic and not photoshopped. Jesus, Emmy. How could you do this?"

"Really, Amir? How could I do this? That's what you want to say?" Acidic bile crawled its way up, choking her almost as much as the emotion. "The privacy of a young woman you've represented for ten years is violated, and you really want to blame her when some jackass—a jackass you advised her to date—releases pictures of her in her underwear for the whole world to see?"

Thankfully, he didn't immediately respond. Otherwise, she might be minus an agent/publicist while she was in the middle of a PR crisis of epic proportions. "Fuck. Sorry, Emmy. This just…out of all my clients, you're the last person I expected to have a sex scandal. In this day and age, I thought you would know better than to let someone take pictures like that. Anyone could hack into the cloud or find a lost phone, or hell, post them out of revenge."

For a man who didn't know how to differentiate time zones, he certainly knew a lot about posting dirty pictures in the digital age. And he had a point. She curled her knees to her chest, wishing like hell the water beside her bed could turn into a big shot of vodka instead.

"I—I wasn't thinking. I never imagined anyone but Kole would see them. I thought that he deleted the damn things after we broke up." She rubbed her forehead. "What do I do? I have a match in…six hours and a press conference after that. How do I go out there with this hanging over my head? And oh God, what about my sponsors? They're going to flip over this, aren't they?"

"You're a trooper, Emmy. You go out there, you play your match, and you avoid the cameras. Let me worry about the press and your sponsors. By game time, I'll have some talking points worked out for you, and I'll clear it with the tour's press people to pull you out of there." He cleared his throat. "I'm sorry this happened, baby doll. You're a good kid, and you don't have to tell me that some of this is my fault. I didn't expect the Naumov thing to spiral this bad."

She swallowed hard, pushing down the tears. "It's not your fault. There's no way either of us could have known how this would go. Just…find out who did this so I can beat them upside the head with my racket."

She ended the call and slid down into the bed, pulling the fluffy down comforter over her head. She should call someone. Zoe needed to know. So did Owen. And Gran. God, what was she going to tell Gran? She pretended to be tough, but she was still recovering from a minor cardiac episode at Christmas time. Gran was going to see those pictures; so were her friends. How could she explain that this was something women today did with their boyfriends? Her grandma still liked to pretend that Emerson was saving her virginity for marriage.

What would Papa Vic think of all this? For the first

time since he'd died, she was glad her grandpa wasn't here. He would be outraged and threaten to beat up Kole, but while he'd never say it, he'd be disappointed in her. It'd be there in his eyes, in the quiet way his broad shoulders would sag and his gray brows would furrow. She hated disappointing him, hated being anything less than the woman he'd raised her to be. Ever since she was a little girl, she'd always tried to be the best version of herself for him, and she'd only failed him twice. Once seven years ago, with Rob and their stupid secret relationship, and once when she let Kole take those fucking pictures.

Giving in to the pelting storm of emotions, she let the tears go for exactly twenty minutes. That's all she could allow herself. As easy as it would be to let it all drag her down, wallowing in the shame and feeling of total violation wouldn't do her any good. She needed to focus on her career. She couldn't afford to be distracted, not if she wanted to keep her career intact and win that Grand Slam title this year.

By the time Zoe and Dera pounded on her door, she'd showered, and all traces of red eyes and puffiness were gone.

"That bastard! How could he do this?" Dera fumed in between bouts of French expletives.

Zoe, frantically typing out a text on her phone, narrowed her eyes at the TV screen where every news channel seemed to be running a story about Emerson. "I'll skin him alive and feed him to the nearest pack of dingoes. Then I'll feed that idiot Amir to them for dessert. I knew you should never have gotten involved with Naumov."

Emerson sat there in a haze. She heard her friend's

unbridled outrage on her behalf and her coach's righteous, almost motherly anger, but none of it seeped in. Numbness had been her friend in the last few weeks, and she clung to it now, only vaguely aware of her brother showing up in her room late in the morning.

"Shit, Squeaker. Are you okay?" Owen pulled her against his massive chest for a bear hug.

Normally, she loved his bear hugs, even when he called her that awful childhood nickname he and Papa Vic had devised because of the noise she made when she hit the tennis ball. His hugs reminded her of when they were little and he'd beaten up the kids at school who teased her for looking too much like their Chinese mother. Unlike her, he'd inherited his six-foot-six height and build from some distant relative on their grandma's side who once rode across the American plains in war paint and buckskin. Like her grandpa, he had that type of presence that made her think everything was going to be all right as long as he had her back. As much as she wanted to cling to her big brother and let him tell her everything was all right, having him with her didn't work today.

"I'm…fine. I'm fine, O." She pulled away, crossing her arms over her chest.

He raised one black eyebrow in a move she swore he'd perfected by spending hours in front of the mirror. "Pull the other one."

"I can't deal with this right now. I have a match," she said, pushing aside his concern. "Have you talked to Gran? I should call her, but I have no clue what the hell I'm supposed to say."

"Gran called me a few minutes ago. Amir gave Gran and the uncles the heads-up after he talked to you in case they started getting calls from reporters." He started to pace. "This is messed up, Emmy. I can't believe that jackass would do this. He's lucky I don't corner him in the locker room and beat him until he's bluer than the hard court."

She sat down on the edge of the bed, her head aching almost more than her heart. She appreciated everyone's support, but she wished they'd give her a few moments alone to process everything and get her head on straight before her match. "We don't know that Kole is the one who released the pictures. Amir's working on that. Until then, we can't rush to judgement. Lord knows, the press is going to do that enough for all of us. How'd Gran sound? Is she okay? This can't be good for her heart."

"Her heart's fine. She's worried about you and shocked, but she's handling it better than expected. Uncle Mike and Uncle Tony are keeping away from the news and the computer, and everyone's taken their phones off the hook so no one can bug them." He shoved his hands in the pockets of his warm-up pants. "Are you going to be okay to play? Do you want me to sit in your box? My match isn't until tonight."

She flopped back on the bed, the weight on her chest growing heavier. She hadn't thought about this affecting Owen. He would have to deal with the press questions too. Everyone on the tour knew they were close, and they'd been mixed doubles partners up until a year ago.

"Shit. They're going to bombard you too. I'll have Amir send you the talking points when I get them. Maybe he can get you out of most of the press conference too."

"Don't worry about me. I can handle the jackals. You focus on winning your match. You've worked so hard to get here, Squeaker." Chocolate eyes studied her with the perceptiveness of one who knew her almost better than she knew herself. Although they were close in age—Irish twins as her grandma liked to say—he'd always protected her, always wanted to step in front of her and take the hit. Now she was in a situation where no one else could take the blow. Whoever released those pictures had executed a perfect shot at her, and there was no going back. She had to swing or risk having her head taken off.

"I've got this," she assured him.

Except she so didn't have this.

All during her warm up, she kept telling herself she did, but as she sat alone in the locker room, she began to realize she was in over her head. Struggling to breathe, she tried to refocus herself and think only about her game. Zoe had kept up a running commentary about what to watch for with her opponent, but now Emerson couldn't even remember a word of it. All she could think about were those fucking pictures. Some idiot was probably jerking off to them right now. Waves of nausea rolled over her, and she hurried to the nearest toilet, vomiting up the little bit of breakfast Dera and Owen had coaxed her into eating.

After splashing water on her face, she went through the motions of ensuring her bag was packed exactly the way she liked it. Then she pulled on her tennis dress, wishing the bright cheery yellow and purple geometric pattern felt more like the armor it usually was for her. She thought the pre-match ritual would set her back on even footing, but from the second she stepped up to the service line, everything felt...off. The wave of peace that normally hit her on the court didn't come. When everything else in her world was wrong, when her dad had rescheduled a trip into town or the kids at school had picked on her, she could come to the court and forget it all.

But not today.

Today all the eyes burned into her, penetrating the protective bubble of the court, and instead of rooting her on, they were all judging her.

Slut. Whore. Wash up. Fake.

That's what they were thinking. Those pictures had given her a rush of empowerment when she first let Kole take them, so sexy and kickass and I-am-woman-hear-me-roar. Now that was replaced with fear and anger and hurt. It hurt that someone thought it was okay to let the world see such private pictures. She'd never hurt quite like this before.

Her knee whispered at her, a dull ache that couldn't compare to what her heart felt. She bounced the ball for her first service game, trying to find her center. She double-faulted instead. Her opponent, a young Brazilian player, ranked number thirty-five in the world, returned each serve at brutal speeds, using every inch of her five-foot-eleven height against Emerson. She wasn't particularly accurate, but soon Em was down a break and struggling to even get her racket to make contact with the ball. This shouldn't be happening; her opponent, an inexperienced wild card, had made it to the quarterfinals on dumb luck and moderate skill.

Yet Em's normally wicked forehand failed her. Her backhand barely cleared the net. Every time she tried to aim a shot to kiss the side of the court before going out, she miscalculated, and the points started to rise against her.

She fought to get where she needed to be. She even managed to win a few games, but the kid—Isabella something or other—took the first set, and before Emerson knew what was happening, they were at match point. They didn't even reach deuce once during the match. She managed to rally for a decent volley on the last point, but the ball sailed over the baseline, and the crowd roared.

She was out.

For the first time in almost four years, she was out of a tournament before the semifinals.

She'd worked her ass off for the last two months, coming back from her MCL tear, getting in the best shape of her life, and she'd let a fucking idiot screw her up so much she lost focus.

Unable to contain herself, she slammed her racket against the hard surface of the court in frustration. Then did it again. She would have slammed it a third time, but the rhythmic clicking of the shutters on the photographers' cameras at the end of the court stopped her. They were lapping this up. A picture of her smashing her racket would be juxtaposed with one of the racier pictures on the tabloid front pages in the states by morning.

She pulled herself together enough to shake hands with her opponent, gather her things, smile and wave to the crowd, and get the hell out of there. Amir's talking points waited in her inbox, but anything she said wouldn't matter. Not today. Today she was just the slut who let her boyfriend take dirty pictures of her, and nothing else mattered.

****

Conversation hummed all around Rob as he sat at the big desk, preparing for the panel discussion of the latest results from the Australian Open. In the midst of a media shit storm, Emerson Grace had gone out in the quarterfinals to an unknown player from New Zealand. Rob was still reeling from both sets of news. The loss itself would have been enough of a surprise. Em had been on fire during the first rounds of the tournament, barely dropping a game. She hadn't gone down in the quarters of a major tournament in years, let alone in straight sets.

But the pictures of Em were what lit a fire under his ass. When he first saw them this morning, he hadn't known what to think. Like any red-blooded man, his first thought had been, "Holy hell, she's hot." As sexy as she'd been at nineteen, she was ten times more stunning now. A man should fall on his knees and thank whatever god he believed in that he had a woman as gorgeous as her willing to wear that lingerie for him.

Once his initial reaction passed, he wanted to punch something—or someone. It took a lot of trust for Em to let someone get so close to her. He hadn't known her relationship with Naumov went that far. It had to be Kole, since the pictures looked like they'd been taken not long after she cut her hair short enough to graze her shoulders. For years, she'd worn it long, down to her shoulder blades, but she'd cut it before the US Open last year. Not that he paid much attention to her hairstyles or anything.

Whoever had posted those pictures was an ass who deserved to have his eyes poked out with hot tongs. Those pictures were obviously an intimate thing that

Em had intended to share with her boyfriend, not the whole goddamn world. Em's trust was hard won—her father's neglect had seen to that—and when she gave it, she didn't do it by half measures. The loss of her trust should hit a man like a high-powered serve to the gut.

Even though he'd lost that trust years ago, Rob's blood still boiled—partly on her behalf and partly because some primal part of him still saw her as his. The body of the woman he'd introduced to how intimate sex could be, how vital the connection between lovers should be, was plastered all over the Internet, and he honestly didn't know what to do about that.

In a roundabout way, it was his fault she was in this position if he wanted to take the masochistic viewpoint. If he hadn't listened to his dad, if some part of him hadn't questioned if she was using him for his name like so many women had before and since, if he hadn't pushed back his instinct to fight for her after the Olympics, she never would have been in a position for Naumov to take those pictures of her. If he'd just told her that he wanted to be with her forever when she assumed he was calling to break up with her, things might be so different now. But he hadn't. He'd let the doubts win.

His next thought had been to blame her, and he was still settled there as the makeup girl came to give his face a final pat. How could Em let this happen? How could she be so naive as to think that no one would post those pictures once they were taken? In this day and age, he barely sexted with a woman he was seeing, let alone took naked pictures with her.

"Rolling in five, four, three, two, one."

Rob looked up from the notes he'd stared at blindly

during the five-minute commercial break. Bruno Watson was leading the panel, wearing an expensive suit and tie, his ruddy complexion mellowed by a strong coating of pancake makeup. The set lights gleamed off the scalp exposed by his thinning hair, but he carried himself with the confidence of a man half his age. Christiane Quinn, one of the network's commentators, was seated between Rob and the older correspondent, a stiff smile plastered on her face, her red hair severely short and perfectly styled. She'd played on the tour for a few years before retiring for a less strenuous life on camera.

"Welcome back," Bruno said. "As you just saw, former number two player Emerson Grace, currently in the middle of a fall from grace, was knocked out of the quarterfinals of the Australian Open only moments ago."

The asshole chuckled at his own cleverness, and Rob barely managed not to roll his eyes.

Thankfully, Christiane stepped in before Rob had to. "I must say, Bruno, it was quite a shock to watch Emerson play today. She's always so accomplished, so in control. Her usual poise was nowhere to be found on the court."

"She was definitely in her head," Rob said. "She's one of the players you can count on for laser focus, for a highly intellectual game. When she loses, it's not because she overthinks her shots or makes unforced errors."

Bruno snorted. "My sources tell me she's been making more than her share of unforced errors off the court, even before she took nearly four months off due to a minor knee injury. Today's loss was merely a symptom of that if you ask me. It's such a shame when the female players let outside drama affect the game."

Rob's temper spiked. He didn't know where Bruno was going with this, but he got the feeling he wasn't going to like it. Bruno's reputation for being more critical and ruthless toward female players was going to be a problem today—likely a big one.

"Now, Bruno—" Christiane started, her jaw clenching a little.

"Come on, Christiane. You were a player. Are you telling me that a fight with your boyfriend or a bad story in the press didn't affect how you played your next match?"

Rob cut in. "I think that's true for all players, not just women. We've all had bad days and lost matches we shouldn't have because of stuff beyond our control off the court."

Just off the camera, Joey gave him a warning look. She wanted him to let Bruno do his thing; she'd made that clear in the makeup room earlier.

"Beyond her control? Gee, Rob, I don't know. I'm not sure any of the problems Emerson is having could be described as beyond her control."

Rob itched to wipe the smug look off the bastard's face.

Christiane's smile faltered a little. "It was sad to see her so off her usual form. I had high hopes for her this tournament. This should be her year to win a Grand Slam. But I'm not sure we should comment on such intimate aspects of players' personal lives when we don't have all the facts."

Bruno shook his head. "I think we are here to comment on the players' personal lives when their personal lives so blatantly affect their game at a major tournament, regardless of facts. I also think that we would be remiss if we didn't talk about Emerson's problems. She's long been held up as a positive influence for women and girls alike, and I must say I'm deeply disappointed in the recent news stories and rumors about her. Aren't you, Christiane? You've got a young daughter who's a juniors player now. Do you want her looking up to someone like Emerson Grace now?"

"Well, I—" Christiane's shoulders sagged. "I don't honestly know what to think of the latest stories and pictures that have come out about Emerson. She's a superb player, and before this there's never been a hint of scandal attached to her, but I do find the pictures in particular problematic."

"Exactly!" Bruno crowed. "She's supposed to be held up as an example to girls like your daughter. What kind of lesson is she teaching those girls if she's taking pictures of herself in slutty underwear? In this day and age, that's just reckless and irresponsible. She should know better. Those pictures combined with the stories of her cheating on world number one, Kole Naumov? I think we know what we can call Emerson Grace, and it's not a champion. Don't you agree, Rob?"

Rob stared at his colleague, then glanced at Joey. She was eating this shit up. Ratings points flashing in her eyes like a cartoon animal spotting a bag of money and seeing dollar signs. As the new kid on the block, he should fall in line and join in with Bruno's commentary or at least take Christiane's stance. That's what they all expected of him, but anger shimmered through him, worse than it did after a bad call on the court or his parents forgot his sister's birthday. Protectiveness roared to life, battling back whatever reservations he might have about Em's decision to let the pictures be taken. Em didn't deserve this. No woman did.

"Is it really fair to judge her, Bruno?" he asked, his voice dangerously soft.

Bruno blinked at him, the smug smile still in place. "What do you mean? I think it's entirely fair. We've got the evidence there in living color. What else would you call a woman who poses for pictures like that?"

"I'd call her a woman who trusts her partner." Rob kept his voice even, doing his best not to betray how he really felt.

If Bruno caught one whiff of any past relationship between Rob and Em, the older correspondent would have a field day shredding them both to pieces on the air. The rest of the world didn't need to know how much Rob wished he hadn't broken up with Em all those years ago any more than they needed to sit and speculate about the pictures she'd let Kole take.

"It's not unusual for a woman to buy provocative lingerie and model it for her guy. It's also normal for a guy to want to preserve that moment, especially when you both have careers that mean you spend a lot of time apart. You're sitting there judging her for sharing an intimate moment with her boyfriend, but what about the people who thought it was acceptable to invade her privacy, release that moment, and turn it into something dirty?"

"She's a public figure," Bruno sneered. "She doesn't get to have privacy. Come on, Ashton, you more than most know that. She doesn't get to have normal experiences, and if she wants to do something like this, she needs to be adult enough to deal with it and not let it affect her tennis game."

Rob leaned forward, forearms braced on the table, hands clasped to keep from punching Bruno. "She's an athlete. Her job is to play her sport and play it to the best of her abilities. That doesn't mean she surrendered her right to privacy. She's a damn good tennis player. That's all that should matter. But she's a human, and when people are attacking you from all sides because someone decided to take a private moment public, that's going to get in your head and lead to losses like today. It still doesn't change the fact that she's one of the top ten players in the world, and she deserves more respect than you've shown her here."

Bruno opened his mouth to say more, but Christiane jumped in at a signal from Joey. "Excellent points, both of you. Let's go to a quick commercial break, and then I believe we're ready to begin the coverage of Cruz Guerra's match against Juan Bassimo on Court One."

They all sat still until the all-clear buzz sounded, then Bruno surged to his feet. "Joey, what the hell is this? Did you not brief the kid here on how our coverage of the Grace story was to go?"

"You were there when I did it, Bruno." Joey sighed. "Rob, what was that?"

Rob bit back a number of sharp retorts before he finally spoke, deliberately keeping his voice as polite and even as possible. "That was me bringing sports coverage out of the 1950s. Slut-shaming one of the top female players in the world? That's really the message you want to send?" His jaw tightened as he reined in his temper. "Think, Joey. Do you think Emerson's team would let us near her for an interview in the next decade if you let Bruno go off on her like that? And dozens of female players would back her up if she decided to boycott us, including Dera Calvet and my sister."

"How do I know this isn't about some crush you have on her? You went soft on her before, and I thought it was charming. Now I'm not so sure." Joey grabbed his arm and tugged him off to one corner. "If you had a problem, you should have said something when I briefed you."

"One, you didn't give me a chance to get a word in. Two, you didn't tell me how far Bruno was going. Alluding to her personal problems is one thing. All but calling her a slut on international TV after she got her ass handed to her by an unranked player is another."

"What's better entertainment? Talking about a relevant story involving a player who lost a match she should have won in her sleep? Or white-washing the same story so as not to offend the player?" she retorted, green eyes narrowing. "I have a responsibility to get us ratings, Rob. I thought you understood that."

He shoved his hands through his hair. "Jesus, Joey. Wake up. I would think you more than anyone would understand. Women are a big chunk of tennis's fan base. Women's tennis brings in just as much, if not more, money than men's, and the viewers and the players are sick of Bruno's sexism. He's a chauvinist and a bully. For once, why can't a network take a progressive stance on a sex scandal? Why slut-shame her? Why not ask the real questions, like who released the pictures? I can guarantee you it wasn't Emerson. Was it Kole? We know the cheating rumors are coming from him, so it's not a huge stretch. Or did someone hack into Kole's phone? Who wanted a story that badly to go after Emerson? You'll win more viewers by treating Emerson like a modern woman than you will taking a Victorian view and placing all the blame on her. Come on, let's be unique for once instead of doing the expected story."

She glared at him for several long moments before sighing and glancing down at her buzzing phone. "Fine. I'll make this work and pull Bruno in as best I can. But do not pull a switch-up like this on me again. And if I find out this is some show of favoritism for Grace, your ass is grass."

That's exactly what this was, but she didn't need to know that. The odds of Em giving him another chance, especially after the shit Naumov pulled on her, were slim.

"Favoritism? There's no love lost between me and Emerson. She'd wring my neck if she had half the chance. I only defended her because if that were Maren, I would want someone to step up and point out how wrong coverage like ours was."

"That better be the truth. I don't have time to train a new correspondent because you've got a hard-on for a pretty girl with a penchant for expensive lingerie." Joey stalked off before he could respond.

His stomach turned as he watched her storm off. Having his say, doing something to help Em, eased his temper—but only a little. Seeing her gorgeous body plastered all over tabloids and blogs made him want to burn down the world. She'd trusted Kole to let him do something so intimate. Moreover, she probably had feelings for the bastard. If he'd released those pictures for the world to see? His ass deserved to fry—or at least be put under the same microscope as Em. And if Naumov hadn't released them, then whoever did had reserved a special place in hell for themselves.

Em didn't deserve any of this. He just wished there was more he could do to protect her and make it go away.

Chapter 4

Emerson sat at the far corner of the hotel bar, as far as she could get from the prying eyes—the accusatory eyes. She ached everywhere; her mind's soreness echoed her body's. Even following Amir's talking points, the press conference had been almost as grueling as the match itself. Question after question, coming at her like body shots from a ball machine turned on too high. Why had she let pictures like that get taken? Did she expect young girls to view her as a role model? Had she released the pictures to get back at Kole? On and on and on.

So here she was, drowning the ache with a very well-made chocolate martini. She'd be in her room, curled up in bed, but Dera had insisted they meet up for a drink. She'd also ordered Emerson to put on a dress and heels and makeup. Emerson hated all three on a good day, but her friend had a point. This had to look like any other loss. If it didn't, there would only be more talk.

God Almighty, she hated the talk. In the locker room before the press conference, she'd briefly heard the TWW team going after her for the pictures and the loss. She'd put her earbuds in, cranking up the Joss Stone as Bruno Watson went on another sexist tirade with Christiane jumping in to try to balance him out and Rob just sitting there, letting him go. It had been the same old story that the gaggle at the press conference had slung. She was a slut for letting someone take pictures of her in her underwear, and she was a bad player for letting the release of the pictures affect her game.

She wanted all of it to stop. To scream at them all to think for two seconds. Deep down, Em knew that this was how the world had always worked—a couple did something scandalous, but the woman took the brunt of it in the public eye. But anyone with half a brain could see that she hadn't been alone when the pictures were taken, and she hadn't been the one taking them. She accepted that she shared some of the blame for agreeing to the pictures, but she'd never asked for any of this. All she'd done was trust a man whom she thought she might be falling in love with. Stupid her. She'd let herself forget what happened to her when she let a man get that close.

"Nice job at the press conference today."

That voice, that deep, rumbly fuck-hot voice. It pissed her off that after seven years of animosity and bickering, Rob Ashton's voice still made her knees go weak and her girl parts stand at attention. It'd happened when he interviewed her too, but it'd been easier to ignore in the newsroom.

All of it came flooding back to her. The heat of young desire. The heady intoxication of first love. The crushing weight of heartbreak when she'd overheard his father telling him she was a gold-digger, a social climber who was using him as a meal ticket because she'd never make it as a professional tennis player. Rob hadn't defended her then, and she'd known what was coming when he took a week to return her phone call after London. Still, her heart had crumbled when he said they'd be better off as friends, better off focusing on their own careers. He hadn't been willing to fight for her, damn him, and he joined the list of men who picked their jobs over her, right up there with her father. Eventually, as she saw him moving on within a few weeks, that heartbreak had morphed into anger soon enough, and the anger still lingered.

She stared at her drink, hoping he was a figment of her very tired brain, but he wasn't. He was there, live and potent as hell, in expensive jeans and a light-blue oxford shirt that brought out the blue flecks in his eyes and emphasized the muscles that he obviously hadn't let go to fat since his retirement. Jesus, he even smelled the same. That mix of eucalyptus and cotton and man that intoxicated her with the smallest whiff.

He slid onto a stool beside her and asked the bartender to bring him a local microbrew.

"You really think I want to talk to you of all people on today of all days?"

Rob shrugged, his gunmetal eyes trailing over her in a lazy assessment. She didn't look at him, but the tendrils of heat his gaze sent across her skin both excited and annoyed her. He was the enemy, damn it. She shouldn't feel anything for him after today.

"Kinda surprised to see you here. I thought you might be on a plane home or up in your hotel room," he said, his eyes never leaving her. "I admire your moxie, though. Showing up at the hotel bar—the same hotel your ex is staying at—in a siren red cocktail dress that teases but doesn't give anything away? That's ballsy."

Apparently, both of her exes were staying here.

She rolled her eyes, taking a drink of her martini to

cool her blood and gain a hold on her self-control. "Wow. That means so much coming from the guy who works for the network that basically called me a whore today. I'll tell you what's ballsy—you coming over to talk to me. I've had it up to here with reporters today. So go jump in the ocean or something."

It felt good to finally take a jab at somebody. She'd much rather it be at Kole, but she'd settle for Rob. Right now, she didn't care what he might say about her on the air. All she cared about was making him go away before she completely lost it.

"Ah. There's the Em I know." He took a long swig from the beer the bartender placed in front of him. "I'm not here as a reporter. I'm here as a—"

"If you say friend, I swear I might kick you. Or rip your testicles out through your nose. Both sound appealing right now." Her fists curled into tight balls against the sleek bar top.

He did not get to call himself her friend. He'd given her up seven years ago. If he hadn't, she might not be in this mess in the first place. After everything he'd put her through, he didn't get to sit next to that chauvinist bastard Bruno and then come up to her and say he was her friend.

He flinched, and out of the corner of her eye, she caught his frown and—was that pain in his eyes? No. It couldn't be. He had proved time and again he didn't give a damn about what she said to him.

"Okay. Obviously, not a good day to talk to you. All I wanted to say was you're handling yourself better than anyone expected, especially in that press conference. Keep your chin up, Em. I'll see you around."

Em.

One little syllable could send her back seven years faster than the time machine on that Doctor Who show Owen loved. "Em" was the girl she'd been during that short, wonderful time with Rob, the girl who laughed more, who let her guy steal kisses as they snuck through the streets of London. Em was the girl whose heart was trampled because she'd given it to Rob without a second thought. Maybe she should go ahead and rip his testicles through his nose. It might make her feel better.

"Wow. Who do you want to turn into mincemeat with your racket?" Dera asked, sliding onto the stool Rob had vacated a few minutes before.

Emerson glanced at her friend. True to form, Dera had dressed to kill in a bright-yellow sheath that hugged her lithe body and left one shoulder bare.

"That arrogant ass," Emerson said through clinched teeth.

"What are you talking about?" Dera sipped the lemon-drop martini that materialized in front of her and gave the female bartender a flirtatious smile. Most people didn't know, but Dera was bi. She didn't hide her "fluid" sexuality as she called it; she just didn't advertise it.

Taking a long gulp of her own drink, Emerson glanced over her shoulder to where Rob sat by himself, tapping away at the screen of his phone. "Did you not hear the post-match analysis TWW did? Bruno and Christiane all but call me a slut and a whore and blamed me for the pictures, just like everyone else. Then Rob thinks he can come up to me and compliment me on how I handled the press conference."

A hand on her arm, Dera turned Emerson to face her. "Wait. Did you listen to the whole panel?"

"Listen to ten minutes of some of the most well-known reporters in the industry slut-shaming me? Uh—no. I put my earbuds in once Christiane joined in."

Anger clawed at her gut, making her question her choice of drink. Maybe a few shots of straight tequila would have been better. She was less than twenty-four hours into this disaster. How much worse was it going to get? Amir was working with her sponsors, but she only imagined what some of them might say in statements if he didn't succeed in persuading them to stick with her.

Sighing, Dera banged her head against the bar. "*Merde*. Emmy, Rob defended you."

The words echoed in her head, but she couldn't make sense of them. Rob Ashton never missed an opportunity to criticize her. When he'd still been on tour, he'd sometimes get up early just to heckle her about her second serve on the practice courts, knowing that she was an early riser. Defending her hadn't been on the table since the day he ended things with her over the phone.

"Defended me?" She shook her head. "Why would he defend me?"

"I have theories on that, but you won't like them. But he did defend you. He called Bruno on being a pig and pointed out that the people to blame for all of this are the people who released the photos. That you didn't do anything wrong. From what I heard, his producer was pissed at first, but he pointed out that pinning a scarlet letter on you wasn't going to win them points with any of the female players."

Rob defended her.

On international TV.

What the hell?

"Am I in the Twilight Zone or something? Rob has never stood up for me before. I'm honestly surprised he didn't join Bruno on the 'Emerson is a slut' bandwagon."

"Oh m'God. You're blind. Rob, for all his Ashton arrogance, wouldn't do that. He likes you, Emmy. He hides it behind the bickering and the sniping, but it's there. Haven't you seen the way he looks at you?" Dera gave a very French shrug. "And more than that, he respects you as a tennis player. Go look up the panel on YouTube if you don't believe me."

Emmy's headache ramped up a few notches. None of this made sense. In the course of eighteen hours, her entire world had been turned upside down, and Rob Ashton defending her was the cherry on top. And she'd been…a total bitch to him. *Shit.* She didn't want to feel bad about one more thing tonight. She flagged down the bartender. "Two tequila shots."

"Are you leaving tomorrow?" Dera asked. "No one would blame you."

Emerson slammed back her first shot, relishing the burn, hoping it'd get rid of the dregs of confusion. "We're checking out of the hotel tomorrow, but Zoe and I are staying with her family until our flight out. It's better that way. Amir says the press are sniffing around my townhouse in Miami, and my grandmother is staying with my aunt and uncle until this blows over."

"How is your gran? Did you talk to her?"

Emerson nodded, glancing over her shoulder. Rob joined her brother and Cruz. *Shit.* What were they doing? This was too much. She couldn't think.

"She's doing better than I expected, but I'm worried. It'd be much easier if Papa Vic were still here. Still, she's not letting on that the pictures have upset her. She's on my side and avoiding the pictures if at all possible. Dad's had a worse reaction than she has, the bastard."

She'd been dodging her father's phone calls since after her match, but she'd listened to the four messages he'd left.

"Ignore him like he's ignored you for most of your life. He deserves a taste of his own medicine." Dera gave Emerson's shoulders a squeeze.

Slamming back the second tequila shot, Emerson accepted the fact that no amount of alcohol was going to numb today. No amount of alcohol was going to make sense of today. And no amount of alcohol was going to quiet the whirl of questions plaguing her, and it was all his fault. Excusing herself from her friend, she hurried up to her hotel room, dodging a few reporters and some well-meaning friends along the way.

The second her hotel room door shut behind her, she kicked off her shoes and grabbed her tablet. She watched the full panel, then watched it again, a dull buzzing noise filling her ears.

None of this made sense. He'd really stood up for her, and he'd done it in a subtle, classy way. He hadn't made it personal or done anything that would make things worse for her. He'd pointed out the sides of the story that everyone else ignored. Amir was still working on finding out who leaked the pictures, but Rob had turned it and made them the story too, shifting the focus away from her as much as possible.

She should dismiss this as him being a stand-up guy, showing integrity in his job. That would make more sense than what she was thinking. Because seeing him there, protecting her when everyone else was skewering her, made her question everything. For seven years, she'd believed he didn't care. Something—or someone—had convinced him to hate her, but now she wasn't so sure. A warmth in her chest started to grow, breaking free of the triple deadbolts she'd put in place when he broke up with her. Did he still care about her? Did she still care about him? This was all…too much. Maybe it would clear up in the morning, but right now she didn't know how she'd deal with the mess that had become her life.

****

Rob left Em and took a seat in one of the corner booths in the restaurant bar. Her rejection stung—a lot. He'd hoped that after today, some of the old animosity might have faded. Honestly, he couldn't blame her for being so mad at him, at any man today. God knew he was disillusioned with his gender after hearing some of the questions the reporters had asked her. He hated how the vultures picked at her. The press team had done a good job of keeping the press conference brief, but there'd been enough time for the gaggle to get some sharp jabs in.

And yet after facing all of that, there she was, sitting at the bar in a dress designed to make a man's mouth water. The fiery red of the slightly shiny fabric made her golden skin glow in the bar's artful lighting. Its loose neckline had dipped low over her full breasts, giving a teasing glance at the upper swells and the tempting cleft between them, without showing too much. From here, he could see how the dress's skirt rode up her thighs, showing off a tempting expanse of soft flesh. His body tightened at the memory of those thighs and how they'd felt around him. He'd spent seven years trying to forget how sweet she tasted, how passionate he could make her.

"Rob. Fancy meeting you here."

Tearing his gaze away from Em, Rob found himself looking up at the towering figure of her older brother. Although Owen hadn't been a full-time student, he'd trained at the same tennis academy in Spain where Cruz and Rob trained from ages twelve to seventeen. Owen had been one of the students who usually came over for a few weeks on school breaks. His grandparents couldn't afford to send him full time, and they'd preferred to have him at home, which wasn't the case for most of the guys at the academy.

Rob stood, extending a hand to him. "It's been a while, Owen. Won't you join me?"

"Care to add a third?" Cruz asked, coming up beside Owen. "Grace and I were getting ready to grab a drink when we spotted you skulking over here by yourself."

"I wasn't skulking," Rob argued, scooting so his friends could join him on the circular bench.

A waitress shimmied up and took their orders, blatantly flirting with each of them in turn, but judging from his friends' expressions, they weren't in the mood for a casual flirtation any more than he was tonight.

"I'm surprised to see you here tonight, Grace," Rob said, sipping at the remnants of the microbrew he'd grabbed at the bar. "Would have thought you'd want to avoid any place a reporter might ambush you."

Owen snorted. "Believe me, I would if I could. But Dera gave me the heads-up that she and my sister were planning to be in the bar tonight. I couldn't hide in my room while Emmy was down here."

"We heard Emmy handing you your ass as we walked in," Cruz commented with a cheeky grin.

"Her tongue's as sharp as I remember it." Rob kept his tone light as he accepted the new bottle of beer the waitress handed him before she gave Cruz and Owen theirs.

"She didn't hear most of the interview." Owen settled back on the bench, taking a drink of his beer. "She tends to tune Bruno out within a few seconds on good days."

The Grace siblings, while opposite in height, shared more than a few similarities. The same easy spirit, the same sense of humor, the same blunt honesty, and the same eyes. Where Em's were more mysterious and assessing, Owen's usually sparkled with mischief. He was known for the little pranks he liked to pull.

"You did a good thing, amigo," Cruz added in. "Did you catch heat from your producers for standing up to Bruno?"

Rob shrugged. "Not too much. Bruno's mad as hell, but Joey's softer side prevailed, for now at least."

"Well, since my sister's not likely to say it, thank you for standing up for her." Owen raised his bottle in salute.

Rob managed a tight smile. Appreciation from Em's brother paled in comparison to a "thank you" from the woman herself, but he doubted he'd get that anytime soon. "Don't thank me for responsible journalism. The vultures focus in on the easiest person to lampoon, and I don't think that's fair to anyone. Everyone deserves privacy and respect, simple as that."

"Here, here." Cruz nodded. "But it was still a big risk to take. You're new at that job. For all you knew, they'd toss you out on your overpriced ass."

Rob watched Em go, her head held high, her dress skimming her curves the way he wished he could. He didn't blame her for leaving now that she'd been seen. He imagined she'd hole up in her room, reading one of the twenty books she always seemed to have with her.

"I hate to see anyone going through this. I've been in the crosshairs before, and it was bad enough when it was an injury. I can't imagine what it's like in Emerson's situation."

The rage that coursed through his veins when he first saw the pictures had boiled down to low-level pissed off, but it still spiked every time he thought of Em's face during the press conference. She'd kept her expression neutral for the most part, which impressed him, but her eyes told a different story. She always had the most expressive eyes; they were his favorite feature of hers. They always told the real story if he looked close enough. He'd seen them bright with joy and the same mischief her brother's usually held, but he'd also seen them swimming with hurt and regret and anger—all because of him.

There'd been so much pain in the warm brown depths during the press conference. He could see it, even through the TV screen. She'd been itching to give them a piece of her mind, but too many years of keeping herself contained, for the sake of her grandparents and under the direction of Zoe, prevented her from going off on them the way she had with him.

"Rob? You with us?" Cruz dragged him back to reality.

"Hm? Yeah, sorry, man." Rob gave his head a mental shake. "What did you say?"

Owen rolled his eyes. "I asked how your shoulder's doing. I've heard a bunch of different stuff, but I thought I'd get it from the horse's mouth, so to speak."

Shrugging, Rob leaned his forearms on the table, studying the sleek wooden surface. "Truth? It depends on the day. It'll never be the same, but a day when it doesn't ache like a sore tooth is a good day."

"I gotta say, I admire you for coming back and doing the whole reporting thing." Owen's brows furrowed. "I don't know if I could be around the courts if I couldn't play anymore."

"Tennis is the only steady thing in my life. Even if I can't play, I want to be around it. And it's really not as bad as I thought it would be." Okay, a small lie. It sucked to sit on the sidelines, more than he'd expected. But at least he had control again; at least he was doing something. He'd spent too much time brooding already. He needed to focus on the here and now, not on his bum shoulder and the loss of the only career he'd ever wanted.

"How's Emmy doing with all of this? Really?" Cruz asked, pitching his voice lower so they wouldn't be overheard.

Owen's jaw tightened. "She doesn't let on, but the last few months have been rough. Getting injured when she was on such a roll was bad enough, but add in the breakup and top it off with the grandparents' health problems and Papa Vic's passing, and last year ended up being pretty shitty. Now to start the season with these fucking pictures getting leaked? She's a lot stronger than I am. I honestly think I'd be curled up in a closet if I were in her shoes."

He remembered how close Em and Owen were to their grandparents, but Em had always been especially close to her grandfather. Her face lit up when she told him stories about her early tournaments and how her grandpa used to fret over her and dote on her.

He'd never know it, but Victor Grace had helped Rob win his granddaughter over in the end.

Em hadn't easily agreed to go out with him, which only made Rob want her more. At almost twenty-three, he'd already been with more than his fair share of women, but they always fell at his feet easily. Not Em, though. He'd asked her out the very first time he met her in London, but it'd taken getting stuck in an elevator with her before she agreed to go out with him. They'd shared their first kiss in that elevator. The first of many kisses. Kisses that stopped because he'd been a complete idiot and listened to his father instead of his heart.

Rob picked at the label on his beer bottle as his friends chatted about some of the matches they'd caught in the men's draw. This felt good. Being here, with his friends. This was what he'd missed in the time he'd been gone. But something was definitely missing from the picture he'd formed in his head.

Em.

She was the missing part of the picture. She'd always been the missing piece. Every time he'd won a major title, even his Olympic medal and his Grand Slam title, something had been missing to make it perfect. He'd realized during his time away from the game that she was what had been missing from all of it.

"Do you have anyone looking into who's behind all of this?" Cruz asked Owen, pulling Rob back to the present.

Owen finished off his beer. "Our agent, Amir al-Tammar, is working on it, but his guys haven't had any luck so far. He's got a top firm looking into it. They specialize in cyber forensics."

"Are the police involved yet?" Rob set aside his beer bottle. He was worried for Em. This was bigger than a prank or revenge. He had some friends who were actors and actresses, and he'd heard horror stories about what happened in situations like this. The crazies came out of the woodwork, and life got complicated.

"Not yet. There's not a lot they can go on right now, and the legality of it all is a bit murky." Owen's eyes darkened dangerously. "But if I find out that it's that dick Naumov who posted them, I may need one of you to come bail me out of jail in whatever city we're in."

"Deal," Rob and Cruz said in unison.

The friends chatted for a while longer before Rob finally stood. "I've got an early call time in the morning, so I'll see you guys later."

After letting himself into his room, Rob flopped down in one of the stylish armchairs and stared out over the Melbourne city lights. Ignoring the ache in his shoulder, he let his thoughts drift into the realm of brooding. He hated this whole situation. He hated that he wasn't on the court, but more than that he hated that he wasn't in the position to do more to help Em. That she didn't know how much he still cared.

It was his own damn fault for letting her go in the

first place. He'd let his dad bully him and convince him that his career should come before everything. He'd let himself believe that Em would hold him back from becoming the best. He should have known that was a load of bullshit after how hard it was to forget her. He'd drunk himself blind for a week straight after things ended between them, but nothing worked.

Now every instinct screamed at him to find some way to help Em, to be there for her as he should have been for the last seven years. But she'd made it very clear tonight that she wanted nothing to do with him or his help, and he wasn't sure he could change her mind after everything he'd done.

****

"All right, let's go over the schedule one more time," Zoe said as they sat in a quiet corner of the Melbourne airport.

Emerson tried not to roll her eyes. In the six days since she'd been knocked out of the quarterfinals, all she and Zoe and—via FaceTime—Amir had done was strategize. Her head spun with all the meetings and events they'd managed to squeeze in between now and her next tournament at the end of February.

"Okay," Emmy said, setting down the book she had been trying to read. "Let's go over operation 'don't lose any more sponsors' for the fiftieth time."

Zoe, with the practice of someone who'd known her since she was six, ignored Emerson's attitude and continued on. "I'm going back to Miami to get things in order and to see my poor dogs. You have meetings with FashFit and hopefully a photoshoot with them in New York. Then the meeting about the exhibition match with Maren Ashton, her mother, and Rosamund

Gilligan to benefit some women in sports charity in May. You and Maren versus the older set. Amir's working on squeezing in meetings with a few of your other sponsors to make sure they understand that dropping you would be worse for their public image than a few pictures. From there, you'll join me in Florida, and we'll go over the video again and see what we need to hone in on."

"Sounds good." She tried to smile but failed as she watched someone buy a tabloid from a nearby news stand with her picture splashed across the front page. Bile rose in her throat. God, when would this be over? Surely some minor royal or B-list movie star had done something stupid recently? It didn't help that one of her sponsors, a hair product line, had dropped her yesterday with a strongly worded release about the "moral character" of the "face of their brand."

Zoe looked to where Emerson's gaze rested. "Don't let it bother you."

"I just—" She took a breath, fighting the lump in her throat. "I thought that it would have died down by now. It's not like I'm that big a name."

"Tennis is hot right now, love. On top of that, Kole is the world number one, and he's got a memorable personality and a body to go with it. You're the girl who broke his heart and took dirty pictures for him, which makes you newsworthy. It'll die down eventually, but right now, there's nothing to distract them from you."

The laugh that escaped Emmy held a rusty quality. She hadn't had much cause to laugh lately. She'd spent the last six days holed up at Zoe's estate, either practicing, plotting, or curled up in the guest room she'd been staying in since she was twelve. She'd lost herself in books and old movies, trying to forget the entire world knew what she looked like in her underwear.

"Well, well, look who it is."

The thick Eastern European accent made the hairs on the back of Emmy's neck stand on end and her breath catch in her chest.

Fuck.

She'd forgotten that before all of this nightmare began, she and Kole bought their tickets so that their planes left around the same time. What seemed like a sweet idea two months ago when they'd still been together now proved the worst idea ever.

"You've got some nerve to even think of talking to me." Emerson didn't look up, didn't do anything that might look like she was acknowledging him. Looking at him would only make things worse. Seeing him with those high, sharp cheekbones and midnight blue eyes and the light brown hair he always kept cut military short would remind her how much she'd come to care for him and what an ass he'd turned out to be. He towered over her and Zoe, so looking at him would give her a cramp in her neck.

"I have the nerve? You broke up with me, Emerson." Kole's voice was cold, but she heard the hurt beneath the words.

She steeled herself against the small twinge of guilt and stood to face him. "Yes, I broke up with you. Do you remember why? Or have you taken one too many tennis balls to the head?"

"Was it because you chose to put your family ahead of your relationship?" His eyes narrowed. "Or is it because you're a ball-busting bitch who didn't want to sacrifice any of herself to be with a man who cared for her?"

"Hey." She took a step back as if he'd slapped her. "I'm not the one who acted like a toddler because his girlfriend wanted to go see her dying grandfather instead of going to some party in New York. And if you really cared for me, you would have understood that. Caring about my life and my career in conjunction with caring for you does not make me a ball-busting bitch— it makes me a modern woman."

Zoe stood up as well, hands on her slim hips, green eyes shooting daggers. "I think you need to go now, Kole."

"Yes, try to shield your precious Emerson like you always do," he sneered. "The poor parentless girl needs her coach to defend her from an adult conversation."

Emerson shot Zoe a warning look. Her coach could be a mama bear when she got the chance, but Emerson needed to handle this on her own.

"An adult conversation? Because it's so mature to take swipes at me about my parents." Emerson crossed her arms, one hip cocked to the side. "You know, I was saying to Dera the other day that it felt like we'd reverted to high school, what with all of the completely false rumors you've been spreading about me. I know you've got quite the ego, but saying that I cheated on you? With multiple men? At the same time? Well, that doesn't really speak well of your…prowess in the bedroom."

He snorted, shifting his leather duffle bag from one shoulder to the other, eyes darting around. "Or it speaks to what a selfish slut you are. Those pictures are worth a thousand words, aren't they?"

She balled up her fist and started to draw it back, but Zoe quickly grabbed her wrist and pulled her back a few steps. At the same moment, a set of broad shoulders appeared in front of her, blocking Kole from her view. She'd recognize those shoulders anywhere. And if she didn't recognize the shoulders, she'd definitely recognize the butt. Whatever the man's faults, he had an excellent ass.

"What do we have here?" Rob asked. "Surely you aren't harassing these ladies in a public place, Naumov. A public place with several members of the press within earshot."

"Mind your own business, Ashton. You know what a bitch she is," Kole retorted.

Rob drew himself to his full height, and Emerson had to step to one side to see Kole's reaction. Rob had a good four or five inches on Kole, and Kole was smart enough to back up a step or two.

"The only bitch I see here is you. A woman broke up with you. Big deal. You've got enough ball bunnies stashed all over the world that you'll have no trouble finding comfort. I suggest you leave now before I get one of my new friends from the tabloids to run a story about you and a nasty STD you picked up from a brothel in Thailand."

Kole and Rob had a stare down worthy of the OK Corral for a minute or two longer before Kole walked away, muttering some colorful words in Serbian under his breath.

"Thank you," Emerson said as Rob turned to face her. "I had it under control, but I appreciate you keeping me from spending the night in an Australian prison."

"They're supposed to be fairly nice, but I think we all prefer that you're not behind bars." Rob's smile wasn't his usual easy grin, mostly because of the worry lurking in his eyes. Plus something else she couldn't put her finger on. "You okay?"

Something caught in her chest and fluttered in her stomach, but she pushed it down. She couldn't let him in, no matter how nice he was being. "I…yeah. I'm fine."

"Zoe. Always nice to see you." With a nod to the redhead, Rob strolled away with his hands shoved into the pockets of his designer jeans.

Zoe and Emerson returned to their seats, Zoe's eyes pinning Emerson with a thousand questions.

"What was that all about? Is there something going on between you and Rob Ashton that I should know about?"

Emerson shook her head. "No. Definitely not."

"Are you sure? The way he looks at you…if I didn't know you two fought like cats and dogs, I'd swear you were—"

"That we were what?" She kept her tone nonchalant, but her heart pounded.

Zoe frowned and sighed. "That you were lovers. Which is ridiculous. Heaven knows I've had to keep you two from fighting often enough."

Not so ridiculous. Her heart clenched as she remembered what it was like to kiss him. He was the first man she'd kissed, instead of letting him initiate the kiss.

She still remembered every detail of it, probably because she saw it so many times in her dreams. The twelve-inch height difference had made the maneuver a little challenging, but Emerson had surged to her tiptoes and pressed a kiss to Rob's mouth. She'd meant for it to be a soft, sweet kiss, over as fast as it started, but he'd followed her as she lowered to put her feet firmly on the ground. Extending the kiss, his lips had moved over hers, gentle but insistent, teasing and coaxing until she opened her mouth. As their tongues twined and danced, his hands had moved over her, his body pressing her into the rough stone wall of the alleyway they'd ducked into.

Every inch of her went up in flames at the memory of how it'd made her feel. That man, that beautiful, strong, talented man had wanted her—little Emerson Grace, the mutt that everyone loved to tease. The power of it had made her a little drunk and a lot turned on.

Later that night, she'd agreed to go to bed with him. Even after all these years, that same feeling still ghosted through her whenever he got too close. Despite everything, she was still glad he'd been her first. Rob had been sweet and considerate and passionate. Everything a girl could want in a lover.

"Rob and I aren't anything. We don't even like each other, like you said." She opened her book again.

Zoe put her hand on Emerson's wrist, drawing her attention up to the green eyes that had been seeing through her bravado since the day they'd met. "A bloke, especially one like Robert Ashton III, does not step in and defend a woman like he has twice in one week if he doesn't like her quite a bit."

Shifting uncomfortably, Emerson looked away. Zoe saw too much and said too much. Emerson didn't want to believe that Zoe was right. The stuff he'd said on the panel could be explained away as human decency, but stepping in today? When he didn't have to? That old fluttery feeling came back in full force, and she had no idea what to make of it. Not that it mattered. With any luck, she wouldn't have to see him again for at least a month or two, and by then everything would be back to normal.

****

Rob couldn't believe his luck. During his conversation with Emerson and Zoe, he happened to get a glimpse at Em's ticket. She was going to be on the same flights to New York as him. A little flirtation with the desk agent and a story about him and Em being old friends who wanted to sit together and spend the trip catching up, and he'd arranged his seat so he was sitting next to her in business class.

He boarded the plane first and got himself settled. Travel was a part of the tennis lifestyle he hadn't really missed. Stuck sitting in a big metal tube for hours on end was not his idea of fun.

He'd rather be moving, exercising, doing anything but sitting still. Stretching his legs out as much as he could, he dug his book out of his carryon and tried to focus on it, all while glancing up so he wouldn't miss Em's face when she boarded and found him in the aisle seat beside her.

As soon as he spotted her dark head over the backs of the seats, he pretended to be absorbed with his book.

"Excuse me." Em's tone was only mildly annoyed—a promising sign.

He glanced up, his most charming smile firmly in place. "Oh. Em. Hi. Fancy meeting you here. Is this your seat?"

"Yes, apparently we're seat mates. Now can you move your giant legs so I can get to my seat, or do I need to step on you?"

"I'll move." He pulled his legs in, enjoying the full-on view he got of her leggings-clad ass under the long tunic-style top as she slid by. "And my legs aren't giant. They're perfectly proportional for someone my height."

Em tossed her short hair to get the swing of it out of her face as she tucked her carryon away. "Yeah, and you're a giant."

"You're just saying that because you're short."

They'd had this little argument so many times during their short relationship, usually when they were sharing a bed and his legs were hanging off the end. He hadn't minded then, because he had her in his arms, naked and satisfied. To be honest, he didn't mind now. It was a far cry from the hostility she'd lobbed at him a week ago in the hotel bar.

While he'd hoped she might at least attempt to make conversation with him, she immediately pulled out a book and didn't even glance up during the pre-flight briefings. Her knuckles got a little white during takeoff, but she still didn't look away from the book. Remembering a conversation they'd had on their first date, he waited until the plane leveled off before speaking.

"Still a little afraid of flying?" he asked softly.

Dark brows furrowed as the sun from the window glinted off her golden skin. She held the book up a little higher, but she still responded. "I'm not afraid of flying. Just of takeoffs and landings and really big bumps. And falling. The whole mom dying in a plane crash thing will do that to a girl."

She talked to him—fifteen-love to Ashton. "Understandable. What are you reading?"

"Why is it," she said philosophically, her nose still buried in her book, "that people feel the need to ask someone what they're reading when they're in the midst of reading? The book in the face should be a universal signal that the person is not in the mood to talk."

He grinned. Nice to know the encounter with Kole hadn't knocked the sass out of her. Sassy Em was his favorite version of her. Well, except for maybe Naked Em. "Maybe, but it's still polite to answer the question, grumpy."

"If you must know, I'm reading *Persuasion*." She turned briefly to show him the cover of the slightly tattered book.

"Is that the same copy you had when we were in London?" he asked, the words coming out before he could stop them. He could kick himself for bringing up London.

She stiffened a little, but she relaxed on a sigh. "Yes. I've had this copy since I was twelve. Zoe brought it back from a trip to England."

"Right. It's your favorite book, isn't it?" Unlike a lot of women who hung out in the players' lounge who spent their time reading magazines or messing around on their phones, Em always had a book with her.

"Yes." Turning the page, she glanced up, her eyes meeting his. "What?"

He shook his head. "Nothing. I just like how you look when you're reading."

Deciding not to overplay his hand, he let her return

to her book, and he returned to his. George R.R. Martin wasn't as intriguing as trying to figure out whether or not Em's feelings toward him were thawing out, but he managed to focus for the better part of an hour. When the flight attendant came by, Em was so engrossed that she didn't look up from her book, so he ordered her a glass of wine Maren liked and himself a scotch and paid for both.

"Here you are, ma'am," the flight attendant said, holding the wine glass out to Em.

She blinked up, startled. "Oh, I didn't—"

Rob took the glass and set it on her tray table. "I got it for you. Didn't want to pull you away from Captain Wentworth and Miss Elliot if I didn't need to."

"Thanks, that was…nice of you." She stared at the wine, the frown back in place.

"It's a glass of wine, Em, not poison," he said, sipping his scotch.

She looked up, her eyes clearing a little. "No. Sorry. Thank you for the wine. I'm…well, I'm confused."

A loaded statement if he'd ever heard one. "Confused about what? I'm a nice guy. I know you like your book, so I ordered your drink for you so you could keep reading. Simple as that."

"If it were only the wine, then yes, it would be simple, but it's not." She set the book down and turned toward him. "Why did you step in with Kole at the airport?"

Ah. He'd hoped they could wait until they were halfway to LA before that was brought up. "Because Naumov is an ass. Owen told me a bit more about the problems you'd had with him, and when I saw him bugging you, I wanted to make sure everything was all right."

"And what about the post-match panel? Thank you for that too, by the way. I'm…sorry I jumped all over you without seeing the whole segment."

Rob's heart tightened a little, finally hearing her acknowledge that he was on her side, seeing the softer look in her eyes. He wished she knew he'd been on her side all along; he'd been an idiot for letting her believe otherwise. She hadn't looked at him as anything other than an adversary for so long; it was nice to see the shift starting.

"You don't need to thank me." He closed his book and set his scotch down, locking eyes with her. "No one, man or woman, deserves to have their private lives thrown out there as part of the criticism of how they do their jobs. And no woman should get blamed for trusting her guy to take private pictures of her."

She glanced down at her hands. "But I chose to have the pictures taken. I bought the lingerie and agreed to model it for him."

A white-hot wave of jealousy hit him, but he tamped it down. She wasn't his, and it was his own damn fault. She had every right to let Kole take those pictures, but God, he wished it had been him and not Naumov behind that camera lens. He would have protected those pictures better than Scrooge McDuck protected his gold.

"So? That's your right. You're a sexy woman with a body any man would give his left nut to touch. Any boyfriend with half a brain would want to have pictures of you to keep with him." He shrugged. "It's not like they were that dirty or explicit. They're no different than those boudoir shots or whatever some women pay to have taken. That doesn't make you a slut or a whore or whatever else they want to try to call you."

For a second, he thought she might be tearing up, but she looked away before he could tell.

"That's…not many guys would say something like that and mean it."

"It's the twenty-first century. If guys can go around snapping shirtless selfies and dick pics all over the place, then I don't think any of us have room to criticize or look down on a woman for taking sexy pictures for her man. I'd say the same thing if it were anyone because I would hope that someone would have the guts to say that if Maren were the one in your position."

He let the words hang between them, part of him hoping that she would read between the lines, the other part of him scared of what he'd do if she did. He wanted her. Wanting her, caring for her, that had never been a problem. He hadn't stopped wanting and caring even after he ended things with her. But so much had passed between them since then, so many snipes and barbs and so much animosity.

"Well, either way. Thank you. I needed to hear that this week, even if it was from an unexpected source." She shifted around in her seat. "I think I'm going to try to catch some shut eye."

"Sweet dreams," he murmured after she'd stretched her seat out to form a little bed.

Once he was sure she was asleep, he let himself study her. So much had changed since they first met. She'd still had the air of innocent girlishness about her that first day; it's what drew him to her. Even at twenty-three, he'd been a little jaded when it came to women.

He'd been with his fair share of women, older and younger, until they all felt the same. Em, with her pretty eyes, golden skin, and long dark hair, had called to him. He shouldn't have asked her out when he did; they were in the middle of the fucking Olympics, but he couldn't help himself.

That same feeling had hit him today in the airport, that compulsion to be with her and damn the reality of their situation. Being with her now was even more stupid than it had been then, especially considering his producer's warning and her current notoriety in the press, but he didn't know if he cared.

Eventually, he nodded off too. By the time they were both awake, the plane was coming in to land in LA. They didn't speak as they gathered their things and exited the plane. Em took off at a quick stride, leaving him in the dust as she sped through customs. He thought about trying to catch up to her, but she'd find out soon enough that he was her seat mate again on the LA to JFK flight.

The look on her face when he boarded the flight and took the seat next to her was priceless.

"You're really cute when you're annoyed. Has anyone ever told you that?" He settled into his seat, noting that she'd put on a little makeup during the layover and grabbed a brown bag full of something that had his nostrils flaring and his stomach rumbling.

She narrowed her eyes at him. "Yes. My grandpa and Owen when I was five. Grown women aren't cute."

"Sorry, angel, but annoyed you is cute. Deal with it." He pulled out his book, then stashed his bag. He watched her take a familiar-looking food out of the bag and spotted the golden arches on its side. "Why Ms.

Grace. Those aren't French fries, are they?"

"Shut up." She took a bite. "They're my weakness."

He laughed. "What would Zoe say if she saw you? It's competition season. You're not supposed to have junk food."

Munching on another fry, she shrugged. "She'd say pass the ketchup, you heathen. One thing of fries isn't going to kill me. I'm pretty good at my diet most days, but when I get on a plane, especially with a layover, I treat myself."

"Fair enough." Quick as a kid stealing from the cookie jar, Rob reached in and took a fry, scalding his fingers a little in the process. "Ow. Those are hot."

"Serves you right, thief." She closed the bag and held it close to her chest. "I wait until just before boarding, then run to get them. And what are you doing stealing my fries? Shouldn't you be watching your girlish figure? I hear the camera adds ten pounds."

A grin tugged at his lips. He'd missed this side of Em. The funny, playful side. The side that made him fall for her to begin with. Most of the world saw the cool, collected exterior her grandparents and Zoe fostered in her, but when they were together, the walls fell down, and the real Em started to come out.

"My girlish figure is fine, thanks. My shoulder may be jacked up, but I can still go for a run to keep in shape," he said, surprised the usual internal wince didn't come when he mentioned his shoulder.

"I'm sorry about the shoulder. I didn't get a chance to say that or see you after it happened." She held out another fry, which he took. "Although from what I hear, no one got much of a chance to see you—not even

Maren."

He munched on the fry to buy some time. "Would you want a bunch of people around if you found out you'd ended your career two points before you won the top seed?"

"Fair point."

The pilot came over the speaker and announced they were preparing for takeoff. She settled back in her seat, tucking the bag beside her and grabbing her book.

"I'm pretty sure the story hasn't changed from the last fifty times you read it." He deliberately needled her, not wanting to lose her to her book again.

She didn't look up. "Doesn't mean it loses any of its effect on me. Distractions are key to me not flat-out freaking out on a plane."

His mind drifted back to the elevator, to how scared she'd been. He was surprised that her mother's death still affected her so much, but he couldn't blame her.

"If I promise to distract you better than the book, will you give me a few more fries?" He stretched his legs out and rested his arms on the armrests so his shoulder was a hair's breadth from hers.

"No. Your producer will thank me later."

He left her alone until the little bell dinged and the fasten seatbelt sign went off. "You need to work on your second serve, you know."

Her jaw tightened, and he could almost hear the wheels turning in her head as she tried not to take the bait. This had been their relationship for the last seven years. He picked at her, while she tried not to respond until she ripped him a new one.

"My second serve is just fine, thank you very

much. What needs work is your ability to read a woman's tennis game," she hissed, eyes still on her book.

"No, pretty sure it's your second serve. I know that everyone thinks it was the whole picture fiasco that cost you the tournament, but it wasn't. Your second serve went to shit while you were out with your knee injury. I noticed it in your earlier matches."

Rolling her eyes, Em closed her book. "Bullshit. You, the king of the sucky second serve, wouldn't know a good one if it bit you in the ass."

They argued like that through the flight attendant bringing them drinks and snacks and kept going until the captain came over the P.A.

"Sorry, folks, it looks like we're about to hit some bumpy air. We're getting close to JFK, so we're going to ask everyone to prepare for descent a little earlier than expected."

Em paled under her golden tan as she fumbled with her belt.

Rob fastened his own belt, then took her hand in his. "Don't worry. Just a few bumps."

"Right. Bumps. Thirty-thousand feet in the air bumps." She tried to pull her hand out of his, but he tightened his grip. Her chest moved up and down as she took deep breaths, mild panic in her eyes.

One thought went through his head—*fix it*.
Make it better.

Seeing her worried or panicked tore at his gut, especially when it involved something neither of them could control. She'd been like this in the elevator in London, palms sweaty, her heart beating faster than a hummingbird's wings. So he did what he'd done then.

Keeping their hands linked, he leaned over and kissed her.

Chapter 5

Holy. Shit.

Those two words blared across Emerson's brain as Rob's lips settled on hers. They were bright enough to be a billboard in Piccadilly Circus or Times Square. She froze, unable to react or move or breathe.

Robert Ashton III, the man who'd broken her heart and then used it for serving practice seven years ago, was kissing her. On a plane. That was going through turbulence.

How many sleepless nights had she spent reliving his kisses? Whatever idiocy he might be guilty of, the man could kiss, and he'd only gotten better with age. After the first few seconds of complete and utter shock, her body responded like the shameless slut it was when it came to him. Even after they were at each other's throats, her body always responded when he was within three feet. It's part of the reason why he infuriated her so much. She didn't want to feel anything for him, let alone desire.

But damn him, he tasted so good—a little salty from the fries he'd snitched from her and something a little darker than just Rob. And it felt so good for him to touch her, even though the only contact between them was his lips on hers and his fingers laced with hers.

She gave herself over to the kiss for a few moments, savoring it. This was better than she'd remembered. Her body went off like a wild fire, sparked and ready to go in zero seconds flat. Kissing Kole had been good, really nice even once they started to get to know each other, but this was—holy shit.

She pulled away, but only far enough to meet those silver eyes, full of masculine pride and unfulfilled desire. She opened her mouth to yell at him, to ask what the hell he was thinking, but all she could say as the plane shuddered a little was "Holy. Shit."

"I was thinking wow, but that works too." A smile tipped up his slightly swollen lips. God, why did he have to be so attractive? They'd been on a plane for almost an entire day, but he might as well have stepped out of hair and makeup five minutes ago.

She loved his hair—she'd always loved the old-gold color and how he kept it at the perfect length for her to run her fingers through it without getting tangled. Those eyes, though, they were the real panty-melters. The dark silver flecked with light blue bore into her, the smile reaching his eyes, a little wickedness entering the mix. She knew that look. He meant to keep her off-kilter. Damn him.

"That didn't just happen. You—you had no right to do that," she said, keeping her voice low. God. This was a disaster. The last thing she needed was for somebody on the plane to take a picture of Rob kissing her and spread it all over the Internet. Amir and Zoe would murder her, and Owen would murder Rob.

Rob's smile didn't falter. "Sure, I did. You were freaking out about the turbulence. I got your mind off it."

Anger bubbled up in her, hot and potent, melding with the lust to have her temper a few seconds from completely blowing. "Of all the arrogant, assholish things—you kissed me to distract me from turbulence? *Who does that*?"

"Someone who doesn't want a beautiful woman freaking out when she doesn't need to. It worked in London, so I thought it'd work again now."

Her heart skipped a beat then. He remembered their first kiss? Why did that make her so swoony?

No, she couldn't let herself get sucked into his crazy. She had enough of her own to deal with.

Emerson rubbed her forehead. "I don't get you. I will probably never get you. You live on Planet Rob, and no one here on Earth will be able to understand the fucked-up processes of your twisted brain. Kissing me in London when we're trapped on a goddamn elevator is nothing like kissing me now. We were two completely different people then. I'm not that girl anymore."

"Uh-uh, Miss Priss. You don't get to go all frosty on me now." He took her hand again so she couldn't hide her face. "You kissed me back. And what's more, you liked it and want me to do it again. And if you deny it, I'll kiss you again to prove that you're a dirty rotten liar."

For a second, she thought about testing him on that. She didn't want to admit she'd kissed him back and liked it, but she also didn't want to risk more pictures getting leaked. It would be ironic if the guy who'd defended her from being slut-shamed contributed to the next wave of slut-shaming.

"Fine. I kissed you back. Whatever. It doesn't mean you had the right to kiss me. Any right you had to do that went out the window a loooong time ago, pal.

You gave it up the second you broke up with me."

"Who broke up with who is debatable. It's not like you were begging me to change my mind during that phone call." Challenge flashed in his eyes. "So maybe my right to kiss you was just dormant, not gone, because I can't get you out of my head."

What the hell? What was going on with him? For seven years, he'd picked at her and antagonized her, and she'd given as good as she got. Neither of them had acknowledged that they went beyond frenemies at one point. Now here he was, being nice to her, defending her on international television, and kissing her because she got seriously wigged out by planes doing anything but flying in a straight line. None of this made sense.

The part of her that still had hot, steamy dreams about him when she was really, really tired wanted to take the challenge and kiss him again. She wanted to revel in this new-old side of him, the return of the Rob she'd fallen for faster than her best ace serve. But she couldn't do that. Her life was chaotic enough without adding Rob Ashton and the Titanic-sized baggage that came with him. Why hadn't she pretended to sleep again? Why did she let him pull her in? At least on the plane from Melbourne to LA he hadn't known how much she wanted to talk to him, to spend time with him even though he drove her batty. Pretending to sleep, she could try to ignore how good he looked and smelled and how it felt to sit next to him for hours on end. Now all she could think about was how easy it would be to take the bait and make him put his money where his mouth was. If he really wanted her back, she could make him prove it.

"Beg you? Seriously? Why? Because you're the

great Rob Ashton, scion of the legendary Ashton family?" She snorted. "What good would that do? I know what it's like to be part of a family where someone doesn't want me around. I got enough rejection from my dad. I sure as hell didn't need more from you."

"Rejection?" His brows furrowed. "What—? Look, I think we need to talk about what happened between us."

"No. This…just no. It's in the past. No use picking at old scars now." She pulled her book out and ignored his attempts to re-engage her. Captain Wentworth sent Anne his wonderfully romantic note when the wheels touched down.

"See? Told you everything would be okay," Rob said as they gathered their carryon items.

Fighting the urge to roll her eyes, Emerson fixed into place the neutral mask she'd forced herself to wear for the last seven years. "Don't try to explain a mild phobia. It's not supposed to make sense."

"Do you need help getting your bags?" he asked as they shuffled down the aisle.

"It might have escaped your notice, but I'm a big girl. I've spent the last ten years traveling all around the world. I can manage my own bags." She didn't care if she sounded a little bitchy. She needed to get away from him before she did something really stupid—like kiss him again.

She pushed through the crowd, tugging her duffle bag and purse higher on her shoulder. Getting away from him as fast as she could was best. Being so close to him after all these years was doing crazy things to her head. Seven years of working really damn hard to forget how he made her feel could not go down the drain after one plane ride—a really, really long plane ride but still.

Thankful for having gone through customs in LA, she sped down to baggage claim. As she walked, she prayed her bags came quickly so she could get out without risking another run-in with Rob.

Pulling out her phone, she scrolled through her messages while she waited for her bags. There were several texts from Amir, mostly giving her the details of the photo shoots and meetings she had scheduled in New York. He mentioned in one a few media requests for interviews, but she didn't plan to acknowledge those.

Out of a long-established habit, she pressed her grandma's name on her favorite contacts list.

"Is that my girl?" Gran's voice warmed Emerson's heart and eased some of the leftover anxiety from the flight.

"Of course it's me, Gran. What, did you think an alien stole my phone and was calling you?" she teased. Her grandmother, while a brilliant CPA, still didn't understand her smartphone.

Gran chuckled. "Cheeky. Did you have a good flight, sweetheart?"

"It was…fine, I guess." She sighed, keeping an eye on the carousel, impatient to retrieve her bag. "You know me and planes."

"Well, it's good to at least be in the same time zone as you again," Poppy said. "When will you be home? Your brother's plane got in a few hours ago."

"I'm stuck in New York for a few days, but then I'll be home. I promise to bring you some bagels from that place you liked the last time we were up here." The baggage belt started to move, and she focused her attention on the chute.

"You're so good to me. I want you to have fun while you're up there, Emmy Anne. I don't want you to worry about what those silly reporters are saying." Gran's voice took the tone she used when Emerson first started playing competitively. She wouldn't let her granddaughter wallow in losses or mistakes.

Emerson took a deep breath, still keeping her eyes on the bags coming out. She spotted her racket case, followed by her roller suitcase. "I promise I'll try to have fun, Gran, as long as you promise you're still taking it easy. I don't want to send Owen over there to make sure you're not trying to attend every garden club and bridge club in three counties."

As her bags came by, she reached out to grab the strap of the racket bag, wedging her phone against her shoulder. She pulled it over easily enough, but when she went to tug her roller suitcase, she couldn't get it over the edge.

"I'm being good, Emmy. I swear. Ask your uncle Tommy if you don't believe me." Poppy's voice took on an officious edge, which meant she was lying through her teeth.

"Uh-huh. Sure, Gran." She followed her suitcase, tugging at it. "Look, I've got to go. I'll call you tomorrow. Love you."

"Love you too, sweet girl."

The phone call disconnected as Em tried again to get her bag over the edge of the carousel, her racket bag swinging down to bang into her side. She was about to give up until the next pass when a pair of hands shot out and easily lifted it off for her.

She turned to find Rob standing right behind her. He towered over her, her head barely coming to his shoulder.

"I almost had it," she said.

He chuckled ruefully. "Would it kill you to accept help? I couldn't stand to see you fighting with that monster bag anymore."

"Yes, it would kill me to accept help, at least from you." The wounds were too close to the surface in this place. "What are you doing, Rob?"

"Helping a pretty girl with her bags." He grinned, making her knees go a little weak, damn him. Being this close to him wasn't good for her peace of mind—or her libido. "Do you want a ride to your hotel?"

She rubbed her forehead. God, why did he make her so muddled? She was a strong, confident woman, for fuck's sake. One of the best strategists on tour. But the second he got within five feet of her, all of that went out the window, and she reverted back to the silly girl she had been before that awful day.

"Um. I don't know. I don't think so. I usually take a cab. It's easier than trying to coordinate a driver."

"Ride with me."

Chapter 6

Rob held his breath as he waited for her to answer. Asking her to ride with him probably qualified as a dumb move. A really dumb move considering where they were. He hadn't fully processed the fact that they were in this airport together. He still kicked himself for not having the courage to face her that day.

Yet here they were.

They'd spent more than twenty hours together on a plane, but he didn't want to let her go. Not yet anyway, not after all the time he'd spent over the last year wondering what might have been.

A helluva lot of tension sizzled between them, and they had to get past years of anger (well, her anger and his stupidity), but something had shifted, even before that kiss. Once she left the airport, he didn't know when he'd see her again, when he'd get a chance like this. The woman had spent seven years honing her ability to avoid him, and testing it didn't top his list of good ideas.

"What? Rob, seriously, what is going on? None of this makes sense."

Those chocolatey brown eyes of hers stared up at him, clouded with emotions he couldn't name. Her brows furrowed, strands of black hair falling out of the high tail she'd pulled it into at some point during the plane ride. Damn, but she looked cute like that, the little tail bouncing when she moved her head. He'd liked her with long hair, but the shorter hair also worked for him.

She wanted an explanation, but he didn't have one. Nothing had made sense to him in the last eighteen months except the fact that he felt alive when he was with Em, and he was an idiot for letting her go. He also wanted to kiss her again and do all the things he'd spent the past year dreaming about.

"I know it doesn't make sense. I don't think this, whatever it is between us, is supposed to make sense. So can we stop questioning it? Can we just go with it? It's not a crime for me to want to help you with your bag or offer you a ride. Think of accepting the ride as being environmentally conscious." Arguing with her was getting old, but he also liked that she wasn't going easy on him. His Em was a firecracker, and he liked that she didn't look as defeated as she had that night in the hotel bar. He was honestly surprised not to see photographers lurking around the airport, but then again, they probably expected her in Miami, not New York.

"Do you really think that's a good idea?" she asked, rearranging her bags.

He shoved his hand through his hair, biting back the niggling frustration. "It's a ride, Em. It doesn't need to be a good or bad idea. You'll be with me for all of thirty minutes, maybe forty-five if traffic's bad. Please?"

Suspicion and calculation flickered through her warm brown eyes. She looked out the window, likely scoping out just how insane the line for cabs was. Finally, her shoulders sagged, and her grip on the handle of her suitcase tightened.

"Fine. For the environment." She tossed her head, defiance in every line of her face.

God, she was gorgeous. Even after almost a day on an airplane, she was still the most beautiful woman he'd ever seen. She had this way about her, how she held herself, how she moved, that grabbed a guy by his balls and made him pay attention.

"But no talking," she warned.

A bark of laughter escaped him as he motioned for her to follow him. He knew better than to offer to take one of her four bags, even though he only had two to maneuver. "No talking? Come on. That's not right. What would be so bad about talking for a little bit longer? We could argue the merits of the Harry Potter movies again."

"Why? I'll win. The books are better than the movies. The end." Her words came in little pants, and he looked over his shoulder to see her struggling with her bags.

"You don't know you would win, Ms. Stubborn." He spotted his usual driver, Frank, waiting outside the sleek black limo. He preferred driving himself, but in New York it wasn't always practical. His father had an account with the same limo company for thirty plus years, so they always had a car waiting when they visited the city. Rob easily handed his luggage over to Frank.

"Good afternoon, Mr. Ashton. Here, let me help you with those, miss." Frank's voice boomed over the noise of the crowd, his smile lighting up his dark face.

Rob nodded to the older man. "Careful, Frank, she might take your arm off if you try to help her."

"Please ignore him," Em said, smiling at Frank.

"His brain is warped from too long on an airplane."

Rob held the door open for Em while she transferred her bags to Frank, admiring the way her dark-green leggings emphasized the muscles of her thighs. Her loose tunic-style sweater and oversized peacoat were expensive but simple. His mother always wore overly flashy, clearly designer-label clothes, and she'd trained Maren—normally a very simple kind of girl—to follow her lead. He liked that Em stayed true to the way she was brought up. By now, she had to have built up a pretty decent bank account, but she didn't flash it around like a lot of their peers.

She climbed in and settled herself on the back seat, as close to the opposite door as she could get. He slid in and let his body fill up the space between them.

"Where to, Ms. Grace?" Frank asked.

"The Library Hotel in Midtown." She gave him some brief landmarks, and Frank pulled into traffic.

Rob let the silence stretch between them for a few minutes before he reached to press the button that slid the privacy screen up, cutting them off from Frank.

"Hey!"

"What happened to no talking?" He shifted to face her, daring her to talk to him.

"Why did you close the screen?" she asked, eyes narrowing dangerously.

Shrugging, he reached out to brush a piece of hair behind her ear, savoring the warm floral scent of her. "Because we've spent the last day surrounded by other people, and this may be the last chance I get to spend time alone with you."

And God, how he wanted to spend more time with her. This was what he'd been craving during all those days of recovery—the peace that only came when he was around Em. She didn't feel the same peace, though, a fact which hit him harder than he'd care to admit. It was his own damn fault, and being this close to her, especially after that kiss, was pure torture. His whole body had been on high alert for almost twenty-four hours, so close to the woman who haunted his dreams and yet not able to touch her the way he'd imagined a thousand times.

With a cute little nose wrinkle, she pulled the loose piece of hair back to where it was. Her jaw tightened, and a hundred emotions played across her face, tearing at him because he'd caused all that hurt.

"It's been seven years, Rob. *Seven years.* Why now? Why are you switching gears on me now?"

You're the one who ended things. You're the one who let your father tell you how awful I was for you. The words hung between them, unsaid, but very much present. So he'd lean into the turn and hope like hell she didn't rip his testicles through his nose.

"Because it's been seven years, and I can't get you out of my head. Can't stop wanting you." He moved so his knee grazed hers, so his body took up more space to remind her he was here and this was real. *Can't stop missing you*—the words stayed on the tip of his tongue, fear holding them back.

"That's all this is?" she asked, clearly looking for something as her brown eyes studied him. "You want me? Shit. Tell me this isn't because of those goddamn pictures."

He shook his head before she finished. "No. Not because of the pictures. Don't get me wrong—they were hot. Like make-a-guy's-blood-evaporate hot, but I wanted you before that. I've wanted you for years, but being away, not seeing you, made it harder to ignore."

She didn't need to know about the doubts that had tormented him in those first days after his shoulder injury. The feeling of complete idiocy that had hit him when he thought about how he gave her up—the one woman he could possibly fall in love with—for the sake of a career that was gone in an instant. Hearing all that would only spook her and send her running in the opposite direction.

"I—" She started to speak but stopped herself.

For what felt like endless moments of his heart pounding in his ears, she stared out the tinted window as the city streets slowly crept by, her jaw clenched and her hands curling into tight fists on the seat. One minute, he thought she was close to punching him, and the next she was in his arms.

Warm, soft lips hit his with the force of a wicked first serve. He fell back against the seat, thrown off balance by the tight package of willing, passionate female. He tasted so much in that kiss. Desire and passion were obvious; every kiss they shared bore a heavy dose of both, from their first kiss in London to the kiss on the plane. But he found more there than just the obvious—bitterness laced with regret along with a big helping of frustration and anger. He understood all of them, because the same emotions battered him every time he thought of her.

He hated what had happened between them seven years ago, that he let her go. It made him sick, thinking of all the time they'd spent sniping and fighting because his stupid pride and need to please his father got in their way. More than anything, he loathed and despised the walls between them. He returned the kiss stroke for stroke, nip for nip, trying to show her what he'd been too chickenshit to say seven years ago. Sooner than he would have liked, air became necessary.

"Em? Wha—?" He struggled to catch his breath, his forehead resting against hers.

"No talking, remember?" She suckled on his neck, just below his ear.

Shit. She remembered that spot? His body went harder than the court surface in Arthur Ashe Stadium.

His laugh came out strangled with need. "You sure?"

Why was he questioning this? She wanted him. He should be celebrating, dancing a fucking jig. But a nagging voice reminded him she'd gone through hell over the last week and might not fully realize what she was doing.

"I'm horny, and we have thirty minutes left before we get to my hotel. Shut up and make me feel," she ordered, her voice husky and full of feminine power. This woman knew what she wanted, and she wasn't afraid to grab it while she could.

He groaned and went back to kissing her, tasting every inch of her mouth before he moved up over her cheekbone and down the curve of her jaw to her neck and her collarbone. She purred and arched against him.

"Please."

"So good, baby. So sweet," he murmured.

He continued to taste her, returning to her lips, his hand slipping under the hem of her oversized sweater. The soft knitted wool contrasted erotically with the lace of her bra. Through the diaphanous web of fabric, her nipples pebbled under his touch. He tweaked and teased them, savoring the ripe weight of her breasts. They fit into his hands perfectly, even fuller than they'd been when she was nineteen.

A cool, slim hand played with the hem of his shirt, trailing over the small of his back, sending a blinding jolt through him. Every cell in his body screamed out for him to bury himself inside of her now and to hell with Frank in the front seat. If he wasn't careful, he'd lose what little control he had left between the desire and rising jet lag fogging his brain. He had to get the upper hand.

Gathering her closer, he switched their positions, pressing her back into the supple leather seat. Long legs wrapped around his waist, and she canted her body against him, moaning into their kiss.

"More," she murmured, lightly biting his bottom lip.

He ignored the insistent bulge that would soon have the outline of his zipper permanently tattooed into it. He began to tease his way along the waistband of her leggings. He first encountered a pair of cotton underwear, a practical counterpoint to the lace of her bra. He grinned into the kiss when he found the material between her legs already damp and hot. So much between them remained unspoken and unsolved, but her body still responded to him, still needed him as much as he needed her.

As his fingers teased her through the thin fabric, she rocked into his hand, her legs loosening from around his hips the more he touched her.

He couldn't take her here in the car, not the first time in so long, but his mouth and his hands mimicked what every cell of his body screamed to do, delving into her, stoking that beautiful passion she kept buried beneath the walls of cool professionalism.

The more he stroked, the more taut her body became. She was close; he could feel it in the edge of their kisses. Thanking God for the stretchy fabric of her leggings, he moved aside the panties, his fingers plunging into the wet warmth of her, his thumb finding that sweet little bundle of nerves, all swollen and ready for him. Cries muffled against his mouth, her body spasmed, going over in a wave as she moved and writhed against him until she came back down again.

When she finally went limp beneath him, he pulled back to look in her eyes. Passion still clouded the chocolatey depths, along with the same questions that battered against the need-locked doors of his own brain. Before either of them could speak, the car eased to a stop, and Frank rapped on the door.

"We're at the Library Hotel, Mr. Ashton, Ms. Grace."

No, not yet. It was too soon. He couldn't let her go now, but he had to.

He cleared his throat, reluctantly easing back from her. "Thanks, Frank."

She struggled to sit up, quickly pulling her sweater back into place and redoing her ponytail. Color rose in her cheeks.

"I should…" She pressed her kiss-swollen lips together. "Thanks for the ride."

Not giving him a chance to speak, she climbed out of the car and shut the door in his face. He sat there, listening to Frank helping her get her bags to the bellhop and making idle chit-chat about the icy weather.

He tried to get his raging hormones under control, but he remained painfully hard for her. He'd been so close to getting through the walls. He wanted more time—he wanted more, period. She was ready for him. Whatever stood between them, their chemistry remained off the charts. What would she do if he followed her to her room? Was that crazy? Then again, when would he get this chance again—the chance he'd spent more than a year praying for?

Chapter 7

"Rob? What are you doing here?"

He stood there, in the doorway of her hotel room, staring at her like he used to when they'd first met, like she was the only woman in the world. She'd thought she was rid of him. She'd made it safely to her hotel room without making a spectacle of herself, and she thought she could finally relax and make sense of what had just happened. Then the next thing she knew, he was in her room, the door was closed, and his mouth was on hers.

Emerson's brain must have started to leak out of her ears. There was no possible way that it was still a solid mass. She'd had the most mind-blowing orgasm ever in the back of a limo in the middle of New York City. Now she was standing in the entry hall of her hotel room, and Rob Ashton was once again liquefying her with that ridiculously talented mouth of his.

Their time in London always had a Twilight-Zone feel to her, and that same sensation colored the last day as well. This wasn't her life. This wasn't what she did. She kept her relationships civilized and contained. She didn't sit and argue with someone for hours on end over everything from Harry Potter to what constituted an acceptable second serve. Making out in the back of a limo wasn't something she ever imagined herself doing, especially with this guy.

But instead of protesting, instead of pushing him away, she pulled him closer, slamming his back against the door before he had time to react. She couldn't deny his body called to hers in an age-old song so difficult to ignore.

This was going to be different than their first time together. Or their last time together. The first time, while sweet, had been awkward. She'd been a virgin, and she hadn't known what to do with a man who made her feel so much. Their last night had been slow and easy, as if they had all the time in the world. He'd spent nearly an hour just playing with her breasts. By the time they finally fell asleep, she'd orgasmed five times.

If she was going to do this, if she was going to let him touch her and make her feel like this again, then she was going to do it on her own terms.

"You sure? We could always just—talk," he said against her mouth, his hand sliding under the hem of her sweater, teasing her spine, and sending sparks ricocheting through her.

Reaching between them, she cupped his erection with a grip she usually reserved for her racket. "Just sex. Dirty, hot, jungle sex. That's all. Make me forget everything but how hard you're making me come."

A wave of pure feminine power surged through her as he groaned. *Good.* If he could make her all squiggly and needy, she should be able to return the favor. She continued to kiss him, the full, open-mouthed kisses that she'd spent so many nights craving. While they kissed, she continued stroking him through his jeans.

Big hands slid down and cupped her ass, pulling her up so he wasn't stooping quite so much to kiss her. "I can do the jungle sex. We'll negotiate the 'just sex' part later."

A warning bell clanged whisper-soft in the back of her head, but she could barely hear it over the need pounding a merengue in her blood. Instead, she went for the buttons of his shirt, tugging them from their moorings. "Get naked. Now."

"You first," he said, running a finger under the strap of her bra.

They moved toward the bed, circling each other with the anticipation of a crowd waiting for the serve on match point. She pushed his shirt off his broad shoulders, but it caught on his elbows as he cupped her face for a particularly soulful kiss.

"Jesus. I know you said to get naked, but are you trying to melt my panties instead of taking them off like a normal guy?" She moved to tease the hollow behind his ear with her tongue, and—just as she expected—he growled that deep rumbling growl that made her girl parts tremble in desperation.

She used his momentary distraction to push him back until his legs hit the giant bed, and he fell back. With him spread out in front of her, she reached down to undo the fly of his jeans. Sweet heavens, the man was sexy. Even after months away from tennis, he still had muscles for days and abs that would make most men weep with envy. Perfectly sculpted with just a hint of golden hair trailing from his belly button into the waistband of midnight-blue boxer briefs.

"Your body is ridiculous," she murmured, running her hands up and down the bare skin she'd exposed.

"Yours is better. Show me." The roughness in his voice sent more quivers and butterflies zinging through her.

She hesitated for only a moment, then gave him her best come-hither smile. She wasn't going to let the stupid pictures or that asshole Kole keep her from cathartic, wildly dirty sex. Standing between his legs, she grabbed the hem of her sweater and slowly pulled it over her head. She reveled in the darkening of his eyes when she tossed the light blue garment aside.

"You've come a long way from the white cotton bras. I thought you bought stock in Hanes or something when we first met." His gaze traced over the pale-yellow lace bra she'd tossed on yesterday morning. It was one of her favorites, even more so now that it made him look at her like she was a slice of his favorite chocolate caramel cake.

"No more white cotton. Especially not bras. Why? Do you miss them?" She hooked her fingers in the waistband of her leggings. She was glad she'd already taken her shoes off.

A tight smile flitted across his face. "I had a thing for them, but wow. Gotta say the yellow lace is climbing the charts."

"Mmm. I may not splurge on fancy limos, but a girl likes to have nice lingerie." She tugged on the leggings, slowly wiggling to help them slide down, but she was careful to keep her yellow panties firmly in place.

"No lace underwear?" he asked, propping himself up on his elbows, eyes raking across her body with enough heat to singe the rest of her clothes off.

She shook her head, kicking the leggings aside as they finally pooled around her feet. "You try sitting on a plane for twenty-plus hours with lace against your sensitive parts. Not as sexy as it sounds."

"The cotton panties work just as well," he assured her.

Purring, she tugged at his jeans. "Come on, hot stuff. Your turn."

"As the lady commands." He bolted upright, easily shedding his shirt. Together, they managed to push his jeans over his hips and off.

They sat there, both in their underwear, their breaths hot and fast on each other's faces.

"No more talking," she said. "In me. Now."

With a grin, he reached behind her to unclasp her bra, his tongue tracing along the curve of her collarbone. "Patience."

His mouth fastened on her nipple as soon as he tossed her bra over his head. With a gasp of pleasure, she tunneled her fingers through his old-gold hair, pulling him closer.

While he drove her crazy, teasing and sucking one breast, then the other, she reached down and pushed her underwear over the curve of her hips. Almost immediately, his fingers danced along her hipbones, tantalizingly close to the hot, wet center of her. She circled one of his wrists with her fingers and gently moved it to where she needed him most.

Her clit was still sensitive from the orgasm she'd had in the limo, her body ready for another, and he was more than happy to oblige. He'd been good with his hands seven years ago, but now he was a master, reading and playing her body with even more skill than he'd displayed on the court. She let herself go over the edge again, a million fireworks going off behind her eyes.

While her body was still riding out the pleasure, he

pulled her onto the bed, flat on her back. He made quick work of his underwear before he returned to cover her body with his.

"Please tell me you have a condom in those fancy jeans of yours," she said.

He reached down to the pile of denim beside the bed and pulled out his wallet, digging around in it until he came up with two foil-wrapped packages. "Always prepared."

"Sure of yourself, huh?" she challenged. "Planning to get laid sometime soon?" She yanked him back to her and used the momentum of his big body to gain the upper hand again.

He gripped her hips, sliding the tip of his erection along the lips of her sex. "I hadn't gotten laid in more than a year, angel. I just like to plan for every eventuality."

She opened the first package and tossed the other aside on the pristine white comforter. She slid it over his erection, savoring the hardness of him, loving how hot he was, how his hips jerked a little as her fingers brushed his testicles. She remembered the first time she'd done this, how powerful she felt as he watched her, trusted her so completely. A man who could have any woman wanted her. How young and naive she'd been. Just to prove she wasn't that girl anymore, she cupped his balls, massaging them lightly with her nails.

He lifted her up and moved her center directly over him. With a self-satisfied grin, she slid onto him, taking every inch of him deep inside her. Almost immediately, his hips started to move, thrusting him even deeper, rolling against her, driving her crazy. Utilizing those amazing abs of his, he levered himself up until they were face to face. Eyes locked, he thrust harder, and she matched him, developing a hard, fast rhythm that drove her higher and higher.

She took his mouth, their tongues tangling and their teeth clashing. One of his strong arms wrapped around her, cradling her as he moved them so her back was braced against the headboard. She caught a small wince as he set her down, and if she hadn't been on the peak of an orgasm, she would have given him a hard time for doing something that might injure his shoulder. Instead, she let him lace their fingers together and press the backs of her hands against the headboard.

With her legs wrapped around his waist, he used his new position to increase the speed and power of his thrusts, sending her over the edge. Breaking their kiss, she cried out, letting the pleasure hit her again. So many emotions hit her, driving her to heights she'd forgotten she could reach. He didn't stop, though; he pushed her up again, his lips kissing all the flesh he could reach.

"More. Harder," she moaned, her teeth sinking into the flesh of his earlobe, then her tongue darting out to soothe it.

"Never enough. So good, Em. So, so good."

His words sparked something inside her, but she pushed it aside, focusing on the here and now. They moved together in a fast, hard dance as old as time. It had never been like this with anyone.

Rob Ashton's power over her body should terrify her, but it only intensified her pleasure. "Please. Come with me. Now."

With a strategic roll of her hips and then another, she sent him over the edge and joined him there, the two of them shouting their pleasure. His thrusts gradually slowed as the spasms of pleasure wracking her body subsided.

They lay tangled together, their hands still linked, now as limp as the rest of them against the pillows. The sound of his panting breath in her ears more comforting than she cared to admit. He shifted a little so the weight of him didn't completely crush her, but he kept every inch of his bare skin pressed to hers.

"Dirty enough for you?" he asked after they both finally caught their breath.

She grinned, every muscle in her body limper than they'd been after Zoe's most grueling workouts. And yet she still wanted more. He made her crazy. She should kick him out now, before she got in too deep, but her traitorous libido stopped her from being smart. "Close, but not quite."

"Is that a challenge?" he asked, pushing up to look her in the eyes. Blue clashed with brown as they had a thousand times before, only it was a sparring match she couldn't bear to walk away from yet.

"Hell, yes."

Chapter 8

Bright sunlight brought Rob back to consciousness. His limbs heavy with pleasure, he cracked one eye, and the night before came rushing back to him. He was in bed. With Emerson Grace. Who was still very, very naked and pressed against his side.

A big-ass grin stretched across his face. When he got to the airport in Melbourne, never in a million years would he have imagined that he would end up in a hotel room with a woman, let alone Em. Last night had been seriously hot—scorching, brain-melting sex that damn near broke the scales. But even better than that, he'd fallen asleep with her next to him.

He loved the weight of her against his side. He hadn't expected it, but she was a cuddler. Normally, he didn't do sleepovers with women; it was too intimate, and he didn't usually like the after part of sex, especially the cuddling. But with Em? He enjoyed drifting off with her arms and legs wrapped around him like well-toned vines. Her soft snores and sleepy mutters were cute. He liked that, despite the years they'd been apart, those little things about her were still the same.

Not wanting to wake her up, he ignored his growing hard-on and focused on what would happen once she did wake up. They didn't do morning-afters well. The first one hadn't been what he wanted for her.

She'd been a virgin, and while the night itself has been off the charts, the morning after was the start of their problems in London.

Rob looked down at the woman sleeping beside him, wishing he could go back and redo that morning. He would have done more to make it clear to his father—and to Em—how he felt about her, done more to make the morning special for her. He couldn't change the past, but he could make this morning better.

He eased her down on the pillow, studying her face. She looked even more peaceful now than she had when she fell asleep on the plane. The worry she'd worn since he first ran into her in Melbourne had eased. An adorable dusting of freckles covered her nose, barely visible against her golden skin. Similar freckles dotted her shoulders. Her cupid's bow mouth still bore traces of their last round of lovemaking at three a.m., the soft, relaxed lips a little swollen, a hint of beard burn marring her otherwise perfect skin.

Thank God she'd found a spare condom in her bag. Unlike their first two bouts, that last round had been slow and easy, both of them still half asleep. Her shoulder-length hair spread out across the white pillows in a wild, inky mass. The slight tilt to her eyes gave her an almost impish quality when she slept, a fairy in repose.

It would be so easy to let her sleep for another few hours so he could study her, memorize every line and curve of her body for when he inevitably had to leave her. He'd never get enough of her. Even her scent intoxicated him; the sharp, flirty fragrance of lemons and rosemary drew him in. He wondered if she'd let him share the luxurious shower with her if he woke her up now.

Knowing she had a busy schedule and no time for jet lag, he leaned down and gave her a feather-light kiss. Then another, each going a little deeper, coaxing her awake. His body leapt with anticipation when her tongue flicked out to trace his bottom lip and her arms stole around his neck.

Unable to stop himself, he pushed the sheet down and cupped her breast, kneading it lightly, a prelude to something more.

Only they never got to the something more.

Em pulled back, big brown eyes blinking up at him as the fog of sleep faded into alert confusion. "Rob? What—?"

"Morning, beautiful. Did you sleep well?" he asked, his hand still resting on her bare breast.

She pushed at his shoulders and rolled away, wrapping the sheet around her. "What are you still doing here?"

"What do you mean? Where else would I be?" He leaned back against the headboard. Shit. He knew that look in her eyes. No sleepy, sweet morning. Not now anyway.

"Um. I don't know. Your apartment? The moon? Anywhere but here," she said as she began to pace.

Pacing was never good. She looked ready to explode when all he wanted to do was hold her close and never let her go.

"We slept together, Em. Why would I leave in the middle of the night?"

He wasn't sure what she wanted from him or what last night was, but he wasn't going to back down now. Not after so long. This might be his only chance to solve the biggest "what if" that'd plagued him every day since his injury, hell, since he made the decision not to meet her in the airport that day. Em was the only woman to ever truly matter to him, and he desperately wanted her to understand that. This wasn't just a one-night stand to him. She'd never been that to him.

She glared at him. "We shouldn't have done that."

"Really, because it felt like we should have. It felt really, really good. Like the first time but without the awkward part of my dad waking us up banging on my door because I was late for practice in the middle of the Olympics," he teased, trying to get her to lighten up, which he knew was impossible.

For a while last night, she'd ignored that they had a past, that he'd been the world's biggest idiot for seven years, and they'd gotten back to those two passionate kids they'd been when they first got together. But the woman before him wasn't a kid. She wasn't the girl who'd called him a coward when he lied and told her that he didn't have time to see her because of their conflicting schedules, and they should break up. This Em had been through the wars, especially over the last few months, and her trust wasn't so easily given any more than her heart was.

Dark eyes flashed at him dangerously. "This is worse. We can't...this is a really bad idea. You need to leave."

Oh, hell, no. This was not going to happen. Whatever this was between them, whatever he'd thrown away seven years ago, he wanted a chance to explore it. He couldn't afford to blow another chance to be with her.

"No."

****

Emerson's world was spinning out of control again. What the hell had she been thinking? Kissing Rob Ashton—stupid enough. Sleeping with him tipped into the realm of phenomenally stupid, and letting him spend the night took that up to catastrophic. All it would take was one bell boy or hotel clerk or maid looking to make some quick cash, and it would be all over the papers that slutty Emerson Grace was at it again—this time with a member of the press who had very publicly defended her.

And they'd be right. God. She was an idiot. *A complete and total idiot.*

"You're not an idiot," Rob said, still sitting there all naked and godlike in the bed, his erection at half-mast under the soft white sheet.

"Did I say that out loud?" She stopped her pacing for a moment, tugging the sheet higher. She needed to find some clothes. At least with some clothes on, she'd be less vulnerable to his…charms.

He shrugged, all lazy male confidence. "Yes. And even if you hadn't, it's written all over your face, beautiful. But you're wrong. You're not an idiot, and this wasn't a bad idea. It was unexpected and impulsive, but it was also inevitable."

"Inevitable?" She found her suitcase and dug through it. "On what planet was it inevitable? Until a week ago, I thought you hated me, and I'm still fairly certain I'm not a huge fan of you."

She couldn't ever be a fan of him, not after everything that had happened between them. Except that he drove her crazy, both physically and mentally.

"Really? Because that's not what your body said

last night, and that's definitely not what the beard burn on your thighs says this morning."

A cool breeze hit the front of said thighs, warning her that she'd lost her grip on the sheet. She quickly tugged on a sweater that covered her ass, then tried to find a pair of panties. Why did he always throw her so off-kilter?

"And I never hated you. Things between us have always been...complicated. But hate does not register on the long list of things I feel for you."

God, why did those words sound so good and so horrible at the same time? Him not hating her made all of this much worse than she'd first realized, and that look in his eyes amped it up five notches. There was a steadiness and a level of affection in them that made Em's entire nervous system stand at attention.

She wanted to believe him—that lonely, needy part of her desperately wanted to believe that there was some hope for them. But she wasn't the naive twenty-year-old any longer. Her heart had been shattered when Rob didn't show up back then, and she'd finally managed to put it back together when Kole left a giant bruise on it. She couldn't let him in. She'd lost too much to open herself up for that ever again.

"So much baggage in one small sentence," she muttered, shimmying into a pair of bright-green lace panties. "Why couldn't you be like a normal one-night stand and sneak out in the middle of the night? I can't do this. We can't do this. You need to leave. Now."

He caught the pair of boxer briefs she picked up off the floor and threw at him. "Not happening. Not until you tell me why we can't do this. Because last night, it seemed we were more than capable of doing this again.

And again. And again."

Waves of heat hit her, coming directly from his smile to between her legs. No. She had to stay strong. She couldn't let him get to her. "Stop it with the panty-melting smile and the charm. I'm serious. We can't do this, Rob. You're a fucking reporter for a glorified tabloid network, and I'm a tennis player you're expected to report on. How is that not a problem?"

"It's only a problem if I show bias toward you. I can be neutral and professional if it means I get to revisit last night," he said as he pulled on the boxer briefs, the scar on his shoulder shining in the light from the window. A tattoo she'd finally noticed during their second—or was it third?—round last night climbed along his ribs. The web of wyrd, he'd said. A reminder of his Nordic heritage and a belief in shaping his own destiny. She'd briefly wondered last night if that meant he no longer believed in his father's outdated sense of family destiny, but she'd immediately dismissed the thought. The Ashtons were raised on family expectations, and nothing could take that out of them.

"Oh, really? And what about what I want, Rob? How do you know that I want to revisit last night?" She tried to ignore how good he looked, his blond locks all tousled from sleep and his arms and chest so muscly and tempting. That tattoo wasn't helping his hotness quotient go down any, either.

No. She was not going there again. The last time she let herself get drawn in by those muscles and that smile, she'd ended up a hot mess and in one of the worst slumps of her career. She couldn't afford to go there again, not when she could almost taste her first Grand Slam win, her chance to show Papa Vic that it was all worth it, even if he couldn't be there to see it.

But damn Rob, he made her feel so…alive. The sex had been toe-curling, wet-dream-inducingly good. The man knew how to play a woman's body almost better than he could read an opponent on the court, but it was more than that. For the first time since the rumors started, she'd slept through the night without anxiety dreams about more stories coming out. And this morning, before reality hit, waking up with him, to his slow kisses and that wonderful scent that was pure Rob—a mix of male and mint and eucalyptus—had been off-the-charts good. Anytime she'd smelled that scent in the last seven years, she immediately went back to their first night together. Not the sex, which had been great considering it was her first time, but the after, when he wrapped his body around her, and she felt so…safe. Safer than she'd felt in years. Except the niggling voice in the back of her head told her that wasn't true, that he'd abandoned her before, and he'd do it again.

"Because I wasn't the only one in that bed last night, Em. And because we matter to each other. I don't want to go back to the way things were. This is the first thing that's happened to me in the last two years that's felt right. Look me in the eye and tell me it doesn't feel right to be here with me."

Right? Right? Was it right to feel torn apart? To not know where she stood or what she wanted?

"I haven't felt 'right' in so long I wouldn't recognize it if I did feel it." She wished she could tell him what he wanted to hear. She hadn't seen that sort of honesty and vulnerability in his eyes in a long time. If she were to lie to him now, it would eat at her even more.

"Rob. Last night was…hormones and lust and a healthy dose of nostalgia," she said, keeping her gaze locked with his but her arms firmly crossed in front of her. "I can't—what do you want from me? You want me to fall into your arms and say, 'Oh, yes, let's have a relationship?' I can't do that."

"Can't or won't?" he challenged, tugging on his jeans, leaving them partially unbuttoned, hanging low on his lean hips, the mouth-watering V of muscles sending a shot of lust straight through her.

"What does it matter? You are a whole mess that I can't even begin to think about. Do you have any idea the shit storm I'd be in if someone found out about tonight, let alone more nights after this? God, Rob. Think about what my poor grandma would have to go through. It's bad enough they've had to spend the last few weeks avoiding all sports news and tabloids so she doesn't accidentally see risqué pictures of me or hear awful stories about what a slut her granddaughter is. The woman just had a cardiac episode, for fuck's sake." She wrapped her arms around herself and leaned against the dresser. "Did you know that Michael even called me after the pictures came out?"

The words were out before she could stop them, but it was a relief at the same time. She hadn't told anyone about that call, not Owen, not Zoe or Maren or Dera. Certainly not Gran. Besides, if anyone knew what it was like to have a complicated relationship with their dad, it was Rob. Except Bobby Ashton at least took an interest in his children.

"Your dad called? He actually managed to find a phone in whatever hellhole he's visiting now?" Rob sat on the edge of the bed, bracing his sexy forearms on his knees, his attention laser-focused on her.

She snorted, pushing her hair out of her face, wishing she had a hair tie. "Yeah, amazing, right? Guess what he said. I can guarantee it wasn't anywhere near as supportive as your little outburst."

Her father's idea of parenting was…minimal, at best. She loved him, but she'd long ago stopped expecting anything from him. It was the same for Owen. Michael had left them with his parents a few weeks after Mai, Em's mom, died. Rob only knew about her relationship with her father because he'd caught her crying after her first match when she realized that, despite being on assignment not far from London, her father wasn't going to make it to watch her play in the Olympics. That was the last day she'd ever had any expectations of her father.

"Fuck, Em. I'm sorry. Did he really give you a hard time about the damn pictures?"

"I swear he was channeling your dad or something. He went on and on about how shameful it was, and how he expected better from me. How I should have thought about my brother's career, how I should care more about my family's reputation." She looked down at her toes, fighting back the tears of frustration. "For a man who spent my entire childhood traveling from one war zone to the next to take pictures, he was really good at laying on the parental guilt. He even talked about how ashamed my mom would be. How Papa Vic's heart would be broken if he were still here."

Rob got up then and drew her into his arms, his body enveloping her like a warm bath. For a second, she let herself nuzzle into his shoulder and breathe him in. The pain and heartache she'd been carrying around since she got the call four days ago eased but didn't fully go away. It could never go away.

"Your mom wouldn't have been ashamed, Em. Any parent worth their salt would be upset for you, not at you. Your grandpa sure as hell would have been pissed off for you. He'd be ready to rip someone limb from limb, just like your brother and I were. Don't let him get to you." His hand stroked her hair.

She hoped that was true. She had no memories of her mother, but she knew she'd grown up in a conservative Chinese family in San Francisco and rebelled by marrying the hotshot American photographer.

"Michael is Michael. But it doesn't change the fact that I can't put myself in a position to open my family up for more scrutiny because of my private life." She pulled away and walked to the open window. On the other side of the glass, the world was alive and bustling. People moved up and down the stairs of the New York Public Library. Yellow cabs wove their way through the streets like snails. Gray, overcast winter skies warned that it'd be bitterly cold when she went outside later, a stark contrast to the warm Australian summer she'd enjoyed the last few weeks.

"I get it, Em. I really do." Rob came to stand by her, a big hand resting on the small of her back.

A pang of sadness struck her to the core. This was it. She wanted him to agree to leave her alone, but it didn't mean she liked it. That lost little nineteen-year-old still wanted the most beautiful man she'd ever seen to sweep her off her feet, but she couldn't let him. Years of experience told her to stand on her own two feet, and the last few months had taught her that opening her heart only led to more pain. "Then you understand why this can't happen again? This can't be anything more than a one-night stand."

When he didn't respond right away, her thoughts began to race. So many scenarios played through her mind. Him getting mad and taking it out on her by telling the world how easily she'd jumped into bed with him. Him walking away and never speaking to her again outside of a professional context. All of it would hurt, but it would be bearable if it happened sooner rather than later. She took a step away, wishing she'd taken the time to pull pants on. Suddenly, she was very aware of how exposed she was.

"No. I get why you're worried, but I don't agree that we can't make this work." Big hands turned her to face him, cradling her jaw with a gentle hand. "I want more than a one-night stand, Em. You have every right to be gun-shy after what you've gone through, but I'm not Kole, and I'm not the guy I was when we first went out."

"Damn straight you're not. You're even more wrong for me than you were back then." She pushed his hand away and walked over to grab her jeans out of her suitcase. Damn it, why was there not a dignified way to put on a pair of skinny jeans? His eyes followed her every move. Irritated at how sexy he looked bracketed by the morning light, she grabbed his shirt from where it'd been tossed the night before and threw it at him. "Put that on and leave. Please."

He pulled the shirt on but made no move to leave, a storm brewing on his face. "We could make this work. All I'm asking for is a chance. I...walking away from you last time damn near killed me. I don't think I can do it again."

Her heart clenched. He hadn't just walked away—he'd let his father convince him she wasn't worthy of him. She'd heard it and known even before he began to pull away that their days were numbered.

"You're the one who listened to your father. You're the one who didn't want to try to make us work because I wasn't from the right background and I wasn't well-known enough for the great Bobby Ashton. That was your choice, Rob. This time it's mine, and I say that there's nothing for us beyond last night."

The words came out colder than she'd intended, but she meant them. She had control now, and a romantic relationship would shift the balance of power. She didn't need that kind of distraction. She still remembered how unfazed he'd been by their breakup after they returned from the Olympics. He'd played even better than he had before and gone on to win the US Open while she went out in the first round and went home to nurse her broken heart. The memory of how utterly lost she'd felt, how worthless and stupid she'd let herself believe she was, put a little steel back in her spine.

His temper flared, his eyes more gray than blue now, but he didn't get angry like she expected. His jaw clenched, and he finished buttoning his jeans. Sitting on the bed, he reached for his shoes, his eyes never leaving her. "So that's it? We go back to biting each other's heads off anytime we see each other and forget any of this ever happened?"

The thought made her nauseous; hating Rob was exhausting and made it more difficult to sort out her feelings. "No. We're polite, friendly even. We simply don't have sex or act like we've ever had sex."

The words sounded weak even to her. Being around him and not wanting to jump him was easier said than done. Half the reason he'd irritated her so much over the years was because even though he broke her, her body still wanted him.

He stared at her, eyes narrowed a little like they did when he was searching for an opponent's weakness on the court. She stayed firm, not willing to give him an inch.

"Friendly? Or friends?" he finally asked, his shoes in place and his expression calculating.

For a moment, all she could do was stare right back at him, her brain trying to process where he might be going with this. Could she be friends with Rob? A year ago—hell, even a month ago—she would have called bullshit, but now? He was there, a glimmer of hope in his eyes, pleading with her to answer him. The what-ifs plagued her. What if friendship wasn't enough? What if he wanted more? Would she have the strength to keep telling him no? It would be so much easier to keep him at arm's length…

"Um. Friends, I guess…" The words came out before she could stop them.

Some of the tension in his broad shoulders eased, and his lips tilted up in the ghost of a smile. "I can work with that."

Deep down, she knew that should worry her, but she was too worried about what would happen if he stayed much longer to think about what he meant. "Great. Can you leave now? It's only a matter of time before someone notices you sneaking out of my room."

Ignoring her, he walked to the bedside table where her phone was. To her surprise, he unlocked it and started typing on the screen.

"What are you doing?" she asked.

"Giving you my number and getting yours. If you're serious about the friend thing, then you'll use it." He handed the phone back to her. "And you should really make your passcode a little more complicated than your birthday."

She blinked at her phone and then him. He remembered her birthday? Would the wonders never cease? Half the time her own brother didn't remember her birthday. Before she had a chance to respond, he leaned down and pressed a quick kiss to her lips.

"Good luck on your shoot and meetings today. I'll text you later."

He left, and all she could do was glare at the door, remembering now why she'd spent the last seven years sniping at him. That confidence—arrogance—was enough to drive anyone nuts. The real question was, would she respond when Mr. Sure-of-Himself texted her, or would she let sleeping dogs lie? Rob Ashton had always been more of a complication than she was prepared to handle, but maybe being friends with him would be easier than falling in love with him.

Maybe.

Chapter 9

"Emerson Anne, you sit back down and finish your breakfast."

Em rolled her eyes at her grandmother's order. "Gran. I know you want to take care of me, but I already agreed to stay here last night instead of going to my place. I've had as much breakfast as I can without puking it up when I get to the practice courts."

"Emmy, don't you sass me. You're skin and bones, little girl." Gran pinched Em's arm in demonstration. "You need to get a good meal before you go out there and run around all day."

She bit back a laugh. She loved her grandma, and it'd felt good to sleep in her old room last night, but she always seemed to forget that Em was twenty-seven, not seven. Her two days post-Rob in New York had flown by. He'd texted her within twelve hours of leaving her hotel room, asking about her photoshoot and meetings, one of which had been with his sister. She wavered between telling him the truth and keeping things light and easy—friendly. The truth was, her body was sore from all the sex, and the stupid photoshoot only made it worse, posing her in awkward positions for "action" shots. But telling him that would only stoke his already massive ego and give him the wrong idea. So she gave him the light, easy answer, and they'd texted back and forth a bit. He'd even told her goodnight with a little kiss emoji.

The next night, he'd called, even though he'd been busy. She'd been worried that it was a booty call, but instead he'd asked about her day, about how her meetings went—off the record. He'd offered advice on how to maneuver around one of the sponsors' scrutiny, and they'd ended up watching part of a movie together while they talked, *To Kill A Mockingbird*, one of her Papa Vic's favorites. He'd called last night too. She'd been busy with her grandma's fussing, but she'd texted him. There was a text waiting for her this morning.

Morning beautiful. Hope you have a good practice today. Don't forget to work on that second serve ;)

She'd sent him an emoji with its tongue sticking out in reply.

"Gran, I love you, but you can't keep me here all day." She stood up and went to kiss her grandma's weathered cheek. It still felt weird not to have Papa Vic there, his eyes twinkling as he silently laughed at Gran's fussing. "I've eaten more than enough, and Zoe will make sure I eat a good lunch. She loves to fuss as much as you do."

"Fine. Go practice," Gran said with a humph. "Just be careful, Squeaker. Those vultures are still lurking around, trying to get a picture of you."

She sighed, her heart warming a little at the childhood nickname. "I'll be fine. Promise."

By the time she was through the first two hours with Zoe, Emerson was wishing she'd stayed at her grandparents' house. "Are you trying to kill me?"

"No." Zoe smirked. "It's not my fault that you didn't practice while you were in New York."

"It's not my fault either," Emerson groused.

"Blame Amir. He scheduled a million things for me to do. I barely had time to eat a real meal, let alone train."

"We'll have to have a word with him about that. You can't afford so many distractions. If you're going to win a slam this year, we need one hundred percent of your focus on the courts. Come on, give me another set of crunches."

Emerson pounded the exercise mat beneath her in frustration but resumed her work out. Between curling her body toward her knees, she said, "It's not like...I like this...but I had to do damage control...to keep my sponsors...which means...doing what Amir says."

She didn't mention that she may or may not have walked into another massive distraction in New York.

Not that she would let Rob be a distraction. When she needed to focus on her game, she'd be a laser. But she had to admit she was enjoying his first overtures at friendship or whatever was going on between them, even if her guard was still up. But it was going to be more of a challenge than she'd thought to keep things platonic. There'd been some seriously hot, wet dreams over the last few nights—the one last night felt really wrong considering she was in her childhood bed.

"Fine. But Amir and your sponsors need to remember that they'll make more money with that Grand Slam under your belt than they'll make by pulling you away all the time." Zoe handed Em her water bottle, which she gratefully gulped. "Let's grab some lunch, and then we'll hit the courts and work on that second serve."

By the time Em drove her Honda Civic up to her reserved parking spot in front of her town house, her body screamed for a long, hot bath, a big glass of ice water, and the comfy embrace of her couch. But first, she had to check her mail, water her plants, and start a massive load or seven of laundry.

Stopping at her box, she pulled out the stacks of mail her house sitter hadn't grabbed while she was in New York and made her way in. The cleaning team had been through yesterday, so there wasn't a layer of dust to worry about. She dragged her bags in from the car and sorted through the laundry before turning her attention to the piles of mail.

"Squeaker? You home?"

"No, O, my car drove itself and parked outside," she called to her brother.

Owen appeared, his black hair cropped closer to his head than the last time she'd seen him.

"Sarcasm. Charming. And here I thought you missed me." He opened her fridge, pulled out one of the lemon waters she loved, and took a big swig of it.

"Remind me again why I gave you a key." She made a face. "I swear it wasn't so you could pick on me here as well as at Gran's house and steal my stuff."

"Because I'm your favorite brother, and I love you. Did you just get home?"

She went back to sorting through the mail. "Yeah. Zo kept me at practice longer today since I missed time while I was in New York."

"Bummer. You'd think Amir would have scheduled some practice time into your schedule." He hopped up to sit on the counter beside her. "Any good mail?"

"Not all of us get nudie magazines in the mail," she said absently, scanning the return labels of each envelope as she piled the bills in one stack, the junk in another, and the miscellaneous magazines and letters in a third.

He snorted. "Please. I haven't gotten one of those in years. It's all about the Internet, now."

"God, O. You are such a guy."

Emerson's eyes flitted over an envelope. The handwriting was the same as she'd seen on two other envelopes she'd tossed in the miscellaneous pile. Blocky, shaky writing, slightly crumpled around the edges. And no postmark…

Frowning, she picked up the letter opener and carefully slit the top of the first one she'd placed in the pile. Fan mail was all supposed to go to Amir's office or her PO box. No one except her family and friends had her home address, and she'd never done any sort of interview here.

You bitch. How dare you betray Kole like that? You deserve to be broken for being such a slut.

Each letter was carefully cut out of a picture of her or Kole. Then another picture of her, one of the ones from the leak, was carefully pasted at the bottom with Xs drawn over her eyes.

"Emmy? You okay?"

Owen's words cut through her stupor long enough for her to shake her head. She quickly opened the next letter, dropping the first as she went.

Slut. Whore. Did you accept payment when you spread for those other men? Or do you do it because you can't keep your legs closed?

The next one had her whole hand trembling, bile rising in her throat. Her breath came in short, shallow pants.

Cunt. If you don't apologize to Kole and admit

what a fucking bitch you are, you'll be sorry!

"What the hell? Squeaker, where did these come from?" Owen snatched the letters from her.

She took a step back, rubbing her chest as if it'd make breathing easier. "I don't know. I...they are in the mail."

"Did you bring it in or did the house sitter?" he demanded, pulling out his phone.

She took a deep breath, closing her eyes to shut out some of the distractions. "I don't know. I think the first ones must have been brought in by the house sitter, but the last one was probably in the bunch I brought in. This is bad. I need to call Zoe and Amir. And Gran."

"First you need to call the police," he insisted.

He was right. Shit. This was a bigger mess than she thought. Police meant more reporters and stories and more of those goddamn distractions she didn't need now.

After she made the calls, she started to pace. Her chest tightened as she moved, her breaths coming in shallower with each inhalation. "Why is this happening? Why can't I have a moment of peace? I can't...I don't know how much more of this I can take, O."

Owen, the family peace maker, who took everything in stride, pulled her into a hug. He cuddled her close, stroking her hair and rubbing her back, just as he used to when they were little and something would upset her. She vaguely remembered him holding her like this after their mom died and their dad left them behind. "Breathe, Squeaker. Slow down and breathe. You're not doing this alone."

She loved her brother more than life. He'd been by

her side for everything, from their mom's death to their first time playing tennis to going pro. He supported her and had her back as much as their grandparents did. But a part of her she always held back, always worrying that there might be too much of their dad in him. She couldn't tell him about Rob, after London or last week, and she didn't know that he could ever understand what was happening to her now.

"Tell that to my subconscious. Intellectually, I know you're here and that everyone has my back, but I'm the only one being attacked. It's getting real old, real fast," she said.

But she let her brother hold her and fuss over her. He even made her some of her favorite tea. By the time Amir, Zoe, and a friend of Amir's from the local police department showed up, Em had downgraded from scared out of her mind to pissed off.

"You were right to call me, Mr. al-Tammar. Given everything that's happened to Ms. Grace over the last few weeks, I think we can safely say the two incidents are connected." Detective Turner Combs slipped the three letters and their envelopes into a protective sleeve of plastic he'd brought with him.

"Do you think you can find who sent the letters?" Zoe asked, her arm protectively around Em's shoulders. Emmy appreciated the support, but she hated that she once again needed it.

Combs frowned. "Maybe. It'll depend on a lot of factors. We'll take Owen and Emerson's prints so that we can differentiate theirs from the ones left by the letter writer. If he left any prints or DNA, we can run them through the system, but it's a crap shoot if we'll find any matches."

"Amir, have you had any luck figuring out who released those pictures?" Owen asked, leaning over the back of the couch near Em.

"Nothing definite, but the PI we hired did confirm that it wasn't Naumov. Kole had some cyber guys check his computer, and some of his accounts were hacked."

Zoe snorted. "And you trust his word?"

"I trust the word of the guys he hired, and so does my PI." Amir glanced at Combs. "You don't think Naumov is behind the letters, do you?"

Emerson's stomach clenched, and her head throbbed with the weight of the emotions hitting her. "No. Kole wouldn't do this. Besides, the letters were written about him. The…the person directed their outrage at me because of him, yes, but I don't think he'd do this. The first one was in a stack of mail from before the Australian Open was over, and Kole left Melbourne the same day as I did."

"Emerson is right. While this person, whoever he or she is, is connected to Mr. Naumov, I don't think he's directly involved. It's more like they're a super fan who's taken a dangerous turn," Combs said.

"What do we do now?" Amir asked. "Wait for this nutcase to show himself?"

Combs stood up, taking the letters with him. "I'd suggest making sure Ms. Grace doesn't go anywhere alone, and forward all of her mail to your office, Mr. al-Tammar."

"What good would that do?" Emerson asked. Her head ached more than her body, which was saying something, and she wanted to curl up in a ball and forget all this had ever happened. "Whoever it is, they didn't send the letter through the regular mail. There was no postmark."

"I'll have one of my guys check your mailbox every few days to see if our friend decides to drop another letter in it, but given that it's a locked box, I'm guessing he found some way to sneak it in with the mail that's already been sorted. I'm going to talk to the guys at the local post office, see if they've noticed anyone suspicious hanging around. Mr. Grace, you and your grandmother should be on the lookout too. If any letters show up at your residences, you call me right away."

"Of course." Owen stood and showed the detective to the door.

Emerson buried her face in her hands. This couldn't be happening. It was all a bad dream, and she'd wake up in the morning to another super sexy dream about Rob.

Amir frowned and started clicking around on his phone.

"What are you doing?" Zoe asked.

"I'm looking into private security. It'll cost a pretty penny, but at least Emmy will be safe."

The ferocity in his voice surprised Emerson. Amir had been her agent since she went pro at nineteen, but he'd always been a cross between a pit bull and an annoying but lovable uncle. The bald man's main focus was usually on earning the money that kept him in expensive suits and ties.

Emerson leaned forward and placed her hand over his phone. "That's really sweet of you, Amir, but I don't need private security."

"The hell you don't," Owen said, returning to the comfortable living room. The soft yellows, purples, and whites had always put her at ease, but today nothing seemed to work.

"You've got a crazy person sending you threatening letters. To any sane person, that's a good sign you need security."

"Before you hulk out on me, think about this, O." She tugged her brother to sit beside her, his big frame eating up twice the space as hers did. "We have no clue where this person is or who they are. We don't even know if they're serious. It could be some weird prank or something."

Zoe gave her a look. "Prank? Those letters did not sound like a prank, Emmy."

"For once, I gotta agree with Zoe. That psycho took the time to cut letters out of your face. That's a lot of effort for a prank," Amir said.

"Maybe. But until the cops think it's something serious, then I think we need to hold off on wasting money on security." Some of her friends, like Dera, had private security with them whenever they were traveling, but she'd worked hard to avoid it. She didn't like the thought of having two or three beefy, muscled guys following her around.

"It's not like I'm ever alone that much. I spend most of my days training with Zoe and the team, then I come home where I have a really good security system and an overprotective brother right next door."

The reason she'd bought her townhouse in the first place was because Owen was looking at one next door. The few years they'd both been away at college felt so odd after being so close all their lives, even though they'd seen each other at tournaments. Having him next door was comforting. They both had different schedules and went to different tournaments, but it was still nice to know that he was a few dozen yards away when she needed him.

"Fine," Owen said. "No private security for now. But you promise me that you'll stay safe. If you need to go grocery shopping, take me or Zoe or one of your team members with you. Only go to and from the training facility and the Grands' on your own."

Her hackles flared. Bossy Owen never failed to tick her off, even when his intentions were good. "I'll be careful, O. I've got too much to look forward to this year to do anything stupid."

The other three started to talk about possible culprits, but Em's mind drifted. Doing something stupid was exactly what she was doing, by agreeing to stay in contact with Rob. It was even more stupid now that she had a nut job sending her letters about what a slut she was. If he got wind of her having one-night stands in hotel rooms, it would probably only make matters worse.

For a moment, she thought about calling Rob. Hearing his voice would calm her down better than anything, but she couldn't do that. They might be "friends" now, but she couldn't tell him about this. Not with his job. Besides, they were the sort of friends who had short, pleasant conversations and casual text message exchanges. Telling him she had a stalker was a bad idea on so many different levels.

****

Rob took a deep breath of the warm California air. It was a nice change from the frigid New York winter he'd left behind. He watched his sister move across the court, light as the leaves blowing off the nearby trees, her long tail of dark blond hair dancing in the wind.

The rhythmic thwack of the racket connecting with the bright green ball took him back to a better time, an easier time. A time when he didn't have a bum shoulder and still had the job he was born for. That sound had been a lullaby for him as a little kid and a battle cry from the time he was old enough to swing a racket. He'd missed that sound, echoing across these same courts, since the day he woke up from his surgery.

His hands itched to pick up a racket again. His legs ached with the need to run across the court to meet his sister's volley.

How many hours had they played here? Despite the seven-year age difference, he and Maren had always been close. He'd taught her how to play when he went to visit her at their grandparents' house in Sweden on a break from the tennis academy. She'd taken to it like a duck to water, and they'd shared that love of the game just like they shared the solidarity of being mostly ignored by their parents. Sometimes he missed the days when he used to coach her. He'd gotten such a kick out of showing her how to grip the racket in her tiny hands and how to serve.

"Watch that backhand, short stack," he called out as the ball thrower sent a cross body shot at her.

Maren missed the shot and turned to fix him with a death glare that had been much cuter when she was five. "I would have been fine if someone wasn't backseat swinging."

"Please. You were a mile off." He stood up and moved down the stairs to the court. "Besides, you promised me lunch, and it's almost one thirty."

His sister winced. "Sorry. I got in the zone and—"

125

"Lost track of time, yeah, I know." He picked up one of the dead balls from the edge of the court and tossed it from hand to hand. "Go get cleaned up."

By the time they got to the cute beachside restaurant they both loved, it was after two.

"At least we missed the lunch rush and got a patio table," Maren said, accepting a menu from the waiter.

"True. I missed this place more than anything." Rob thumbed through the menu, even though he knew exactly what he'd get.

Laughing, she took a sip of her water. "What, no ocean views in NYC?"

"River views? Sure. Harbor views too. But nothing like this. I miss the sandy beaches and the warm weather. I've bought more sweaters in the last two months than I have in the last ten years combined."

"Hey, you're the one who wanted to move to New York, big brother. I told you it was a stupid plan." She grinned at the waiter. "I'll have the grilled shrimp with the squash and zucchini chips and a side salad."

"And I'll have the fish tacos with the avocado crema and extra cilantro." Rob handed the menu over and accepted the soda the waiter handed him in exchange. "I like the job well enough, Mare. Just not the location."

"Do you really like the job? I saw your face earlier. You miss being out on the court." She fiddled with the end of her ponytail, a habit left over from childhood. Their mother always insisted Maren keep her hair long but pulled away from her face. She'd rebelled against a lot over the years but always kept the long hair.

"Of course I miss it. But unless my shoulder magically goes back in time to before my injury, I'm not going to be playing again anytime soon." He kept his words light, doing his best to hide the bitterness that lingered. Saying he missed being out on the courts was like saying a fish missed water flowing over its gills. But he'd had to come to terms with his life as it was and not focus on the fact that he'd never play competitive tennis again.

She rolled her eyes, the long-suffering sister look down pat. "You didn't answer my question, Robby."

"Okay, *Mary*. Do I like my job?" He shrugged. "Some days I do and some days I don't, like every other poor schmuck out there. Some of it's not great. Working with Bruno sucks, but I don't mind the rest of it."

"You could be coaching, though. You love working with kids," she insisted. "Mama would love to have your help with the tennis academy, especially her program with the foster kids."

He shrugged. "Working with the parents isn't an option. Besides, I get to tell stories about the people worth knowing about. I'm in a position to make sure that the people who deserve attention are getting attention and that people are hearing the truth about the phonies."

The breeze from the ocean eased the lingering tension from his time at the court. He'd spoken the truth, but not all of it. Being a reporter was harder than he'd expected, especially as a junior reporter. Bruno had tried to railroad him into stories that were meaningless. More than once, the older reporter had pitched follow-up stories on Em that would directly counteract all the good Rob had done for both the network and for Em. Thankfully, Rob had managed to convince Joey to nix the ideas and focus on other stories, like Dera Calvet's new coach or Chessa Pavlich's mysterious absence from the press events following the Australian Open.

The stories about Em were thankfully dying down, but that didn't mean she was far from his mind. He'd gotten into the habit of talking or texting with her every night before bed. Hearing her voice made it a little easier for him to sleep, even if it did inspire more wet dreams than he'd had since high school. Before the network sent him out here, he'd been trying to think of an excuse to go down to Florida to see her for a few days.

"As much as I hate you working for that slimy network, that was a good thing you did for Emmy Grace after those pictures came out," Maren said, munching on some chips and salsa. "I've never been more proud to be your sister than I was when I saw the segment."

Heat crept up his cheeks, and he was pretty sure it had nothing to do with the salsa. "It was nothing. Really. I just...I said what I'd want someone to say if you were in that position. Not that I ever want you to be, of course, but I did what any guy with a conscience would do."

"Well, we all appreciate it. If it weren't for the whole conflict of interest thing, you'd be scoring with a lot of the female tennis players." She winked. "Not that you had any issues in that area before."

There was really only one woman he wanted to score with these days, but he sure as hell wasn't telling his sister that. He waited until their food arrived before revisiting the topic of Em. He had to be careful, or her annoying sister radar would go off in a second. She'd always been able to tell when he was really interested in a woman.

"How is Emerson doing? The stories seem to be dying down," he said, taking a bite of his fish tacos. The flavors burst in his mouth, the mix of sea and spices so good he almost moaned.

She finished chewing her chip before responding. "She's all right, I guess. She seemed a bit scattered at our meeting in New York. She's still a little depressed about everything that's happened, but she's been keeping busy with training. She's dead set on winning a slam this year. But I did get the sense she wasn't telling me everything. I'd planned to try to pry more out her, but she hung up before I got the chance."

"I've heard tell she's a woman on a mission." He sipped his soda, mulling over his sister's words. He'd gotten the feeling Em was holding something back too, but he'd written it off as her keeping distance between them because of their past.

"Speaking of missions, have you heard from the parents lately? Is Bobby still riding you pretty hard?" He wanted to ask more about Em, but he didn't know if he could do it without tipping his sister off.

Her mouth tightened, and she stared out over the ocean. "Dad is Dad. He's so focused on his legacy, you know? Thank God for Mom. She's been keeping him distracted as best she can, but I half expect him to show up and start butting in at any second."

He hated that his injury made life harder for his sister too. All their lives, when their dad did decide to pay attention to them, it had been to focus on Rob and his career. The next piece of the Ashton legacy. He'd done his part and added as best he could, but Bobby wanted more. He wanted a calendar Grand Slam and a record as the world number one. Since Rob couldn't do that now, his sister was in the hot seat.

"Don't let him bully you, Mare. I know you want to please him, but you've got to remember to put yourself first over whatever it is he wants." He gave his sister's arm a squeeze.

She laughed. "Is this a 'do as I say not as I do' thing? You sure as hell couldn't stand up to Bobby. How do you expect me to?"

He swallowed hard. Damn his sister for a wicked gut shot. She was right, of course. But it didn't sting any less. He'd let his father bully him about his life choices for most of his life. But he'd also been free for more than a year, and it felt...so fucking good not to have his father watching his every move, personally or professionally. "Learn from my mistakes, short stack. Dad's all hot air. At the end of the day, you need to be happy. That's all that matters."

They finished their lunch, slipping away from the high-octane topics and into the realm of easy conversation about movies and books and current events. He'd dropped his sister back off at the courts when his phone rang.

"Joey? What's up?" he asked, leaning back in the seat of the convertible he'd rented for the trip.

"I've got a story I want you to start looking into right away." She didn't waste time on any pleasantries. "How soon can you wrap up the Casterman story?"

He closed his eyes, letting the breeze wash over him. She already had him out here doing a story about a prodigy playing at one of the local high schools. The kid was fourteen and already playing better than some of the WTA vets. "I've got another interview scheduled for tomorrow night, then you'll have all the footage to edit the piece."

"Good. Once you wrap things up there, I want you to go to Florida."

In the background, the echoes of Joey's fingers flying over a keyboard provided a soundtrack to their conversation. The woman didn't slow down for a single second. He'd yet to see her not multitasking. The hair on the back of Rob's neck stood up. Florida was the home of a lot of tennis players, but he doubted Joey would send him to do a story about just anyone.

"If this is a story about my parents—"

She interrupted him. "No, it's not about your parents. We wouldn't have you do that kind of story anyway. No, this is about Emerson Grace."

Em. Shit. Not again. He'd tried to get Joey to leave her alone, but the network just kept coming. He couldn't contribute to the circus, not now, not when Em was finally seeing him as a friend. "I thought we decided we weren't doing any more stories about the photo leak."

"Bruno's doing a follow-up piece about investigators determining that Naumov wasn't behind the leaks," she said distractedly. "But I want you to look into a separate story."

This was news to him. Em hadn't said anything about the pictures since they left each other in New York. When they talked, they kept things light and non-specific. She didn't tell him much about her day to day life.

"Wait, if Naumov didn't leak them, do they know

who did?" he asked, his mind already turning over the different possibilities. If Kole hadn't leaked the pictures, Em had a bigger problem than they'd originally thought.

"That's what I want you to look into," Joey said, "or at least part of it. I've heard rumors that Emerson has been receiving threatening stalker-type letters. I want you to see if it's true and look into a connection between the stalker and the leak."

A thousand feelings hit him faster than a ball machine, all of them more visceral than the next. Confusion came first, but fury and an inexplicable sense of betrayal followed quickly. Em hadn't said a word about this. They'd talked for at least fifteen minutes last night when he got back to his hotel after his interview. How had she left out something like that?

"Where'd you hear these rumors? I haven't heard anything about this." He struggled to keep his voice neutral.

"I've got a source with the Miami PD that says they've been ordered to make more frequent patrols in the same neighborhoods as Emerson's practice facility and her townhouse. They heard some whisperings, but they don't know anything for sure. I want you to confirm the story so we can get an exclusive."

He bit his tongue. He had no intention of letting Joey run a story like this if it were true, but he couldn't pass up this chance. "Okay. I'll finish up here and head down to Miami day after tomorrow."

He let her rattle on a few minutes about travel arrangements before he finally got her off the phone.

Fuck. He'd thought he and Em were in a good place, but he'd been right. She was keeping something from him—a big something. He thought friends told friends about stuff like this.

Punching Em's code name on his favorite contact's list—Anne for the heroine of her favorite book—he listened to the phone ring through the rental's Bluetooth.

"Hi. You've reached Emerson Grace. I'm either on the court or too tired to look at my phone. Leave me a message, and I'll get back to you when I can."

He bit back a bellow of frustration. "Em. It's me. Just heard some interesting news about you, and I think we need to talk. Give me a call back."

That ought to get her attention, but it didn't. He went through his day, finished up a meeting with his camera crew, and went back to his hotel, but still nothing from Em. Not even a text message acknowledging that she'd gotten his message. Worry warred with flat-out pissed off as he ordered room service and took a stinging-hot shower. Still, no call from Em. He tried her again and got sent straight to voicemail.

Damn it. He glanced at his watch. It was only ten thirty on the east coast. She would normally be awake now, curled up in her bed while she read or watched one of the ten thousand TV shows she followed.

She was avoiding him. The walls were going back up, higher than before, and he couldn't let that happen. He needed to talk to her, to see for himself she was really okay.

More than that, he needed to know they were okay. Losing the slimmest chance he had to finally have an answer to the what-ifs that stood between them was not an option. There was too much left unsaid, too much he wanted. If he lost her—even if it was just her friendship—it couldn't be like this.

Chapter 10

"Any more letters?" Zoe asked as she watched Emerson practice her serves. Her practice partner, Yvonne, easily returned the serve, and Em let it fall off to one side.

Emerson tossed the ball in the air and caught it, then bounced it a little. "One more yesterday. The police dusted for fingerprints and everything, but nothing came up that helped."

"What did it say?"

Completing the serve, Em sighed. "I didn't see it, but Detective Combs said it was mostly taunting me for keeping a low profile, calling me scared and shit like that. Nothing too crazy."

"We need to talk about what we're going to do at the Qatar Open as far as security goes." Zoe stood up and demonstrated a serve. "Try to angle yourself more like this."

Emerson followed her coach's movements on the next two serves. She aimed the ball to hit on the edge of the service box, just out of reach of her opponent. "Do we have to? I really don't want to make a big thing of this."

Zoe gave her a look, and Em immediately wanted to revert to her six-year-old self; the little girl who wanted to do anything to please this rock star of the tennis world so she'd stay and coach her still lurked under the surface. The tall, redheaded glam-azon had stepped in and was a mother to Em when she needed one most. Gran was great and had gone above and beyond to take care of her, but Zoe had really helped her become the woman she was. When Zoe got that no-nonsense look on her face, Emerson knew not to mess with her.

"The Qatar Open is our chance to do a dry run before Indian Wells. I've talked to Amir and Detective Combs, and they agree that the letter writer probably won't make it to Qatar. Indian Wells is another kettle of fish." Zoe demonstrated another service technique. "It'll be a lot easier to get to, and he or she won't stand out in the crowd. We need to have a protocol in place to keep you safe."

Emerson went through the motions of a few more serves, hating that they had to have this conversation. The shit storm of the pictures was dying down, and the photographers had gotten bored with her. All she did was practice, visit her family, grocery shop, and stay in her house. That wasn't much of a change from her normal routine. She'd always been focused on her practice. If she'd had a normal job, she probably would have turned into a workaholic.

Tournaments, though, were different. While she didn't have many close friends, she enjoyed the camaraderie of the tour. She got along with everyone and liked to go out for drinks or dinner when they weren't working. She didn't want this nutcase interfering with that.

"I don't want to make a big deal out of this, Zo. Qatar is always really contained, so it's not a big deal. And it's not like I'm going to have time to go out or do much at Indian Wells. When I'm not with you and the team, I'll be with Dera, who always has a side of beef following her around or with Maren or Owen."

"Emmy, I don't think you realize how serious this is. You have someone threatening you, who wants to do you physical harm. You can't brush this aside," Zoe said, pulling Em to face her.

She felt bad for the older woman. She was scared, and Em didn't blame her, but it also wasn't her life that would be affected if they gave in to panic. "Freaking out is exactly what this person wants. He wants me to miss out on my life, to let him be the one in power. I can't do that. I'll take all the usual precautions, but I'm not going to let him see me blink. Not until we know something more about him."

Zoe clearly didn't like Em's answer, but she thankfully let it go. They went through more drills on the court and then went into the gym for conditioning work. Emerson tried to keep her focus on her routine, but her mind started to drift to Rob, something that was happening way too frequently.

For the first time since she left New York, she'd ignored his texts and phone calls yesterday and the day before. Twinges of guilt and the inexplicable need to talk to him almost had her responding to the last call, but she'd stopped herself. She'd spent too much time thinking about him the last few days, and her dreams kept getting hotter, more erotic and sensual than most of her real-life encounters. A little breathing room might do her some good. Her focus should be on the court, not on if she'd talked to Rob that day. Besides, a woman didn't obsess about talking to someone who was just a friend, and that's all he could ever be. A friend with absolutely no benefits.

By the time her physio worked her over at the end of the day, Em's body resembled a wet noodle. She poured herself into her car and drove home by rote, avoiding the heavy traffic areas in favor of the sun-dappled streets lined with houses. It took a little longer to get home, but it was worth it to get to destress instead of worrying about idiot drivers.

She pulled up to her townhouse but stayed in her car. There was a strange Jeep parked across the street with a man sitting in it.

Her fingers hovered over Detective Combs's contact on her phone when she realized who was in the car. Brows furrowed and annoyance flaring, she grabbed her workout bag and marched up to the Jeep. Of course he would show up when she was wearing a pair of ratty jeans and a T-shirt of Owen's she'd stolen in college. It was gratifying to see him jump a little when she knocked on the window. He quickly put on that charming, dimpled smile that made her panties go a little damp.

"Hi. I was just about to call you," he said, opening the door and unfolding his long, lean body. He wore a slate-gray oxford shirt with the sleeves rolled to his elbows and a pair of dark wash jeans that probably cost more than her prom dress. Those muscular, sexy forearms were seriously unfair.

He moved to give her a hug, but she put a hand on his chest, keeping him at bay for the moment.

"Really? I thought you were in California all week. Imagine my surprise to find you here, lurking outside my house like a creeper."

Her head started to spin a little. After all that had

happened since she last saw him, she didn't know how she felt about letting him in. But instead of taking the hint, he'd shown up on her doorstep looking so damn good and safe, and she couldn't decide whether to slap him or bury herself in his arms.

"Creeper? I'm just a guy who decided to surprise his friend since he was unexpectedly in town. Since you weren't answering my calls, it's not like I could warn you I'd be waiting at your house." Rob shut the door to the car. "You'd think a guy would at least get a hug after traveling across the country to see said friend."

She hefted her bag on her shoulder and glanced at the house next door. Luckily, Owen's car wasn't waiting outside his townhouse, but she expected him to pull up at any moment.

"O lives next door. For all we know, there's a photographer lurking in those bushes over there." She led the way to the door, walking quickly in the hopes that he'd get the message. The last thing she needed was for the stalker to see him walking into her house, especially not this close to dark.

"Nice place." He took in the open entry hall. "If I didn't know you lived here, I'd still know it was yours."

She laughed, setting down her bag on the entry hall bench. "What does that mean?"

"It means it looks like you. It's not fussy or cluttered. Bright but comfortable colors. Pretty but functional furniture, and lots of books everywhere." He followed her into the living room.

"Thanks." She shoved her hands into the pockets of her jeans. "You never answered my question."

He smiled at her, all charming and sexy and infuriating. "What question is that?"

139

"Why. Are. You. Here?" Annoyance still spiked, mixing with low-level temper and fatigue. She'd reached her maximum level of socialization for the day, and her stomach was ready to eat itself. Playing games with him wasn't on the agenda.

He took a seat on her yellow-and-gray polka dot chair, still managing to look hot and masculine even in the girliest piece of furniture in the room. She took a seat on the purple-checked couch, sinking deep into the cushions to keep as much space between them as possible. Tension crackled through the air; he might look pleasant and affable, but Rob was pissed about something.

"I'm here because you and I need to talk, and you've been avoiding my calls." He still kept his voice even and pleasant, but temper lurked beneath the surface. "Besides, I had to be down here anyway to visit my parents before I head to Qatar. Mom insisted."

That took her a little off her guard. She'd forgotten that he and his mother were close because his dad always overshadowed so many of her memories of Rob. "I haven't been avoiding you. I needed some space, and I've been busy. It's not like I talk to Dera or Maren every day."

"Really? Because you seem to be pretty good at keeping me at arm's length even when we *are* talking every day." A dangerous edge crept into the charming smile, and she went back on alert.

"What are you talking about?" she asked, curling her legs up to her chest, hoping that it might muffle the sound of her rumbling stomach and the crying of her aching muscles.

He didn't give anything away; his face kept the

easy expression he'd worn thousands of times in interviews and on news reports she'd watched over the last few weeks. "I got a call from Joey the day before yesterday. She wants me to investigate an interesting rumor she heard about."

"Oh?" A dozen scenarios flashed through her head, dread pooling in the pit of her stomach. She couldn't think of what Joey could have him investigating that would get him so pissed off at her.

"Yeah. She said that she's heard some rumors about you receiving letters. Letters she heard might be from a stalker. I gotta say, I was a little surprised that this was the first I'd heard of them. Maren didn't mention it when we had lunch, but she did say she thought you were holding back." He shrugged, anger creeping into his steely eyes.

For a moment, a wave of guilt hit her, but she pushed it back. What gave him the right to be pissed at her about this? Especially since he was here because his boss had sent him. They weren't dating, and they'd just started this whole friend thing. "It's just some weirdo getting his rocks off by intimidating me. Seemed a bit much to toss into early stages of friendship. It's not something I would tell someone I'd only known for a few weeks. I sure as hell wouldn't tell them about it if they worked for a gossip news network."

"It's not a gossip network." The temper crackled around him. "And a few weeks? I'm pretty sure I've known you for seven years, Em. I would think you'd know that I wouldn't use that kind of information in a story and that I would give a damn that someone was fucking threatening you."

Em let out a startled laugh of disbelief. "You're

kidding me, right? Your boss sent you here to do a story about this very topic. Can you not understand why I wouldn't tell you something like this?"

"I'm not an idiot, Em. Do you honestly think I'd actually go through with this story?" He got to his feet and started pacing, sizing her up as if they were on the court instead of in her living room. "I only agreed to it so I could come down here and check on you without anyone getting suspicious."

She wanted to believe him, but temper and seven years of mistrust flared. He'd abandoned her, but now he expected her to suddenly trust him with something as high octane as her stalker. If he went to his network with all the intimate details, they'd probably build a statue in his honor.

"I don't know what you'd do, Rob," she shot back. "I didn't think Kole would keep those stupid pictures either, but he did, and now they're everywhere. If the news of this were to get out, it would make everything ten times worse than the photo leak."

He looked ready to punch something. "Do not compare me to that jackass, Em. I don't know what went on between you two, but I am nothing like him."

"And I'm supposed to believe that?" She buried her face in her knees, then looked back up. "Before you disappeared, you slept around almost as much as Kole did, a new leggy model on your arm at every event. You walked away because I didn't match your ideal woman, just like he did."

And you broke my heart, just like he did. She left those words unsaid, but she hoped he remembered. She might be the one keeping the wall up between them now, but he was the one who built it in the first place.

Rob shoved his hands through his hair, the blond strands catching the light from one of her antique lamps. "I'm not that guy anymore. I haven't been that guy since I hurt my shoulder."

She wanted to believe that. She wanted to believe he'd changed. He certainly wouldn't have stood up for her so publicly before his injury. But at the end of the day, he was still the great Rob Ashton, and she was still that little nobody scrapping her way to the top. "Maybe that's true. I don't know. In my life, I trust a very small group of people. The last person I let in turned out to be a complete jerk on a monumental scale. Do you get why I didn't call and tell you right off the bat that I have a stalker?"

Finally, he stopped pacing and looked at her with such intensity that her knees went weak and her breath caught in her throat. With a level of speed she hadn't seen since the last match, he swept her up off the couch, his arms around her waist, her legs dangling limply so her toes brushed his shins.

"What are you doing?" she asked breathlessly. "I thought we agreed—"

"To hell with what we agreed to." Rob's mouth crashed into hers, and without thinking, she tangled her fingers in his hair, losing herself in the moment.

So much bad shit had happened since she last saw him, so much hung between them still unsaid, but it all went up in flames the second he kissed her. All it took for her body to respond to him was a single touch. Her girl parts had been ready and raring to go before he even left her hotel room in New York.

She really, really shouldn't be doing this. Every time he got involved in her life, she ended up even more of a mess than before. She should pull away, make him let her go. Remind him again that friends don't kiss friends, at least not in ways that threatened to burn down the house around them it was so hot.

But God, it felt so good.

She'd had some good sex since he took her virginity, but none of it was quite the same as with him. All her senses came alive as his hand strayed down to cup her butt.

"Mmm…Rob. We—we shouldn't—" She tried to get the words out, but her lips stayed fastened to his, desperately craving more.

He groaned, lifting her so the apex of her thighs rubbed against the erection growing underneath the rough denim of his jeans. "Tell me you don't want me, Em. Tell me and I'll stop."

Every rational part of her brain that hadn't been obliterated by that kiss told her that having sex with him again was beyond stupid, but her libido gave those parts the finger and told them to shut up. Instead of answering, she pulled him in, kissing him even deeper than before. He started moving backward, blindly navigating her living room. Unfortunately, climbing the stairs without looking required more coordination than he had, and Rob tumbled back against the stairs with her sprawling on top of him.

"You okay?" she asked, breathless.

His grin flashed bright and blinding, his dimple deepening. He took her hand and pressed it against his erection. "What do you think?"

His mouth moved to trail along the neckline of her T-shirt, kissing and nipping the bare flesh. His hands began to fumble with the buttons on her skinny jeans when an idea struck her. With a few quick movements, she had his jeans unfastened and her hand clasped around the rock-hard shaft. If she was going to do this, she was going to be the one in control this time. If she could keep the power dynamics in her favor, maybe she wouldn't lose herself completely. Slithering down a few steps, she grinned up at him, an awareness she hadn't felt in a long time coursing through her blood.

"Em? What are you—?" Before he could finish his question, her lips fastened around him, sucking and licking until his breath hitched. Working him with both her mouth and her hand, she enjoyed looking at him through her eyelashes, watching the interplay of desire across his face. His hips bucked against her, and her body went up in flames. Her hand went down her own pants, stroking through her panties to ease the ache until it was merely painful instead of completely breathtaking.

"Please, doll. I don't know how much more I can take." His words came out jagged and strained, his knuckles white as he gripped the stair behind him. "Fuck. You're so hot. I need to touch you. Let me touch you, please."

She pulled back, continuing to stroke him as she raked her gaze over him. "Uh-uh. I like you like this. Horny. Needy. Totally at my mercy. Makes me feel…powerful."

"From where I'm sitting, you look like a freaking goddess. Let me make you feel like one," he urged.

"If you insist."

Keeping their eyes locked, she got to her feet, shimmying out of her jeans, slowly, as seductively as she could—no mean feat in skinny jeans. He caressed her body with his eyes, his expression that of a dehydrated man spotting water for the first time in days. She deliberately kept her panties on, knowing how much he'd like them. She hadn't thought that he'd ever see these, but she'd taken to wearing sexier lingerie because of how it made her feel. Like she was reclaiming the part of her Kole had violated when he saved those pictures.

"A red lace thong? Fuck, Em. Are you trying to give me a heart attack? Do you want to kill me?" He reached for her, but she took a step back. Yes, he wanted her. All thought of messy emotions was gone, and they were back to the basics, back to where they'd never had any problems.

"Now why would I kill you, when it's much more fun for me to have you alive?" And God, he was fun, especially to look at. In his current position, the man was so fucking sexy, his cock poking out of his expensive jeans, his hair rumpled, and that mouth-watering V of muscles barely visible over the open waistband. If she unbuttoned his shirt a few more inches, she'd see that delicious tattoo climbing his rib cage. She wanted him now. She needed it hot and dirty and fast. Anger and confusion still coursed through her veins. This man ignited her, both her anger and passion, and she couldn't stop until she'd had him.

Reaching into the purse she'd hung on a hook by the stairs when she dropped her bag off, she pulled a condom from the secret side pocket and opened the package.

"Planning on getting laid at the tennis court?" He raised an eyebrow, his abs contracting a little as he spoke.

"Ha. No." She knelt between his legs, stroking him a few times. Taking her time, she rolled the latex over his erection. "I just like to be prepared."

"I like that in a woman," he said, his chest rising and falling rapidly. His hand reached out to cup her sex through the silky fabric, his finger teasing along the edges of the thong. Her hips undulated against him of their own volition. He tried to pull her in for a kiss, but she dodged him.

She took a step back, fighting to regain control. "Uh-uh. My house. My rules."

To prove her point, she pushed aside her thong and straddled him, taking him inside her in one slow, easy movement. Her body was more than ready for him, and she loved how he groaned in pleasure. Using the stairs as leverage, she started to move, letting out a moan of her own when his hands cupped her ass. He locked his mouth over hers, their tongues dueling for supremacy as their bodies moved together.

"Em. So beautiful. So good," he murmured against her mouth.

"Rob. God, yes. Right there. I'm close. Harder. Faster." She urged him on as one hand left her ass to play with her clit. The waves of pleasure started to hit her, and she increased the tempo, wanting more, wanting him to go over the edge with her.

Even with her in the position of power, this man knew what to do to win her over. Their current position put them exactly at eye level, and when he pulled back from another soul-searing kiss, his eyes were a steely gray storm of emotions. Biting her lip, she muffled a cry as she lost control again.

"God, doll. You're so tight. So wet. Come for me

again." He nipped at her ear, sending shivers on top of shivers through her.

She chuckled, giddy with breathless pleasure. This man. What he did to her body was indescribable. All she could do was crave more of it. "If you insist. You've got to come with me, though."

Deliberately rolling her hips and grinding against him harder, she met him move for move, moan for moan. His body worked into hers, his hips pounding faster in spite of the less than ideal location, urging them both up and up and up. They both went over the edge within moments of each other, his roar of satisfaction mingling with her gasps of pleasure.

They both sat there together for several long moments, struggling to catch their breath, eyes never moving from one another. Rob opened his mouth to say something when her stomach let out a noisy rumble.

Laughing, he raised an eyebrow. "Someone work up an appetite?"

"Someone was already starving when you showed up." Em stood, tugging her underwear back into place and grabbing her jeans. "I supposed I should feed you or something too, huh?"

"Or we could go out," he suggested. "I know a great little Italian place not far from here. Come on, it'll be great. A little candlelight. Good food. Good company."

She narrowed her eyes at him. He looked like some sort of pagan god, sprawled on her stairs, tempting her. She'd already given in once. She couldn't do it again. This wasn't how it was supposed to be. He wasn't supposed to have this much of an effect on her. He should be the last guy that made her this hot, but he did.

She didn't want to feel this. She didn't want any of this. Except that she did. For the first time in a week, she'd felt safe, and she'd forgotten about the stalker and her career, and she'd just let herself go. Despite that, she had to keep him at a distance. He was too much of a distraction, and he worked for the enemy.

"That sounds awfully close to a date."

"What if it is?" He stood, removing the condom with a tissue she handed him and casually fastening his jeans, then his shirt. "Would that be so terrible?"

Terrible? No. One date wouldn't be terrible. It was when one date turned into another and another, and before she knew what was happening, she'd be left alone in an airport again wondering why he hadn't showed up. Then it would be disastrous.

"I don't go on dates with my friends," she said, keeping her tone light. "But I will make them dinner. If you don't mind some sort of pasta dish, I could whip us up something here."

He studied her for a few moments, his eyes drifting over her face, leaving hot trails of awareness as they went. She could tell he wanted to fight her on the date part of the equation, but he didn't—smart man.

"A gorgeous woman cooking me a meal? How could I refuse?"

She led the way into the kitchen. "Come on. You can be my sous chef."

"Oh, I don't know. You sure that's a good idea?" he teased. "I'm more of a take-out or pre-prepared meals kind of guy. The most I can cook is scrambled eggs and mac and cheese."

"What a surprise. Although if you're going to cook, those would be two of the most important dishes

149

to have in your arsenal. Come on. You're a smart guy. I think you can at least be trusted to cut vegetables for the salad."

She gave him his task and then went about getting ingredients together. "I would prefer to make pasta from scratch, but between Zoe kicking my ass in practice today and someone distracting me with sex, I don't have the time or energy."

"You can make pasta from scratch?"

She turned to see him staring at her as if she'd sprouted a second head.

"Yes. Papa Vic's mother was Italian. She taught Gran, and Gran taught me. I swear Nona rolls in her grave every time I use dried pasta."

Emerson used the pot filler on the bigger of her sauce pans and added a healthy dose of salt to the water. She thanked God that, for the moment at least, he was distracted from discussing what had just happened between them. She had no damn clue how to feel about it, and she needed the time it'd take to prepare the meal to gather her thoughts. Cooking always helped her think, even more than playing tennis sometimes.

The steady rhythm of Rob's chopping filled the room. "It's official. I might have to marry you. I don't know a single woman who knows how to make pasta from scratch."

His words were light and teasing, but there was an undercurrent that sent shivers up her spine and a stab of pain through her heart. If he'd met her that day, they would be married. But Rob Ashton and marriage were two things that did not go together. She shook off the confusing emotions, matching his tone as she grabbed a

Tupperware dish full of sauce and meatballs out of the fridge.

"A big pasta fan, are you?"

"Oh yeah. Any sort of pasta, although gnocchi in pesto is probably my favorite." He tossed a piece of carrot up and caught it mid-air.

God, why did he have to look so damn good in her kitchen? She should want to rush him out the door, but instead the slutty, horny part of her whispered that she should feed him, then take him upstairs and have her way with him all over again.

"Good to know." She got out the skillet. "Tonight, you'll have to settle for spaghetti with meatballs, though. Gran sent me home with leftovers from Sunday dinner. Owen was pissed."

He groaned. "Okay. This is officially my favorite side perk of this job."

His job.

Shit.

Why did he have to bring that up?

Reality crashed back in at full force, and she stared at the pan of sizzling meatballs, trying to make sense of what was going on here.

"Your job. Right. You're here because of a story. About my stalker."

This was why she could never let him all the way in. He was a member of the press. Even if he had the best of intentions, if she let him in now, he could hurt her on a scale monumentally worse than anything Kole had done. Seeing Rob here in her space, cooking with her, it did something to a part of her she'd buried all those years ago. Something that she couldn't begin to think about now. She needed to focus on her career. She was twenty-eight years old, and she was tired of being second best—on the court and in relationships with the men in her life. She needed that Grand Slam title, not another complicated relationship that would only end in heartache.

Chapter 11

Rob sensed the shift in the room. The air crackled between them, and his temper came back to the surface, albeit significantly more mellowed thanks to her screwing his brains out not fifteen minutes ago. He still couldn't believe she hadn't trusted him with that news. As she stirred in leftover sauce to go with the meatballs, her shoulders visibly tensed. He let the silence stretch for a few moments, trying to gauge her reaction, but she didn't say anything. She just went about sticking the pasta in the now boiling water. Finally, he decided to try to make her see reason and remind her that he hadn't been the bad guy in this scenario.

"The stalker you neglected to tell me or any of your friends about," he said. He dropped the knife and turned to face her. "Em, I get that you're still getting used to me being back in your life. I do. But this is one of the areas where the more I know, the more I can help protect you."

She gave the sauce a vicious stir, the lid clattering on top of the pan so loudly it echoed through the small kitchen. "Protect me? You think you can protect me? How do you figure that one, Sir Galahad? You can do a story but make it slightly less unfavorable to me? Your magic smile will make people forget that everyone sees me as a slut?"

"You're not a slut," he retorted, his words fiercer

than he intended. "But if I had known about the story in the first place, I could have thrown Joey off the scent when she gave me the assignment. Suggested another, more interesting story that wasn't likely to egg this guy on."

"Do you really think that would do much good?" she asked quietly. "If Joey's got a source telling her about it, the other networks or the blogs or papers are bound to find out eventually."

"If I throw Joey off the scent, then the others are likely to stay distracted for a while." He tossed the salad in the bowl she'd given him. "And I have connections with other reporters now."

Her shoulders sagged, and she braced her hands on either side of the stove. He could almost hear the wheels turning in her head. Finally, she moved to finish the dinner preparations, draining the pasta and mixing it in the skillet with the sauce and meatballs. "I…appreciate that you want to help, Rob. I really do. And if you can distract Joey, that would be great. But I want you to know that I can take care of myself."

"Okay," he said, wishing he had ten years to unpack everything she'd just said.

Even though the words were conciliatory, tension stretched between them all through dinner. He relished the awareness that always buzzed around him when she was anywhere in the vicinity. This was different; it was like before his injury.

Fuck.

He thought they'd made progress. Their little session on the stairs sure as hell had felt like it.

"That has to be the best meal I've had in weeks," he said, standing to help her carry dishes to the sink.

"You're an easy guy to impress." She pulled out a hidden shelf and brushed the bits of foods into a bin marked "compost."

God, she was pretty. He liked her like this, a little rumpled from sex, her feet bare and her hair falling around her shoulders in a black cloud. He especially liked the way her athletic lifestyle did nothing to detract from her natural curves. Her whole body was tight with muscles where it should be, but soft and full elsewhere.

"Think I can distract you again?" He came up behind her, trailing kisses along her neck, his fingers stealing under the hem of her shirt, a pretty yellow number that brought out the light caramel tones in her skin.

Sadly, her hands clamped around his wrists and stopped him. "Not so fast."

The walls coming up around her echoed between them. Damn it. For every two steps forward, she pushed him back three.

"What? You don't want to see if we can make it to the bed this time?" His penis stirred back to life at the prospect of spreading her out on a bed and using his mouth to drive her crazy a few dozen times before taking her again, slow and easy, making it last as long as it took to pull those walls down again.

"I—" She pushed at his chest until his back hit the island, and she stepped out of his reach. "You can't stay here, Rob. We can't—I thought we were supposed to be friends, not friends with benefits."

"I won't lie to you, Em. I'd like us to be more than friends with benefits, but I'll take what I can get. We both enjoy the benefits. What's so wrong with that?" he asked evenly. He wanted to scream that he didn't want to just be her friend. Her pushing him away was starting to piss him off. He wanted to be with her, damn it. To sleep beside her, to wake up making love to her. Hell, he even wanted to make her breakfast in bed. Why couldn't she let him?

The laugh that bubbled out of her closely resembled a sob, the sound as rough and harsh as the surface of a hard court. "It would take an entire five-set match to list all of the reasons that are wrong with that. We've been over this, Rob. I can't—I can't afford to be anything more than friends with you. My focus needs to be on training, not on whether you're going to show up for a booty call—and that's all this was."

"A booty call?" His temper spiked again, and he gripped the island behind him to keep from grabbing her and giving her a shake. "Huh. Is that what you think? Because I could have sworn I came down here to check on you since you have a fucking stalker, and I wanted to see for myself that you're okay. That's what friends do."

That scored a hit, and she winced.

"Look, I...I appreciate the concern, but I'm fine. Everyone gets letters like this. It's not a big deal." She grabbed her wine glass off the table and chugged the remaining ruby-red liquid.

"It is a big deal, Em. You need to be careful, and you need to have people around you watching your back." He caught her hand as she walked by to put the salad dressing in the fridge. "I want to be one of those people."

"I know you do." She pinched the bridge of her nose. "I—please, Rob. I can't do this right now. You...you confuse me. There's so much history between us, and I can't think straight when you're around. When I'm not thinking about having sex with you, I'm paranoid that some tabloid reporter is waiting outside my door and is going to catch you or that I'll be so busy thinking about all the problems you present that I'll blow a major match."

The knot in Rob's gut tightened, and it had nothing to do with the meal he'd just eaten. The anxiety and worry and need this woman inspired scared the shit out of him, almost as much as he scared the shit out of her. "So, what? You want me to stop caring? To go back to not being your friend?"

He held his breath as she stood in front of the fridge, her forehead resting against its stainless door. When she finally responded, he barely heard her.

"No." She cleared her throat, but her voice still came out hoarse. "I've missed you too much to go back to the way things were. But you also confuse me and piss me off in equal measure. I just need some space and for you not to be so damn attractive."

A tiny spark of hope glowed in his chest. She wasn't completely shutting him out.

"Okay. I'll go now, if you promise that you'll answer my phone calls and return my texts so I won't worry so much."

"Fine." She sighed and turned to face him, propping her shoulder against the fridge. "I'll return your calls and texts, but you have to promise to give me some space at least through Qatar. I need to stay sharp and get on a roll."

"That's fair. In the meantime, I'll squash the story with Joey for now. I've got a few ideas I can use to get her onto another story." The Qatar tournament was too insular for him to sneak away to spend time with her anyway, and it would be the first tournament he'd covered without Bruno. He let her walk him to the door. "But at Indian Wells, all bets are off. I want to spend time with you, even if it's just dinner in your room."

"We'll see." She gave him a sassy smile before holding the door open. For a moment, he thought she wanted him to kiss her, but he didn't. Let her miss him a bit even if it killed him.

The street was thankfully quiet after the echo of Em's door closing faded and empty of any suspicious cars. Walking to his rental, he climbed in and punched Joey's number.

"Tell me you have some juicy news for me," Joey demanded.

Rob had hoped to get her voicemail, but that was too much to hope for on a day that definitely hadn't gone his way. "Sorry. Checked around with a couple of reliable sources down here. Looks like the stalker rumors were just that—rumors."

"Really?" Her voice deflated a little. "Nothing we can use? Not even another source confirming it?"

It should have bothered him, how easy it was to lie to his boss, but even as annoyed as he was with Em, he wasn't going to let Joey go down this path. It was too dangerous. Giving this guy national media attention would take this to a whole other level of bad for Em. "Nope. No one knew what I was talking about when I asked."

"Well, shit." She paused. "Maybe we should go with one source. Emerson Grace is a hot name now. Any story about her boosts our ratings and our website traffic by double-digit percentages."

His gut clenched. That's all Joey thought about. Driving up site traffic and ratings were part of her job, but the woman was more intense about it than anyone he had ever met. Reining her in on this would be harder than he'd expected. "I don't think we want egg on our face with this one. If we're wrong, it's going to cause a lot of problems for everyone involved. And it's not fair to stir shit up if there's nothing to the rumors."

"Fine. I guess you're right. There are some big tournaments coming up. Maybe she or Naumov will do something that'll get us some ratings there," she mused. "Get your ass back here ASAP so we can get a game plan in place for Qatar and Indian Wells."

"I'm on a flight tomorrow night," he said before hanging up.

He sighed with relief. That bullet was dodged, at least for the moment. She wouldn't let this go, but he'd deal with it if it came up again. His plans for the evening shot, he drove through the cool February night, finding himself at his parents' Miami house, his frustration with Em for pushing him aside still churning under the surface. Seeing his dad now was the last thing he needed, but the last time he'd checked, they were supposed to be gone until tomorrow. Using his key, he slipped into the house and let the darkness embrace him.

This was not the way he'd seen his night going. Going to bed—alone—at his parents' house? God, he'd been such an idiot to think that she'd welcome him with open arms and give him a real chance. Okay, so deep down he'd hoped that's exactly what would happen, but nothing ever went as expected when it came to Em. She was the most complex woman he'd ever met. A smart man would give up, but no one could ever accuse him of being smart, especially not when it came to her.

Drained from the worry over Em's stalker, the anger over her rejection, and the mind-blowing sex, he dropped off to sleep the second his head hit the expensive guest room pillow. He spent the night drifting between dead sleep and vivid dreams of the night he'd planned with Em.

By the time he woke up, he was as tired and angry as he'd been when he went to sleep, and he was hallucinating the scent of coffee. Pulling on his clothes, he padded down the sleek, modern wood stairs to the kitchen. As he approached, voices and the sounds of pans banging and sizzling food drifted toward him.

"Mama? Dad? I didn't expect to see you here yet." He stood in the doorway, blinking sleepily at his parents. His mother, still as whip-thin and blond as she'd been the day she first stepped onto the court as a pro, stood at the stove with a spatula in her hand. His father, hair more silver than gold now, sat at the glass breakfast table, tablet in front of him and a mug of coffee in one hand. Both were perfectly pressed and dressed, the picture of an older married couple ready to start their day.

"Well, we didn't expect to see you either, *Älskling*. What are you doing in Florida?" Brigit offered up her cheek expectantly, and he obligingly went over to kiss it, snatching a piece of turkey bacon off the plate at her elbow.

"I had to do a quick research trip and visit a friend before my trip to Qatar. I'm heading back to New York tomorrow." He poured himself a cup of coffee and went to sit across from his father.

Robert Ashton Junior was still a giant of a man, his very presence filling the room. As a kid, Rob admired how Bobby's personality drew everyone to him, but as an adult, he found it abrasive and unsettling. So different from Robert Ashton Senior. Rob's grandfather, the one who'd raised him more than his parents ever did, had a big personality, but he used it more gently, more thoughtfully. He let his tennis speak for him, rather than flashing his talent to whoever was closest or trying to impress them with his pedigree. Granddad had always taught Rob to follow his lead, whether it was on the court or in the quiet hours before dusk when they sat and whittled together, and somewhere along the way, Rob started to lose that in his need to please Bobby.

Bobby glanced up at his son, a narrow-eyed look. "A friend, huh? What kind of friend?"

"Just someone I know. We try to see each other a few times a year. I'd planned to stay at my friend's house last night, but she—they had something come up, so I needed a place to crash."

"You're welcome here anytime, *min son*." Brigit ruffled Rob's hair as she placed a platter of pancakes and bacon on the table. She took a seat beside him. "I've been so proud of your work. Your stories are much better than that slob Bruno."

Bobby snorted. "A blind man could do a better job covering tennis than Watson."

Rob gritted his teeth and kept his attention on his food. His already raw temper didn't need to deal with his father's bombastic opinions and not-so-subtle digs.

"Bobby!" Brigit gave his father a look across the table. They'd always had an unspoken language that

Rob and Maren couldn't decipher. This was loud and clear, though. Since his injury, she had become more protective of Rob, and she didn't like it when his father criticized him.

"Don't 'Bobby' me, Bree. Our son could be doing so much more with himself, but instead he's working as number two to an idiot like Bruno Watson. I want what's best for him. You know that." Bobby's tight smile did nothing to make Rob feel any better. His father wanting what was best for him was how he'd gotten here in the first place, sitting at his parents' kitchen table instead of laying curled up in bed with Em. His father had been the one who convinced him all those years ago that Em was a nobody that would only distract him from becoming another star in the Ashton constellation.

"You could be great. You could be better than me if you had half a chance. But she's an upstart, so her career will always come before you. You need a woman who will sit in your box and cheer you on, not one you'll have to battle for time on the practice court."

That's what Bobby had said when Rob refused to break up with Em after the Olympics. He still remembered how those words ate at him as a twenty-two-year-old. Hearing his father finally say he could be as good as the great Robert Ashton Jr. was everything he'd wanted to hear. Growing up, he'd craved his father's attention, for him to see how hard Rob worked, how much Granddad Robert taught him. Then, the first time Rob thought about a life beyond tennis, his father had decided to see him and his potential, the bastard.

Looking back, Rob hated that he'd taken those words as gospel. His father's whole life had been about tennis. He'd managed to retire with minimal injuries and still in the top five players of the world. Bobby Ashton didn't know what it was like to have the choice taken from him, to have his work taken from him in an instant. He had no clue what it was like to realize he may have missed the chance to have a life with the woman who meant the most to him, all because of stupid pride.

"I like my job, Dad. If I can't play tennis, I can at least report on those who can and help drive the conversation. Not all of us can play in charity matches or sit on our high horses doling out advice on things we don't know anything about." He stood up and gave his mom a tight smile. "I'm going for a walk. Thanks for breakfast, Mama."

He wandered around the expansive backyard, barely seeing the tropical flowers that filled the beds his mother's gardener lovingly tended. Without realizing where he'd gone, Rob found himself on the tennis court they'd built at the back of the property. The sound of the hard court under his shoes, the breeze across the net—this was home, more than anywhere else could be. Grabbing a racket from the small equipment shed, he gripped it, savoring the coarse texture of the grip against his palm. He grabbed a ball canister and removed a fresh green ball.

Yeah, this was where he belonged.

His grandfather had a court like this at the house where Rob had spent most of his childhood. They'd spent hours on that court, Gramps's withered hands gently guiding Rob's, laying the foundation for the techniques that Rob relied on until the day his shoulder died. He could almost see Gramps sitting on the bench along the side of the court, his long fingers moving whatever piece of wood he was whittling then, his eyes sharp as he watched Rob practice.

Bouncing the ball, he gave in to the urge to hit it against the backboard set up for solo practice. The ball flew back at him, and he hit it again with an easy forehand. He repeated it twice, three times, then four without his shoulder reacting. Wanting to test it, he moved back and used a backhand on the next shot.

"Robert. What are you doing?" His mother's voice cracked through the air as a shard of pain arrowed through his shoulder.

He winced and let the ball bounce past him. "Just blowing off some steam."

"Hmm. Like a true Ashton," Brigit said, stooping to pick up the ball. "I can't tell you how many times I've found your father hiding on one court or another, hitting a ball rather than talking."

"Talking won't do me much good with Dad, will it?" He already knew the answer. It'd been the same his whole life.

His mother shrugged. The wind barely mussed her long, blond hair thanks to the tight bun she contained it in every morning. "Your father isn't the easiest man to live with. You and I know that better than anyone in the world. But I also hope that you know he does what he does and says what he says from a place of love."

So many things popped into his head to say, but he bit them back. His mother's love for his father let her overlook a lot. She didn't see how much criticism his father targeted at him. Maren got her fair share of the pressure, but she was the first Ashton female to play tennis, so she had more room to breathe. Rob had the family legacy resting on his shoulders, and he never did enough in his father's eyes. Brigit's family wasn't demonstrative, but they always let her know how proud they were of her career, no matter what she did. Coming from that sort of family, she didn't fully grasp the politics of the Ashtons.

"Yeah, maybe. I don't know, Mama. I'm—I like my new job as much as I'd like any other job. Would I rather play tennis? Hell, yeah." He twirled the racket in his hands. "But I think I'm good at this. I…I'm back in control and doing something well. I have the chance to change the conversation for the better."

"You are, *Älskling*. I have never been prouder than when you stood up for Emerson Grace." She wrapped an arm around him and led him back toward the house, setting the racket aside as they went. "That showed real maturity, *min son*. Much has passed between you two, but I'm glad you stood up for her. Overlooking all of the hurt tells me that you are more than capable of doing your job admirably."

Emerson. Even her name made a smile tug at his lips. He was glad his mother was too short to look him in the eyes from her current position. Things with Em were still a mess; anger and hurt lurked deep down between them. Anger from how they'd ended things before and anger that they couldn't pick up where they'd left off now. But being with her felt right—more right than anything else in his life, including his job— and that gnawing ache that tore at him all during his recovery had slowly started to ease, despite the lingering questions.

He wanted to show Em it was safe to be with him, but he didn't know what he'd do once he did. Loving

165

someone terrified him more than his first professional match. After growing up playing second seed to the great love of Bobby and Brigit, he couldn't contemplate the idea of giving himself over to another person with that level of commitment. All he knew was he needed to spend as much time with Em as he could. The only problem was convincing her to let him.

****

Em stood at the service line, bouncing the ball to draw the moment out. Her final round opponent, Annika Mattherson, shifted on the opposite side of the court, her body coiled to spring. The twenty-year-old put up a good fight, but she'd faded early under the hot California sun. All Emerson needed was one more point, and she'd have her second title of the year.

Tossing the ball up, she relished the sound of the ball connecting with the racket's sweet spot. It sailed toward Annika, landing just shy of the baseline, barely leaving room for Annika to take a swing at it. Her weak swat and a lucky wind sent the ball into the net where it limply rolled back toward the Norwegian player.

The crowd roared their approval, and Em indulged in a moment of contained celebration. Zoe gave her a nod from her player's box. It took her back to her early tournaments when she and Uncle Leo and Uncle Nathan sat there with Papa Vic, cheering her on through every point.

She took Annika's hand and gathered her things, nodding to the big burly bodyguard Amir and Owen insisted follow her around throughout the tournament. They'd made it through the Qatar Open without security, but another letter while she was gone made it impossible for her to deny their request.

Rather than showering first, she went to the press room, Amir by her side. The questions—thank God— mostly focused on the match until the last one.

"So tell us, Emerson, now that you and Kole have split up, is there a new man in your life? Or is it men?"

The question came from a snide little reporter from one of the local papers, his bow tie and plaid shirt screaming pretension. Em struggled to keep her expression neutral. "I'm not sure what that has to do with the tennis match I just finished."

"Come on. You're the sex kitten of tennis. Everyone wants to know who your latest conquest is," the reporter pushed. "What lucky guy have you lured into your bed this week? I've heard there's talk of you and Ryan Gosling hooking up over the weekend."

"I heard it was Chris Evans the night before. Naughty girl," another reporter chimed. They all jumped in with their own theories, hurtling them at her faster than the balls Annika had hit during the height of the match.

The sex kitten of tennis? That better not stick. Anger boiled inside her, pushing all the buttons she'd kept control of throughout most of the original sex scandal. She hadn't expected any of this. She'd thought she could get back to tennis being the focus and not who she was screwing or not screwing. Men like Kole and Rob and Owen never had to deal with this level of bullshit. She glared at Amir before fixing the reporter with her back-the-hell-off stare. "I don't comment on my personal life or tawdry, fictional stories about my personal life. Have a good evening, everybody."

She floundered out of the press room, the bodyguard trailing behind her. The last thing she wanted to deal with right now was more stories about her sex life—especially when she barely had one—but apparently, the press wasn't willing to let it go. Hearing those questions, being called a sex kitten in front of a room full of reporters, took her back to the worst of the shit storm that had followed the photo leak. All she wanted to do now was escape and forget that the idiot reporter had even tried to drag her back there.

The sun was starting to creep low in the horizon. They'd been the last match of the day, and she knew exactly what she wanted to do once she'd showered off the thick layer of sweat. She'd been in California for twelve days, first doing press events, then playing through today's final match, and she'd yet to see Rob except in passing or on TV.

Those twelve days had been spent trying to convince herself that he didn't matter. That she didn't want to see him. But damn it—he'd been slowly waging war on her defenses since he left her house. Sweet text messages and long phone calls when they had the time. He reminded her of the boy she'd met that first day in London, so considerate and funny. While she enjoyed the attention, it did little to help her make sense of what he made her feel.

He didn't press her for more, he was just—her friend. He said all the right things and asked the right questions. The second she won the Qatar Open, he'd sent her a text congratulating her and teasing her about her second serve again.

A few times, their texts drifted dangerously close to sexting, especially the longer they were apart. Only her own sense of self-preservation stopped them from crossing that line. If her smoking hot dreams last night hadn't been enough to convince her that maybe she was ready for them to revisit the "benefits" part of their friendship, that stupid reporter's comments sure as hell had been. She wanted mind-blowing sex that made her forget everything—all the awful comments and the doubts and the reasons why this was a horrible idea for her to have anything to do with Rob Ashton.

As she dressed after her shower, she sent Rob a text.

Hey, handsome. I think it's time we have that dinner you mentioned. Want to meet me in room 445 for a little room service? ;)

"*Merde*, Emmy. You have exquisite taste in underwear."

Em jumped and turned. "Jesus. Warn a girl if you're going to sneak up on her. I thought your match was earlier this afternoon. What are you still doing here?"

"The men's doubles match before mine went to three sets with a tie break in every set, so we got a late start." A towel-clad Dera rubbed lotion on her dark bronze skin, her braids falling in her face, free of their normal band. "What's with the fancy lingerie? Does someone have a hot date?"

Wincing, Em pulled on her blue wrap dress. To lie or not to lie. That was the question.

"No. I have a weakness for La Perla. Everyone knows that now."

"Huh. I would have thought that might make you shy away from it. I'm proud of you, cherie. Don't let them get you down. But red lace underwear like that is clearly meant for someone to look at."

Her friend had a point, especially after the damn

reporter's nosy-ass question, but she wasn't about to let what other people thought about her affect her underwear choices.

"Yeah. Me." Em grinned, shrugging. "I like wearing sexy underwear."

Dera narrowed her golden eyes. "Sure. Whatever you say. Tell whoever it is to treat you well. You've earned some sheet-scorching fun."

Em's phone chimed. *Room service, huh? I'm done with work in twenty. Can't wait to see you.*

A smile tugging at her lips, Em grabbed her bags and hurried out of the locker room before her friend could ask any more questions.

By the time she got to her hotel room, anticipation surged through her, replacing the adrenaline that had kept her going through the match and the post-match interviews. Agitation lingered, but she channeled that into the sexual energy racing through her blood.

Zoe, thankfully, had already gone off to have dinner with old friends, and the rest of the team was busy, so she didn't have to worry about interruptions.

Checking her phone for the time, she scanned the room to make sure everything was ready. A box of condoms on the night stand. No stray shoes on the floor. She pulled the sheets back, neatly folding the blankets at the foot of the bed. Now the real dilemma. Did she leave her dress on or take it off and wait for him in her underwear?

A scrap of diaphanous fabric spilling out of her suitcase caught her eye. With an evil grin, she tugged the ties of her dress loose and pulled on the white lace robe she'd tossed in her bag on a whim.

God, what was she doing? She stared in the mirror.

If she'd hoped to keep Rob at arm's length, this was not the way, but her libido and her pride didn't give a damn at the moment. That high she'd gotten from making it to the second straight finals in a tournament died in the press room after those ridiculous questions, and she wanted it back. She wanted him—wanted what he made her feel, like she was a beautiful, powerful woman that no one else could touch.

More than that, she wanted to reclaim her private life. While she didn't sleep around or have one-night stands, she'd always enjoyed sex. Aside from Rob and Kole, the men she'd dated had been easy distractions for when she had the time or inclination to explore that part of herself. Now that part had been tainted by prying questions, crazy stalkers, and those fucking pictures. It might be insane, but screwing Rob Ashton's brains out sounded like the perfect step back toward the woman she'd been before this mess started.

The confident knock on the door sent shivers down her spine, but she didn't rush to answer it. Taking her time, she slicked on pin-up-girl red lipstick and fluffed her hair.

"I'm sorry, do you have the right room?" she asked, holding the door open a crack, keeping her body out of sight.

Rob stood there in his full, masculine glory. He still wore his suit, but he'd lost the tie somewhere along the way. The dark blue of his shirt brought out the blue flecks in his gray eyes, a perfect contrast to the slate-colored suit. His rumpled old-gold hair gave him a rakish appearance that made her weak in the knees.

"God, I hope so," he said with a weary grin. "I'm supposed to meet this really gorgeous woman I haven't seen in a few weeks. She's about your height, really smart, pretty brown eyes, and a dynamite body. You seen her?"

Charming man. Fucking sexy man. She held the door open, keeping the door in front of her body until he was in the room. Keeping her back against the door, she rested one foot against it, letting the robe fall open enough to give him a small, unobscured glimpse of the red lace thong.

The look in his eyes when he turned around made all the day's annoyances worth it.

"Careful, handsome, you might scorch my clothes off if you keep looking at me like that."

"That's the idea."

Biting her bottom lip, she crooked her finger at him, beckoning him closer. As soon as he was within reach, she grabbed the lapels of his jacket and pulled him to her.

The second her mouth slammed into his, a fire sparked in her body.

He didn't stand there passively; he fought her for control like he had that day in her house. His big hands slapped against the door, his long, lean body pinning her in place. He dipped low, pressing his erection into the crease of her thighs, and she bit back a moan. One hand moved between them to fumble with the tie of her robe.

"Mmm. Did someone miss me?" she murmured against his mouth, loving how his teeth nipped at her bottom lip.

"Shit, Em. Are you trying to kill me? Because the robe alone is enough to do it, but this underwear?" Moving away from her lips, he nibbled his way down her neck, along her collarbone to the strap of her bra. Insistent fingers shoved it aside, but the excellent construction wouldn't budge.

His growl of frustration sent shivers down her spine, and she couldn't resist shoving her fingers into his hair. Giving up on the strap, his mouth fastened around her pebbled nipple through the thin lace.

"There's a clasp, you know," she panted, savoring the contrast of wet, hot mouth around lace. "Then you could have the full experience."

He grunted, moving to the other nipple. She let him go for another minute before she regained enough brain power to remember that she was seducing him, not the other way around. She pushed at his jacket until he let it slide down his muscular arms. She tried to unbutton his shirt, but that was not an easy task with his mouth all over her breasts and her brains turning to Jell-o.

Before she knew it, he'd managed to free one of her breasts, and she'd undone half the buttons on his shirt and popped off another two, revealing a delicious expanse of tanned, slightly furred chest.

"Are you sure about this, Em?" he asked, his breath rough against her cheek as he tugged at her earlobe. "I seem to recall you not wanting to explore the benefits side of our friendship."

"God, Rob." She ran her fingernails over his chest, arching her body against his ever-hardening erection. "Do you really want to talk now? Or do you want to screw? Because I really, really want you in me now."

To prove her point, she guided one of his hands into the waistband of her panties—her soaking wet panties.

He looked like he wanted to say something else,

torn between being a good guy and being a red-blooded male with a warm, willing woman in expensive lingerie in his arms. His fingers found her over-sensitized clit a moment before a knock echoed through the door behind them.

"Expecting someone?" he asked, both of them freezing in place, his breath dancing over her heated skin.

She shook her head, struggling to catch her breath. "No. Shit. Hold on."

Pushing him back, she turned to look out the peephole. What she saw on the other side of the door sent her heart into her throat and her stomach to her feet. This couldn't be happening. They weren't supposed to be here. Her thoughts went skittering in a million different directions, and instinct kicked in. She had a half-naked man in her room, moments away from sexing her up, and they couldn't see that.

"You've got to hide. Now. It's my grandma, and she's got my dad with her."

Chapter 12

One moment Rob was a second away from watching Emerson Grace explode in his arms, and the next he was being shoved toward the closet.

"Hide? What? Why—?" He stopped, blinking at her. "You do realize you're an adult, right?"

She glared at him, scrambling around for clothes. Pulling a blue dress off the back of a nearby chair, she wrapped it around her body in frantic, tight movements. "Not to my gran, I'm not. And my father? What should I do? Tell them that we're occasional fuck buddies?"

Ouch. That stung more than he'd expected. It was the truth, but hearing it put so bluntly hurt when he wanted her to see him as something more than a fuck buddy. Deep down, he wanted her to be excited to introduce him to her grandma. He got why she was freaked out about her dad, but he wanted her to want him there with her to face him instead of wanting to hide him.

The knock sounded again, more insistent.

"We'll tell them that I was here visiting as an old friend."

"Please. Sneaking, we can do. Lying? Not so much." She clasped her head between her hands. "This is so, so bad."

"I'm going into the bathroom." He pulled out his don't-fuck-with-me voice. "Answer the door. I'll come

175

out in a minute when it's not so obvious what we were about to do."

A hysterical laugh bubbled out of her. "I think the missing buttons will give us away."

"Trust me. Go, answer the door."

Grabbing his suit coat and vest, he let himself into the spacious bathroom, audibly shutting the door behind him. He waited until he heard Em open the door before he turned on the water, splashing some of it on his face. The muffled murmurs of an older woman's voice and a man drifted in. Rob took a breath and stared at himself in a mirror. He was really going to do this. Meet a woman's family. He tried to remember the last time he'd voluntarily done this, but nothing sprang to mind.

He was both nervous and oddly excited. He'd heard a lot about Poppy Grace from both Em and Owen. The formidable matriarch who played the other half of the mythical grandparents the Grace siblings worshipped. He felt a small pang for Em. When he'd pictured meeting her family all those years ago, it was her grandmother and grandfather he imagined charming. The one hesitation Em had had about eloping was the fact that her grandpa wouldn't be there to walk her down the aisle. He should be here for this now, to help Rob act as a buffer between Em and her father, but he wasn't.

Bracing himself, Rob did up the loosened buttons of his shirt, thankful that the two that popped off were lower down. He'd hide their absence under his vest and coat. With his damp hands, he smoothed down the hair that Em had clutched as he teased her. She responded to him so beautifully, but at the first sign of something beyond physical intimacy, she put up walls higher than the walls of Arthur Ashe Stadium. He'd deal with that later. Right now, she needed backup.

As he opened the door, a woman an inch or two shorter than Em hugged her, the woman's white-streaked black hair pulled into an old-fashioned knot at the nape of her neck. She wore a soft gray dress with black buttons and a pair of sensible black shoes his mother would never be caught dead in. Her frame was thin and her face drawn, but there was a glow about it when she looked at her granddaughter. Behind Poppy stood a man that Rob never imagined meeting. He stood a few inches taller than his mother, his hair more pepper than salt. Owen had obviously gotten his build from some other ancestor because while his height was slightly above average, he didn't resemble his son at all.

"Emerson? Who is this?" Michael Grace asked pointedly, his undertones clear.

"Is this your new fella, Emmy?" Poppy teased, and a wave of gratitude hit Rob. She might be a battle ax, but she was a battle ax who wasn't rushing to judgement.

Emerson's cheeks flushed, and she opened her mouth to speak, then immediately shut it. The room was silent except for the wheels in her head turning as she tried to come up with a way to explain to her family why he was there.

No way was he letting her wiggle out. He stepped over, placing one hand on the small of her back, and held out his hand to her father. "Rob Ashton. I'm a good friend of Em's and Owen's. It's nice to finally meet you."

Michael shook the offered hand, but his eyes held a calculating look Rob recognized from dealing with other reporters so much. He was trying to find a weak spot, and Rob couldn't let him find one.

"Friend, huh? And you said your name was Ashton? Didn't realize my little girl was friends with one of the newest sports reporters for TWW. Especially not the one who so vocally defended her."

"Rob and Owen have known each other since they were teenagers," Em said, her voice tight with annoyance. "And Rob and I met during my first Olympics. The tennis scene is pretty insular, so we all know each other."

Rob's hackles rose a little on Em's behalf. The accusatory look in her father's blue eyes, the posturing. The last time Michael talked to his daughter had been to lambast her about those damn pictures and make her feel two feet tall.

"What is this, Emerson?" Michael demanded. "Do you really think it's a good idea to have a man—a man who works for a sleazy gossip network—in your room alone? Haven't you made the headlines enough this year?"

Rob gritted his teeth as Em stiffened beside him. He pressed his hand into the small of her back, reassuring her that he was with her.

"Dad, that's none of your business."

"Really, Michael. What a thing to say," Poppy clucked, moving to sit on the nearby sofa. "We're here to spend time with Emerson, not interrogate her friends."

"Owen and Em are my friends first and always." Rob led Em to sit next to her grandma, perching on the arm beside her. "I'm able to keep my personal and professional lives separate."

Still posturing and puffing himself up, Michael raised an eyebrow. "Really? Is that what you were doing when you defended my daughter so publicly?"

Rob glanced at Em's grandmother. He wanted to make a good impression on the older woman in addition to not totally alienating her granddaughter, but he had a strong urge to punch Michael, partially because he was acting like a jackass and partially because he'd spent years ignoring his daughter before deciding to pretend he was any sort of father.

"Would you prefer I had let my colleagues bad mouth her when she didn't do anything wrong?" Rob asked. "I did what any man with an ounce of respect for women should have done. Em didn't ask for those pictures to be leaked, but she was the only one paying for it."

Michael snorted, standing with his feet apart and his arms crossed over his narrow chest. "Those pictures never should have been taken. What woman with an ounce of self-respect lets a man take pictures like that?"

"Michael!" Poppy gasped.

"Jesus. Do you spend so much time in third world countries that you've adopted their medieval moral standards?" Em surged to her feet, eyes blazing. "It's the twenty-first century. Women are allowed to own their sexuality."

"Not a woman in your position. Letting someone take pictures like this was asking for trouble," Michael retorted. "God, what would your mother say if she saw you now? Or God forbid, your grandfather? This certainly isn't the behavior they expected. Your mother wanted you to be a lady, a scholar, not some sort of—"

"Michael. That's enough," Poppy snapped.

Rob ached for Em. She stood facing off with her father. He'd been there, feeling the weight of parental disapproval, but he'd always known that eventually his parents would accept his decision. But Em? She'd been more or less abandoned by her father for years on end.

Instead of shrinking back, she went for the body shot with the same ferocity she would during a match.

"No, Gran. Let him get it out. He needs to pretend to be a father once every five years, and I'm guessing this is the criticize-his-daughter's-life-choices addition. Never mind that he wasn't around for my first day of school or my first date. He doesn't know me, and he doesn't know Rob. He doesn't get to stand there and judge me for my life decisions."

"You're my daughter. I have every right to have an opinion on what you do with the life that your mother and I gave you," Michael argued. "I expected so much more from you, Emerson. It's time you went out and found a real life for yourself. You can't waste your life on tennis forever. You shouldn't waste your time hanging around with a guy who is probably only looking for a way to use you and information on you to advance his career. How long before we see the Emerson Grace exposé, Rob? A week? A month?"

Fury and protectiveness bubbled to the surface, and Rob opened his mouth to speak, but Em cut him off. From his position, Rob caught the glimmer of tears in her eyes, but she didn't let them loose. *That's my girl. Don't give him that power over you.*

"Dad, at this point, you are nothing more than a sperm donor. I know you don't approve of my career or Owen's. God knows you've made that clear enough over the years, but it was not a waste. I may not risk my life taking pictures of starving children in war-torn countries, but I don't sit on my ass either." She braced her hands on her hips, a warrior refusing to back down. "Owen and I have a fantastic charity foundation I set up to help inner-city orphans get an education and have enough food. How many people do you know that have their own charity foundations by the age of twenty-three?"

"Anyone with money can throw it at a problem," Michael snarled. "You could be doing so much more with your life. Your mother wanted so much more for you. When you were a baby, we talked about how you could become the first female president or run a major company. Instead, you prance around the world in little skirts, taking pictures like you're some sort of Playboy bunny."

"Hey! That's enough." Rob shot to his feet. "You show up here out of the blue, and you treat your own daughter like shit in front of your mother, who raised her for you because you couldn't man up and stop 'prancing around the world' taking pictures. She's got a fucking stalker after her, but all you care about is being like every sexist asshole out there judging her."

He didn't stop to think about what he was saying. He didn't stop to think about what Em and her grandma might think. He just knew this guy was hurting Em when he was supposed to be her father, the man who should protect her from the world.

"How dare you? You have no right to stick your nose in our business." Michael sneered. "And what are you talking about? What stalker? Is this a story you're drumming up to boost your ratings?"

"Stop it. Damn it, Dad." Em stomped her foot.

181

"Get out of here. Now. You don't belong here."

Michael didn't move until Poppy stood and tugged at him, her eyes as stormy as Em's. "Yes, Michael. I think it's time we left. You can see me to my room and get on with your trip. I'm sure Owen or Emmy or Zoe can get me back to Florida safely. You've outstayed your welcome."

Rob and Em stood in silence as they watched her grandmother manhandle her father out of the room, bristling with rage. It wasn't until the door shut that Em turned to Rob. The tension hadn't left her body, but some of the fire died down. Unfortunately, he was still mad as hell.

"Thank you," she finally said. "I…you're getting really good at defending me against assholes."

"Of course I am," he snapped. "Damn it, Em. Don't you get it? You matter to me. A hell of a lot more than fuck buddies, but you won't admit what we are, even to your own family."

He knew he shouldn't take his anger out on her, but she'd pissed him off when she tried to shove him in the closet, and he wasn't over it yet. He loved her, or at least he thought he did, and she kept shoving him away.

"I don't know what we are, Rob. Do I like having sex with you? Hell, yes. What heterosexual female wouldn't? But do I want to have to answer all the questions that come with anything beyond the sex? No. My life is complicated enough. Our past is complicated enough. Telling everyone would ramp that up ten notches. Being more than that almost broke me last time. So can't we go back to where we were before we got interrupted?"

She moved closer, giving him a glimpse down the

plunging neckline of her dress. He hesitated, his brain flashing back to the memory of how smoking hot and fierce she'd looked in those sexy red lace panties and that mouthwatering bra. Instead, he took a step toward the door. "Maybe another night. The moment's gone, and we both have busy days tomorrow."

She blinked at him in shock. "Seriously? You get me that turned on and just leave?"

"Sorry, doll." A trace of bitterness colored his words. "Like you said, things between us are complicated. And I'm not sure how I feel about being your dirty little secret."

His hand rested on the door for a moment before he turned on his heel, and long strides ate up the distance between them. Leaning over her, he took her mouth in a hard, hot, passionate, and all too brief kiss. She might have even whimpered when he pulled away. "Think about how that made you feel. Because I think you and whatever complications there might be are worth it because of that, Em. Am I worth it to you?"

The satisfaction of the door slamming behind him faded thirty seconds later when he came face to face with Owen and Cruz, staring at him dumbfounded down at the end of the hall.

"Dude. Tell me you weren't just in my sister's room," Owen growled, coming up to him. Rob shifted uncomfortably; Owen Grace might be a gentle giant, but he was still a giant who worked out a hell of a lot more than Rob did lately.

"If it makes you feel any better, you missed your dad and your grandma by only a few minutes," Rob said, trying to get a rein on his temper.

Cruz's eyes widened, but he never lost his usual

easy facade. "Ah. I think this might be best discussed over alcohol. Join us in the bar?"

"Lots and lots of alcohol," Owen muttered.

Rob couldn't agree more.

****

"Emerson Grace, as I live and breathe. I thought that you were spending the evening with your fuck buddy." Dera patted the seat of the tall stool beside her in the upscale hotel bar. The French woman sat with Maren Ashton, both dressed to kill in short, strapless dresses and high heels. Em had changed into a red silk dress to match her mood. Damn her father. And damn Rob. Why did he have to make everything so complicated?

"Well, the mood kinda got ruined when my dad and my grandma interrupted us," Em said, setting the tumbler of bourbon she'd grabbed from the bar on the table.

Maren winced. "Ouch. I heard shouting from your room, but I didn't know what was going on. Your dad showed up?"

"Yep. Gran strong-armed him into bringing her out here to watch us play." Em bolted back the bourbon and nodded to the waitress to bring her another. "God. Why are men such unmitigated asses?"

She'd tried so hard over the years to keep the peace with her father out of some misguided need to have a relationship with him, to maintain that connection to her mother, but hearing him say those awful things broke that last tie. He didn't care about her or what she did, only how it reflected on his idealized picture of what a daughter should be.

And Rob. He'd stood up for her again and then

completely turned her world on its head—again. Why couldn't he accept that she wasn't willing to let him in? They were working as friends with the occasional benefits. If they went deeper than that, things would get messy, and she didn't have time for that. She was on a roll, and she couldn't afford to lose her focus now.

"Uh-oh. Did things go south with the fuck buddy as well as your father?" Dera asked. "Where is your bodyguard? Aren't you supposed to have him trailing you everywhere? And do we need to do damage control? Maybe distract you? Because there are at least five guys checking you out right now."

Some of the tension in Em's chest eased, and a rusty laugh escaped her lips. "Oh, D. I wish that would work. I gave the bodyguard the slip, and I'm down here to get pleasantly drunk and spend time with my friends, not flirt with guys."

At that moment, one of the guys Em assumed Dera was referring to showed up. His name was Ian, and he was an investment banker from LA.

"So can I get your number?" he asked after making the usual mundane chit-chat, clearly ignoring the signs that the three friends were in a serious conversation.

He was cute, in a Wall Street hotshot sort of way, but definitely not her type. She should want to date a guy like him; it'd be so much easier if she did. Falling for athletes or anyone associated with sports was a headache and a half, but Ian didn't make her body tingle even a tenth as much as Rob had before they'd been so rudely interrupted.

"You seem like a nice guy, but I'm from out of town," she said, going for the easy let down. No need to bruise his ego this early in the night. Her spine tingled, as if someone was watching her. Glancing around, she spotted Rob sitting at a table in the opposite corner with her brother and Cruz. Fuck. She really couldn't escape him.

Ian's grin turned wolfish. "I know. I've read a lot about you lately. But I travel all the time. Bet we could meet up and have a lot of fun."

"*Mon Dieu*," Dera muttered, rolling her eyes.

Em's stomach churned. God, how many of these guys were there in the world? He was the fourth so far this tournament and the tenth since the pictures came out.

"Mm. Tempting, but I'm really not interested." Em gave him her best brush off smile, but she doubted it was as effective as usual. The confrontations with her dad and Rob left her with very little bullshit tolerance at the moment.

Ian shrugged. "Guess the rumors aren't true."

As he walked away, a tall, leggy blonde sauntered up to the table in a skin-tight tube dress in violent pink. "Breaking hearts all over the place, aren't you, Emerson?"

"It's not breaking hearts if you turn the guy down before the first kiss, Chessa." Emerson eyed the Croatian Amazon suspiciously. Chessa Pavlich didn't get along with most women on the tour, least of all Maren, Dera, and Em. Their philosophies for play and their careers were completely different. Chessa craved the attention and thrived on being outrageous. Unfortunately, she had the skills to back up the showboating.

"What are you still doing here, Chessa?" Maren asked. "I would have thought you'd be on your way home after Em here whipped you in the quarters."

Chessa looked down her perfectly sculpted nose. "As the world number one, I'm expected to stay around for press obligations."

Now it was Em's turn to roll her eyes. Trust Chessa to toss that in their faces. The four of them had spent the last four years duking it out for the top positions, but Chessa had settled comfortably at number one eighteen months ago, and they hadn't managed to budge her since.

"Well, I guess we'll see you in Paris." Emerson hoped Chessa took the hint. Her politeness filter had started degrading during the fight with her dad, and it'd only gone downhill from there.

Thankfully, Chessa walked away, her attention homing in on some slick guy who waved to her from the bar. Em returned her attention to her friends, hoping they could move into safer conversational territory.

"So I understand why you're pissed at your father," Maren said. "Been there, done that, got the T-shirt. But what'd your fuck buddy do to make you start slamming down bourbons like they're chocolate milk?"

Dera sipped her lemon drop martini that perfectly matched her dress. "More importantly, *who* is your fuck buddy? He must be very special for you to even let him into your bed after what that bastard-who-shall-not-be-named did to you."

Em chewed on her lip, her gaze returning to Rob for a moment before flitting away. She didn't miss how his attention had drifted to her as well, gray steel boring holes in the back of her head. The alcohol burned through her system, leaving behind a pleasant haze, but it didn't cut through the confusion clouding her mind as much as she'd hoped.

She shouldn't say anything to them. She should keep her mouth shut and let them think she was fucking some random guy. But it wasn't some random guy. It was Rob, and he came with so much emotional baggage she didn't know if she could keep it in.

"It's Rob," she murmured into her glass as she tossed back the fresh double the waitress set in front of her. The smooth alcohol scorched its way down her throat.

Her friends froze mid-drink, their eyes almost cartoonishly wide. Em motioned for another drink, waiting for them to respond.

"*Excusez moi*. I'm going to need you to repeat that," Dera demanded, setting her glass down slowly.

"I don't. Emmy said my brother is her fuck buddy, and now I need brain bleach." Maren shuddered and drained the remnants of her cosmo.

Dera's perfectly sculpted eyebrows rose almost to meet her hairline. "Rob Ashton? Aren't we daring?"

"It just—happened. No big deal." Em shrugged. "At least at first."

"You don't have fuck buddies." Dera studied Em, sipping the remnants of her cocktail. "That's usually my modus operandi, not yours. You have boyfriends. They're few and far between and short-lived, but they're still boyfriends."

Dera spoke with the certainty only a best friend could, and Emerson looked away. She didn't like where Dera was going with this. "And look how well that's worked out for me in the past."

"It's still a little weird," Maren said. "I mean, no offense, but I never pictured you and my brother together. You were always so…hostile toward each other."

"Well, there's a fine line between love and hate, you know," Em said lightly, ignoring the pang of guilt for not telling her friends the whole story. "We were stuck on a plane together on our way back from Melbourne, and one thing led to another."

"Hmm…and I suppose it had nothing to do with him defending you after the pictures came out?" Dera raised one dark brow, challenging Em to deny it.

"Look, he's an attractive guy who finds me attractive for reasons other than those damn pictures, so I'm enjoying myself." She hated to dismiss her friend's questions, but she didn't want her prying too deep, not after today. The last thing she wanted was to think about what Rob made her feel. "And like you said, he gives really fantastic orgasms. Or he did last time we got together. Which wasn't recently because, well, my dad and grandmother interrupted us."

Maren winced. "Okay, enough. New topic. Like what he did to piss you off."

Em couldn't even begin to unpack that question. "He…Rob wants us to be something more than fuck buddies, and because I've been burned one time too many and have way, way too much going on right now, I want to stay strictly in the FWB territory."

Just then, one of the impeccably dressed concierges came up to the table and held out a folded piece of paper. "Ms. Grace? Someone left this for you at the front desk earlier."

"Who?" she asked, wondering if her father had decided to continue to berate her in letter form now.

"I'm not sure," he replied. "It was waiting at the

desk. Someone must have left it when I stepped away to help another guest about thirty minutes ago."

Ignoring the debate going on between her friends about whether FWB was a viable option for her, she unfolded the paper, her blood running cold when she saw that it definitely wasn't from Michael.

Bitch. Bet you think you're the shit now that you finally won something. Did you whore yourself to the umpire for those calls? You never deserved him. You spread your legs around like all the other cunts out there who think they deserve all the glory. I saw you, smiling for the fans, with that slab of beef following you everywhere. Are you fucking him too? All those men are hitting on you thanks to me. I'm surprised you haven't set up a rotating schedule by now. Go crawl under a rock where you belong.

"Emmy? What's wrong?" Dera asked.

Em struggled to breathe, the paper shaking as she clutched it. God, why now? The last letter had come three weeks ago, and there hadn't been a sign of problems here. Everything had started to go back to normal. "He's here. That bastard is here, and he's watching me."

"Shit, Em." Maren glanced around. "We need to get you out of here."

Shaking her head, Em gulped some of Dera's water. "No. Not here as in at the bar. Here as in Indian Wells. And at this hotel. But he's probably gone now."

"Either way," Dera said, glancing around. "You shouldn't be here without your guard."

"I let him go for the night. This guy won't try anything in a crowded place like this." Em rubbed her chest, trying to get control of her breathing.

Maren rubbed her hand up and down Em's arm. "Breathe, sweetie. You need to calm down and breathe."

Ha. Easier said than done. She was scared—really, truly scared—and frustrated. She hated feeling so helpless, like someone else had control of her life and there was no way she could get it back. She stared down at the letter, trying to make sense of what was happening. She was vaguely aware of Dera getting up, but she didn't look to see where her friend went.

"Maybe you're right. Maybe I should go back to my room," Em said eventually, looking up into Maren's worried blue-gray eyes.

"Uh-uh. Your brother and your *cher amie* here need to hear this now, not after you've had time to hide and process." Dera's accent grew thicker when she was stressed. It was subtle but hard to miss.

Em looked up to find Owen, Cruz, and Rob standing behind Dera, all of them looking at her full of concern.

"Wait, you two know?" Owen demanded.

Maren let out an impatient huff. "Yes, we know these two are screwing each other's brains out. Keep up, that's old news. We've got bigger problems."

"Bigger problems than my sister having a secret relationship with someone I thought she hated?" Owen's glare hit Em full force, but she couldn't focus on that now.

Rob reached out and took her hand. "Em? You okay? What happened?"

"Yeah, Emmy, you look like you did that time Grandpa and I made you go deer hunting with us." Her brother's glare faded into worry. "And if you're going

191

to puke, please aim away from me this time."

That got a weak laugh out of her. "Jerk. I'm not going to puke. I swear. It's just…I got a note. From the creeper. He dropped it at the concierge desk while it was unattended. And someone thinks it's a bigger deal than it really is."

"It is a big deal, Emerson," Maren insisted. "The jackass has been watching you the whole tournament. *He was in the freaking hotel!*"

"What?" Rob's bark made Em jump a little. She didn't blame him for being upset with her about earlier, but he didn't get to be in a snit about this.

Owen pounded a fist on the table. "Goddamnit, Squeaker. I knew I should have said something when you showed up here without your guard."

"He hasn't done anything, O. He's trying to scare me, and it's not going to work," she said, silently cursing when her voice trembled.

Shaking his head, Rob slid onto the stool beside her, his big body facing her, almost shielding her from the door. "He's dangerous, Em. He's taunting you for now, but what are you going to do if he goes beyond taunting and decides to really come after you?"

She fought back a shudder at the thought of what might happen. She hated that Rob was right. On any other night, she might have been able to shrug it off and not let it bother her. She'd go up to her hotel room, chug some water, and go to sleep without a second thought. But tonight, after seeing her dad, after hearing the venom he spewed at her, her armor had more than a few chinks in it.

"I'll be careful. I promise. Both of you, stop worrying. I'm a big girl."

The words held more bravado than she felt, but she needed to say them. She loved her brother for worrying, but he had his own life to focus on just as she had to focus on hers.

"Fine, you're a big girl," Owen said, "but that doesn't mean we're leaving you on your own until you're tucked into your room for the night. All of us are sticking with you like glue. Got it?"

The others nodded, even the silent Cruz. He stood by Maren, his brown gaze steady and sure as ever.

Sighing, she nodded. "Okay. I should probably call it a night anyways."

They all moved toward the elevator in a huddle, her friends forming a protective circle around her, with Rob and Owen flanking her. The others chatted about this and that, but Rob remained silent until they got to her door.

"You good?" he asked after everyone turned to walk toward their own rooms. His face stayed impassive, but his eyes spoke volumes. There was so much there Em didn't know where to start.

"Stay with me?" The words came out from a place deep within her. She hadn't planned to ask him in. It was a stupid, stupid idea, but tonight she couldn't bring herself to care.

He reached up to brush a lock of hair behind her ear. "Are you sure?"

"Yes." She opened the door. "I'm not a fan of the caveman tendencies you're showing, but I don't want to be alone tonight."

He slammed the door behind him and pulled her into his arms. The warmth of his body pressed into hers; the smell of his mint and eucalyptus soap and the rough feel of his scruffy jaw did more to calm her than a dozen shots of bourbon. He was here. She was safe.

"Do you get how much you matter? To me, to your brother, to our friends? I know you don't take these threats seriously, but we do." He spoke by her ear, teasing the sensitive skin there. "We couldn't handle it if something happened to you. I couldn't handle it."

A lump formed in her throat. It wasn't a declaration of love or anything close, but for the first time since letting him back into her life, she almost believed that he would actually stick around this time. Having him here, after today felt…good. Right, even. "I really will be okay. But right now, I…I want to fall asleep with you holding me."

"Whatever you want, doll."

Sleeping in his arms wouldn't chase the pain away forever, but it would get her through the worst of it. She needed him tonight, more than she should, and she was beginning to think she might need him for more than tonight.

Chapter 13

Rob stood toe to toe with Joey, his blood roaring in his ears and his fists clenched at his side to keep from taking a swing at the oversized man-child standing behind her.

"This is the goddamn French Open. You're really going to let him get away with pulling this kind of shit an hour before we go on the air?"

Joey straightened the jacket of her impeccable tailored suit jacket and rolled her eyes. "Bruno's the senior correspondent. He has first choice on stories and interviews. What part of this aren't you understanding?"

"I've spent weeks convincing Dera to let us do an in-depth interview while we're here. She and I have a rapport. She agreed to sit down with me, not Bruno. You really want the world number three to think we're pulling one over on her? The tennis players are just now starting to trust us and think that we might not be going for the lowest common denominator on stories."

Bruno smirked, his arms crossed over his barrel chest. "Exactly. This is a major coup, and I'm sure the network would want to see their top correspondent conducting the interview, not someone greener than a grass court."

It took all Rob's self-control not to take a swing at him. This was the third story in the last week and a half

Bruno had tried to steal from Rob. The first two, he'd had to admit defeat, but he wouldn't back down on this one. Interviewing Dera and her family at her home tournament was too big a chance to waste on Bruno. Knowing the ex-football player, he'd offend Dera within the first five minutes, and she'd drop him flat.

"Dera Calvet is not going to agree to let Bruno interview her, Joey. You know that. Why are we even having this conversation?"

Rob and Joey both knew exactly why they were having this conversation: because Bruno was a pompous ass who liked to throw his weight around. He'd been worse than usual at this tournament. That's why Joey was here instead of a local producer they usually used. Bruno had thrown a fit to get someone who he could "work with" in Paris, which meant someone he could bully into doing his bidding. Rob silently prayed Joey grew a backbone before Bruno completely ruined their coverage.

Finally, her shoulders sagged, and she rubbed her temples. "Rob's right, Bruno. He's done the prep work and got the athlete's agreement. He's doing the interview."

"Thanks, Joey." Rob nodded to the producer and walked away before Bruno could continue the argument. He had a few hours before Dera was scheduled to come to the studio, and he needed to do some last-minute prep.

His phone chimed as he returned to his temporary office. *Hey, handsome. Headed to dinner with Owen and the uncles. Wish you could join us. Maybe we can meet up after?*

He smiled. Ever since their last night in Indian

Wells, something had changed with Em. She was more…open. The walls were starting to come down, and he liked it—a lot. During the Miami Open, he'd managed to spend a few nights at her house. She'd been quiet, but she'd done a hell of a job showing him how she felt with her body.

So far, she'd been playing well. She'd had her quarterfinals match today, and she'd kicked some serious ass. He loved watching her play; the way she moved, the intensity she put into every second of the game, it was like watching a dancer at the ballet. He wished he could have been in her box with her family and Zoe like a normal boyfriend, but that wasn't an option. As long as he had this damn job, it would never be an option.

On days like this, when Bruno's assholish tendencies went off the charts, Rob considered quitting. Every time he did, he reminded himself there wasn't another job that would let him be this close to the game, that would let him keep an eye on Em and his sister the way he could now.

So far, there'd only been a handful of signs that the stalker hadn't given up. The police intercepted a package with a doll dressed like Em that'd been sliced in a few places, and there'd been a few emails from different accounts, but they hadn't been able to trace them.

"Thanks for making that relatively painless, Rob." Dera met him after her interview as he headed for the elevators. While they'd always gotten on well, he knew she didn't like the interviews that went beyond her role as an athlete. He got that; living in the shadow of your parents' legacies was harder than most people thought.

That's why he'd insisted on doing the interview with her instead of Bruno.

He chuckled. "I promised, didn't I? Not all journalists are ogres."

She made a very French sound of disbelief. "I heard what that ogre you work with tried to do. My agent got a call this morning. She and I were not pleased. I'm glad you managed to talk sense into them."

"Bruno's an idiot. He's been trying to steal my stories this whole tournament, but I wasn't letting him win on this one." He gave her a wink. She'd really opened up, talking as if the cameras weren't there. She still kept stuff back, and he didn't try to push her beyond what they'd talked about in the pre-interview meeting. They steered clear of her personal life. It was common knowledge on the tour that Dera was bisexual, and while she didn't go out of her way to hide it, she didn't discuss her personal life with the media.

They emerged into the tennis complex together, the sun just starting to set behind the sea of courts.

"What's that?" Dera asked, pointing to a small group off to one side. Looking closer, Rob noticed it was a small gathering of cameramen and reporters, and they were surrounding someone coming out of the players' facility.

"I don't—" His stomach dropped. Bruno led the pack, and he had a microphone shoved in Em's face.

"*Merde*. What's that bastard up to?" Dera started toward Em.

Rob's mind kicked into overdrive, trying to decide what to do. If he went and got into Bruno's face, not only would the whole thing be caught on camera, but Bruno would get suspicious, maybe even leap to conclusions—he was an expert leaper. There was no way Rob would be able to handle this calmly. Right now, he was ready to pummel Bruno for cornering Em, and he didn't even know what it was about yet.

"Dera, call Zoe. I'll call Owen. Damn it, where's her security team?"

As they got closer, Rob could make out the questions Bruno hurled at Em.

"Emerson, is it true that you now have a stalker? Is that why you've had increased security at the last few tournaments? Do you have a message for your stalker?"

Shit. This was not good. Not good at all. He thought he'd buried the story. If Joey had pursued this story behind his back…

He stopped, pushing Owen's name on his contact list. "Owen. Get your ass to the players' center now. Bruno's ambushed Em, and her security's AWOL."

He ended the call before his friend could respond, taking in the scene and trying to come up with a plan. Dera didn't hang back; she waded in among the reporters who had joined Bruno, picking up on his line of questioning and running with it.

"Leave her alone. Did you not hear her say 'no comment'?" Dera growled, golden eyes flashing. She spouted off some choice insults in French, and with her arm wrapped around Em, she tried to push her way through the throng of reporters. Unfortunately, they couldn't move. Rob couldn't push through even if he wanted to.

"Come on, Emerson. This is just another scandal in a long line of problems," Bruno jeered. "Do you have a comment? Did the sex photos incite the stalker? Are you sorry about those photos? Do you wish you hadn't taken them?"

Rob's heart clenched as Em's face paled, and so many emotions ran through those dark eyes. Last time he'd seen her in person, those eyes had been so at peace; she'd given him that wonderful, sleepy smile and pulled him in for a long, thorough kiss. Now she resembled a caged animal, searching for a way out.

Rob was about to say to hell with it all when Owen came sprinting out of the players' center door. "What the hell is this? All of you need to back the fuck off."

"Oh, come on, Owen. Did you know about your sister's stalker? Do you think she deserves this?" one of the other reporters shouted.

"Yeah, give us a comment, Owen," Bruno said, shoving a microphone in Owen's face. Em's security guards came jogging out not far behind Owen, moving to put themselves between the reporters and Em.

Rob spotted his opening and took it. "All right, everyone. Let's back off. I'm sure the Graces will make a statement when they're ready. You're not going to get anything from them right now. Barry, Jeff. That means you guys. Let's go."

He grabbed the TWW camera guy and sound technician by the shoulders, tugging them away from the crowd.

Bruno was harder. "No, Ashton. This is my story. I want a quote from the new scandal queen of the WTA. What do you have to say for yourself, Emerson? Are you proud of yourself now?"

Something snapped on Em's face, and pure rage surfaced from the fear and the hurt. "Proud? No, you jack—"

"Bruno. Back. Off." Rob got between Em and his

colleague. The last thing they needed was for Em to go off on Bruno with all those cameras around. "Let's go back to the office and talk about this. This is not the way to do this."

"You arrogant little shit. Who are you to tell me how to do my job?" Bruno bleated as Rob forcefully guided him away from Em, Dera, and Owen. The security guys were dispersing the other reporters, and Barry and Jeff had lowered their equipment after Rob called them off.

"You were ambushing one of the top players and bullying her about her stalker," Rob hissed as he followed Bruno inside. "That's not doing your job. You're not some dumb paparazzo. You're supposed to be a journalist."

"I was going after one of the best stories of the tournament." Bruno's voice boomed through the halls. "What, are you trying to get in Emerson's pants or something? Why are you always defending that bitch?"

Rob's fist clenched, but a hand on his shoulder stopped him from actually throwing the punch.

"What the hell is going on here?" Joey asked, her hair standing on end and dark circles under her eyes. "Shouldn't you be back at your hotels by now?"

"You would think," Rob snapped. "Except that Bruno was outside ambushing Emerson Grace about her stalker."

Joey's shrewd blue eyes widened. "A stalker? I knew it! Did you get a comment from her?"

"No, because this arrogant asshole wouldn't let me," Bruno said. "I almost broke her, but he got in my face and dragged me away."

"Ashton, is this true?" Joey braced her hands on

201

her hips, her don't-fuck-with-me face firmly in place. "You said you couldn't verify the story two months ago. Now you're interfering with Bruno doing his job. What the hell?"

"He was bullying a major tennis star, Joey. Harassing her. Shoving a microphone in her face, and not taking no for an answer is not the way to get a quote for a story," Rob retorted. "She has a stalker. The police are involved, and it's a serious situation. We shouldn't be giving this creep air time and stroking his ego and egging him on."

Bruno's eyes narrowed. "Wait. How do you know there's police involvement? That wasn't in the tip I got."

Rob's stomach sank to the floor. Shit. He'd overplayed his hand. "You're not the only one with sources."

"You lied to me, didn't you?" Joey accused. "You confirmed the rumors back in March, and you lied. You buried a fucking gold mine, Rob. Do you know how much traffic we'd bring to our site and the show if we'd run this story as an exclusive three months ago?"

"This is a serious situation, Joey. A dangerous one. This guy's been following her to tournaments and sending her threatening letters and emails. If we report on it, we make the police's job harder, and we encourage this guy." The thought of the creep getting off on them running this story sent waves of nausea through Rob. He hated that Em needed security guards and that she couldn't even check her own mail without getting worried. Running this story would make it ten times worse.

Joey's face hardened. "You're a reporter. Our job

is to report the news, not coddle the players. I know this is hard for you, Ashton, but this is a story, and we're going to run it."

"And I'm going to make sure the executives know that you buried a story because of your friendship with one of the players," Bruno said, smugness oozing off him.

"I withheld information for safety reasons, nothing more. And this isn't the type of story we should be focusing on if we want to be seen as a creditable news source. This involves an athlete's personal life, and it's only a story if we make it one," Rob argued.

Bruno snorted. "We'll see."

Rob watched Bruno and Joey walk away, their heads together. They were going to do the damn story. He wanted to scream and kick something. He thought he'd made a difference with how Joey was starting to see stories, even if he would never change Bruno from a slimeball to a halfway decent person. Instead, the second a juicy bone flashed in front of her face, she reverted to the scandal-hungry viper she'd always been. Not for the first time since taking the job, Rob felt like a layer of muck and filth clung to him. He worked for a network that fed off other people's pain and weakness, and he wasn't sure what he was doing here.

He wanted to lock Em in a protected tower and throw away the key until this asshole was found. He had the sinking suspicion his job was suddenly on thin ice, but he couldn't bring himself to care. All he cared about was Em and making sure she was all right. She was all that mattered, and she had been for a long time.

****

"Focus, Emmy. Half the Grand Slams are done.

Dera took you out in the semifinals in France. There's no room for error at Wimbledon."

Zoe ended her diatribe on how poorly Em had performed during her latest training session, and a weight settled in Em's chest, the same way it did any time her grandma or grandpa gave her the "we're disappointed in you" speech because she'd gotten a bad grade or skipped a class to get more practice. She hated letting Zoe down, especially now, after everything she'd done for her over the years.

"What do you want me to do?" Em asked, glancing away from Zoe's hard blue eyes.

Zoe placed her hands on Em's shoulder, her eyes softening. "I want you to get focused. Shake all of this off. You've got to put one hundred percent of yourself into the game if you want to beat Chessa. She's on fire, and nothing but your best is going to get you that title."

Focus. Easier said than done. After everything she'd been through this year, it was a miracle she had any focus left. With Rob becoming part of the mix more and more each day, Em's attention was only further divided. It was only a matter of time before someone found out about them if she kept seeing him. But Zoe was right. She needed to go back to basics and re-center her attention on her goal—a Grand Slam title.

"Okay. I can do that." Em hoped she sounded convincing, because she didn't believe her own words. She didn't think she knew how to focus anymore.

Zoe tilted her head skeptically. "I want you to go have dinner with your grandma and your brother. Take a nice long bubble bath. Get some sleep. Then come back and be ready to work tomorrow. Got it?"

As much as it chafed, Em did what her coach

ordered. She didn't remember getting to her grandma's house, but she remembered being pulled into Gran's warm embrace and letting the rest of the world fade away.

"You're too skinny," her grandmother fussed. "Even skinnier than when I saw you in California."

Em winced at the mention of Indian Wells. "It's been…a long year, Gran. Skinny is the least of my problems."

"I know, sweetheart. I know." Gran cupped Em's face, stroking her cheek with her age-softened thumb. "Come on. Your big brother's already in the kitchen. I put him to work making the salad so he doesn't eat all of my cheese sauce before it's done."

Em let her grandma link their arms and lead her into the cozy kitchen of the condo the Grands had occupied for most of Em's life. She and Owen grew up in this place, doing their homework at the butcher-block peninsula while Gran and Papa Vic cooked together. Even after a long day at her job as a CPA, Gran still insisted on helping to cook dinner. It was their time to be a team again, she'd argue any time Papa Vic tried to get her to stay off her feet. As they grew up, Owen and Em were slowly allowed to join the team on occasion, but it was always Papa Vic's special time with Gran.

"Cheese sauce?" Em sniffed the air. "Are you making mac and cheese?"

Gran's eyes twinkled. "Well, when Zoe called to say that my girl was having a rough time of it, what else could I make? Comfort food is the order of the day. Besides, that brother of yours has been bugging me nonstop to make some for him."

"Not nonstop," Owen protested from his spot at the

counter, a chef's knife in his hand. "I just…made a request or five."

"We were just in France. World capital of cheese. But the second we get home, you con Gran into making you mac and cheese?" Em teased, her smile genuine but weak.

He shrugged, popping a slice of tomato into his mouth. "Gran's is still the best. I will be a hundred and still want her mac and cheese."

"Aw. That's why you're my favorite grandson." Gran patted his arm since he was too tall for her to reach his face. "Now pay attention to those vegetables. I didn't teach you to use poor knife skills."

"Yes, ma'am." He grinned, going back to his task.

Em lifted herself onto the counter beside him, too drained to do anything but watch her family. Her heart ached as it always did when the three of them were together lately. Being with her brother and her grandmother went a long way toward soothing her, but it also reminded her how much she missed her grandfather. He should be here, bustling around, maybe popping outside to grill something—he'd loved his Big Green Egg grill she and Owen bought him three Father's Days ago.

Gran dumped the pasta into the cheese sauce and began stirring the gooey goodness together. "Emmy Anne, you go set the table. Owen, take that salad in with the bread. I'll bring this along in a minute."

"You doing okay?" Owen asked as he followed Em into the little dining nook located off the back of the kitchen.

She sighed, setting the plates on the table in three spots. They always left Papa Vic's chair empty now.

"Define okay."

"Hmm. 'Aside from the jetlag, you aren't five minutes away from collapsing under the weight of the world' would work as the definition today." He set the salad down and helped her with the napkins.

"Ah." She pursed her lips, thinking. "In that case, I think I'm probably a little past okay, but not much. Why? Is it that obvious?"

"Only to someone who shared a bathroom with you for eighteen years." Her brother winked. "Besides, anyone else would have curled up into a ball by now if they were in your position."

"Our Emmy's made of sterner stuff than that," Gran said, carrying a giant fiesta ware bowl full of noodles and cheese. "Both of my grandchildren are."

Em smiled and went to pour sweet tea into the glasses of ice Owen brought to the table. "How are you feeling, Gran? Are you still going to that yoga class at the community center?"

"Yes. I'm getting quite good at it. Your grandfather would laugh at me for looking so silly, but I feel much more limber." Gran wiggled her shoulders. "And ten years younger to boot."

Em bit her lip as she spooned some mac and cheese onto her plate, then passed it to Owen. She desperately wanted to ask her Gran some things, but she couldn't bring herself to ruin the mood. "Don't hurt yourself. We don't want you to have to have a hip replacement or something like that."

"You worry too much," Gran chided, helping herself to some bread. "I'm fit as a fiddle and doing everything my doctor says. Besides, the instructor at the community center makes everything gentle on old bodies like mine. I'm not nearly as hard on my body as the two of you are on yours. That was a nasty tumble you took in your last match, Owen. Are you all right?"

Em took a bite of the mac and cheese, savoring the bite of the cheddar and the smoothness of gouda. Gran put three or four different cheeses in her sauce to make it extra flavorful and creamy. The taste took her back to simpler times, when she didn't have to worry about secret boyfriends or stalkers or winning Grand Slams. God, what she wouldn't give to go back to that time today.

"The clay courts don't hurt nearly as much as the hard courts, Gran. I had a few bruises, but nothing too bad. Would have had Cruz if it weren't for that fall, though." Owen pulled a face. "Oh well. Both Graces in the semifinals ain't half bad, huh?"

"Oh, I wish I could have been there," Gran said. "I miss traveling with you two."

Owen coughed. "Yeah, last time you showed up didn't go so well."

An awkward silence stretched for a few minutes before Gran finally spoke. "Your father has always been a difficult man. You two know that better than anyone. And I don't know how a son of mine and my sweet Victor's turned out like that, but he's still your family. Family has always been at the center of our lives, and at the end of the day, we love each other."

"We might love each other, but it doesn't mean we have to like each other," Em muttered.

"Speaking of my visit," Gran said. "How are things with you and that nice young man who was in your room?"

Em cringed at the memory of her grandma

interrupting her having sex with Rob. Even in high school, they'd never had a situation quite like that. "Um. Rob's…Rob's fine. I guess."

"You guess? Isn't he your boyfriend?" Gran asked.

Owen flashed her a wicked grin. "Yeah, Emmy. Isn't he your boyfriend?"

"God, what are you, five?" Em glared at her brother. "Rob…my relationship with Rob is complicated, Gran. I wouldn't necessarily call him my boyfriend. It's not like we've gone on a real date or anything like that."

"Ah. So it's one of those friends-with-benefits things I've read about?" Gran nodded wisely.

Choking on her food, Em took a gulp of her tea, hoping it would cool the embarrassment burning her cheeks. "Oh. Wow. Gran. Um. I—I don't—"

"Because I've got to tell you, from where I was standing, it seemed like he was your boyfriend," Gran pressed.

"What makes you say that, Gran?" Owen asked, mischief still twinkling in his eyes. "Inquiring minds want to know."

"Nosy minds, you mean." Gran gave him a reproachful look but continued. "It was the way he looked at you, I suppose. And the way he positioned himself beside you. It reminded me of your grandfather and me."

Gran's words sent a jolt through Em's system. She wished that Gran knew everything that had gone on seven years ago. When she'd come back from London with Papa Vic, Em honestly expected him to tell Gran about everything, but he didn't. At the time, it had been easier for her not to talk about it. Now she desperately wished Papa Vic were here to help her make sense of everything going on.

"Oh, Gran. We're not—" Em shook her head. "Rob and I aren't like you and Papa Vic. You two were a fairy tale. Meant to be together and partners to the end."

"And you don't think you could have that with your Rob?"

Em sent a desperate look to Owen, but her brother raised an eyebrow at her.

"Yeah, Squeaker. What's going on with you and Rob? Are you going to live happily ever after?"

She raised an eyebrow right back at him, taking a bite to buy herself some time. "Are you and the D-list TV star you're dating going to live happily ever after? Why is it guys never get asked that question about a casual relationship?"

"Sorry, sis, but I don't look at Tonya the way you and Rob look at each other. Good try at deflection, though," he said easily.

She hated how he could be so calm and cool in the face of everything. She tried to be like that, but in the last few months she'd been failing—epically. "Gran, Rob and I aren't serious. He's…a friend."

"A friend who you have sex with," Owen put in.

Em aimed a well-placed kick under the table at her brother. She did not want to talk to her grandmother about sex. Ever. Zoe had even had "the talk" with her in junior high so she didn't have to talk about sex with Gran.

"I know things have changed since the days your grandfather and I were dating, dear, but I recognize that a man and woman can simply have a physical relationship," Gran said coolly. "But that's not what I saw when I met your young man."

"Really?" Owen broke off a piece of bread.

"Surely you've seen them together," Gran said. "The way he looks at her. The way he defends her, both in public and in private. Wish you could have seen them lay into your dad. I was about to jump in, mind you, but he got there first. Reminded me of one of those old movie heroes."

Em shifted uncomfortably in her chair. "He wasn't doing anything that Owen or Cruz wouldn't have done if they'd been there. Dad was being a jerk, and Rob called him on it. You're reading too much into this."

"And that's not to say anything about how she looks at him." Gran sent Em a pointed look. "Not that I blame you. He's certainly a handsome devil. If I were twenty-five or thirty years younger, you'd have yourself some competition, young lady."

Em's jaw dropped. "Gran!"

"What? I may have spent fifty years married to the love of my life, but that doesn't mean I can't appreciate a fine specimen of manhood. Especially once I saw him smile and look at my granddaughter like she hung the moon."

Groaning, Em took another bite of her food. The conversation moved on, but the words kept swirling around in her head. Rob was always there, in the back of her mind. This was why she couldn't focus. Rob and all that had passed between them had become intrinsically entwined in her thoughts, and she needed to untangle them before it was too late.

During clean up, Owen got a text message. "Hey, I've gotta go and meet some…friends."

"Tell Tonya hi," Em called after him as he kissed

Gran and left.

Now that it was just the two of them in the house, they fell into an easy rhythm. Filling Tupperware with leftover food, putting the salad dressings in the fridge. They stood side by side, Gran rinsing the dishes before Em loaded the dishwasher. As much as she enjoyed this time with her grandmother, she couldn't escape the tight feeling in her chest that something—*someone*—was missing.

"Gran, do you still miss Papa Vic?"

The words came out before she stopped to think about them. She'd hoped that as time passed, she'd start to miss him less, but with every loss, she had felt her grandfather's loss more keenly. The clock over her head kept ticking. Her knee had started aching mid-way through the French Open, and it only served as another sharp reminder that she didn't know how much time she had to honor the promise she'd made to herself and to Papa Vic to win a Grand Slam title.

Gran froze, her hand dripping with soapy water. "Oh, sweetheart. Of course I do. Every day. What makes you ask that?"

"I just..." Em put some forks into the basket in the dishwasher. "With everything going on, I miss him. So much. I find myself wishing he was here so I could talk to him. He always made things seem so...simple. No problem was too big for him."

That earned her a chuckle, albeit a watery one. "You say that now. You should have seen your grandfather with you and your brother after your mom died. We'd kept y'all a few times when your parents were in town, even one overnight stay, but you'd spent more time with your mom's family than us. We hadn't had small children in the house in decades, and we'd never had a little girl before."

"I don't remember that. I always remember him being so good with us."

Gran nodded, returning to her work. "Oh, he was. But not at first. You especially. You were this sweet little bundle of energy who wanted to have tea parties and wear princess dresses while you wrestled with your big brother. He kept fretting that you were going to get hurt or break something."

"Only I didn't. At least not then." So much had broken in the years since. Most notably, her heart.

"You were so fierce and fearless. You didn't back down from anything, even your brother and your cousins. You had to run as fast and as far as they did, even though you were so tiny." Gran smiled. "By the second week, you had him wrapped around your little finger for good. He loved you so much, sweetheart."

Em's throat burned, and her eyes stung. "I loved him too. He was with me through so much. I…I wish he were here now. There's so much I need help making sense of, and I don't know where to start."

"Would this have anything to do with your Rob?" Gran handed Em a large pot.

Em placed the pot beside the colander, sighing at her grandmother's mind. "He's not my Rob. But yes. There's…a lot that's happened between Rob and me. And with everything else going on, it's becoming distracting. I need to do better, to win a Grand Slam, but the world keeps intruding and distracting me."

"You think Rob is part of this?" Gran guessed, scrubbing at a sauce pan.

"Well, yeah. He's probably the biggest part of it.

Ever since he came back into my life, everything's gotten so tangled and messy." Em leaned back against the counter as her grandmother worked.

Nodding, Gran didn't respond for a moment. "By back, you mean after the way he treated you all those years ago?"

"You know?" Em stared at her grandmother, genuinely surprised. She'd never said anything about knowing about Em's past with Rob. Not in Indian Wells and not at dinner.

"Of course I do. Your grandfather didn't keep things from me. We told each other everything for fifty years." Gran smiled fondly at Em. "How else do you think we stayed together for so long?"

Em sagged in relief. "But you never said anything. Never even hinted that you knew."

"Because I saw how broken you were when you came back from London." The older woman wiped her hands on the ancient dishcloth she kept on the drawer by the sink. "Your grandfather had a special relationship with you, and I respected that. If you'd wanted to talk to me about it, I knew that you knew I was here for you. But you didn't even talk to him about it after that first day, so I didn't push."

A well of love bubbled up inside her. This was why she'd always pick her family over anyone else. Her grandmother was one of the most gracious women she'd ever known, and it was because of stuff like this. The bond between her grandparents was another reason. They'd worked seamlessly as a team, even when it came to dealing with their granddaughter's broken heart.

"I…thank you for that." She reached out to hug her

grandmother. The two women moved toward the living room together. "So if you know about our past, you can understand how things between us now are…messy. Really, really messy. And more importantly, Rob and my feelings for him are a distraction that I'm not sure I can have right now."

Gran pulled Em onto the couch, wrapping her in a hug and a quilt. "You've been through so much in your young life, Emerson Anne. You've dealt with more heartache than I saw in the first four decades of my life. But why on earth do you think that a boy who loves you is a distraction?"

Love. That word shook Em to her very core. Love couldn't be part of the equation, not now. Not ever with Rob. Not again. "He doesn't love me, Gran. We like each other. We have really, really good sex together. But he doesn't love me. And I don't love him. Even if I did, he's a reporter. If anyone were to find out that we were seeing each other, it would be…a disaster of epic proportions. That's part of the distraction."

"I suppose that's fair." Gran ran her fingers through Em's hair like she used to when Em had a nightmare as a kid.

"Between the stalker and the news and Rob, I haven't been able to get my head in the game." Em snuggled closer to her grandmother. "Zoe even yelled at me today."

"You've been doing so well. Why would she yell at you?"

Em let out a bitter laugh. "I haven't been doing as well as I could. I should have made it to the finals at Roland Garros, maybe even won, but I wasn't as focused as I should have been."

"So you're questioning if you should continue your relationship with Rob in the wake of the other distractions?" Gran eased back to study Em's face, her brown eyes thoughtful.

"Exactly. Being with him is starting to feel…right, but I don't think I could ever trust him again after last time. It might be easier all around if I told him that we shouldn't even be friends again, let alone friends with benefits." The words stuck in Em's throat, and she hated them even as she said them. Rob did something to her, to her body, that wouldn't be easy to let go of, but she had to if she was going to do what she set out to do this year—win a Grand Slam, no matter what.

Gran sighed, cupping Em's face. "Sweetheart, if it's starting to feel right now, if it was 'right' enough for you to give your whole heart to the boy seven years ago, then it wouldn't be easier to give him up. Love isn't a complication. It's the solution. A man like Rob Ashton would be your partner, if you gave him the chance, just as your grandfather was with me. The other things are momentary distractions. In time, they'll fade into memory, but those feelings will still be there."

But Em wasn't sure she wanted those feelings to still be there. It had hurt too much last time, and with everything else, she wasn't sure she was strong enough to be hurt again. The partnership her grandmother described sounded so good, though. Maybe if she redoubled her focus and worked even harder in the next few weeks, she could get her win without giving Rob up. It was at least worth a try.

Chapter 14

"I can't believe I let you talk me into this," Em grumbled as Rob met her at the door to the upscale Miami hotel ballroom.

Rob grinned at her, pulling her off to one side so that an oversized palm tree hid them from view. "It's for a good cause. You like my mom's charity, remember? Helping foster kids and at-risk kids is one of your things. And you look gorgeous."

She really did. The warm, dark yellow color of the gown turned her skin a rich golden tone, and the plunging neckline and thin shoulder straps made his mouth water. She'd even managed to pin her hair up in a sexy, curly up-do thing that left her neck and collarbone exposed.

"I lost the French Open, Rob. I should be practicing or studying my last match. I shouldn't be attending a charity gala with the guy I'm secretly sleeping with." Em wrinkled her nose. "And compliments aren't going to distract me from that fact."

Sighing, Rob slid his arms around her waist, pulling her close. She was taking this loss a lot harder than the others. "It was the semifinals, and you were playing against Dera on her home turf. She's a beast on clay. You saw how she smashed through everyone else at the tournament. You at least took her to three sets."

To prevent her from arguing further, he leaned in

217

for a kiss. He missed being able to kiss her. He'd been stuck in New York for the last week, dealing with his bosses yelling at him for not running with the story about the stalker. Joey had taken it as a personal affront that he didn't confirm the story for her two months ago, but he couldn't bring himself to care.

The back of his neck tingled, like someone was watching him, but he brushed it aside. As concealing as the palm might be, they were in public. Thankfully, it was dark enough that the odds of someone identifying the couple making out behind the big leaves were slim.

"You're lucky I'm wearing smudge-proof lipstick, mister."

The breathy quality of Em's voice made him hard in less than two seconds. "Mmm. Now, are you done with your guilt freak-out? I promise you, it's okay if you take one night off. I'd like to enjoy getting to see your face instead of your text messages. I missed it."

"I missed your face too," she admitted. "Fine. We can go in. But remember, none of the couple-y stuff. There's too many people we know here, plus I just had to walk past fifty photographers."

"Fine, but one last kiss." He leaned down for another kiss, letting his tongue tease hers a little, savoring the sweet taste of her. "Okay. I'm good. For now."

"Good to know." Em giggled, glancing pointedly down at the crotch of his tuxedo pants. Damn it. He was as hard as a rock. "Why don't I go in, and you can stay here until you're more...presentable?"

"Right." He stayed where he was, watching her walk away. Her hips swayed, making the floaty fabric of her dress flutter seductively around the silver heels peeping out from under the hem.

After she left, the reality of the situation started to come back to him. He was at his parents' major charity gala of the year. The woman he wanted more than his next breath was here, and so was his dad, the person who'd driven them apart the first time around. At the time he invited her, this had sounded like a good idea.

Waiting behind the plant for a few more minutes, he reminded himself this wasn't London. He wasn't a kid trying to please his father anymore. Tonight was about putting on a good face for his family, and it was about getting to see Em somewhere other than at a tournament or at her townhouse. Thankfully, Owen and Cruz were here somewhere. So was Dera. His sister was always his wing-woman at events like this, but it was nice to have the additional backup.

Rob emerged from behind the plant once he got his body under control, and he straightened his tie and his hair. He'd barely made it halfway down the stairs into the ballroom before his mother came gliding up to him.

"Rob! *Älskling*, where have you been? I thought I saw you earlier, but then you disappeared," Brigit said, lifting her cheek for him to kiss. She looked lovely in an ice blue gown that draped over her willowy body as if it had been designed just for her—which it probably had.

"Sorry, Mom. I saw a friend I needed to talk to. You look stunning as usual." He kissed her cheek. "This is some party."

Brigit shrugged. "Your father and I never do things by half measures. Have you seen him yet?"

"No. I haven't seen him or Maren. I'm sure I'll run into him eventually." He shoved his hands into his pockets and scanned the room. His eyes caught on a flash of rich yellow through the crowd of pastels and black. Em was standing by one of the perfectly set tables, talking to Maren and Cruz, her head thrown back in laughter. God, she was gorgeous. He wished he could go up to her and kiss her, taste that laughter and the flavor that was just Em.

"Is that Emerson Grace?" Brigit asked, following his line of sight. "She looks quite lovely. I'm so glad she decided to come this year. I really admire the work she's done with her foundation."

A smile stretched across his lips, unconscious pride in Em. "Yeah, she's great."

"Great, hm?" She got this look in her eyes that put him on alert. It was one of those mom looks that threatened to turn a man's world upside down if given half a chance.

"What?" He shuffled his feet and avoided his mother's gaze, hoping to catch Maren's eye so she could rescue him.

Brigit linked her arm through Rob's, that look never wavering as she nodded to people walking by. "You still have feelings for the Grace girl."

Oh. That's why she had the look. She was matchmaking or something. He quickly ran through his options. He could deny the hell out of it, and she likely wouldn't believe him. Or he could tell her the truth. He and his mom hadn't always been close, but since his injury, they'd developed a deep bond. She'd braved his black moods and been by his bedside after every surgery. She'd stepped up in a way he hadn't expected. His relationship with his father overshadowed so much of his childhood years that his mother somehow faded into the background. Back when he and Em first met in London, he'd never talked to his mother about how he felt. He'd assumed she agreed with his father about everything, but things were different now. He could rely on her.

"I might," he proceeded cautiously. "What would you say if I did?"

Her eyes softened. "I would say that look in your eyes when you watch her is enough to make any mother happy for her son. Does she still have feelings for you?"

He stopped, considering his words carefully. He didn't want to think too much about all the walls Em put up between them. Better to take a different tack. "We've been seeing each other for a few months now."

"A few months?" Her jaw dropped in surprise. "Is that why you've been in Miami so much lately?"

"Yeah. We've been trying to keep things quiet, so I've been coming down to see her when I can. It's a little easier to keep things on the down low here than in New York. Less crowded."

It was also because he felt more at ease here than in New York. New York didn't…fit him. He only lived there because his job was based there. He'd rather be here, close to his mom, close to his girl.

"I'm sure it's been hard for both of you, spending so much time apart. I assume that your employers don't know about this?" She raised an eyebrow.

His stomach clenched. That was the tricky part in all of this. His bosses would hang him up by his toenails if they found out about him dating Em. "Nope. Like I said, very few people even know we're together, and we want to keep it that way for a while, what with

Em's stalker and the photos and all the press attention."

"Understandable." She tugged him to walk with her. "But how long can you keep this silent? The two of you aren't A-List celebrities, but you're very well known in certain circles. Eventually, someone will see the two of you together, and it will be big news. Do you think you'll be able to keep your job after that?"

Trust his mother to go straight to the heart of the matter. She didn't pull punches or try to coddle him. She was supportive, but fair. And she had a damned good point. That question had been at the back of his mind since Em started to loosen her grip on their secret and let people in. The longer he spent with Em, the more he wanted to be with her for good. He could care about his career, especially now that his options were limited if he wanted to stay in the tennis world, but he wasn't sure that he did.

"I don't know, Mom. I'm trying not to overplay my hand on this one, and I can't worry about the minor 'what ifs' now." He sighed, nodding to one of his dad's old tennis buddies. "I'm focusing on the big 'what if'— what if Em's the one, and I threw my chance away seven years ago because I let my dad and my career come between us?"

Brigit had the good grace to look down, color staining her cheeks from more than just the blush she'd used. "Your father meant well, *Älskling*. He really did. He wanted you to focus on your tennis career. You know how he gets. He wanted the best for you, and in his own way, he was trying to show you that he cares. Even now, he's worried for you. He doesn't show it in the most obvious ways, but he wants to see you happy and settled with someone who will give you the same kind of partnership we've enjoyed for so long."

Best for him? His father wanted what was best for him? Rob had so much to say on that little pronouncement, but he held it in. His mother would defend her Bobby until her last breath. He both loved and hated that about her. And he really didn't like the sound of that last bit. His father's worry for him usually led to the two of them nearly coming to blows over something.

"Like I said, I'm focused on here and now. Em means a lot to me, and I want as much time with her as I can."

She turned to face him, a warm, concerned expression on her usually cool face.

"I understand, and if you are happy with Emerson, then I couldn't be happier for you. Just…be careful, *Älskling*. I don't want to see you get hurt." Brigit reached up and straightened his tie.

"Don't worry, Mama. I'm going into this one with my eyes open." He leaned down and kissed her cheek again. "Now, if you'll excuse me, I'm going to go check on my friends."

Brigit chuckled. "Say hello to Emerson for me. Be sure you two dance later. I want to see how lovely my grandchildren could be."

Rob was still shaking his head when he walked up to the small group waiting at the table he'd been assigned to.

"What?" Em asked as he came to stand beside her, lacing his hand with hers under the cover of the folds of her dress.

He opened his mouth to speak, then shook his head again, mesmerized by the sight of her. She was so gorgeous. The thought of losing her sent a sharp pain through his gut and into his heart. Hearing his mother speculating about potential grandchildren should have scared the shit out of him, but it didn't. The thought actually comforted him. He and Em could make it. They could be together and have children. He just had to ensure that he didn't let anything—not even his father—ruin it this time.

****

"Ms. Grace, I believe it's my turn for a dance."

Rob held out his hand to her. She'd been up and down all evening, dancing with Cruz and Owen and other friends from the tour. They'd taken a break to eat dinner, but couples were once again starting to trickle back onto the floor.

It'd killed her not to dance with him, though, especially when she saw him dancing with other women. Obviously, it didn't bother her if he danced with Dera or Maren, but she'd been surprised by the pangs of jealousy that hit her every time Rob danced with someone else. She expected her face had been as green as the courts at Wimbledon when she saw him dancing with Carrie Webster, another product of tennis royalty. Carrie and her twin brother, Clayton, were the darlings of mixed doubles tennis, like their parents before them. There'd been a rumor a few years ago that Rob and Carrie were a thing, but Maren assured her that the rumors were more wishful thinking on the part of their parents than anything based in reality.

In spite of the blips of jealousy that tugged at the back of her mind, they'd had a wonderful evening. Under the guise of talking with friends and acquaintances, she and Rob spent time together without actually appearing to be a couple. It had been…nice to be out in public with him. But dancing with him? That might be testing their luck too much.

"Do you think that's a good idea?" she asked. It was really hard to resist him right now, standing there looking all handsome and sexy and suave in his tux.

"Yes, I do. I think it's an excellent idea for me to dance with you right now since I can't do any of the things I really want to do with you right now." Rob kept his voice low, but Owen still made a face.

"Oh, gross, guys. Seriously. You're going to make me puke up my dinner," Owen moaned.

Dera smacked him. "Stop being a child. Go dance with the man, Emmy. You look fabulous in that dress, and you'll look even more fabulous dancing with him. Go."

"Fine." She put her hand in Rob's. "One dance."

Rob grinned, linking their fingers together. The band began playing a cover of Ed Sheeran's "Thinking Out Loud," and she couldn't help but smile back.

"So you're happy to be dancing with me," he teased, pulling her into his arms, his hand resting on the small of her back, their hands clasped together still.

She tilted her head to meet his eyes. "Maybe I like this song."

"Why do you think I asked you to dance?" His eyes softened, and all she wanted to do was kiss him. He remembered this was one of her favorite songs. She vaguely recalled mentioning it in passing a month or so ago when they'd been talking about their days. She'd told him it was one of the songs she had on her playlist to listen to when she'd had a long day. It was just so hopeful. For the first time, she was as hopeful as the song. Being here with Rob, dancing at a party full of people they worked with, filled her with that level of hope.

"Some days, Rob Ashton, you are the biggest pain in the ass," she said. "Then other days—like today—you're Prince freaking Harry or something. How do you do it?"

With his golden hair and blue eyes, he was a near-perfect specimen of a man. Never in a million years had she thought she would be here now with a guy like this. She'd always worried that she would find a man who would turn out to be like her father, charming but distant, more intent on saving the world than saving his family.

"Talent. And if I'm a prince, then you're definitely my tennis-playing princess. You bring out my romantic side." To demonstrate, he dipped her a little before bringing her back upright.

"Very smooth," she teased.

"Thank you. My grandma insisted on giving me dancing lessons. She convinced Gramps that it would make me lighter on my feet on the court." He made a face, but she laughed.

"Clever grandma." She let him lead her through the gentle steps of the rumba, loving how in sync their bodies were. It was so comfortable to dance with him. She didn't worry about him not leading her or fumbling a step. They simply flowed. For a little while, she could forget about losing in the semifinals of the French Open and the fear of being too distracted to prove herself to her grandparents. She could leave behind the weight of guilt and disappointment and just be a woman dancing with a man who made her heart flutter.

"You and Carrie Webster looked pretty cozy earlier. She certainly appreciated your dance skills," Em prodded. She didn't want to ruin the moment, but that niggling voice in the back of her head needed reassurance.

He shrugged, his gaze moving over her face in a lazy caress. "Carrie's an okay dancer, but she doesn't work with me. I have to do all the work. You, on the other hand, move with me perfectly. Almost as well as you do in bed."

He said the last part in a husky whisper, moving so his cheek rest against her. As if to prove his point, he brought her body flush to his. A wave of desire pulsed through her, bringing her back to the steamy encounter behind the palm earlier. If it wouldn't earn them endless ribbing from their friends, she might suggest they sneak out early.

"Mmm. We do know how to hold a conversation with our bodies at least," she said, breathing in the eucalyptus and mint that clung to his tux, mixing with the underlying aroma of maleness and Rob.

"You really do look gorgeous tonight," he murmured in her ear before spinning her out and back in.

She smiled. She never got tired of hearing him say that. She never doubted for a minute that he meant it. "Careful. Someone might start getting suspicious if you keep looking at me like that."

"Does it matter?" he asked. She quickly looked up. The laughter was gone, and his gray eyes were suddenly serious for the first time all evening. "Would it be so bad if everyone knew?"

Her stomach dropped to her surprisingly

comfortable Jimmy Choos. She was not ready for everyone to know about them. Her chest tightened, and her insides rolled as she remembered how bad it'd been when the pictures came out. How much worse would it be now, especially since Rob had defended her both on TV and so publicly in front of other reporters in Paris? Besides, once everyone knew, they'd be under a microscope. That wasn't what she needed right now.

"I—" She stopped herself from spewing all her concerns at him. This was not the time or place, plus she was having problems breathing now at the thought of it all. "Can we talk about this later? I just want to enjoy the evening."

His face fell a little, but the gleam in his eye told her he wouldn't give up easily. "Okay."

The song ended, and he led her back to the table. Their friends grinned at them, and a flush crept up Em's face. "Shut up, all of you. Not a single word from the peanut gallery."

"But you're so cute together," Maren teased, keeping her voice low enough it couldn't be heard by anyone not at their table.

"Be glad you don't have a little sister," Rob muttered, unbuttoning his jacket before he took a drink of the scotch a waiter had brought him while they were gone. Another glass of rosé sat by Em's plate.

"I'll trade you one annoying little sister for an annoying slightly older brother," Em said, forcing a tight smile.

Owen narrowed his hazel eyes at her from across the table. "Hey. You like me, remember?"

"Most of the time. I seem to recall you getting me in trouble a time or twelve, and then there's the whole overprotective thing."

"I think I'll stick with the sister. She keeps the parents distracted better than Owen would." Rob winked at his sister.

Em let the conversation flow around her for a few minutes, hoping the knot in her stomach would ease the further she got from the question about going public with her relationship with Rob. When it became clear the knot was there to stay, she stood. Rob got to his feet as well, but she waved him away. "I need a little air. I'll be back in a few minutes."

She left before anyone could stop her, praying none of them followed her. The door to the veranda was near their table, so she slipped out, letting the humid night air wash over her. Despite the thickness of the air, she started to breathe easier without the sensation of hundreds of eyes on her.

"Ms. Grace."

Em jumped at the deep voice coming from the shadows of the veranda. She turned to see Robert Ashton Jr. standing off to one side, staring out at the ocean. She tried to remember the last time she'd seen the tennis legend in person. He'd been at one of her and Maren's Grand Slam semifinal matches a few years ago. Normally, Bobby Ashton didn't show up for his daughter's matches, so that appearance had been a shock to Em and threw her off her game. The last time the man said two words to her had been in London, when he told her she'd never be good enough for his son, for his family.

"Mr. Ashton. This is a lovely party. You and Mrs. Ashton have really outdone yourselves."

Bobby Ashton strolled farther into the light cast

from the French doors behind them. Seeing him was like seeing into Rob's future. As much as Rob detested his father, they shared more than a name.

Rob had inherited his father's height as well as his chiseled features and gold hair, although Bobby's had faded to silver in places. The only things he seemed to have gotten from his mother was his easy smile and his eyes.

"Thank you. Brigit's got a knack for these things. I just smile and tell her 'yes, dear.' It makes life easier." Bobby stopped beside Em.

She instinctively wrapped her arms around her middle, the knot returning full force. "That sounds like what my grandfather would say."

"I heard about his passing. I'm sorry for your loss." He shoved his hands in his pockets, not looking at her directly. "I must say, I'm pleased with the turnout this year. Everyone who's anyone in tennis showed up."

"It's quite a crowd. But we're all happy to show up for a good cause." Her hair stood on the back of her neck and up and down her arms. He was up to something. She didn't trust the man any farther than she could throw him.

"It does a father's heart good to see his children enjoying themselves. Rob looked like he was having a good time out there." He glanced over his shoulder, back into the crowded room. She followed his gaze, stopping when she saw what caught his attention. Rob was standing near the door, Carrie Webster at his side. The statuesque blonde leaned close, tossing her hair and laughing at something.

"They make a lovely couple, don't they?" Bobby turned back. "Corbin and I have always hoped that they'd end up together one day. So much talent in one match. They'd be quite the power couple, although not as much now that Rob's tennis career has ended."

Anger roiled inside Em. "Rob's talent didn't get damaged along with his shoulder. He's still the same man he was before his injury."

"True. But he's wasting himself working as a journalist for a glorified institution of yellow journalism. He could be doing something more worthwhile."

She bit her tongue. On some level, she actually agreed with the pompous asshole, which she hated. "Rob's an adult. He's made his choice about how he wants to spend his life."

"Fair point. My wife mentioned in passing that you and my son have been seeing each other for the last few months. Is this true?"

"Um. Yes." She hadn't known Rob had told his mother about them, but she didn't think he expected his mother to tell his father. If he knew, then why was he talking about Rob and Carrie Webster like that? "Well, kind of. It's…complicated."

"Really? Either you are or you aren't seeing each other. That does not seem very complicated." Bobby's voice dripped with the same condescension that he'd shown all those years ago.

She gritted her teeth. "We're together, but we're keeping things casual. Nothing too serious. I'm focused on my career right now." She wanted to believe her own words, but after that dance she didn't know that she could.

Bobby didn't seem to believe them either. "That's good to hear. You know when I saw the two of you dancing earlier, I thought it might be something more than casual. My wife certainly thinks so. She told me that she'd never seen our son so infatuated with a woman. I wouldn't be surprised if she started to pick out china patterns and designs for a nursery for grandchildren soon."

Grandchildren? Nausea hit her harder than the waves lapping at the beach not far from where they stood. She could barely take care of herself right now, let alone a husband or children. She and Rob hadn't ever talked about if they wanted children. Had Rob given his mother the impression that they were headed in that direction? God, she hoped not.

"We're not anywhere near that stage." She cleared her throat. "Rob's got his life and I've got mine, and we get together when we can. No need for china patterns or nurseries."

"Are you sure? I saw your match against Dera Calvet at Roland Garros. You seemed unfocused. Off your game. Usually when someone plays like that, it's because something off the court is distracting them."

"Did you play poorly when you and Brigit first got together?" she challenged. She really didn't like this man. How someone like him had children like Rob and Maren flabbergasted her. Then again, from what both of them had said about their childhoods, Bobby Ashton had been a supporting character rather than their main parental influence. He'd been too busy for them, not unlike her own father, following his career instead of being there for his family.

Bobby snorted. "Of course not. I knew how to keep my personal life off the court. I trained with some of the best, and my coaches would never accept anything less than my complete and total focus."

She shook her head. God, this man was an ass. He'd spent so long as the top dog he didn't remember what life was like before he was the great Bobby Ashton. She doubted he'd been so cool and collected when he and Brigit first met. She'd seen the stories about how in love the Ashtons were. She remembered as a teenager studying the tennis greats and wondering how Brigit could give up her career to follow Bobby around. Now, especially after attempting to have a long distance whatever it was with Rob, she saw that Brigit had made the decision to focus on her marriage and her relationship rather than her career. She'd been a good player, but never a great one, so she'd switched gears to be with the man she loved.

"Well, Zoe's one of the best, and even with everything going on, she's done a good job of keeping me focused," she said, even though she wasn't nearly as confident as she sounded.

"I suppose we'll have to wait and see. After all, there are only two Grand Slams left in the season." He plucked a flower from a nearby pot, twirling it in his fingers. "I'm honestly surprised you've done as well as you have given the circumstances. For someone of your background to make it as far as you have with so much media attention and outside stress is impressive. Unexpected, but impressive."

She curled her fingers into her hand, her nails digging into her palms. It was really hard not to punch Rob's father. On the surface, the words were complimentary, but she could read between the lines better than most to find the insults he was too polite to come right out and say. She was used to people like

Bobby after all these years, but it didn't make his words sting any less.

"It's probably wise of you and Rob to keep your relationship quiet," he continued. "I'm sure it would be problematic if he were to announce he was seeing you. I've heard a bit about the situation you're in. A stalker is nothing to be ashamed of, but I can imagine it would only complicate matters if you were to date someone publicly right now. And besides, when you end things, it will make life much simpler for you both."

When they ended things. Like it was a foregone conclusion. Em glanced back inside to see Rob still talking to Carrie, looking as at ease as he did talking to any other woman. The fears and worries she'd confessed to her grandmother came flooding back to her, but she couldn't let Bobby see them.

"Like I said, we're keeping things casual and quiet," she replied, the words hollow to her own ears.

He patted her shoulder as he turned toward the doors. "Smart girl. I should get back before Brigit has my hide. Lovely chatting with you."

She stood there, colder than she should be on an early June evening. Thoughts swirled around in her head, battering her heart and sending her deeper into the well of panic that had started during her dance with Rob. As much as she loathed him, Bobby Ashton had made some valid points. With Wimbledon only days away, she couldn't afford any distractions.

Telling the world about her and Rob wasn't even remotely an option, but for some reason that made her inexplicably sad. Dancing with him had been…nice. Being out in public with him still felt odd, like she was committing a crime in broad daylight. He obviously wanted to take that next step, and she wished that she could, but his father was right. Going public wouldn't only draw more media attention than she wanted; it would taunt her stalker and likely make him worse.

Em braced her hands on the stone balustrade of the veranda. What scared her most about the thought of agitating her stalker wasn't the idea that he would come after her. She'd accepted that as a possibility a long time ago. No, what now haunted her was that Rob could be in the line of fire too. The image of him getting hurt because of her made her want to curl up in a ball in the corner and sob.

Oh God.

She was falling in love with him.

She was falling in love with Rob Ashton.

Again.

Shit.

This wasn't supposed to happen. This was supposed to stay easy and casual and not remotely in the realm of something that would involve love. Love was what left her devastated last time. Love left her vulnerable to heartbreak. She knew Rob had said he wanted more, but she didn't trust that, especially not after her little chat with his father. At the end of the day, Rob was an Ashton, and he'd follow the Ashton party line.

She had to keep things between them the same as they were until she figured out what to do. And that would have to wait. She had to focus on Wimbledon. She wouldn't let Bobby Ashton be right. She was going to kick ass and win the tournament in spite of the mess that was her life, just to piss him off.

Chapter 15

Em stood in the corner of the refurbished warehouse, sipping a club soda and watching Amir work the room. Outside, London stretched around them, shrouded by gray clouds she hoped went away before Monday. Wimbledon was only two days away, and she really wanted perfect weather. She'd worked her ass off for the last few weeks, had another tournament win under her belt, and she was ready to take this Grand Slam.

At least she thought she was. The vague sense of confusion that'd settled on her during the Ashtons' charity gala still lingered, only fueled by the rumors swirling about Rob and Carrie—no doubt planted by his father. Her feelings for Rob and her indecision on what to do about them made it hard to concentrate, but she was determined. She'd told Zoe to push her harder than ever and not let up for a moment. Rob had tried to come visit her before she left for London, but she'd managed to put him off. Talking to him every night was one thing. She could keep her distance when she didn't have to see him and those blue eyes of his and that body that sent her libido down a dangerous path. It would be harder to keep him at arm's length here. She only hoped that the network kept him so busy he wouldn't have time to see too much of her until the end.

"You look nice tonight, Emerson," an accented

voice said in her ear.

She whirled around to see Kole standing close behind her. He looked good—his ice blue eyes were accentuated by the deep blue designer shirt that had obviously been tailored to fit him perfectly. The same could be said for his medium gray suit. Emotions hit her harder than a battering ram. So much had happened since they last talked. With distance, she remembered what she'd first seen in him, but she still hadn't forgiven him for what he did. It might be easier if she did, if she could still care for him instead of for Rob who came with so many complications and mountains of emotional baggage.

"Kole. Um. Thanks. You look nice too."

"I always liked you in blue." He took two flutes of champagne from a passing server. "Although you do seem a little bored."

She tugged on the top of her strapless sheath dress before accepting the champagne. "I hate these things, but Amir bullied me into coming."

"Yes, my publicist was insistent that I needed to put in an appearance as well." He turned and scanned the crowd. "There are quite a few sponsors here tonight. I'm surprised more players didn't choose to attend. Doesn't your brother usually keep you company during these things?"

She shrugged, trying to figure out what was going on. Why was Kole suddenly so chatty? He'd ignored her through most of the tournaments this year since their little talk in Melbourne. And she'd been more than okay with that. It was easier to keep her anger and hurt in check when he avoided her. She didn't understand why he decided to stop the avoidance now of all times.

"Owen had a late practice session, and he didn't want to rush through it. Dera's here somewhere. I think Maren Ashton was here earlier, but she managed to make her escape before her publicist noticed. Mine, on the other hand, has the senses of a blood hound and won't let me out of his sight for long enough to escape."

"I noticed you've added a security detail." He nodded to Lance, the black-suited man standing off to one side. "I thought you detested having a security detail. You certainly didn't like mine."

She'd hated his. They'd been overzealous at times, and then they hadn't kept the groupies back when they should. He'd also used them as an excuse for why he couldn't go with her to see her grandpa in the hospital or why he couldn't help with her charity work. Now that she had her own security detail, she was a little more sympathetic, but not much. After all, it was his fault she needed the security detail in the first place.

"Yes, well, after the pictures came out and the stalker popped up, I lost the battle and had to get a security team, at least for the tournaments." She tried to keep her tone light, but a blush stained Kole's knife-edged cheekbones as he took the full meaning of her words.

He cleared his throat, gulping down some of his champagne and nodding to one of the models brought in to add atmosphere to the party. "Ah. About the pictures—"

"You really don't have to say anything about them," she insisted. "I've spent more time than I ever wanted to talking about them."

"No, I—I want to say this, Emerson." He placed a

hand on her arm, keeping her from walking away. "I didn't release those pictures."

She sighed, pushing a loose strand of hair behind her ear. "I know. The police and Amir's PI figured that out a couple months ago."

"But you're still mad at me about them, I suppose."

"You suppose correctly." She took a drink of the champagne, wishing it were something stronger. Just then, her phone chimed. Hoping it was a text from her brother or Amir or anyone to get her out of here, she immediately looked at the screen. And froze.

Mmm. I'm loving all the airtime your friends at TWW are giving me. I'll be watching you this week. Maybe the lords and ladies of London can teach you to be a lady instead of a fucking whore.

"Emmy? Emerson, what's wrong?"

Someone removed the glass from her hand, and an arm went around her shoulder. She didn't know how, but she somehow ended up in a chair, with Kole sitting beside her.

"What's wrong?" he asked again.

Her hands shook as she stared at the phone. This was the first time he'd managed to find her phone number and text her. Fighting against the tremors, she took a screenshot and forwarded it to the head of her security team and Detective Connors. "It's…it's nothing," she said, trying to force her voice into some semblance of normal.

Kole tilted her phone to see what it said. "*Срање*. Emerson, who would send this to you? Who would dare call you a whore?"

She thought about lying to him, but the words came tumbling out before she could stop them. "I have a freaking stalker after me. They're so obsessed with you that they now hate me for cheating on you and being a 'slut' or a 'whore.' It changes in each message."

"What are you talking about? A stalker?" His brows furrowed, and he shifted closer.

She sniffed, searching the crowd for Dera or Cruz or anyone to come rescue her. She didn't want to get into this, now or ever, but she'd opened her damn mouth, and now she had to deal with it. She honestly didn't believe he didn't know about this already.

"Please, Kole. It was all over the papers during the French Open. Some nutter started sending me threatening letters thanks to those pictures and the stories you were spreading about me. And now he's apparently moved on to text messages."

An ache took up residence in her chest. She'd actually cared about Kole, and it still hurt to think about all the shit he'd said about her. She really had the worst luck with men. Between her father and Rob and Kole, it was a wonder she hadn't taken a card from Dera's book and started to try to find a woman to date.

"I—I didn't know, Emmy. I'm—sorry doesn't begin to cover it, does it?" He leaned back against the brick wall beside her as if his body couldn't hold him up any longer. "I didn't start those stories. It was—my publicist thought it would be a good idea to put it about that I broke up with you. That it would make me more sympathetic and human. I didn't want to do it, but Patty insisted. I didn't realize that it—fuck. I'm so sorry."

She looked at him, her eyes widening in surprise. He was sorry? The great Kole Naumov was sorry? She almost checked to make sure the sky wasn't falling or something. He hated to apologize even more than he hated to deal with anything resembling family.

She studied him, really looking at him for the first time in months. He looked older and more serious than she'd ever seen him. And as much as she hated to admit it, he did look sorry. She also thought she might believe him about the stories coming from his publicist. From the interviews she'd seen, including that one with Rob and Bruno, he hadn't done much to stop them, but it did make more sense for his publicist to be the mastermind.

Kole never cared that he was seen as kind of an asshole, but his publicist was always going on about how to make him more likable. She was exactly the type of shark to come up with the "ex-girlfriend is a slut" line. It was unimaginative and totally below the belt.

"I believe you. I think. I don't know. This is all so weird," she admitted.

"I know. And I truly am sorry. This isn't how I wanted things to play out with us." His lips tilted up in a ghost of a smile. "Guess I have a lot to learn before I can keep a woman like you for long."

She stood and moved to lean beside him, a small, weary smile of her own coming to life. "You can be a really sweet guy when you want. You have the capacity for more emotions than you give yourself credit for. You…need to learn to let people in. And not be so paranoid about family stuff."

"You have a point. But your grandparents are a little intimidating. Well, not your grandfather so much. He was a kind man. Your grandmother is a different story. She scares me."

She giggled. "Gran can be a little scary, especially if you decide it's a good idea to use her cheese grater to play tennis with the garlic. Owen and I learned that the hard way when we were in junior high."

A tap on her shoulder drew her attention away from her ex.

"Ms. Grace. Mr. Hodgkins contacted me. He feels we should get you back to your lodgings for the night while he examines the information you sent him," Lance said, the bodyguard's frame rigid, his eyes scanning the crowd.

"I think that would be best." She gave Kole a tight smile. "Good luck this week. I mean, I hope my brother kicks your ass, but good luck until you get there."

Outside, Em gratefully sank into the car, relieved not to have to schmooze the sponsors anymore. All she wanted to do was go back to the flat she'd rented and take a long hot bath. She briefly thought of asking Rob to meet her there, but she pushed that aside. As much as he relaxed her, she couldn't let herself rely on him. She needed to survive the next two weeks and win the whole tournament, then she could worry about Rob.

****

Rob gritted his teeth as he sat at his temporary desk, glaring at the pictures on one of the tennis blogs he was checking out before his next broadcast. Em stood beside Kole Naumov, who was turned toward her, a solicitous expression on his chiseled face. From this angle, it almost looked like he might be thinking about kissing her. But Em's face was what caught Rob's attention. She was actually giggling about something that Kole said.

An inexplicable jealousy surged over Rob. Again. He'd seen different angles of this same shot since the tournament began eleven days ago, but more pictures had trickled in of Em and Kole stopping to chat outside the locker room or shots taken from other players' Instagrams of Kole and Em talking in the lounge.

He'd tried to find Em to ask her about it, but she hadn't answered his calls, or she told him she was too busy to meet up at her flat or his hotel room. If he hadn't been run off his feet from dawn until dusk every day, keeping up with Joey's demands and the stories Bruno thought were beneath him, he might have had a chance to go see her. He didn't understand what she was doing even talking to that asshole. Kole was the reason she was in all this mess to begin with. The guy had treated her like shit, and she was standing there giggling with him?

On an intellectual level, he understood that it was a social function, and she couldn't exactly kick the guy in the balls, but did she have to look so happy to be talking to him?

All of it wouldn't have mattered if the stupid blogs weren't jumping from zero to sixty with the story. All of a sudden, Em and Kole were reconciling. One stupid site even tried to claim that Em and Kole were planning to elope to Paris after the finals. Rob's temper had been on a low boil ever since that one came out. It wouldn't be if his fucking girlfriend—because that was what she was, even if she didn't want to admit it—would let him go public with their relationship. But she'd refused, and now he was stuck, sitting here brooding because he couldn't approach her about it in public and he couldn't get her to pick up her phone.

Sighing, he pulled on the summer-weight light-gray suit jacket his wardrobe stylist had laid out for him to wear today. He was expected to do the pre-game interviews with the women's finalists before watching the game.

As he walked toward Centre Court to take his place, Rob's phone rang.

"You watching the match today?" Owen asked by way of greeting.

"Of course." Rob wove his way through the crowds moving toward Henman Hill. "Your sister might be avoiding me like I've got the plague or something, but I wouldn't miss it. I mean, I'll have to work before and after, but I wouldn't miss it."

An awkward silence echoed through the phone. "I'm sure she's not avoiding you, man. This tournament has been insane. Between the rain delays and all the promo stuff Amir's scheduled to keep her sponsors interested, she's been crazy busy."

"Is she doing okay? I've been"—*jealous, pissed, annoyed*—"worried. She still got her security with her?"

"Yeah, they're still around as much as she hates it." Owen coughed. "Good news is, the stalker seems to have gone away for now."

Rob paused, ignoring the crowd jostling him, his mind flitting back to those damn pictures. "Really?"

"So far, aside from a text right before the first day, she hasn't heard anything the whole tournament. It's made a difference."

"I'm proud as hell of her for making it this far. She's been damned near flawless," Rob agreed, picking up his pace. He had to be ready to start the first interview in ten minutes.

"Not even a single set dropped, let alone going to a tie-break," Owen bragged. "Just wish she wasn't going up against Chessa. Chessa's her kryptonite, man."

Rob opened the door to the Centre Court players' area and flashed his press pass to the security guard. "No joke. Don't worry. Em's got this."

Ending the call, Rob nodded to his cameraman. "Hey Jerry. If we're set, I'm going to go check on the players and see what our ETA is."

By players, he meant Em. He made his way back to the locker room reserved for the top female players. Before he could knock, the door flew open, and Em emerged.

For once, she didn't have a crowd of people around her. Zoe must already be up in Em's box with Owen.

"Rob! What are you doing?" She glanced around nervously.

"Just came to check on you." He took her in, his whole body standing at attention now that she was finally in front of him. God, he'd missed her. It took every ounce of his self-control not to sweep her in for a kiss.

She shifted her equipment bag higher on her shoulder. "Oh. Um, well, I'm fine as you can see."

"Yeah. Nice to actually see you in person. You've been avoiding me, Em." He leaned against the doorway, blocking her path. "Wouldn't have anything to do with those pictures of you and Kole, right?"

Brown eyes narrowed at him. "Is this really the time? Chessa will be out any minute, and you're supposed to be interviewing me on live TV in two minutes."

No denial. Huh. His stomach clenched, but he pushed it down. For now. "You're right. We'll talk after the match, though, yeah? I…I need to see you, Em. I've been worried."

Her gaze flickered away. "Okay. We can talk later. Right now, I have a title to win."

He made it through both Em and Chessa's interviews with minimal effort before he slipped out to his seat in the back row of one of the lower sections. His stomach churned and roiled worse than the River Thames during a storm. He wished it was only nerves for Em. By the third set, he was a fucking mess. He was tempted to slip back to the studio early—he had to be there as soon as the match ended, but he couldn't take his eyes off her. She wanted this so badly, and she wasn't going to give up without a fight.

Through it all, he kept straying back to the way her little white tennis dress made her almost glow in the unseasonably warm sun, the dark coppery tone of her skin richer as the sweat glistened off it.

The look on her face right now told the whole story; her eyes narrowed, her jaw set, she resembled a warrior queen, ready to fight to the death. He'd never seen someone so determined to win a Grand Slam. He remembered that drive, that intense focus, and he missed the hell out of it. Em took her service game easily, but Chessa wasn't backing down. The Croatian woman was a machine. She'd taken out her first four opponents without losing more than five games a match.

This match was a battle of the gladiators, each woman playing full-tilt, neither giving the other quarter.

"I don't think I can watch," Cruz muttered from his seat beside Rob.

Rob sent him a sidelong glance. "You can't watch? How do you think I feel?"

"Feels like everyone's here. Even the royals sent some delegates," Cruz said, nodding to the royal box where senior members of the Windsor clan sat.

Chessa went on serve after Em took the first game of the set. Rob winced as the Croatian aced her first serve and sent her second serve at a fierce angle that was almost impossible for Em to hit effectively. Em's frustration radiated off her. Sweat glistened on her brow, and her shoulders sagged a little. Chessa was getting in her head.

Rob's eyes never left Em as the final set continued. She matched Chessa game for game until the eighth game, then something happened. Chessa broke Em's serve, and she lost steam. By the time Chessa served for match point, Rob's heart ached for Em. She'd been so close. She'd fought for every inch of ground, but it hadn't been quite enough to beat the world number one.

Around him, the crowd cheered as Chessa secured her victory, but Rob's attention remained on the curvy figure of one person. Fuck. He wanted to go to her, to hold her and make that crestfallen look go away. The jealousy, the confusion, all of it faded in the face of Em experiencing the hardest loss of all—the almost win. Rob's shoulder ached as a not-so-subtle reminder of his last almost win, the one that had ended his career.

While the officials prepared for the awards ceremony, Rob slipped back to the studio, a mess of emotions swamping him. He wanted to be with his girl, not having to clinically break apart her lost title on international TV.

The second he stepped into the studio, Rob was bombarded.

"Don't pull your punches," Joey snapped as she

bustled around the studio. "I don't want any white knight antics today, Ashton. Bruno's going for the throat, and I don't plan to hold him back."

"What's that supposed to mean?" Rob asked, pinning his microphone in place and letting one of the makeup techs powder his face.

Bruno smirked. "I've warned Joey that you've got a soft spot for a certain player, and she's not having it. The best player won today—the worthy player. Emerson Grace is too busy spreading her legs for any man she can for her to actually win a Grand Slam."

Rob's hand curled into a fist, and that was only the first time he wanted to punch Bruno during the broadcast. Every chance he got, Bruno alluded to, hinted at, and even expressly blamed Em's recent "poor personal decisions" and her "sudden reunion" with Kole to her loss. Rob and Christiane both attempted to steer the conversation back to the mechanics of the match, the statistics and the calls that could have changed the course of the match, but Bruno's ability to pivot was both impressive and sickening.

By the time the broadcast was over, Rob could barely sit still. He wanted to completely go off on all of them, to tell them how sleazy they were for going along with Bruno's plan. Despair and anger warred for supremacy. He'd thought he could change things from the inside, but every day it was becoming clear that he was fighting a losing battle. He couldn't deal with this now, though. He had bigger things to worry about.

He made it back to the City Centre as the local church bells struck ten p.m. He'd texted Owen to ensure that Em was in for the night. The Grace siblings were sharing a townhouse in Knightsbridge during the tournament. Thankfully, Owen had plans to attend a party at the request of his publicist, so Rob and Em would have the place to themselves.

Glancing around, Rob knocked on the front door. Thankfully, the cobblestone street was quiet and deserted. At least he thought it was. There was a movement in the shadowed doorway across the street, but after a moment, a stray cat darted into the pool of light coming from the street lamp. Good. He didn't need to worry about Em freaking out or giving her an excuse not to let him in. When she didn't immediately answer, he knocked again. And again. Finally, he heard slow footsteps coming down the stairs. A moment later, the door opened.

Em stood on the other side, the opposite of the woman he'd watched earlier today. Gone was the fierce warrior in tight tennis whites. In her place stood a woman with sad, angry eyes, slumped shoulders covered by an oversized black sweater and dark-gray leggings encasing long, powerful legs. With her face free of makeup and her dark hair, still damp from her shower, falling around her face in waves, she resembled the girl he'd first met in London, young and lost.

"Jesus. What are you doing here?" she asked, her voice hollow and flat, but he didn't miss the underlying tension crackling between them.

"Oh, just out for a stroll." He pushed his way in, shutting the door behind him. "I thought you could use some company, and I'm done letting you avoid me."

She looked away, crossing her arms over her chest. "You thought wrong. I don't need company, and I haven't been avoiding you. I've been busy, and I'm tired. I'd like to be alone. You more than anyone should understand that."

"You're right. I've been where you are, but I know you don't want to be alone, not really." He moved past her, climbing the narrow stairway to the main floor of the converted mews. A cozy room dominated the first floor with its rough-hewn wood floors and overstuffed furniture. Exactly like he'd expected an English apartment to look.

She followed him up, her bare feet stomping on the stairs. "Where do you get off, pretending to know what I want?"

"Oh, I'm not pretending any such thing," he snapped, shrugging out of his suit jacket. "I don't know what the hell is going on with you, Em, but you can't keep shutting me out."

He wouldn't let her do that. He'd worked too damn hard to get here with her now. The rest of his plans for his life post-tennis were going up in smoke around him, but he wasn't giving Em up without a fight. She mattered more than all the rest of it combined. He just needed to convince her of that.

Chapter 16

You can't keep shutting me out.

Direct hit. Rob didn't miss a trick. She'd been avoiding him since the gala. It seemed her luck had run out on that score now. He was here, and he wasn't going to let her out of this, damn him.

She'd spent the last few hours in a daze of total disbelief. She'd felt it. She had that match. She was finally going to hoist that Grand Slam trophy over her head. And then it'd slipped through her fingers—again.

She'd searched her mind for the exact moment the match went against her. Maybe it was in the first set when she lost the tie break. Maybe it was in the third set when Chessa broke her serve for the first time. But all she kept coming back to was that moment before the pre-match interview when Rob found her. He'd brought up the pictures of her and Kole that had plagued her through the whole tournament, and she'd just…frozen.

"What do you want, Rob?" She curled up in the corner of the sofa. "Do you want to offer me words of comfort? To tell me that I played my best and I'll have another chance? Well, save it. I'm not interested."

Gray eyes remained fixed on her, steady and storming. In his rumpled shirt and gray suit, with his tie pulled loose, he looked like a business man recently arrived home from a long day at the office. Handsome and worn, but also glad to be with the woman waiting for him. Only she hadn't been waiting for him. He'd shown up to make her confront the emotions she'd desperately hoped she could ignore.

"If I thought it would work, Em, I would spend tonight pampering you. I'd get your favorite wine and desserts, maybe some of those peonies I know you love, and I'd make sure you understood that you're important to me because of who you are, not because of any titles you've won."

He started to prowl the room, his long, lean body tense and alert. She'd never seen him so agitated before, not even after going three rounds with Bruno. She wished she could believe what he said. It would be so easy to let him comfort her and tell her that the titles didn't matter. But they did to her.

"Then why are you here?" she demanded.

"Where do I start?" he mused, bracing his hands on the back of the chair opposite her. "How about with why you've been avoiding me? With why you don't want to talk about those pictures of you and Kole? You both looked pretty cozy at that party."

Her temper flared and snapped at her, cracking through the air between them. "God, Rob. I think those cretins you work with are getting to your head. Kole and I talked for maybe ten minutes at most. He was…he apologized. For everything. We were polite to each other. But of course, the world sees me as a sex maniac, so it was automatically something more than just a conversation. How could you think I would do that? I'm not the type to cheat on my—on someone I'm seeing."

"On your boyfriend?" he challenged. "Is that what you were going to say? Because that's what I am, Em.

Whether you want to admit it or not, I'm your boyfriend."

She shook her head. "We talked about this, Rob. You aren't my boyfriend. That implies so much. I don't have room in my life for a boyfriend."

"What are you so afraid of? Why won't you accept us already? Everyone else has. Your brother, my sister, my mom, our friends. Even your grandma. They all know what you're too scared to admit. That we belong together." He resumed his pacing.

Panic clawed at her throat, her mind flitting back to what her grandmother had said. *Love isn't a complication. It's the solution.* Except that it wasn't. Because loving someone had never done anything good for Em. All it had done was hurt her and cost her what she'd worked so hard to achieve. Gran thought that Rob wasn't a distraction, but she was so, so wrong. He was the reason she'd lost her focus today. After a nearly perfect tournament, the day she talked to Rob was the day she went off track. She couldn't do this anymore. The years of pain and anger and rejection swelled inside of her until she was surging to her feet, the two of them circling each other like combatants in a boxing ring, ready for someone to take the first swing.

"We belong together? We belong together?" She kept her tone cool, her expression neutral while inside she seethed. "Now, after all this time, you think we are supposed to be together. It's convenient for you now, so it's okay for us to be together, is that it?"

His body shifted, watching her like he would an opponent on serve. Suspicious but ready. "We were always meant to be together, Em. I knew that the first day I saw you. I was the one who had to convince you

253

to go on a date with me, remember?"

Of course she remembered, damn him. She remembered everything. "I remember overhearing my supposed boyfriend's father telling him I was trash. A slutty opportunist who only wanted to use him. We belonged together so much that my boyfriend used my heart for serving practice by breaking up with me after I lost the Olympics because of his father's opinion, only to come back seven years later, suddenly ready to commit."

He froze, his face a mask of regret. "Em, I never wanted to hurt you. I—we were barely older than kids. We both had our whole careers in front of us. Being tied down at that point, we would have come to resent each other. At least that's what I told myself at the time. And damn it, you agreed with me."

On some level, he was right. They would have resented each other. She'd seen that a month or so later, once the choking pain had faded to a dull ache covered by simmering anger.

"Of course I did. What else was I supposed to do? God, I thought I was in love with you, and then you didn't say a single word to defend me against your dad. Would things be any different now?" She braced her hands on her hips to keep him from seeing how badly she was shaking. "It would be worse, Rob. Especially for me. The media attention from those fucking pictures would be nothing compared to what would happen if it came out that I was dating the man who so publicly defended me. I would be called every name in the book and then some."

He shook his head. "You wouldn't be. If we played the story right, no one would dare say anything bad about you. I would protect you, Em. I love you. Why won't you believe that?"

A thousand answers came to her lips, but she held all of them back, save one. "Because the last time I believed that, I had my heart crushed. I've lost too many people I care about to buy that love will magically fix everything. Every man who's ever mattered to me has abandoned me in one way or another except for my brother. Even my grandpa died when I needed him the most. And no matter what you say, you're no better than my dad or Kole. How can you honestly expect me to get past everything?"

His shoulders slumped as he stopped behind the couch, staring at her. "Is that what you really think? That I'm like Kole? Like your dad? I would never treat you the way they have. If you'd let me, I would spend every single day of our lives showing you that you are the most important person in the world, because to me you are. Even when I was trying to forget you, you were everything to me. Everything. When I was stuck spending months at home recovering, all I could think about was that I was the biggest idiot in the world not to show up at the airport that day. If you'll let me, I will be your partner, Em. I will be there for you, no matter what. Given the chance, I'd never leave your side again. What do I have to do to convince you of that?"

She turned her back on him, unable to bear the hurt and betrayal in his eyes. She wanted to believe him. Every ounce of her screamed at her to jump him and tell him she wanted that partnership, that she wanted him with her and had since she was twenty. But that was the easy way out. Ever since he came back into her life, she'd lost control of everything, but more importantly she'd lost her focus. Without him, without worrying about what would happen if someone found out about him, without worrying that he might decide to leave her—again—she could focus on her tennis again.

It was time to give him back, to get him out of her life before he did more damage. In her heart, she'd known it was time the moment the crowd roared and Chessa's arms shot into the air in victory. It'd taken every ounce of self-control for her not to vomit right there on Centre Court as the Duke of Kent handed Chessa the winner's trophy. The overwhelming sense of loss and pain had been unbearable, and all she'd wanted to do was scream in frustration. Her dream had been tantalizingly close, and she'd let it slip away again. All through the press conference and the painful meal with her brother and Zoe, her only thoughts had been that it was her fault she lost and that she had to give up the one thing keeping her from devoting one-thousand percent of her energy into achieving her goal.

"There's nothing you can do, Rob. We…we're too broken to ever work as a real couple. There's too much that's passed between us." Tears stung her eyes, but she brushed them off, fighting for control.

Before the pictures, before that plane ride, she'd been in control. Grieving for the loss of her grandpa, but in control. In spite of her knee injury, she'd trained her ass off during the off-season, and she was ready to win her first Grand Slam.

Then the distractions came in. The pictures might have started the spiral, but it was Rob who amped it up to another level. When she was with him, it was hard to focus on anything but how he affected her. He made her think of a life beyond tennis, a life she might have had if she'd chosen the more conventional career path her father always harped on and on about. In the quiet moments, ideas would seep into her brain, ideas about sharing a life with a man—this man. She beat them back mercilessly, reliving those awful hours waiting and watching for him to show up for the plane ride they'd never taken. Even with all of that, the ideas refused to let go—and that scared the hell out of her.

Since the first time she'd met Zoe and heard her tales of winning Grand Slams, it was all Em wanted, and Papa Vic had joined her in those dreams. Over the years, it had evolved from a simple desire to win, to a desire to prove herself. To her grandparents, to her father, to the world. To the men like Bobby Ashton who said she wasn't good enough because of her background, because she didn't fit the mold.

And she couldn't do that with Rob in her life. That had been clear enough today. This time, she was the one who had to pick her career over the person she could love.

She'd come too far, put her family through too much—especially this year—to go back now. She needed to turn all her attention toward Flushing Meadows and the US Open. She didn't have room for anything more—she couldn't allow herself to have room for anything more.

"What are you saying, Em?" His body was eerily still, the full power of his gaze on her, the waves of denial rolling off him. "Look me in the eye and tell me what you want."

Taking a shuddering breath and brushing away the stray tears that escaped against her will, she turned and looked him in the eyes. The pain there almost brought her to her knees, but she forced herself to remain strong. "I'm saying I'm choosing my career over you. I want you to leave. Now. I want you to let me get on with my life. I can't risk being hurt again, and I can't afford any more distractions."

He stared at her, his jaw clenched and his body tense. "You're sure? This is what you want? Because the Emerson Grace I knew was brave. She wouldn't hide or back down in the face of fear."

She answered him with a bitter laugh. "I'm older and wiser. I have to protect myself, Rob. And I'm dead sure I want you to leave. So, please. Just go."

And he did. Without a word, Rob turned and left. Each echoing footstep on the old stairs made her want to call to him, to tell him to come back, but she didn't give in. Her attention had to remain on the US Open. Winning there was the only way this whole ordeal would be worth it.

Chapter 17

Every inch of his body ached. That's all Rob could think as he trudged into the TWW offices three days after the end of Wimbledon. The only other time he'd felt so shitty was when he destroyed his shoulder. That's what it was like; like losing the function of an entire limb. Except this time, it was his heart.

He'd gone over to her flat, expecting them to have a rational discussion, and suddenly they'd broken up. If he could call it that. She'd kicked him out, and he'd been too stunned to fight back. He'd tried to call her, tried to get Owen to tell him what he knew, but nothing worked. Owen refused to get in the middle of it, and Em refused to take his calls.

So here he was, trying to get to work and pretend like his heart hadn't been completely shattered just when he thought he might stand a chance to win a permanent place in her heart. He'd thought about going down to Miami to try to talk to her in person, but Owen and Maren pointed out that Em needed time to get her head on straight, that she needed space.

Space.

God, what a loaded word. He wished he could have some space. Instead, he had to go back to work and deal with whatever new crap Bruno threw at him. He'd been numb enough during the men's finals broadcast that he hadn't cared that Bruno looked unusually smug or that

Naumov beat Cruz—again.

Over the last twenty-four hours, it'd all started to hit him. Em was gone. He'd started to make their usual pre-bedtime phone call last night, and he'd stopped himself because she wouldn't answer.

Now he had to deal with reality. He had to face the fact that he was back to square one. He had no tennis career and no Em. All he had was his job as an on-air sports reporter at an unrepentantly sleazy network.

Fuck.

"Ah. Ashton. Just the man I was looking for."

Bruno's voice had Rob's skin crawling as he stopped in the door of his office. The last thing he wanted to do right now was deal with more of Bruno's bullshit.

"What do you want?" he asked, shoving his leather bag higher up on his good shoulder.

Bruno crossed his arms over his massive chest, a sneering grin on his face. "I've got a story for the morning sports news, and I wanted to know if you'd like to comment before we go on air."

"What are you talking about?" Rob massaged his temples, wishing the ibuprofen he'd taken on the ride here would start working.

"I wanted to know if we could get a comment on the story about how you were seen in intimate situations with Emerson Grace in the last few months."

Blood roared in Rob's ears, and the pain went from a dull ache to damn near blinding. Bruno had to be playing him. Trying to catch him out or something. They'd been careful. The only people who knew about his relationship with Em—his former relationship with Em—were his friends and family, and none of them would dare say anything to an asshole like Bruno. "What the hell? Is it April Fool's Day?"

"The innocent act won't work, Ashton. I've got pictures to prove it." Bruno pulled his phone out of the pocket of his ugly green suit.

He held up the oversized phone, scrolling through a set of pictures, and Rob's stomach dropped.

The bastard wasn't bluffing. Damn it. He knew exactly when these were taken. The first five were from his parents' gala, some of them were from when he'd cornered Em behind the palm tree, and others were from this weekend. There was one of him and Em at the door of her townhouse.

Rob tried to grab the phone to throw it across the room, but Bruno held it out of his reach. For a minute, he considered punching the guy, but he had a feeling that would only make things worse.

"Ah, ah, ah, Rob. You wouldn't want to compromise an important part of my research, now would you? This is going to put our ratings through the roof."

"You sick jackass. What did you do, have me followed?" Rob shoved his hands through his hair. "You think the network is going to let you run a story like that?"

Bruno sniffed. "Maybe. It's not like I had time to dig up dirt on the Golden Boy myself. I needed to find out if you had a weakness. Turns out you do."

Rage seared through Rob's blood stream. Bruno was about to blow the lid off his relationship with Em after months of them sneaking around—and the relationship no longer existed. As much as he hated Bruno's snooping for what it would mean for Rob's position at the network, he hated it more for what it would do to Em and her feelings toward him. He hated the pictures of her and Kole from that damn party, but they'd kept the stalker quiet for a while, according to Owen. This story would send the sicko through the roof.

"You can't air this story, Bruno. Emerson's still dealing with a stalker. This story will only provoke him. It could be dangerous," Rob said.

Bruno pursed his lips. "Hmm. The theoretical reaction of a stalker or a story that will ensure you never get my job? Such a tough decision."

Rob itched to tear him limb from limb. He was sick and tired of blindly ambitious men. His father, Bruno, Kole—they were all cut from the same cloth. They only saw things from the angle of how they would be affected; they never thought about the effect their choices would have on the rest of the world. If it weren't for men like them, he might have a completely different life. He and Em might be married, and they might even have a kid or two. A girl with her mother's dark hair and his eyes or a boy with his spirit and Em's eyes he could teach to play tennis like his grandpa had taught him.

He ached at that thought. He wanted that life more than anything, and now he'd probably never have it.

"I don't give a rat's ass about your job, Bruno. I care about the fact that Emerson's life could be in jeopardy if you do this." He pushed past Bruno and headed down the hall, frantically looking in the open doors.

"What are you doing?" Bruno asked, hot on his heels.

Rob stopped, his mind racing. "I'm trying to find Joey or Peter or anyone with the authority to shut this down."

"You'll find them in the conference room. Probably discussing if they have grounds to fire you," Bruno sneered.

The conference room. Rob jogged through the halls, checking the time on his phone. He had less than fifteen minutes before the morning news went on the air.

Sure enough, he found the executive producers gathered in one of the smaller conference rooms, grim expressions on their faces. They glanced up when he entered.

"Mr. Ashton. We were about to send for you. Won't you sit down?" Peter Townsend, one of the network's top producers, said, gesturing to one of the leather chairs.

"No. I won't sit down. Are you really going to let Bruno run this story?" Rob demanded.

Joey raised an eyebrow. "In case you've forgotten, this is a news network. Last I checked, one of the top female tennis players having an affair with a reporter—even one of our reporters—is news. News we should be the ones to break rather than another network."

"It's not news. It's tabloid gossip. More importantly, it's stupid to run the story. You remember the story about her stalker? You think this is going to help that situation any?" Rob braced his hands on the back of the chair. "Do what you want to me. I don't care. But you cannot run this story."

"Are you the news director now?" Bruno scoffed. "It's their choice if we air this story. Do you know how much of a rating's boost we could get out of this? It might even surpass when those sexy pictures of your girlfriend came out."

Bruno wanted him to lash out, but Rob settled for rolling his eyes. "Do you know how bad this story will make the network look? Turning on one of its own employees? Not knowing about the relationship in the first place?"

"Whose fault is that?" Joey slammed a hand on the table, eyes blazing. "How could you be so stupid, Rob? Getting involved with one of the players?"

"I don't see how my, or Emerson's, or Dera's or Cruz's or any other public figure's personal life is anyone's business but their own. Why should it matter to you who I'm dating? Would you care if she were a high school tennis coach?"

Joey rubbed her forehead. "Of course it wouldn't. At least not to the same degree. But come on, Rob. This isn't new to you. Your parents dealt with this for your whole life. Your personal life has always been tabloid fodder. So has Emerson's. Look what happened after the Naumov photos broke. She's big news. Both of you together are huge news."

"That doesn't mean you should run this story. Why should this network continue to be on the level of tabloids and gossip blogs? We should be better than that. Set a better example for our contemporaries. Maybe then the top athletes wouldn't avoid us like the plague."

"Please. If this story were about anyone else, you wouldn't give a damn," Bruno said. "This conversation is ridiculous. The news director already approved it to air. All I wanted was a comment from you."

Rob struggled to breathe. He wanted to scream or punch something or kick a hole in the wall. The train was barreling toward the cliff, and there was nothing he could do to stop it. Only one thing came to his mind.

"Here's my comment. If you run this story, I quit." He straightened.

Peter's eyes narrowed, and he leaned forward in his chair. "Be careful, Ashton. You don't want to say something in the heat of the moment you'll regret later."

"I am being careful," Rob said. "If you want to air invasive stories that have the potential to cause serious harm to someone, then I don't want to be a part of it. And before you try to spin this, even if Emerson weren't someone I care about, I would still take this stance given the stalker. Never mind the fact that this story is no one's business but mine and Ms. Grace's."

Tension crackled in the air, reminding Rob of a tennis match before the first serve was made. The moment where the outcome was uncertain, where two combatants faced off to see who would have the upper hand. Rob waited, hoping Peter and Joey would take the chance to rein in Bruno before he took things down a path Rob didn't want to travel.

"I'm sorry, Rob. We can't pass this up. Our numbers need the boost, or the execs are going to start beating the war drums. If they were to find out we had this story but let someone else break it—especially after almost losing the exclusive on the stalker news—we'd be out on our ears and blackballed," Joey said. "Bruno, you need to get to the studio. You won't mention any of this in the broadcast. Say that Rob refused to comment."

The big man left without a word, but the cloud of smugness he left behind choked Rob.

He glared at the people seated at the table. "You do realize what you've done, don't you? No tennis player is going to trust this network. It's not just me or Emerson. It'll be everyone. They already hate Bruno. Running this story, where he violated my and Emerson's privacy, simply cemented it. If something happens to Em because of this story? You'll never get an exclusive with any of the top players again."

"Is that a threat?" Joey challenged.

"No. Consider this my exit interview," Rob said, struggling to keep his tone level. "Free advice if you will. Bruno's just alienated a lot of important people, and your tennis coverage is going to suffer because of it. It's simply a fact. Now, if you'll excuse me, I'm going to go pack up my things and be on my way."

Rob stormed out of the conference room, temper blazing. He was back in his office before his brain caught up to him. Tossing his belongings into a box, he dug out his phone and pushed the first number he came to.

"Oh, it's me." He grabbed a picture of him and Maren, setting it in the box. "We've got a problem."

By the time he finished the story, Owen's voice echoed through the room, cursing up a blue streak. "Fucking hell. This isn't good."

"Understatement of the decade." Rob collapsed in his desk chair. "You need to sound the alarm. Let the detective know, let Em know, and more importantly, you need to let the security firm know. The vultures are going to swarm, and no matter what Em says, you need to have them at the house."

Owen groaned. "Right. Shit. Thanks for the heads-up, man. You didn't have to."

"Yes, I did. She matters. So much," Rob said.

"I know." Owen ended the call, leaving a lot unsaid, but Rob could sense what his friend was thinking.

His heart clenched. He didn't want to think about what this meant for his chances with Em. He couldn't begin to think that they were over for good. He'd waited so long, but after today, he could feel everything he'd hoped for slipping away from him in a way he hadn't felt, even when Em kicked him out of her flat in London.

****

Em sat on her couch, staring at the TV screen, shell-shocked. She hadn't believed it when Owen called three days ago to tell her that Bruno had snuck around and found out about her and Rob. The media frenzy had been almost immediate. It came at her from all sides. There was still a flock of photographers camped outside her house, and more were staking out the practice courts.

All she wanted to do was hide from the world. She'd ended things with Rob so she could focus and eliminate the risk of discovery—to avoid this exact situation. Now she didn't have him, and she was alone in the storm. Her grandma and Owen tried to make things easier where they could; her grandparents had even offered to let her come and stay with them, but she refused. This was her own mess, and she couldn't bear the thought of them being caught up in another public scandal that was caused by her. She'd have to ride this one out on her own.

A knock echoed through the empty house, and Em's phone started to vibrate. Dera's face smiled up at her from the display, and she immediately answered.

"Hey, Dera."

"Open the door, cherie, before these vultures pick my bones clean," Dera said cheerfully.

Em got to her feet. "What? What are you doing here?"

"Open the door, and I'll tell you."

Jogging to the door, she opened it cautiously. To her surprise, the reporters were standing on the curb, and Dera was alone on her porch. She tugged her friend into the house before throwing her arms around the taller French woman. Dera's arms closed around her immediately, the bag dangling from her hands hitting Em's back softly.

"I can't believe you're here. You should be at home practicing." Em gave her friend a final squeeze before pulling back.

"I was here for an event with my charity, and I couldn't leave you on your own. And I brought vodka to help keep us company."

Em's eyes teared up a little. She hadn't expected to see anyone tonight, let alone have her best friend show up with exactly what she needed—a lot of alcohol. "You shouldn't have."

"Cherie, I should have been here two days ago. I can't believe this is happening." Dera led the way into the living room, pulling two bottles of vodka out of the bag and setting them on the coffee table.

"It's…a nightmare. I thought I was through with all of this. Now it's ten times worse." Em collapsed on the couch, letting her legging-clad limbs flop onto the footstool she'd pulled up to the couch.

Dera snorted. "I can't believe the audacity of that bastard Bruno. It takes a lot of balls to dig into someone's life that way, especially when that someone is your colleague."

"This was exactly what I was afraid of, D. I didn't want to get into this—this thing with Rob, because I didn't want this to happen." She grabbed the vodka closest to her and opened it, then took a swig straight from the bottle.

Dera went to the kitchen and came back with two large glasses. She took the bottle from Em and poured until the tumblers were half full. "It's called a relationship, darling. I realize you didn't want to think of it that way, but it was. You need to accept that."

"Relationship, affair, whatever you want to call it, it shouldn't have happened." She bolted down some more vodka, enjoying the sting of the alcohol as it slid down her throat to fill the hollows inside of her.

Dera studied her, gold-brown eyes serious as she sipped her own drink. "Before you broke up with him, I thought Rob might be the best thing to come out of the last year."

Sniffing, Em burrowed deeper into the sofa. She'd thought the same thing, so many times over the last few months. As scared as she'd been that someone would discover them, she'd been content, even happy with Rob. All the fire and passion, mingled with the cozy familiarity, the sense of rightness that came any time they were together. Now it tore at her heart to think of it.

"God. It's been a seriously sucky year, hasn't it?" Em slugged back more vodka, staring at the muted TV.

Thankfully, they'd moved on from her and Rob, and they were talking about pre-season football training or something. She couldn't tell.

"*Oui*, I suppose. Your grandmother's illness was a terrible blow, to be sure, especially after your Papa Vic." Dera made a very French gesture, stretching her long legs out, her short shorts riding up. "That nonsense with Kole—abysmally unfortunate. I still want to wring his neck every time I see him."

Em shook her head, sipping her vodka. "He's apologized for the photos, and I've forgiven him. Mostly. Okay, not really, but I'm on my way toward forgiveness. As shitty as it was, all of that was a series of bad shit piling up at once."

"He still should have called his press team off. They fanned the flames. He has a shark for a publicist, and it's not going to do him any favors in the long run."

Em smiled at her friend. Dera's loyalty went bone deep. She didn't let people get too close, but once someone was in, they were in. She never wavered in her support, and she'd fight tooth and nail to protect her people. It felt so good to have that kind of support now.

"You're right. But that's a lesson he'll have to learn on his own." She gulped down more vodka, pulling her knees to her chest. "Just like I'll have to learn that celebrity and relationships don't mix, at least not for me."

"Oh, Emmy." Dera reached out and squeezed Em's hand. "I know this has been hard for you. I can't imagine going through what you went through, let alone trusting someone after all the shit your father's done. But you can't write off relationships forever."

Em pulled her hand away from her friend, curling

tighter into herself. Dera didn't know what it was like. She'd grown up with both of her parents. They'd loved and spoiled her, taking her with them everywhere. They still talked three or four times a week, and they all went out of their way to visit each other. She never had to ask herself why her father never stayed, why he put a job ahead of her every chance he got. She didn't know what it was like to see another man put his career before her. She hadn't had to see her private life blasted all over the Internet and newspapers and social media after seven years of not trusting a man.

"The hell I can't. I don't exactly have a lot of opportunities to meet a guy who isn't part of the tennis scene. Even if I do, how would I find a guy who could look past those damn pictures even if he does get over the fact that I'm a professional athlete?" Em stared at her hands. "I certainly can't date someone associated with tennis again. It's a disaster. If we're not being followed around by awful photographers, we're having to sneak around, avoiding the photographers and keeping everything so secret that it feels like we might suffocate."

She'd been the one to suggest the secrecy with Rob, and it'd made sense at the time, but now it felt so futile.

"Besides. Men are a distraction I can't afford right now. It's my year, remember? The year I'm supposed to win a Grand Slam, and I only have one more chance."

Dera didn't say anything then. They both sat there drinking for a few long moments before Dera switched the subject. They argued about who had better movies, the Americans or the French. After a heated argument

271

about whether escargot was disgusting or delicious, they briefly considered ordering a pizza before dismissing the idea and downing more vodka.

As the evening went on, Em's body went blessedly numb and her head pleasantly swimmy. "I can't remember the last time I drank this much," she mused, staring at the now empty vodka bottle. "I didn't drink this much when Kole and I broke up, did I?"

Dera shook her head, unable to lift it off the back of the couch where it rested. "Nope. You kicked him to the curb, remember? We had a few girl-power drinks, but no getting drunk."

Em frowned, her thoughts floating around, unable to settle on the single thought she wanted for a moment. Then it came to her. "But I kicked Rob to the curb. So why are we drunk?"

"Because you were stupid to break up with him." Dera immediately clapped a hand over her mouth, giggling hysterically. "Oops. I did not mean to say that."

Blinking at her friend, Em tried to make sense of it all. "But he was—he was distracting me. I'm supposed to win big. Gotta make my grandparents proud. Show my dad he's a dummy for thinking I should be something boring like an accountant."

"Maybe it's not Rob." Dera blew out a long breath. "Maybe it was the sneaking around and the secrets that have gotten in your way."

"What d'you mean? Without the sneaking, we would have been in this mess sooner." She gestured toward the front door, the only thing keeping them from the horde of photographers.

Dera snorted. "Maybe. But it wouldn't have been

this bad. They would have made a fuss for a week or two, then you could have gone about being a normal couple. It's the secrets, though. They're what drag you down, distracting you from your goals."

"How would you know?" Em scoffed, setting her empty glass aside.

"Because I've been there, Emmy." Dera's eyes grew heartbreakingly sad. "Keeping your private life secret tears at you a bit more each day until you're in shreds."

Her words cut through the haze of alcohol. She liked to be flippant about her personal life, but Em knew there was a lot her friend kept locked away behind her free-spirited facade.

"What happened to you, D?" Em asked quietly.

For a long while, Dera didn't speak; she stared into space, her jaw flexing and her breathing labored.

"I dated someone. Recently. Well, it's been almost a year, I suppose." She swigged down some more vodka. "We kept things quiet because she asked me to, and it tore us apart."

Em's heart twisted. "What happened, D? Who was she?"

"She…I can't tell you who she is. She's still pretty deep in the closet. She's not on the tennis scene, so seeing each other was difficult, but we managed it." Dera shifted, curling more tightly into herself, tumbler dangling loosely from her fingers. "She'd fly in to wherever I was playing, using business as an excuse, or I'd go see her when I could get away. Since no one knew she was interested in women, it was a little easier for us than it probably was for you and Rob, but *merde*, Emmy. I wanted to shout from the rooftops that she was mine. I wanted to take her dancing and kiss her whenever I felt like it. But she…she wouldn't let me."

"Why?" Em reached to rub her friend's arm, doing what she could to reassure her.

Dera shrugged, her features twisting into a very French look filled with bittersweet remorse. "Her parents. Her friends. Her job. What the world might say. *Je ne sais pas*. Mostly? I think she was scared to admit who she was. Who she could be. And to a certain extent, I think she wanted to keep a buffer between us. I was merely a fantasy to her. A youthful indulgence she allowed herself before she took her place as a proper wife to some blue-blooded American millionaire."

"Oh, Dera. I'm so sorry." Em moved to wrap an arm around her friend, tears burning her own eyes. "Why didn't you tell me?"

Dera leaned her head against Em's shoulder, tears streaming down her brown cheeks. "It all happened while your grandpa was sick, and I didn't want to burden you. Besides, I—I was ashamed of myself."

"What? Why would you be ashamed?" Em knew that Dera had struggled with her sexuality when they first stepped on the tour, but she'd long since become confident and comfortable with the fact that she was attracted to both men and women.

"Because I let myself be her dirty secret. I didn't even tell my parents about her. I think that's what eventually broke me. None of the people who mattered, who'd supported me for so long, knew that I was falling in love." Brushing at her cheeks, she straightened a little, pulling away to look at Em.

"You are the sister of my heart, Emmy, but I think you've been stupid when it comes to Rob. Keeping your relationship a secret has done you both more harm than good. Look at you—my beautiful, kickass friend—turning yourself inside out because of a man you could have easily had."

A lump grew in Em's throat, and she drank more vodka to try to push it back down. Hearing how badly her friend had been affected by her lover's need for secrecy only made Em's guilt worse. She'd thought keeping things secret was best for both her and Rob—but what if she was wrong? Their situation was different. They didn't have the same stigmas to worry about—at least not to the same degree. Her background had always been there between them, but in this day and age, it wouldn't break them as it might have thirty or forty years ago. But they would still be the target for more attention than Em ever wanted off the tennis court. So she pushed him away.

"I could have had him—I did have him. But I didn't deserve him, Dera. I—we're not meant to be together," she croaked.

"Bullshit. You two were perfect together," Dera retorted. "I love you, and I'm all about being a supportive friend, but anyone with half a brain could see how you and Rob are together."

Perfect. God, she hated that word. That's what she'd tried to be for so long. The perfect daughter. The perfect granddaughter. The perfect tennis player. The perfect girlfriend. That last one had been what got her into this mess in the first place. Amir had convinced her that she and Kole would be perfect together, and now look at the mess her life had become.

"I'm not, though. Look at the mess I've gotten us into. I'm not perfect for anyone, Dera. Rob should be

275

with someone who isn't such a train wreck, who his family actually likes."

"Like who?" Dera demanded. "Who on earth do you think would make him as happy as he's been with you?"

Em took another big gulp of vodka, wishing that it still numbed the pain wrenching through her at the thought of Rob with anyone else. "Carrie Webster. You. Anyone who doesn't come with a seven-forty-seven full of baggage and a bad reputation to boot."

"Me? Carrie Webster?" Dera burst out laughing. "Carrie Webster would bore him to tears within a day, especially after almost six months of dating you. And while he's a very charming, attractive man, Rob and I could never be more than friends. It's you he wants."

Em didn't speak for several beats. The words bubbled inside her, threatening to spill out. God, why couldn't they get wasted and laugh hysterically like those girls in the movies and talk about how awful her ex was? It would be so much easier than this.

"I want him too, Dera. But I can't have him."

Dera set her drink down. "Why the hell not?"

"Because he left me once before. Seven years ago, he let his dad talk him into breaking up with me, and, and—"

"And deep down you can't bring yourself to trust him." Dera sighed, flopping her head against the back of the couch.

Em slowly nodded, reaching to pour herself some more vodka. "It's not just that. I—he's a distraction. His dad was right back then. And now I've given up my chance with him. It doesn't matter if everyone knows about us. I need to move on. I need to move on and fix myself, and maybe someday I won't be such a mess anymore."

"Oh, *cherie*. You're not a mess. You're human. And you should be with the man who appreciates you for who you are."

"It doesn't matter!" Em's voice grew louder than she'd intended as the hollowness inside threatened to consume her. "I can't look back. I can only look forward. I need to focus on my career, not on what I've given up."

It was the only way she'd survive. Even through the haze of alcohol, she knew she couldn't keep wishing she'd done something differently. All she could do was ignore all the outside bullshit and make sure she was in the best shape of her life going into the US Open. She'd worry about the rest of it later.

Chapter 18

"Oh, so now you're unemployed you find you have time for your mother?"

Rob rolled his eyes, leaning down to kiss his mother's cheek. "I always have time for you, Mama. You know that. I just have more of it now."

"Oh, *Älskling*. It's so good to see you." Brigit's hug eased some of the pain that pounded at Rob since the end of Wimbledon. "You're too thin, though. And you haven't been getting enough sleep."

Rob followed his mother into the house, setting his duffle bag down by the door. She was wearing a bright-green tennis dress, her long hair pulled back in a sleek tail, a visor shading her face.

"I'm fine. Don't fuss. Did I catch you at a bad time?"

"Not at all. You caught me at the perfect time." She studied him. "Your father had to go out of town unexpectedly, and I need some help at the academy today. Did you bring workout clothes with you?"

He narrowed his eyes suspiciously. "Yeah. Why?"

"You're going to help me teach a clinic we're hosting today. Go. Hurry and change. We need to leave in five minutes."

He opened his mouth to argue, but his mother didn't give him the chance. Before he knew what had happened, she had him standing in front of a group of short people, a tennis racket in hand.

"Mr. Rob! When are we going to get to play?" one of the bigger kids asked. She couldn't have been more than nine, but she was scrawny as hell, and her eyes said she'd seen more than her fair share of sorrow in her short life.

All the kids were part of the Miami foster care system. Some of them lived in group homes, but others lived with foster families. They all came to the Ashton Academy as part of an outreach program his mother had launched a few years ago.

"Well, let's see. Does everyone have their rackets?" Rob looked around, knowing full well they did. He'd helped his mom hand them out as the kids arrived and were checked in by the harried-looking social workers assigned to chaperone.

"Yes, sir!" the kids shouted, wiggling with anticipation.

"Does everyone have a tennis ball?"

"Yes, sir!"

"Okay. Let's get started."

He sectioned them out by age, letting the older ones who had been here before go meet his mom on one of the far courts, while he stuck with the littler guys.

None of them were very skilled, but they all had a boundless energy he envied. An hour into the clinic, and he was wiped.

"Good job, Ivy. But I want you to try holding the racket like this." He repositioned the little girl's hand on the racket grip, smiling at the intense concentration furrowing her brows. Her dark braids and fierceness reminded him of what Dera Calvet must have looked like when she was six or so.

The little girl took a swing and bounced on the toes of her worn sneakers when the ball bounced over the low-slung net. "I did it! I did it, Mr. Rob! Did you see?"

The sense of pride that washed over him surprised him. He'd never expected to feel this way again. Since his surgery, he'd written off any hope of feeling this level of accomplishment again, like he'd done something worthwhile. He'd enjoyed his job at TWW—at least he thought he had—but it hadn't satisfied that deep part of him like playing tennis had.

"I saw. That was great. Before you know it, you'll be up forty to love at Wimbledon," Rob said. "Okay, Juan. Let's see what you've got."

He turned his attention to the seven-year-old boy who was next in line, chuckling at his enthusiastic "practice" swings that had him spinning in circles from the force of them.

He helped the boy adjust his arm placement, showing how to move so that the ball came into contact with the racket at the right time, in the right spot. They were cheating a little, using a bounce serve instead of an overhead, but with how little they were, their arms wouldn't reach high enough.

"All right, Denny. I want you and Juan to stand on the two white lines and practice hitting the ball to each other. Ivy and Sally, you stand here and practice." He set each pair up seven or eight feet apart, giving them room to swing their rackets and hit back and forth a bit.

Leaning against the fence, Rob watched them for a minute. They made up for any lack of skill with their determination. He went and corrected a few of them before he went back to his post.

"How's it going over here?" his mother asked, coming to lean beside him.

"Pretty well. They're hard workers."

"Did you see, Mr. Rob? Did you see? We hit it five whole times before it stopped," Ivy cried.

He nodded, smiling at the girls. "You did great, shorty. Try going for six this time."

When he looked over at his mother, the smile on her face almost blinded him.

"What's got you grinning like the Cheshire cat?"

She shrugged. "Can't a mother enjoy being right about her child?"

He frowned at her. "What? What are you right about this time?"

"You. This. You're meant to do this," Brigit said.

"To do what? Ride herd on munchkins?" He didn't know what he was meant to do anymore. He didn't regret leaving TWW for a second, especially not after the media frenzy set in, but he was at loose ends. Hiding in his apartment brought him back to those awful days after his surgery. He'd gone to visit Maren and Cruz in California for a few days, but once the photographers found him, it was time to move on. Besides, he'd needed this. His mother managed to soothe a lot of his hurts, even though she hadn't been there to do so when he was little.

"No. Coach. Teach. You've always had a knack for it. Ever since Maren was little," Brigit said. "You're great with kids especially. Much more patient than your father. He has a tendency to become a bit…"

"Intense?" he supplied. "I remember. He and Gramps almost came to blows a few times when Dad tried to teach me."

281

She giggled. "I recall that as well. Your father's excellent for our teenage students who are more serious about the game, but he doesn't do so well with the little ones."

"They need some encouragement and a smile." He winked at Juan as he did a victory dance for hitting the ball past his partner.

"*Älskling*. It's so much more than that. It takes someone special to work with the children. We need someone like you here, Rob. You're a brilliant coach, with such a warm heart, and you could be such an asset to this program."

Here. His mother wanted him to teach here? With her and his dad? Rob almost immediately rejected the idea. Working alongside his father would lead to World War III or worse. Then his attention returned to the kids, and he hesitated. They all beamed with pride as their skills started to develop, and it gave him another little kick of satisfaction.

"I don't know, Mama. Being here with Dad? It doesn't sound like the best idea." His jaw tightened when another thought occurred to him. "And I don't know that I can stay here, so close to Em—not when things are so messed up between us."

He didn't wait for his mother to respond. Pushing down the pain that hit him every time he thought of Em, he returned his attention to the kids. They continued practicing for another hour or so before the chaperones rounded up the worn-out kids and loaded them into the worn-down vans. Rob waved them off, smiling at the little faces pressed against the windows.

"Are you happy, *min son*?" Brigit asked as they repacked the kids' rackets.

The question blindsided Rob. He froze, unsure of how to respond. If she'd asked him three weeks ago, he might have said yes. Even though they'd been keeping their relationship off the radar, he'd had Em and there was hope for something more. He'd had a job that he thought he could stick with long term, and he was able to do something to help his friends and make sure the sport remained the focus instead of their personal lives.

Now all of that was gone. He had his family—such as it was—and a few friends, but he'd lost his job, and more importantly, he'd lost Em. Or rather she'd left him.

"How can I be happy? My life's gone to shit—again—only this time I don't even have the hope of getting Em back," Rob said, his voice rough.

"Are you sure about that?" Brigit asked, closing the plastic bin that housed the rackets.

He snorted. "Pretty sure. She kicked me out, refused to answer my calls, and now the whole world is watching us, which proves her point. No matter how much I care about her, how much I want to be with her, she'll only see me as a distraction."

"A distraction?" She frowned. "How could you be a distraction? You love her, yes?"

"Of course, I do. I told her as much, but it didn't matter." His heart still ached at the memory of that night in London.

She bent to pick up the ball basket. "But love isn't a distraction. Real love could never be a distraction. It's strength. Protection. Comfort. Hope."

He thought so too, but Em…she couldn't see that. "Maybe she doesn't love me, Mama. Or maybe it's not me that's the distraction. Maybe it's all the baggage that comes with me. I—I don't think I realized how much I hurt her when I ended things with her all those years ago. I was stupid to let Dad persuade me to break up with her, to leave her there, waiting for me to show up. I don't know that I blame her for pushing me aside. I put my career before her last time; now it's her turn, I guess."

Her lips pursed, and he could hear the wheels turning in her head. His father might bluster and roar, but his mother was the one with the real temper in the family. It took a lot to chip at the ice around it, but once she let lose, his mother could burn down the road.

"I love your father. He's been the center of my world for so long, but sometimes he is a jackass." She slammed the ball basket down on a loose ball, scooping it up and moving to the next one. "He should never have interfered with your relationship. I told him so back then, but he thought he knew best."

"Dad always thinks he knows best," he muttered. "Did you know he told Carrie Webster to call me last week? He fed her some line about me saying I'd wanted to get in touch with her."

Huffing, she collapsed on the nearby bench. "That man. If I hadn't lost my heart to him thirty-five years ago, I might strangle him. He's had it in his head for years that you and Carrie belong together."

He joined her on the bench. "Believe me, I know. Carrie's a nice woman, but she's not…"

"She's not your Emerson." His mother linked her arm with his. "I understand, *min son*. My parents weren't too fond of your father, either. Not at first. But they saw how much he cared for me, and they grew used to having a brash American around."

Chuckling, he looked out over the court. He enjoyed this, being here with his mother. He'd missed so much time with her growing up, but they'd always shared this love of tennis.

He studied his mother, realization only beginning to dawn on him. His mother had been his rock over the last eighteen months, but she'd had his back for a lot longer than that. Brigit Ashton's backbone of steel was the secret of his parents' marriage. She'd given up so much for their family, but she always made the best of it, finding her own place in the whirlwind that surrounded their family.

"Are you happy, Mama?" he asked. "Do you ever wish you'd put your career first?"

She reached up and brushed his hair off his forehead. "I have a talented, beautiful daughter, a charming and handsome son, a husband who for all of his bluster loves me to the moon and back, and I have this academy. I couldn't be happier. Playing tennis professionally was a wonderful part of my life, but this, what I have here? It's so much more fulfilling. The roar of the crowds, the thrills of the win, all of that faded once I fell in love with your father and realized my place was with him."

He nodded. "What would you have done if you were in my position? Would you have let Dad walk away?"

"Never. And your father wouldn't have let me walk away either." She tightened her arm around his. "When you love someone, you fight for them no matter what. You respect their need for space and for time apart, but you don't give up. You're an Ashton; it's not in your blood to give up, especially when it counts."

When it counts.

Em counted. Being with her meant everything to him. But he needed more than his love for her. Maybe his mom had a point about coaching. He didn't think his shoulder would let him coach at a professional level, but he could do what he'd done today. He could foster the love of tennis in the way his grandpa had done for him, the way Zoe did for Em. If things went well, he could even look at expanding the program. Even if he lost Em, it might be enough for him.

Losing her wasn't an option, though. He'd give her time and space, but at the end of it all, he wanted her sitting here beside him, sharing in the peace and quiet after a day spent doing a job that made a difference.

Chapter 19

Rob moved through the crowds at the Billie Jean King National Tennis Center, tugging his hat farther down until the brim met the top of the sunglasses. The beard he'd spent the last two weeks growing itched in the late-summer heat as the New York sun beat down on his back, but he didn't mind it.

What he minded was the torrent of memories flying at him. The last time he'd set foot in this place was the day his life changed forever. When he first took the job at TWW, he'd dreaded this tournament and the memories it brought back. His shoulder twinged a little at the thought of his last game here—or maybe it was the training session he'd had yesterday with five eight-year-olds from the Ashton Foundation. His mother had insisted he get in one last session before he came up to New York for two weeks. He didn't mind the small twinges that came with his new job. He finally felt accomplished, like he was doing something satisfying again.

"Rob? Is that you?"

He froze for a second, before relaxing when his mind recognized the lightly accented voice of his best friend. Cruz stood off to one side, his tennis bag resting on a bench behind him. Thankfully, he wasn't surrounded by the entourage that usually followed him around during tournaments.

Rob hurried over to his friend, clapping him on the back. "Good to see you, man."

Cruz flicked the brim of the hat. "What's with the lumberjack routine? I don't think I've ever seen you go more than a few days without shaving."

"Trying to blend in." Glancing around nervously, he adjusted his hat again. "The last thing I need is every reporter in the place following me around everywhere."

The Spaniard raised an eyebrow. "Since when does press attention bother you? They used to follow you everywhere except the toilet."

"I'm not here as Rob Ashton, former tennis star. I'm here as Rob Ashton, supportive big brother." He shoved his hands into the pockets of his pale-blue Bermuda shorts, keeping his eyes down toward his boat shoes so as not to catch anyone else's attention.

"And supportive boyfriend?" Cruz prodded.

Cheeks burning, he shrugged. "If you're asking am I here to watch Em's matches, then the answer is yes. But I don't want anyone to know. The press has just started to lay off both of us, and I don't want to give them anything more to work with. She wants to focus on her game, so I'm letting her focus on her game."

Cruz let out a low whistle, motioning for Rob to follow him through the crowd. "You're really here to support her after she broke up with you?"

In his darker moments, he'd asked himself the same thing. After breaking up with him, after what she'd said, he shouldn't still want her. His heart should be ripped to shreds, but he couldn't give up hope. Not yet. "Em's been through a lot over the last year. She's pushed me away because she's fixated on winning a Grand Slam this year. I can't—I can't give up on her until all the craziness dies down, and we have a real chance to talk. And until then, I want to be there for her, even if she doesn't know I'm there."

"*Amor. Dios* save me if I ever lose my head over a woman the way you have," Cruz scoffed, keeping to the sides of the crowd so as not to draw too much attention.

"Someday you will." Rob smiled at the thought of his quiet, contained friend finally meeting a woman who could break past his walls. It'd take an explosion, but it'd be well worth the show.

Rob followed Cruz into the mostly deserted players' lounge. It'd been updated slightly since the last time he visited. The TVs and a few of the couches were newer, but it still felt the same. An oasis from the crowds. A place for only the players and those closest to them to hide away between matches and practices. He hadn't been able to enter the lounges since he came back, as reporters were strictly forbidden. He had at least thirty minutes before Maren's third round match started in Louis Armstrong Stadium, so he sat down with Cruz in a secluded corner, enjoying the coolness of the air conditioner.

"So what's the plan?" Cruz asked, propping his feet up on the low wooden coffee table.

Rob mimicked his friend's pose. "Plan?"

"To win back the heart of your lady love." Cruz pulled a sports drink out of his bag, tossing a spare one to Rob. "I assume there's a plan. You wouldn't have shown up here without one."

"You assume a lot. I don't have a plan. Having plans never works when it comes to Em. She's got a mind of her own, and she's got it made up that we don't belong together. It's going to take more than a plan to convince her otherwise."

Cruz nodded, a smile tugging at his mouth. "She's a stubborn lady. But what will you do if she won't be convinced?"

"I don't know." He'd tried to imagine his life without Em a thousand times, but he couldn't. Every future he saw had her with him. "I've started to build a life for myself in Miami. Did I tell you about Mom's latest scheme?"

He filled his friend in on his new role working with his mother and the kids.

"And *el jefe*? How are the two of you working together?"

Rob scratched his chin, the stubble there still unfamiliar, chuckling a little. "We're...muddling through. Mostly we stay out of each other's way. He's here somewhere, rubbing elbows and playing the former champion. I'm avoiding him when I can. He's tried to get me to set up a dinner with Carrie Webster at least five times since I moved down there."

"Ah, Bobby Ashton. As unchanging as the Pyrenees. You'd think that after—what is it, fifteen years?—he'd give up." Cruz took a long drink.

"No such luck," Rob said, sipping his own bottle of bright green liquid.

"Is your mother still crusading with him?"

Rob smiled at the thought of his mother. She'd surprised him more and more every day since he decided to stay and work at the academy. Slowly, the woman who'd unflinchingly followed Bobby Ashton through every step of life was fading. She'd deflected his dad from some touchy topics on more than one occasion, keeping peace between the Ashton men.

"She's actually pulling for Em on this one. She saw us together at the gala, and she was already planning what her grandkids would look like. Brigit Ashton is nothing if not adaptable. And she's never been as tied to my father's ideas about good breeding. She came from old money, but that wasn't what was most important to her or her family."

"I hope Bobby sees the error of his ways this time around," Cruz put in.

After Em left London, Rob had told Cruz everything, about the Olympics, about how his father convinced him to break up with Em the first time. About the regret that plagued him every time he'd seen her for the next seven years.

"It doesn't matter if he does or not. I don't need his approval anymore. I know who I am now and what I want. If he makes trouble, I have the money to start my own academy and do the same work I've been doing with Mom. I may do that anyway down the line. Maybe I'll even get you to help me out." That sense of certainty did more to ease his concerns about Em's decision to take him back than anything else. Nothing was going to come between them if she really wanted to be with him. That had been true even back in January, but now he had more people at his back. His mother, Maren, Cruz, Dera, Owen. They all saw what he knew in his heart. He and Em belonged together.

Cruz snorted. "Glad you finally learned to ignore him. The tennis academy's a good idea, and I think you'll be a much better coach than you were a journalist. Now you need to learn how to sweep your girl off her feet."

"I've got a few ideas. Most of them are cheesy and

over the top. Like in those sappy movies Maren makes me watch," Rob admitted. "Singing to her after she's won the tournament. Sending her thousands of peonies. Declaring my love for her in front of everyone. But…"

"Gestures like that would send her running as if the bulls were chasing her through Pamplona."

Nodding, Rob sighed. "And on top of that, until the nut job who's after her is caught, I can't do anything quite so public. I'll just have to hope she'll talk to me after she wins and go from there."

"She'll talk to you. From what Owen says, she misses you more than she's willing to admit. Once the tournament's over, I doubt she'll be able to keep you at arm's length."

Rob hoped his friend was right. All through his sister's match, Rob tried to find a way to get through to Em. He still had a week before he could see her. A week to decide how to ensure the woman he loved spent the rest of her life with him.

****

"Are you sure you haven't gotten any good leads on him?" Em asked Detective Combs. The detective had flown up to New York to work with the NYPD to catch the stalker.

The detective shook his dark head. "Unfortunately, no. We know he's here, and the venue's tightened security as much as they can, but we don't have a lot to go on. He's good at hiding his cyber footprint, but the NYPD and the FBI have got their top people tracing the posts made on the tournament's site, as well as the emails we've intercepted."

The posts on the site had shaken both of them. They'd been much more intense than the previous emails. They'd detailed what they'd do to her if she won the tournament in graphic language. The emails had been even worse. Apparently, the stalker had gone off the rails. He'd sent pictures of her at her home, at the training courts, at the grocery store. All of them had been distorted and manipulated into a sideshow of horror.

"I can feel someone watching me during my matches." Em shivered, glancing around the sitting room of her suite. It was the same hotel where she'd stayed last time she was in New York, although thankfully a different room. The memories of Rob already threatened to overwhelm her. She'd done a good job of keeping them at bay in the weeks leading up to the tournament and even during the tournament itself, but at night they swamped her. She ached to have him beside her, even as she hated herself for missing him.

Detective Combs frowned. "Forgive me, but there are a lot of people watching you during the matches."

"I know that. I mean, watching me like someone's hunting me or something. I don't know. It sounds silly, but it's like when a photographer is lurking behind me. I can sense it," she explained.

"Ah. Well, if you notice anyone suspicious, be sure you let your security detail know. They're on the NYPD's radio frequency, and they'll get the word out." He gave her what he probably thought was a reassuring smile. "We'll catch him, Ms. Grace. I promise you."

She sighed. "Sooner rather than later would be best. I don't know how much longer I can take living under a microscope."

Her security detail had been following her

everywhere since TWW broke the news about her and Rob's relationship. They sat around while she practiced, and they parked outside her house most nights, taking turns on watch. She'd spent the plane ride to New York with one of them in the aisle seat. Even now, one of them stood outside her door while the other watched the hotel's security feed.

"You worry about winning your match this afternoon. I'll worry about stopping this guy." Detective Combs gave her a fatherly pat on the shoulder and left.

She ran her hands through her hair. She needed to focus, to get ready for her match. It was the fucking semifinal match. She couldn't believe she was this close now.

"Are you ready?" Zoe asked as she came in from the bedroom where she'd been making some phone calls.

Em giggled, on the edge of nervous and hysterical. "God. Can you ever be ready for something like this? I've been in the semifinals every year for the last five years. Why the hell am I still so terrified?"

"Because it's the semifinals of a Grand Slam. Because you want it so much you can taste it. I've been there, sweetheart. But you're in a better place than you've ever been before. You haven't dropped a set the entire tournament. Your first four rounds you only lost seven games total. You only lost four games on Tuesday. You're well-rested and in the best shape of your life."

Em tried to find solace in her coach's words, but she couldn't. "Maren's done just as well. She's also four years younger than me and a former champion."

Playing her friends in the high-stakes matches was the worst. Any other day, she'd be cheering Maren on, but today, her one mission in life was to beat her friend as quickly as possible.

"Maren Ashton is good. There's no denying that. But right now, at this tournament? You're better," Zoe argued. "You've got more passion, more drive, and more focus than you've had at any other tournament. You can do this."

You can do this. You can do this.

She repeated the words to herself over and over and over. She continued repeating them as she went through her pre-match preparations. Pulling on her bright-blue tennis dress and lacing up her sneakers, she focused on her breathing. Keeping calm and centered was her best bet for getting through this match. If she let herself think too much about the stalker or the fact that her opponent was her friend and the sister of the man she cared for, she might completely lose it.

"Time to go, Ms. Grace." One of the tournament officials broke into her thoughts, motioning for Em to follow her. She gathered her bags and made her way out to Arthur Ashe Stadium, the dull roar of the crowd around her somehow distant as she zeroed in on the mission at hand.

She took her designated side and started to unpack her bags. The place was full, the sun starting to set in the early September sky. Glancing over at her box, she was pleased to see her grandma there with Owen and Zoe. Gran had insisted on coming, in spite of Em's worry that the stalker might target the older woman. Even when Papa Vic was so sick last year, they hadn't missed a chance to watch her at the biggest US tournament of the year.

Continuing to scan the crowd, her gaze caught on a man sitting directly across from her. At first, she didn't recognize him, but realization dawned. The scruffy beard and baseball cap might fool a lot of people, but she'd recognize that jaw and those dimples anywhere.

Rob was here.

Sitting in the front row, waiting to watch her match.

Only that was stupid. He wasn't here to watch her. He was here to watch his sister.

He didn't know she'd spotted him, his attention on the crowd instead of her, but she drew a little bit of strength from knowing he was here.

She still didn't know what she'd do about her relationship with Rob, if she even still had one, but he'd been such a big part of her life for so long, having him here made sense. He'd pushed her for years, his little digs only making her better, more determined. Losing him the first time was what had made her fight so hard to get to where she was today. She'd wanted to prove his father wrong, to show all the tennis world that she could be as good as anyone with piles of money and years of nonstop training at the best academies in the world.

Soon, Owen joined Rob in the front row. Now, all the people she wanted to have supporting her were here, except one. Her dad was off in Belize or Bolivia or somewhere, working on a new assignment. He'd sent her a text before the tournament, wishing her luck, but she hadn't heard anything more from him since the dinner he crashed.

She'd gotten used to disappointment over the

years. He'd never showed up to support her before, so she couldn't say she was all that surprised. But now, as she got closer and closer to her goal, she wished he were here to see it.

Moving for the requisite handshake, Em returned her attention to the match. She looked her friend in the eyes and knew she could do this. She could make it to the finals of the US Open—and win.

****

Rob settled into his front row seat in Arthur Ashe Stadium, his body vibrating with tension. He'd managed to make it to every match his sister and Em played in, and he'd known today was coming. They were both too good not to make it to the semifinals. It sucked that they were in the same half of the draw, but it'd probably be worse for him if they met in the finals.

He leaned forward, watching the crowd settle into their seats as match time approached. The stadium lights flicked on, working in conjunction with the fading twilight. Almost the entire stadium was full of spectators, all eager to watch a match between two of the WTA's top players. Cruz and Kole were slated to play after Em and Maren finished, but the ladies were the main draw today.

All of the sportscasters had been buzzing about this match since the semifinal contenders had been determined two days ago. They'd tried to spin it as a grudge match, Maren wanting revenge for her brother's broken heart. But his sister and Em refused to play into that. He loved that they were friends and that all the drama that passed between him and Em hadn't dimmed that friendship.

Even now, as they shook hands before taking their

positions on opposite sides of the net, they smiled and chatted as if it were a practice match instead of the semifinals of the last Grand Slam of the year.

"So who are you rooting for?"

Rob tensed before realizing Owen had taken the empty seat beside him. Em's brother had played earlier in the day, knocking out the number five player from Sweden. "Who says I'm rooting for anyone? I'm simply taking in an enjoyable tennis match."

"Please. Your sister is playing the girl who broke your heart," Owen teased. "You have to want someone to win."

He did want someone to win, not that he'd admit it out loud. He loved his sister and always supported her, but today, for the first time in her life, he was rooting against Maren. Em's ferocity throughout the tournament had impressed him. She'd refused to give an inch. She'd charged forward, intensely focused on making it through each match.

She took first serve, pounding a firecracker across the court at Maren, forcing her to hit it with a slightly weak backhand.

"Em's on fire," Rob said. "Have you ever seen her like this?"

"Once. After her seventh-grade teacher told her she'd never win the geography bee. She studied so hard that Gran thought she might keel over. But she went out there and managed to make it all the way to the state championships."

"Sounds about right," Rob murmured. His eyes darted back and forth, following the ball. Em's forehand kept returning Maren's shots with deadly accuracy. He was surprised by the number of unforced errors his sister racked up in the first few games.

By the time Em led four to two, Rob's heart swelled with pride. His girl was unstoppable. She showed no fear, no hesitation. She had one thing on her mind—winning.

During a break, Rob managed to tear his gaze away from Em long enough to scan the crowd. He'd made a habit of watching the crowd, searching for anyone suspicious ever since Detective Combs called to warn him about the new threats. So far, no one had jumped out at him. He looked at all the people in the front row across from him. A few celebrities and socialites he recognized dotted the crowd. Directly opposite him, he spotted a sallow-skinned man wearing an ill-fitting dark suit, too shabby for someone who could afford premium seats and too warm for the heat wave beating down on New York. His dark eyes fixed on Em, he barely moved during the next two games.

"What's your read on that guy?" Rob asked Owen during the next break. His friend had just returned from checking on his grandmother, who was sitting in Em's box, intently watching the match. Owen claimed it stressed him out too much to sit and watch a match with Poppy Grace.

"Which one?" Owen asked.

"Suit guy. With the thin brown hair and the pug nose."

Owen's eyes narrowed. "A suit? Here? In this heat? It's a little weird, but maybe he's one of those Wall Street types who came straight from the office."

"He's got a creepy vibe, though, doesn't he?" Rob shifted in his seat. Maybe he was being paranoid. He'd had more than a few nightmares about something happening to Em over the last few weeks. Nothing could keep them away.

"Yeah, but nothing too weird. Relax, man. The security on this place rivals the White House this year. No one's getting anything through that could hurt Em. Just watch the match. Your sister's about to get her ass handed to her."

It was true. They were creeping deeper into the second set now, and Em had only given up two games. She was a game away from taking the match.

The stadium grew quiet except for the soft clicking of camera shutters as Em let loose another powerful serve. It hit the net, and a ball boy ran to retrieve the dead ball. Let for service. Em took her stance again, her next serve as deadly as the first. Maren returned the serve with a two-handed backhand stroke, the ball hurtling back toward Em as her grunt of exertion echoed through the otherwise silent court. Em hit it back across the court with a neat forehand, sending Maren running for the ball.

They went on, both battling for supremacy, but Em continued to keep the edge. "I'm not sure I can watch," Owen murmured as Em set up for match point.

"I can't take my eyes away. She's amazing," Rob said, leaning forward in his seat. He pushed the brim of his hat up so nothing obstructed his view.

Em's final serve was perfect. Maren returned it, and the battle was on. The only sounds in the entire stadium were the thunks as the ball hit the rackets and the women's grunting with effort as they lobbed the ball back and forth between them. Em kept Maren on her backhand side for every hit, while Em moved up gradually. One well-placed shot kept his sister from reaching the ball before its second bounce.

The crowd exploded with cheers. It was rare to have the two best American women playing each other, but that had been a grueling match. Rob jumped to his feet, arms raised in the air. Em was going to the US Open finals. She was now only a handful of sets shy of the win she'd been chasing all season—for her whole career.

Em's celebration was more contained but no less enthusiastic. She and Maren met at the net, exchanging a warm hug, both laughing and crying. No egos involved there. They both would have been supportive whatever the outcome. After thanking the judge, they both waved to the crowd, arms around each other, laughter on their faces.

Something across the court caught his eye. It was suit guy. He was scrambling over the low wall around the court, his hand reaching into his pocket for something.

Acting on instinct, Rob vaulted the wall on his side, scrambling to get to Em. His brain vaguely registered the security guys converging around them, but he got to Em first, putting himself between her and suit guy.

"Rob? What—?" She struggled against him, but froze just as a sharp, stinging pain flashed up his side.

The world began to fade around him. Shouts and scuffling came from behind him, but all Rob could focus on was Em. Her beautiful brown eyes wide with fear, the victorious smile replaced with a look of horror and pain.

Oh God.

Had Suit Guy gotten her? Was he too late?

Chapter 20

Em couldn't process the pandemonium around her. One minute, she and Maren had been celebrating. She loved that her friend didn't hesitate to share in her joy, even though it meant Maren's chance at a Grand Slam title for the year was over. Then the next minute, Rob was rushing at her, pulling her against him and into his arms. Before she'd had a chance to process what was happening, a strange guy had shoved something into Rob's side mere seconds before the burly security guys converged around him, slamming him to the ground.

Rob's big body went weak against her, his knees buckling. Blood blossomed along the side of his light-blue shirt.

"Oh God. Rob. You're—"

"Are you okay? Did he hurt you?" he asked, his voice panicked.

She shook her head, easing him down into a nearby chair. "No. No, he didn't get me. Rob, you're hurt."

"What? No. I need to—I can't let him hurt you." His skin turned the sickly gray-green of a tennis ball left too long in the wind and rain.

"They've got him, babe. It's okay. You're the one that's hurt. We need a medic here," she called out. "He's hurt."

The walls of dark-suited security guys around them parted for the on-site medics to swarm around them.

They tried to push her aside, but Rob refused to let go of her hand. "No. Can't lose you."

"I'm not going anywhere," she assured him. She moved to stand behind him, keeping a hand on his shoulder. "Let them look at you."

"Don't go away," he insisted as the medics pulled up his shirt, examining his side.

"Knife wound to the lower abdomen. May have nicked an artery," the dark-skinned female EMT reported. She pressed a button on the radio stationed at her shoulder. "We need the ambulance to AA stadium. Male, early thirties, stab wound with significant blood loss."

Maren appeared beside Em. "Is he okay? What happened?"

"I don't know. That guy—" Em struggled to breathe through the tears burning her throat. "That guy stabbed him or something. I don't know."

"Sir, what's your name?" the medic asked, her voice calm as she and her partner pressed more and more gauze to Rob's side.

Rob's grip on Em's hand tightened, his fingers shaking. "R-Rob A-Ashton."

"Okay, Mr. Ashton. It looks like you've got a pretty nasty stab wound here. We're going to take you to the hospital to get you checked out." She glanced up at Em and Maren. "Are you family?"

"I'm his sister and she's…she's his girlfriend," Maren said, her voice choked. Em opened her mouth to protest, but Maren shook her head, stopping Em from speaking.

"Okay, one of you can ride with him to the hospital. The ambulance team is on their way in." As she spoke, the crowd parted for a gurney being pushed across the court.

Em turned to Maren. "You should go with him. I'll—I'll meet you there."

"No." Rob shook his head, struggling to get up. "Can't leave you here. What if—?"

"Whoa. Stay down," Maren said. "You should go with him, Emmy. He needs to stay calm, and he's not going to stay calm if he's worrying about you."

The paramedics in their dark-blue uniforms started maneuvering Rob onto the gurney, but he refused to let go of Em's hand.

"Okay. Will you—will you let everyone know where I've gone?"

Maren nodded. "You just worry about Rob. I'll worry about everyone else."

The whole ride to the hospital was a blur. The paramedic hooked Rob up to all sorts of machines as they trundled through the streets, sirens wailing. Em sat by his head, running her fingers through his hair and along his cheeks. The beard felt foreign and scratchy, but it was still her Rob. Her heart threatened to burst out of her chest.

"So pretty. My Em. So pretty and so strong," Rob murmured. "So proud of you."

"I know." She pressed a kiss to his temple. "I love you. I should have said it earlier, but I love you."

His eyes fluttered closed. She sent the paramedic a panicked look, but he gave her a tight smile. "He's all right. Just unconscious. He's lost a good amount of blood. He'll be in and out until we get him some platelets and blood."

She fought back tears but nodded. Her mind went

to the worst. Her mother had died from catastrophic blood loss after an accident. She knew Rob's injury couldn't possibly be as bad as that, but fear still clawed at her.

She should be celebrating right now and doing interviews. Instead, she was scared to death that the man she'd stupidly broken up with was going to die before she had a chance to make it right with him.

By the time they got to the hospital, she was almost in a blind panic. She followed the paramedics into the Mount Sinai emergency room, but thanks to Rob's slack grip, she fell behind. They wheeled him into a cubicle not far off the entrance, pulling the curtains closed.

She stood there, unsure what to do. She desperately wanted to push her way in and stay by Rob's side, but she couldn't do that. She had to let the doctors work on him. Reflexively, she reached to dig her phone out of her pocket before realizing she didn't have anything with her. No phone, no purse, nothing.

"Um, do you have a phone I could borrow?" she asked the nurse at the main desk. "My—my boyfriend was just brought in, and I left without any of my things."

"Sure, hon. Dial nine to get an outside line." The older woman gave her a motherly smile. Em stared at the phone for a few minutes, trying to remember a phone number to call, but her mind was completely blank, worry and fear drowning everything else out.

Before she could dial, the doors behind her opened. "Emmy!"

She turned to see Maren and Owen, both out of breath, her purse hanging off Maren's shoulder. Setting down the phone, she rushed over to them, throwing her arms around them both. Tears fell freely down her cheeks.

"Any news? What'd the doctor say?" Owen asked, pulling back.

"They haven't said anything." Em brushed at her cheeks. "They disappeared behind the curtain, and they haven't said anything."

Maren sniffled. "Okay. I'll see what I can find out. Mom and Dad are on their way. They missed the last half of the match for some fundraising event. Hopefully they'll make it through the crowd outside. I think every reporter within fifty miles is already outside."

Owen pulled Em off to the overcrowded waiting room and forced her to sit down. She started to shiver, although she wasn't sure if it was from shock or from the icy blast of the air conditioner trying to combat the heat.

"It'll be okay, Emmy." He wrapped an arm around her shoulders, comforting her as he used to when they were little. "Rob's come through worse."

She shuddered. "Worse than this? Why did he do that, O? Why did he step in between me and that knife? It should be me in there, not him."

"Because the man is stupid in love with you. And if he could talk right now, he'd tell you that he would much rather be the one in there than the one out here. He's been worried sick about you the last few weeks. Poor guy's called or texted me every night to make sure your guards are around and that you're still okay."

Em's heart fluttered, and fresh tears flooded her eyes. She'd been so wrapped up in her own head, in her own drive to make it to where she was. But Rob hadn't let it stop him from worrying about her. She didn't deserve him.

Maren came over a few minutes later, her face drawn but calm. "They took him up to surgery. He should be out in an hour or so."

"But he's going to be okay?" Em asked, brushing at her cheeks.

"The doctor said he's lucky. The knife or shiv or whatever it was missed most of the major organs, and it only nicked one of his arteries. Once they do the repairs, he'll be fine."

Em's shoulders sagged in relief. "Thank God. I don't know what I'd do—"

"Don't go there," Maren said, pulling her into a hug. "We didn't lose him. He's going to be fine and you're both going to pull your heads out of your asses and fix whatever went wrong between you."

Em nodded, her heart ready to burst. Together, the three of them followed a nurse's instructions to the surgical waiting room, and she sat between Owen and Maren as they waited for news.

She was only vaguely aware of the Ashtons showing up. She must have said something to them because Rob's mother gave her a hug and his father's expression was only mildly hostile. At some point, Zoe showed up, trying to urge her to return to the tennis center and engage in the usual post-match rituals, but she couldn't leave. She wanted to be here when Rob woke up. She wanted to be here to tell him she was stupid in love with him too. Tennis, the press, the police, none of that mattered. Rob was the only person she wanted to talk to right now.

****

307

Beep. Beep. Beep. Beep.

The steady rhythm of the beeping pulled Rob out of a really good dream. He wanted to open his eyes, but he was pretty sure a whole bus full of his students were weighing them down. It took a few minutes, but he finally pried them open.

His mother's sleeping form greeted him as soon as his vision cleared, her willowy frame curled up in an ugly green chair. Rob slowly took in his surroundings. Machines and cords surrounded him, but he at least wore his own pajamas. His sister sat in another chair at the foot of his bed, and his father stood staring out the window.

"Dad?" His rusty voice hurt his ears.

Bobby turned to face him, eyes widening. "Robby? 'Bout time you woke up. Brigit. Wake up. Look who's decided to join us."

Brigit stirred, blinking in surprise. "Oh, *Älskling*. It's so good to see your beautiful eyes."

"What happened?" He tried to remember how he'd gotten here. The last thing he remembered was Em winning the semifinal match and— "Did they get Suit Guy? Is Em okay?"

"She's fine," Maren said. "She refused to leave your side until Zoe came and dragged her away late last night."

"What about the stalker? Did they get him?" Rob gratefully accepted the water his father held out to him as Maren ducked out to grab the doctor.

Bobby's jaw tightened. "Yeah, they got him. Bastard had stashed a shiv in a bathroom a few weeks ago before security tightened. He got you but missed anything vital."

"Who was he? Why was he after Em?" Rob struggled to sit up more, but a twinge in his side stopped him.

"He's an unbalanced man," Brigit said. "He fancied himself Kole's best friend, and he took offense to Emerson's rejection of his idol. The psychologists the police brought in think he had some sort of psychotic break and fixated on her until he had his chance to attack."

Rob's blood chilled, and he was pretty sure it wasn't due to the IV fluid. What would have happened if he hadn't taken the hit for Em? Would the guy have done serious damage? Would he have killed her? The very idea of it broke his heart.

"How long have I been out?"

"You've been in and out for the last thirty-six hours, Mr. Ashton." The doctor's booming voice hurt Rob's head a little. His family stepped out as the efficient doctor and his equally efficient nurses buzzed around Rob, checking his incision and vitals and a lot of other things that Rob didn't understand.

By the time they left, Rob could have sworn he'd played at least three straight sets. His family trickled back in, each carrying a cup of coffee and some sort of pastry.

"What? None for me?" Rob asked, eying Maren's chocolate croissant.

She shook her head. "Doctor said you had to take it easy for the first few days, which means boring, bland foods."

"How's that supposed to make me feel better?" he grouched, crossing his arms.

"Hey, you're just lucky Mama convinced them to

let you wear your own pjs." She took an exaggerated bite of the pastry, reverting back to the five-year-old who used to taunt him with ice cream when he was stuck practicing.

Brigit shook her head. "Oh, Robby. You had us so worried."

"Everyone's calling you a hero," Bobby put in. "But I can't believe you did something like that, son. What were you thinking?"

Rob opened his mouth to respond, but a knock on the door stopped him. Maren opened it, and Em entered, a Tupperware bowl in hand. Rob's heart jumped into his throat, and he worried for a minute that they'd be able to tell on the monitor. Thankfully, it remained even. Seeing her did more to ease his concerns than anything else. Jesus, she was beautiful. Her hair was pulled up in a dark tail, and she wore a warm-up jacket over her bright-yellow tennis dress. Most people wouldn't notice, but he could feel the nerves vibrating off her. So many things rushed to his mind, but he couldn't say a single one of them in front of his parents, especially not with his dad obviously spoiling for a fight.

"Oh. You're awake." Em froze in the doorway. "It's—you look a lot better than the last time I saw you."

He chuckled, wincing.

"Couldn't keep pulling the Sleeping Beauty act for your match," Maren said, pulling Em into a hug.

Her match. Shit. Had he been asleep that long? He glanced at the paper on the table by his bed and saw the date. It was the date of the women's final match. Em still had five or six hours before she had to be on the court, but match day involved a lot of prep work and warm ups that were vital to getting ready.

"I know. I wanted to stop in before I headed to the tennis center. Gran made some gnocchi in the kitchen in my suite. She thought Rob might prefer it to the hospital food. She made it for Papa Vic a lot when he was sick," Em explained.

"Your grandma is officially my new favorite person," Rob said. "I was not looking forward to hospital food."

Brigit came over to wrap an arm around Em. It was so strange to see his mom and Em together, but he liked it.

"It's so good of you to come back, Emerson. I know this is a busy day for you, but I'm sure it's good for Rob to see for himself that you're all right."

Rob nodded. "You have no idea."

"Hopefully it'll be easier to convince the boy that it's all right for him to take it easy until they give us the go ahead to take him home," Bobby said. "The sooner we can all get back to our normal lives the better."

The sooner he's away from you.

Bobby didn't say the words, but they hung there, heavy with meaning. Rob wanted to throw something at his father, to tell the old blowhard to shut his mouth. His father was trying to get rid of Em, even though the rest of them wanted her to stay.

Em's face fell a little, but she recovered quickly. "Well, I'm glad to see that Rob's doing better. You had us…" She hesitated, swallowing hard. "You had us worried for a minute there. Anyway, I should go. Lots to do." Em handed the bowl to his mother and gave Maren another hug.

Brigit stopped her, pulling her into a hug of her own. "We're all rooting for you. Play well, sweetheart. Hopefully we'll see you later."

Em lingered for a minute, their gazes locked, and Rob silently begged her to stay.

He had so much he wanted to say, so much he wanted to hear her say. If he could, he'd kick his family as far out of there as he could, but there was no way he'd get his parents out of here in time to talk to Em. Besides, she needed to focus. It was bad enough that she'd be worrying about him—he could tell just by the look she gave him as she left that she'd barely gotten any sleep last night.

She left before Maren could stop her, and Rob's heart sank.

Damn it. He didn't want to be here. He wanted to be at the stadium to watch Em play. Over the last eight months, he'd imagined watching her win her first Grand Slam title a thousand times. Being with her in that moment would be a priceless memory. He still remembered every Grand Slam he'd won vividly, but they'd always felt a little empty without someone by his side. Having his family had been all well and good, but usually it was just Maren and his mom there with him. He'd desperately wanted a partner to share the moment with, and he didn't want Em to feel the same.

But would she even want him there now? There was so much unsettled between them. Maybe she'd shown up at the hospital out of guilt or obligation. That would be like her—to do the right thing, even out of a sense of obligation.

"Damn it, Dad. Why couldn't you have kept your mouth shut?" Rob growled. If his father hadn't been such a jackass, maybe he could have gotten a better read on her, figured out why she was really there.

Bobby glared at his son. "You really wanted her here? She's the reason you're in that hospital bed. There were security guards everywhere, Robert. Why the hell didn't you let them do their jobs?"

"If it were Mama, would you have sat back and trusted a bunch of strangers to protect her from a guy you knew was trying to hurt her?" Rob asked.

"You're really going to compare that woman to your mother?" Bobby scoffed.

"Enough, Bobby." Brigit's icy words had both Ashton men flinching. "Do not presume to know your son's mind or his heart."

"He doesn't know what's best for him, sweetheart. Look at him. He's in the hospital because of that girl." Bobby began to pace. "Our son could have died because of her."

Rob slammed his fist onto the tray table, the flimsy plastic clattering and almost tipping over. "I would have died if something happened to her. Don't you get it? I don't want someone like Carrie and Chessa or whoever you want to throw at me. She's it for me. You're not going to change my mind again. I'm not some dumb kid anymore. When are you going to understand that?"

Bobby continued to bluster, but Rob was distracted by the entrance of a nurse.

"I'm sorry to interrupt, Mr. Ashton, but this was left at the front desk for you." She handed him a sheet of paper, her eyes wide at his father's ranting.

"Thanks." Rob gave her a reassuring smile before letting her escape. He opened the folded sheet of hospital stationery, his heart leaping when he recognized Em's handwriting.

Rob,

I can't tell you what I felt when I saw you get stabbed. My heart shattered into a million pieces a hundred times over until you were moved into your hospital room. I only hope I'm not too late to tell you the truth about how I feel. I've been so stupid ever since you sat down on that plane beside me. I let years of pain and bitterness cloud my judgement, and I fought too hard to keep my walls in place. You hurt me when you listened to your father that day, when you let me go—you broke me, and that feeling has haunted me every day since.

I didn't want to trust you, to let you in and share my life with you after everything I'd been through with you, with my dad, with Kole, but there you were, so steady and sure and constant. I began to realize that maybe last time timing or the universe hadn't been on our side, but they could be now. You made me feel again, and that scared me. A lot.

So I was selfish. I pushed you away, and I've regretted it every day since I left London. I wanted to call you so many times, but I let my pride get in the way. Again.

Seeing you, bleeding in my arms, was the worst moment of my life.

I don't deserve to be with a man as wonderful as you, but I can't stop my heart from wanting you. I wish I could have stayed by your side until you woke, and stay there now, but I have to finish what I started. The second I can get away, I'll be back. I'm going to fight for us this time.

I only hope you'll be mine as I am yours,
Em.

He read the note again. And again. And again.

"Robby, what is it?" Brigit asked.

He struggled with what to say, his mind racing. Staying in this bed was not an option. Missing Em's win tonight was not an option. "I have to get out of here."

"What?" Bobby looked at him as if he had two heads. "You had surgery two days ago. You can't go anywhere."

Glancing between his mom and his sister, Rob pleaded with them. "I have to get out of here. I can't stay here and miss it."

"Miss what?" Bobby demanded.

"Dad. The woman I love is playing in the US Open finals tonight, and she's going to win." He pushed himself into an upright position without the support of the bed. The twinge in his side wasn't as bad as what he'd felt after his shoulder surgery. "I can't not be there."

Maren pressed a hand to her lips as she squealed with delight. "You're going to get her back?"

"I think I already have her," he said, holding up the note. "But I need to be there tonight. Mama, will you help me?"

Brigit's eyes shone with tears, and her smile was warm enough to melt Bobby Ashton to mush. "Of course. Let's find that doctor. We only have a few hours to convince him to let you out of here. We can't miss my future daughter-in-law's first Grand Slam victory of many."

315

Chapter 21

Em wiped at the sweat sneaking past the band of her visor. They'd barely been on the court for twenty minutes, but already the early September heat had her dripping. The sun crept low in the early evening sky. Around her, the crowd quietly buzzed, waiting for her to set up her next serve.

Two games in, and they were tied. She'd struggled during the last game a bit, letting Chessa get a few points she should have won, but she couldn't let that get in her head. She needed to focus. Chessa was a wily player, unpredictable and deadly, but Em was determined to beat her this time. She'd done it before, but never on this scale. Chessa led their matchups, sixteen to six, but half her victories were on clay. On hard courts, Chessa had won five to Em's three. Not great odds, but not terrible either.

Out of the corner of her eye, Em saw movement coming from the direction of her box. Turning, she watched as her grandma and brother and Zoe moved over to allow a group to join them.

Rob.

All at once, worry and jubilation crashed over her. What was he doing here? He should be in the hospital. While he looked normal, she caught the wince of pain as he eased into one of the seats. His skin wasn't as pale as it'd been when she saw him earlier that morning, but he still shouldn't be here.

She still hadn't recovered from seeing him laid out on the hospital bed, unconscious, hooked up to a dozen different machines, nurses bustling in and out all day. The fear of losing him gripped her and hadn't let go until she came by his hospital room that morning and saw him awake.

Had he read her note? Was that why he was here? God, she hoped so.

Pushing down her worry, she zeroed in on the fact that he was here. Right now, every person in the world who mattered was here to watch her, to support her. Tennis might be an individual sport, but today she wasn't alone. The thought overwhelmed her at the same time it filled her with a renewed sense of purpose.

Winning today wasn't just about her or about proving something to her father. Winning was about showing the people who supported her that their support did more for her than anything. They'd all been there for her over the last year, seeing her through the worst days of her life. Even though Papa Vic was gone and her dad couldn't care less. Gran, Owen, Zoe, Maren, Dera, and Rob—they all stood at her back, cheering her on even when she couldn't cheer for herself.

Turning her attention back to the game, she bounced the ball on the vivid blue surface of the court. Across the net, Chessa crouched, ready to spring into action as soon as Em let her serve fly, her bright-red skirt and top a taunt in the otherworldly quiet of the stadium. Tossing the ball in the air, Em brought her racket crashing down on it, sending it hurtling over the net. It hit with perfect precision, firmly kissing the corner of the service box farthest from Chessa's racket, without any chance for the Croatian player to return it.

The crowd cheered as the umpire boomed out the score of fifteen to love. Some of the nerves tightening Em's muscles left, and she settled in, pulling another tennis ball out of her pocket to prepare for her next serve. This one Chessa managed to return, but Em won the point after a handful of returns. Before long, Em won the game without Chessa scoring a single point.

After a short break, it was Chessa's turn. Em studied her every move, watching for telegraphed signs of where the blonde would send her first serve. Barely waiting for the echoing thunk of Chessa's racket making contact with the ball, Em bounced off the balls of her feet, easily moving to meet the fluorescent green projectile and send it back across the net. This game cost a bit more effort than the last, but Em kept pace with Chessa until the umpire announced "Deuce"— she'd managed to tie up the score forty to forty.

Both of them scrapped for the next point, but Em won the advantage. Break point. If she won this, she'd be two games ahead of Chessa going into her next service game—a comfortable place to be. She couldn't let up. Chessa's serve was wicked fast, but Em was ready for her. Using her backhand, she sent the ball hurtling across the court to the opposite side from where Chessa currently stood. Long legs ate up a lot of ground, though, and the ball came flying back toward Em. She beat it back again and again until she managed a passing shot that won her the point and the game.

The crowd roared, and Em looked over in her box to see the beaming expressions on the faces of her family. Rob gave her a nod of encouragement, his blue eyes steady on her from under the brim of his ball cap. He'd shaved since she saw him this morning, and his dimple winked at her.

The match continued under the bright stadium lights as the sun fell and a cool breeze drifted into the court. Em won the first set six games to three, but Chessa rallied in the second set, winning in a tie breaker. Em refused to let it faze her. She won her service game, then Chessa's then hers. Chessa battled back to win her next service game with some nasty shots, but Em kept going. Soon they were at the breaking point: one set each, five games to four in the last set. If Em won this game, she took the match. If Chessa won, they'd have to go at least two more games, risking a brutal tie break.

Thanking whatever god made this situation fall on her service game, Em set up to serve. Every muscle in her body ached, especially the knee she'd injured almost a year ago. They were well into their second hour of play, fast approaching the third. This was what she'd trained for, what she and Zoe and her team had spent hours preparing for. She couldn't give in to the fatigue now. She had to push through.

The little smirk on Chessa's face spurred Em on. Chessa didn't believe she could win this, still had the arrogance to think she could win the match.

Not this time.

Em went into an almost fugue state as she played through the last game of her US Open finals match. Her instincts, her years of training, and muscle memory took over. She put every last ounce of energy she had left into that game, hitting the ball as hard as she could, giving it the right spin at the right time.

It finally came down to match point. Em served the ball, but it didn't make it over the net, bouncing limply along her side of the court. A ball girl ran out and grabbed it.

She served again, this time sailing it perfectly into the service box. Chessa returned the serve, but Em was ready for it. Stroke by stroke, she moved forward, making it a little harder for the world number one to hit the ball back to her.

Em went in for a drop shot, flicking her wrist in a neat little move that had the ball barely clearing the net, bouncing once, then twice.

Before it bounced a third time, the stadium exploded. Cheers and shouts echoed around Em as she sank to her knees in disbelief.

She'd won.

The US Open title was hers.

For a second, she knelt on the rough surface of the court, letting it all sink in. After more than twenty years of work and training and fighting, she'd won a Grand Slam. Tears welled up in her eyes, and she tilted her head up. The softly fading light tinged the sky purple and hazy pink, but that wasn't what she was looking at. Somehow, she knew with absolute certainty that Papa Vic and her mother and her maternal grandparents were all up there somewhere cheering along with the rest of the crowd.

Getting to her feet, she went to shake Chessa's hand after she brushed the tears away. It didn't take a genius to know the Croatian was pissed as hell, but Em couldn't bring herself to care about anything but the unrestrained jubilation and giddy disbelief coursing through her.

She'd finally won, and she worried she might explode out of her skin. Keeping her cool until she shook hands with the umpire, Em gave a little bounce of celebration, waving both hands at the still roaring crowd. Turning in a slow circle, she accepted the applause until she spotted the people she really cared about.

Ignoring everything else, she climbed the stands, and hands reached out to help her as she made her way to her box. Her brother's hands closed over her arms, pulling her up and over the edge of the box and into another man's chest. She'd know that eucalyptus and mint scent anywhere.

Rob.

Reaching up, she cupped his cheeks, pulling his mouth down until it met hers. The crowd went wild, hooting and hollering, but she couldn't care less. Kissing Rob again after everything, after all that had passed between them, after seeing him bleeding in her arms two days ago, felt like she was waking up from a nightmare. He tasted so good, of joy and Rob with the faint underlying sweetness of soda. She clutched at him, desperate to feel if he was real or not because none of this felt real.

Rob pulled back, his forehead resting against hers. "You did it, Em. You did it."

Emotions clogged her throat, and long, callused fingers brushed wetness off her cheeks. She didn't even realize she was still crying. Staring into Rob's eyes, she saw so much that made her hopeful, but she didn't dare believe it yet. They had so much to say to each other, and no time to say it now.

Unable to speak, she moved to the next person

waiting for her. Her grandmother.

"Oh, my girl. You were magnificent," Gran whispered fiercely.

Owen joined the hug. "We're so proud of you, Squeaker."

"Thank you," she said, her voice choked, both from joy and from missing the other person who made up their little family. "Thank you both, for everything."

She quickly accepted hugs from Dera and Maren and Owen, before she finally came to Zoe.

"This isn't just my win," she told the redheaded Amazon who'd stood by her side for every step of this journey. "It's ours."

"You did this, Emmy. You and no one else." Zoe kissed her cheek. "Go enjoy your victory."

Before leaving her box, Em returned to Rob one last time, wrapping her arms around him.

"I'm so glad you're here. I—I don't know if I could have done this without you," she said, her lips pressed to his ear. "There's no one else I wanted to see in my box as much as you."

"I couldn't miss it," he said. "I'm only sorry your dad's not here to see this."

She shook her head. "It doesn't matter. I don't need his support or approval or whatever. I'd rather win a thousand titles without him than to win one without you and my real family there to watch."

Giving him one last kiss, she pulled away and made her way back down to the court. The cheers hadn't yet subsided, but the stadium staff were preparing for the trophy ceremony. Taking a moment as she packed her gear back into her bags, she pushed the tears back.

It was…overwhelming to finally achieve the goal she'd worked so hard for. Joy blazed through her, along with anticipation. She glanced back at her box to where Rob stood, his skin a little pale as he clapped and cheered with everyone else. Winning the Grand Slam had once been everything to her, but now, winning the heart of that man meant more than a thousand wins. She only hoped her letter had really done its job.

Chapter 22

Rob stood outside the women's locker room, bouncing on the balls of his feet, waiting for Em to emerge. Thankfully, the security was still tight, even though they'd caught the nut job who stabbed him, and they'd kept the reporters outside the building, giving him a place to wait in peace.

"Robby, you should go home and rest," his mother said from beside him. She'd been fretting over him since the match ended, trying to convince him to go back to the hospital or at least go back to his apartment.

"Mama, I'm fine. I swear. You go find Dad and Maren and go to dinner. I'm not going anywhere without Em." He kept his gaze fixed on the door across from him as his mother walked away, muttering about stubborn, lovesick boys who didn't listen to their mothers.

It felt like days since he'd kissed Em in the player's box with the whole world watching. Maren had shown him the pictures that spread across social media like wildfire. Everyone was saying how romantic it was, what a fairy-tale romance they had. They all seemed to forget that only a few weeks ago, they'd been lampooning Em and insinuating all sorts of things about her character.

He didn't give a damn what the rest of the world said, though. All that mattered was seeing Em and reassuring himself that she'd really meant what she said in the letter. That kiss had certainly felt like she meant it, but he needed to hear the words from her. He'd waited so long to hear them.

He'd never been more proud than when he watched Em hoist that trophy over her head. It erased the lingering pain that hit him every time he stepped into that stadium. His new life, the one where he was a coach for kids who needed him and—God willing—Em's partner, really started in that moment. He no longer missed his career or the thrill of the win. He'd finally made peace with himself and his father's expectations.

After a good twenty minutes more than he felt necessary, the door of the locker room opened, and Em emerged, her eyes down, staring at the screen of her phone.

Fuck, she was gorgeous. It never ceased to hit him in the chest every time he saw her. She'd showered and taken time to style her hair, the black silk falling in gentle waves around her face, kissing the tops of her shoulders. She wore a loose dress that fell across her body, kissing her curves, the fabric dotted with bright mixes of turquoise and blue in abstract shapes. The dress bared a great deal of smooth, long legs, leading down to the low wedge sandals he knew she wore for comfort rather than fashion.

"Most people would look like hell after playing as hard as you did today, but you manage to look like the most beautiful woman in the world. Not sure that's fair," he said.

Her head shot up, and her eyes widened. "Rob. What are you—? I mean, I didn't expect you to still be here."

"Where else would I be?" He pushed off the wall to walk toward her. It took all his self-control not to crush her in his arms and kiss her silly.

"Um, the hospital?" Worry clouded her brown eyes as they traveled his body, as if taking inventory to make sure he still had all his parts. "You were stabbed two days ago, Rob. You should be in your hospital bed, charming the pretty nurses, not lurking in hallways."

He shrugged, keeping his expression light, ignoring the slight twinge in his side. "Here's the thing. The nurses? Scary, all of 'em. And besides, there's only one woman I want to be charming right now. I honestly haven't really felt my injury since she left me this note earlier today."

"I can't believe your doctors let you come today." She shifted her bag on her shoulder, looking down shyly. "I'd planned to come back to the hospital after the match to see you."

"Well, the doctors didn't really let me come. I told them I was leaving whether they liked it or not." He reached out and took her hand, pulling her a little closer. "I couldn't lay there in a hospital bed and watch the match on TV. Not this one."

She bit her bottom lip, and he ached to kiss her. For now, he settled for breathing in the citrus-and-rosemary scent of her, savoring the feel of her hand in his. To make sure she couldn't escape, he linked their fingers together.

"I want to be mad at you for risking your health like this," she said, "but I can't tell you what it meant to have you there. Seeing you there, with my family, with your family. I don't—I don't think I could have done it without you there."

"You would have, Em. You were on fire today." He glanced around the abandoned hallways. "It's getting late. If you want to go celebrate with your family, we can do that. Or…"

She gave his hand a squeeze. "Or what?"

He took a deep breath, laying his cards on the table and hoping she picked them up. "Or we could go back to my apartment and talk. Tonight might not be the best night for it. I'm sure you're exhausted, but—"

"Going back to your apartment sounds perfect." A smile tilted up her lips. "It's weird, but I'm the opposite of tired right now. I'm wired, like I might jump out of my own skin."

"It's a rush." He tugged her down the hallway toward the door. "Are you ready to face the hordes? They'll be outside waiting. I could go around another way if you prefer."

It hurt to offer that, after all they'd been through, but he wanted to respect her wishes. If she didn't want to be seen with him, he'd deal with it—for now.

"No. No more hiding. Besides, I think the whole world saw me kiss you earlier," she teased.

Grinning down at her, he pushed the doors open and let the cool evening air hit them along with the storm of flashing cameras. The questions came pelting at them, buzzing through the air like a swarm of bees. At first, he simply shouldered his way through the crowd, keeping a tight hold on her hand. Then Bruno put himself in Em's path and refused to move.

"Emerson. It seems the rumors are true. Are you and Rob together again? Is it true you slept with him to try to get better press coverage after your boudoir pictures were leaked?"

Rob's fist curled, and he seriously considered punching Bruno, but Em stopped him. He'd seen the same ferocity in her eyes earlier when she faced down Chessa, and she approached Bruno, her spine ramrod straight.

"I thought you were supposed to be a journalist, Bruno. Not a scandal-monger," she snapped. "You can go to hell if you think I'll give you any sort of interview after the shit you've pulled."

"What about that kiss after the match, Emerson?" Jodi Barnes, a reporter for one of the New York dailies, asked. "Seemed pretty steamy from where I was sitting."

Em sighed, moving closer to Rob, their hands still entwined. He didn't say a word, waiting to see what she did. If it were up to him, he'd shout how he felt from the rooftops. But this was Em's show, her career, her decision how much to say.

"Look, I get you all want a good story, and everyone eats up a romance subplot. But I'm only going to comment on my love life once. Rob Ashton is one of the most important men in my life. He's not someone I'm screwing or using for whatever twisted purposes you dream up to sell ad space. He's my partner and the man I've loved for seven years. Now, in case you didn't notice, I've had a long day, so if you could let us through, that'd be great."

Unsurprisingly, Em's pronouncement set off a new melee of questions, but now Rob took charge. His heart swelled as he wrapped an arm around Em's shoulders to lead her through the crowd. She'd claimed him in public, twice in one day. She'd left no room for interpretation. Now it was time for him to do the same.

They didn't speak through the entire ride back to his apartment. In fact, Em dozed off not long after they left the tennis center. It was a miracle that he'd convinced both of their families to give them tonight. They'd all wanted to celebrate with her, even his father, but given the fact that she was gently snoring beside him minutes after sitting down for the first time in what must have been hours, Rob knew he'd made the right call. Tonight would be for them. And hopefully, tomorrow they'd celebrate more than just her Grand Slam title.

"Wow. What a view," she said as he led her through the industrial metal door of the converted warehouse. His apartment looked out over the Hudson, the lights of the city twinkling in the night.

"It's one of the reasons I can't bring myself to give this place up. As much as I don't like living in the city, when I'm up here, I forget how noisy and crowded and busy it can get."

She set her bag down and went to stand in front of the floor-to-ceiling windows. "I can see why. I love looking at the water. One day, I want to get a house on a little canal or lake so I can sit and watch it for hours."

"Sounds nice." He wandered over to the couch and took a seat, his eyes never leaving her. He still couldn't believe she was here in his apartment. Three days ago, he wouldn't have ever believed this was possible. Eight hours ago, he'd woken up in a hospital bed, unsure that Em would ever want to talk to him again. Then she'd written him that note, and everything changed again, just as it had that day on the plane.

For so many years, he'd regretted giving her up,

regretted listening to his family, to his father. Then, when she walked away in London, he'd almost given in to his anger and given up on her. But he couldn't because something in him clung to her, to how she made him feel. And now she was so close, yet there was still something lurking between them, keeping them apart.

"We didn't come here to talk about the view," she said, her voice hollow, her shoulders hunched, and her arms wrapped around her middle.

He desperately wanted to go and wrap his body around her, to feel her in his arms again, to savor the scent of her, the warmth of her. Every night without her had been worse than the last.

It would be so easy for him to pour his heart out to her, to tell her that he still loved her and wanted to be with her. If he wasn't careful, he'd even tell her all the plans he'd cooked up in his head while waiting for the doctors to sign his discharge papers. The house they'd live in, the children they'd have. How they'd work together after she decided she wanted to retire. How he'd hold her every night and wake up to her beautiful face every morning for the rest of his life.

"No, we didn't." He leaned back, watching her carefully. "You...you said a lot of things in your letter. And that you had more you wanted to say. Ball's in your court, Em."

She didn't turn around to face him for several long moments, but when she did, her face was awash with a hundred different emotions that Rob struggled to place. He thought love lurked there, but it was masked by— pain? And anger? Sorrow also tinged her gaze. As her face crumpled a little, he realized that everything had finally caught up with her.

"I—I don't know where to start," she said, sniffling a little, her arms still crossed. "No, wait, I do. How could you be so damn stupid, Rob? You were so, so stupid, so many times."

Anger bubbled up inside him, but he kept it at a low simmer. "I'm the stupid one? How did you work that out? Seven years ago, yeah, I'll own wearing the stupid hat then. But not this time."

"Yes, this time," she lashed out. "You don't see me jumping in front of a crazy man with a knife and ending up in the hospital. Why did you do it? Why didn't you let the security guys take care of it?"

"Why do you think?" He narrowed his eyes at her. Did she really not know? Or was she trying to find an excuse to take back what she'd written earlier?

She brushed at her cheek with one hand, keeping the other arm around her middle. "I—I don't know. All I know is you scared the shit out of me when you did. Seeing you lying there, bleeding? Yeah, that proves it was incredibly stupid."

"Imagine how I felt, know that guy was coming straight at you." He shot to his feet. "Jesus, Em. Do you think I could stand by and watch you get hurt two days before the finals? To see you lose your dream when you were so close?"

His heart still stopped at the thought of Em taking that stab. He'd died a thousand times in those few moments before he put himself between her and the knife. Seeing her out there today, so fierce and fit and whole, had been the only thing to really ease that terror, that convinced him she was really all right.

Her jaw tightened, and her body folded over as she

331

gasped for breath. Without a second thought, he went to her, pulling her to him and kissing her for all he was worth. He needed to stop her tears before they broke his heart, and she needed to know that he wasn't going to give her up until the last breath left his body.

****

Em lost herself in the kiss for a moment, and the sobs clawing at her throat dissipated. She didn't know what to feel. Ever since she'd scored the winning point, her head had been spinning. Every emotion on the scale battered her from all directions, threatening to overwhelm her. So she clung to Rob for a little longer, letting him protect her once more.

But she finally had to pull away, had to say what she needed to say. She let him lead her over to the couch and let him sit beside her. She tried to remove his arms from around her, but he refused to let her.

"I—God, Rob. For so long, I've wondered if I was good enough. Good enough for my father, good enough for my grandparents, good enough for you. Especially you. When you didn't fight for me that day, I knew your father convinced you that I wasn't good enough." She looked away, keeping her gaze on the windows. "Now I know for sure. I don't deserve you. You've done so much for me, risked so much, and I've been— I've been the world's biggest bitch."

She bit back another sob, trying not to give in to the emotions. She needed to be strong now. She couldn't be one of those girls who crumpled because of a guy, who needed a guy to make her feel worthy. She could do this without him and be totally fine— eventually—but she didn't want to.

"Emerson Grace." Rob's voice cracked through the

air, cutting through the roaring in her ears. Big hands came up to cup her face, forcing her to look up into those gorgeous blue eyes. "You are anything but a bitch. You are kind, compassionate, selfless, and fiercely loyal. You would do anything for the people you love, including giving up on a relationship you really want to make them proud. You push aside your happiness because you've made a promise to yourself and your dead grandpa that you'd win a Grand Slam this year to prove all of the work was worth it. What you don't realize is that, title or not, your grandparents have always thought you hung the moon, and Zoe loves you like her own daughter. They just need you to be you, and that's all I need too."

She sniffled, trying to move away from him and the wave of feelings he conjured up, but he held her where she was.

"Come on, Em. You said in that note you were going to let your walls down, that you were ready to put the past behind us. Part of that is trusting me and what's between us. Did you mean what you wrote? Because from those kisses, I think you meant it."

Her cheeks burned a little, and she glanced down. "Yes. Of course I did. It's just…so much so fast."

"We can take things slow, if that's what you want. I've waited seven years for you. Going a little slower won't hurt me as long as I know that you really want this. That you want me."

Her heart ached as she watched the flicker of uncertainty in his eyes. He was usually so confident, so sure of himself. It was usually nice to see the cracks in his armor, but now she wanted that confidence back. He needed the words as much as she did, and this time it had to be her turn to say them, to take the leap.

"I want you, Rob. So much." She reached up to cover his hands with hers. "I've missed you every day since I left London. It's like I said—I got scared, and I lashed out, and I was the stupid one then."

"Okay, then no more tears, beautiful." He brushed the wetness off her cheek and pressed a kiss to her forehead. "We both want to be together. We can work with that."

She squeezed her eyes shut, a little giggle escaping her lips. "Yeah. I guess we can."

He eased them both back onto the couch, his arms wrapped around her, her head resting in the crook of his good shoulder. "In case I haven't said it already, I was crazy proud of you today."

She snuggled in, savoring the scent of him. This smell had haunted some of her steamier dreams over the last six weeks. "When I won? That was pretty good. Not as good as when I saw you awake this morning, but close."

"Yeah, the whole achieving your life-long goal thing was awe-inspiring to watch." A teasing smile lit his eyes with that spark she loved so much. "But I was talking about when you stood up to Bruno and told him to shove it up his ass. When you told the world I was your partner."

Burying her head in his chest for a moment, she glanced up at him, slightly embarrassed. "I did do that, didn't I?"

He nodded, leaning in for a kiss that was only long enough to make her toes curl. "Yeah, you did. It was almost as great as when you kissed me in your box after you won."

"That was pretty good," she admitted. "Once I got over being annoyed that you didn't stay in the hospital like you should have, I was so glad to see you there. To share that with you. For the first time, I had the person I really wanted in my corner when it counted."

For years, she'd dreamed of having someone there for her besides her grandparents. They were wonderful, but she'd always felt like something was missing. Like someone was missing. She used to think it was her dad or her mom. But now she could admit it to herself—it was Rob. It was someone to love her, to be there for her not because they were her family, but because they chose her, because she mattered to them.

"It's the first of many times I'll be there. I promise." He brushed her hair behind her ears. "I'll be there for every match if you want."

She raised an eyebrow. "Oh, really? And how do you plan to do that?"

"Well, I'm sure you've heard that I no longer work for TWW."

"I seem to have heard rumors to that effect. So what, you're unemployed, which means you can follow your girlfriend around the world, watching her play tennis?"

He grinned. "Girlfriend? Definitely like the sound of that. But I actually have a job. Just one with a very flexible schedule and a convenient location. Do you want some dinner? I think I want some dinner."

He stood up, leaving her on the couch as he made his way over to the kitchen on the other side of the great room. He pulled something out of the oven and puttered around grabbing plates, and all she could do was stare after him. He acted so nonchalant, as if they weren't discussing pretty significant parts of their life together.

"Hold up. You can't drop something like that, then go talk about food, Mystery Man. What is this job?" she asked, getting up to join him, leaning back against the concrete countertop as he poured wine into two glasses.

"I'm working as a coach at my mom's tennis academy." He dished up what looked to be panang curry over steamed rice that already rested on deep-lipped stoneware plates. "My job is to help coach the kids who attend the academy through the foundation's work with foster kids. And I actually kind of love it. If it goes the way I think it will, I may ask Mama to let me take over the whole program for her."

Em listened as he explained his work, his face lighting up as he talked about the kids he worked with. He looked so...satisfied. More comfortable in his own skin than she'd seen him since before his injury.

"It sounds...amazing," she said, accepting the plate of food and joining him at one of the stools by the breakfast bar. "But wait. Isn't your mom's academy in Miami?"

Rob chuckled, taking a bite of his food. "Catch up, lady. Why do you think I agreed to help?"

"But what about your dad? You and he don't exactly make the best colleagues."

"We're learning to work together. Mom's helping him realize that it's okay to let me live my own life."

She gave him a skeptical look. "You really think that's going to last?"

Bobby Ashton was not a man to give up his ways easily. Both Ashton men had heads harder than the courts of Arthur Ashe Stadium, and neither of them liked to back off if they didn't have to. She almost felt sorry for Brigit, having to manage the two of them all day.

"We'll see how it goes. Like I said, I'd like to eventually grow the program and oversee it on my own. For now, I'm doing a job I love, and I get to be in the same city as the woman I love." He sipped his wine. "At least when she's in town. And if I need to rearrange my schedule to travel with her, I have the room to do that."

Love. Such a little word packed a really big punch. Her heart swelled as she tucked it in close, enjoying how freely he used the word.

"The woman you love, huh?" She leaned closer to him.

"Yep. Love, adore, worship, take your pick. It fits." He sat his fork down and pulled her in for another kiss. "The woman I want to take on dates and show off at parties and sleep with every night and wake up with every morning."

Her heart fluttered. "Love definitely works for me. I'm pretty crazy in love with you too. So crazy that I think I could get on board with most of that list, especially the last two."

His eyes darkened, desire sparking in their depths. "Oh yeah?"

"Definitely." She pushed their plates back and boosted herself onto the counter, moving to sit in front of him, arms around his neck. "In fact, I have a proposition for you."

She leaned in for a nibbling kiss, teasing, tasting, but not sinking in. Not yet.

"What might that be?" he asked, his big hands sliding around to cup her ass, his fingers dancing along the hem of her dress.

She hesitated for only a moment before diving in, keeping her tone light, as if she were simply spitballing ideas. "Well, with this job, have you found a place to live yet?"

A slow smile stretched across his face. "Now that you mention it, I haven't really had a chance to house hunt yet. I've mostly stayed with my parents when I haven't been flying back up here to finish things."

"You know, it'll be really challenging to accomplish the whole falling asleep together and waking up together thing if you're living with your parents or in some apartment." She stroked his hair, loving how the light from the pendant over the bar caught the old gold tones, making them glow. "What would you say to moving in with me?"

His hands slid up her thighs, pushing her dress up, sending sparks of desire zinging across her skin. He leaned in to trail kisses along the column of her neck. "I would say that sounds like an amazing proposition that I plan to take you up on as soon as we get back to Miami. But for now, I want to get started on the loving you part of this whole thing."

His fingers dipped into her panties, teasing her wet folds. She let him play with her for a few minutes, drinking in the fact that he was here, with her. This wasn't a dream. It was for real, and Rob intended for it to be their reality from now on.

When she reached to pull the hem of the loose dress over her head, he stopped her. "Not here. If you take that off now, I'm not going to be able to stop myself, and I want you in my bed."

Together they moved through the apartment toward

the sliding barn door that led into the bedroom. The second they crossed the threshold, they began tugging at each other's clothes, sending piece after piece flying until they were both naked save for her lacy panties and his black boxer briefs. She would have pulled those off him too, but the sight of the angry red wound on his side stopped her.

"Rob." She almost reached out to touch it, but she stopped herself. "Are you sure we should be doing this?"

He leaned in, taking her mouth in a deep kiss that sent most of her rational thought running in five different directions. For added effect, he cupped her breasts, his thumb rolling around her nipple in the way he knew drove her crazy. "I probably shouldn't join in the fun tonight, but that doesn't mean I can't watch you have fun."

To prove his point, he spent the next hours driving her up and over the edge of pleasure, urging her on until her muscles turned to Jell-o and her cries of ecstasy grew hoarse. Then when she couldn't take any more, he settled her under the blankets and pulled her close into his uninjured side.

"I love you, Rob Ashton," she said, leaning up to give him a kiss.

He smiled into the kiss, his arm tightening around her a little. "I love you too, Em. I lost so much time with you, but I don't intend to miss another minute. You're it for me."

She returned his smile, loving the feel of his hot, sculpted body beside hers. Yeah, she could definitely get used to this, to the certainty that he'd be there when she woke up tomorrow and every morning for as long as she wanted as her partner, her friend, and her lover.

"You're it for me too. Winning you might be the best thing that ever happened to me."

A word about the author…

From the time she figured out how to turn the Disney Read-Along cassette tape over in the dark, Taylor's been addicted to reading—both authorized and unauthorized. By the time she was thirteen, she'd started writing Newsies fan fiction and reading romance novels late into the night. A champion multitasker, she's been known to read, write, and watch TV all at the same time, especially if there's an HEA ending involved. In addition to being a frequent stress baker, she's spent the majority of her free time becoming fluent in most dialects of nerdiness, starting with musicals, and is mildly obsessed with all things British (especially the Royal Family and tennis champ Andy Murray). Growing up with a village of strong women as an example, she doesn't miss an opportunity to weave community engagement and feminism into each of her books in one way or another—her heroines are always sassy and smart, and her heroes wouldn't have them any other way.

She's represented by Julie Gwinn of The Seymour Agency.

~*~

Find Taylor online at:
http://taylormlunsford.com

Thank you for purchasing
this publication of The Wild Rose Press, Inc.

For questions or more information
contact us at
info@thewildrosepress.com.

The Wild Rose Press, Inc.
www.thewildrosepress.com

To visit with authors of
The Wild Rose Press, Inc.
join our yahoo loop at
http://groups.yahoo.com/group/thewildrosepress/